RESOLUTION COLLECTION

Other Books by D.I. Telbat

Dark Edge: Prequel to The COIL Series
The COIL Series: Christian Suspense (5)
Distant Boundary: Prequel to The COIL Legacy
The COIL Legacy Series: Christian Suspense (3)
COIL Legacy Collection: 3 Books in 1 Volume
The ELM Series: America's Last Days (3+)
The RESOLUTION Series: America's Last Days (4)
RESOLUTION Collection: 4 Novellas in 1 Volume
The STEADFAST Series: America's Last Days (6)
STEADFAST Collection: 6 Novellas in 1 Volume
Last Dawn Series: America's Last Days (4)
Leeward Set: Where Christians Dare (2)
Never Lost Series: Trafficking Rescue Novels (2)

Arabian Variable
Called To Gobi
God's Colonel
Soldier of Hope
Short Story Collections (7)

RESOLUTION COLLECTION
America's Last Days

4 Novellas in 1 Volume

D.I. TELBAT

Only the resolute will prevail!

IN SEASON PUBLICATIONS
USA

RESOLUTION Collection Copyright © 2024 by D.I. Telbat
(Individual novellas first published July 2019.)

All rights reserved. No part of this publication may be reproduced, distributed, or transmitted in any form or by any means, including photocopying, recording, or other electronic or mechanical methods, without the prior written permission of the publisher, except in the case of brief quotations embodied in critical reviews and certain other noncommercial uses permitted by copyright law. For permission requests, contact the publisher, In Season Publications, Attn: Dee at ditelbat@gmail.com.

Publisher's Note: This is a work of fiction. Names, characters, places, and incidents are a product of the author's imagination. Locales and public names are sometimes used for atmospheric purposes. Any resemblance to actual people, living or dead, or to ministries, businesses, companies, events, institutions, or locales is completely coincidental.

The Hymn, *It is Well with my Soul* by Horatio Spafford, was used from public domain in *Resolution Book Four*.

Printed in the United States of America

RESOLUTION Collection/ D.I. Telbat -- 1st ed.
Futuristic Christian Fiction; Christian Suspense; Collection

D.I. Telbat / In Season Publications
https://ditelbat.com
https://books2read.com/DITelbat

ISBN 979-8-9917076-0-2

Cover by Angie Alaya at Fiverr

To the resolute who find Jesus Christ
as the solution to every need and problem.

Acknowledgements

My thanks to God for opening our eyes to the good things He gives us; to Dee who sees these ideas through from beginning to end; to my helpful proofreaders and Beta Readers who whip each manuscript through the finish line; to Brian L. for his gracious help with the book covers; and to my readers, who encourage me to keep writing more. It's an honor to share these adventures with you!

Table of Contents

-MAP 1 – for the Resolution Series	i
-MAP 2 – for Resolution Book Four	ii
Note from the Author	iii
RESOLUTION Book One	1
RESOLUTION Book Two	75
RESOLUTION Book Three	147
-Bonus Chapter – Valles	207
RESOLUTION Book Four	215
-What's Next?	287
-Character Sketch	289
-Glossary	291
-Bonus Chapter – *Steadfast Book One*	293
-About the Author	304

RESOLUTION COLLECTION

Map 1 for the RESOLUTION Series

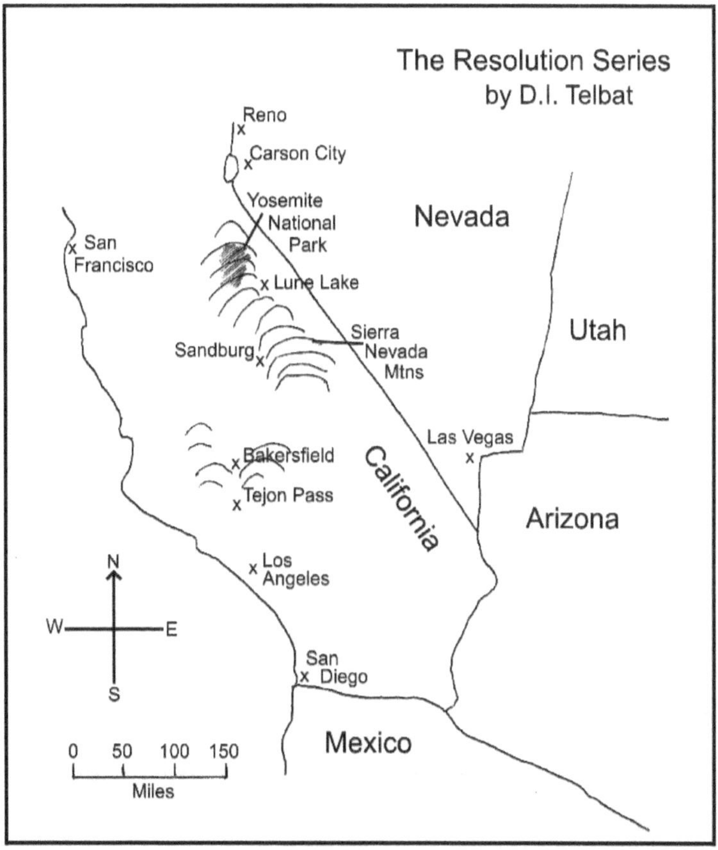

D.I. Telbat

Map 2 for RESOLUTION Book Four

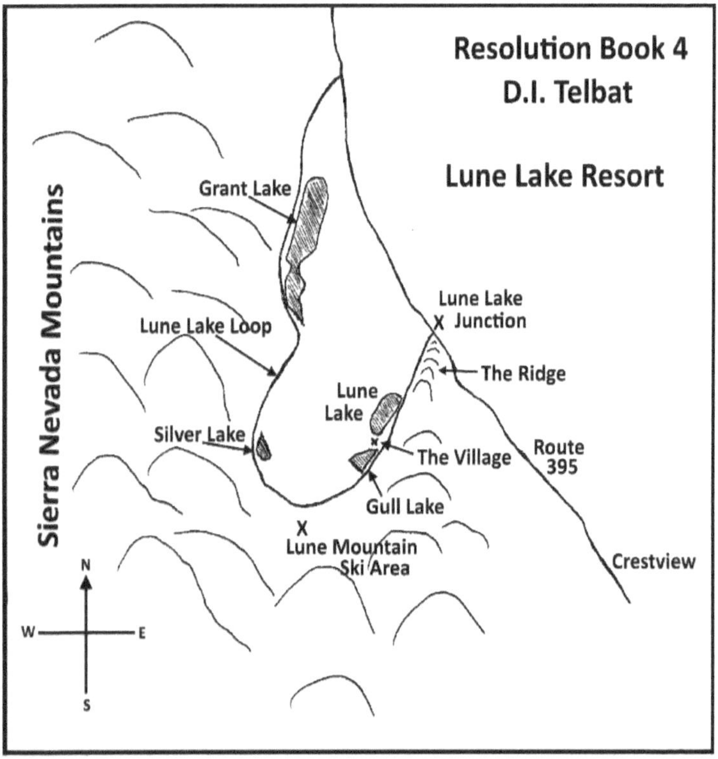

A Note from the Author

Dear Friend,

The following series consists of four consecutive novellas that fit into the COIL timeline one year after Pan-Day (the fictional collapse of America). I wrote this story about Wes Trimble and Chevy to reveal the strength of their faith as Christian men who stand firmly yet also separately from the Casperteins. After all, one-eyed Wes Trimble was living for Christ years before he ever met Titus Caspertein or his sister Wynter.

In chronological order that relates to this series, *The COIL Series* (with the Dowlers) comes first as five full-length novels. *The COIL Legacy Series* comes next (with the Casperteins), as three full-length novels, as well as in a one-volume collection. Following those, we recommend: *The ELM Series* (Casperteins), *The Resolution Series* (Trimbles), *The Steadfast Series* or *Collection* (Radners), and the *Last Dawn Series* (Casperteins). We'll be adding full-length novels indefinitely to *The ELM Series*, my current project, so go ahead and read other D.I. Telbat novels while you wait for the next *ELM* book!

As you read *The Resolution Series*, it is our hope that you are encouraged and inspired to live as a disciple of Jesus Christ, even when the world is against you. May we each resolve today to trust our Lord and Savior, even in the face of conflict and intimidation. After all, we know as believers, our soul is safe in the Lord's mighty hand!

See you on the next page!
David Telbat

RESOLUTION BOOK ONE

America's Last Days

D.I. Telbat

~*~

To Christ, whose life and love shows us
what it means to be sacrificial.

D.I. Telbat

Book One, Prologue

My Dear Wes,

I'm leaving this letter in your pack, knowing you'll find it once you start north after us. We'll see one another within a couple of weeks, but for me, it'll feel like eternity. We've been together every day since we were married, so part of me will be missing until we're back together.

While we're apart, I'll pray for your safety as you help Titus and Oleg make peace with people who prefer war. We couldn't have known that our lives would take this strange turn, but as you often remind me: our circumstances don't determine our reality; our faith in the truth of what God has made us to be determines our reality.

For this reason, I hope that as we part ways with people in San Diego, you'll see that you're much more than my brother's shadow, as you've called yourself for several months. I've known you were joking, but I hope that you see yourself in a new light soon—as a man who is just as much a leader as Titus. The Wes I know is no man's shadow. As God calls us to step out alone, you'll see how God wants to use you in a way that best fits how He designed you. You and I have been called elsewhere, my love, and I'm desperate to see what God will do next!

Don't fret over me going on ahead of you. Chevy is reliable, and what he lacks in experience, he makes up in commitment. The great company we're with should guarantee our safety on the road, but if something should befall either one of us before our child is born—we both know without any doubt that we are safe and secure in God's hands. We are His children, and for this little while on earth, I've been blessed to have been your wife.

I hope you find this letter within a couple days after you get started behind us. Soon, you'll be telling me of your journey alone, and I'll be sharing about my journey with this diverse crowd of refugees. God is with us both.

Until we see one another again, my love,

Wynter

Chapter 1

One-eyed Wes Trimble squeezed the brakes on his mountain bike and came to a stop in front of six highway bandits. He planted his feet on the pavement of the Los Angeles overpass and unbuckled the chest strap of his eighty-pound backpack. Without the chest strap hindering him, he could easily reach into his winter parka and draw his forty-five-caliber handgun from the shoulder holster. The holster was already unclipped and ready for action.

The six bandits had appeared suddenly, emerging from behind abandoned and burned-out vehicles left on Interstate 5. For two hundred miles, ever since leaving San Diego, Wes had been weaving his way through the cars on every highway and freeway. Drivers had left them wherever they'd run out of gas a year earlier. Pandemic-Day had crippled America. Few people had been prepared for the virus. The nation-wide quarantine hadn't stopped the panic. Crisis had ensued, followed by tragedy, crime, and death—oh, so much death.

It was January, so the six bandits were wearing heavy coats and hoodies. Their faces were unshaven and scarred. Wes didn't have to wonder what weapons they had concealed under their bulky winter gear, because their shotguns and mini-machine guns were in plain sight, aimed straight at him. None of them were older than thirty. The leader wore a dark beard and a scowl so deep that his eyebrows formed a unibrow. They appeared to be a hard lot, but Wes had been wrangling criminals, thugs, and terrorists his entire adult life. His real confidence came from God. Since Wes was a Christian, God was not absent from his life—not now, not tomorrow, not ever again.

"What're you doing all alone out here, boy?" Unibrow asked, holding an assault shotgun in both hands like he knew how to use it. "Nobody travels this highway without paying their respects."

Wes turned slightly, angling his head enough to see to his left with his right eye, the only eye he had. There might've been one or two more people hiding behind the abandoned van on his left. These men were wary, and definitely vicious if they had survived the Pan-Day riots that had burned across Los Angeles.

"Just passing through, friend." Wes sighed as the six drew closer. He didn't have time for these kinds of delays. His pregnant wife was with Avery "Chevy" Hewitt a few days ahead of him. Red spray paint marked the highway every few miles, indicating that his wife had indeed passed that way. "My name is Wes Trimble. I'm on my way up to the mountains, just this side of Yosemite. I've got people waiting for me."

The six continued to advance, and Wes wondered if they were showing uncharacteristic courage since they couldn't see how well-armed he was. His shoulder-holstered sidearm was concealed. The twin Desert Eagle forty-five in a leather holster was on his hip under the bottom of the parka. He had a nine-millimeter Baby Eagle handgun on the outside of his calf, and a .308 bullpup battle rifle in his pack. The bullpup's stock was compact enough to fit the whole rifle within the internal frame of the backpack, but he couldn't draw it out unless he had a moment to undo the weatherproof top. All of his firearms were loaded with COIL's non-lethal, gel-tranquilizer rounds, capable of putting a grown man to sleep for an hour. Since he was a man who knew the love of Christ, Wes no longer had the heart to kill someone made in God's image.

"Where you coming from, boy?" Unibrow asked. He stopped on the left side of the bike's front tire.

"San Diego." Wes allowed his eye to wander across the other five men, who covered him in an arc. There seemed to be no one behind him, but with so many abandoned cars, ambushers had many places to hide. "I left five days ago."

"San Diego?" Unibrow seemed surprised. "We heard San Diego burned to the ground. Like what happened to us."

"We had a few fires. Some rioting. But troops from Coronado moved in to keep the peace. Where they didn't help, other good people took charge. Half the city is still habitable."

"Good people took charge, you say?" Unibrow shook his head. "There ain't no more good people left on this earth. Only bad. You got some fancy gear, San Diego. What's with all this stuff you got?"

"I'm going prepared for the mountains. A lot of people will need help when they reach that snow level, or they'll die. Many have never lived outside the city before. Survivors from Pan-Day are looking to the mountains, thinking they'll be safe. Seems they need to be taught a little something about winter survival if they're going to make it."

"And that's you? You're going to teach them to survive? You think you're one of the good people?"

"I think God made us to be good, but we've all gone our own way." Wes nodded at the shotgun still aimed at his chest. "Nice shotgun. Looks like a Mossberg twelve gauge. That used to be a twenty-eight-inch, vent-rib barrel, before you sawed off part of it. It's a good bird gun, actually. I saw some quail off the freeway about a mile back. Seems the wildlife are already moving back in to take back their land, huh? Might make hunting easier."

Unibrow studied Wes in silence for a moment, tilting his head left and right.

"How'd you lose your eye, old man?"

Wes smiled a little, realizing he'd graduated from "boy" to "old man" rather quickly.

"I like to think I lost it in a violent gun battle overseas where I was the self-sacrificing hero. But the truth is, I was fly-fishing years ago." Wes chuckled at the memory of a different time. "The hook caught right in my eyeball. It didn't hurt much at first, but after I got it worked on, it turned out the hook gave me an infection. Sometimes God helps us appreciate what we have when we lose what we took for granted, you know?"

"Losing what we took for granted." Unibrow snorted, and lifted his shotgun to rest over his shoulder. "I never heard anyone talk so much about God nowadays. San Diego really isn't burned up?"

"Most of it's still standing. Like anywhere, there was a lot of looting, but hundreds are living peacefully around the waterfront now. A guy named Brogdon sort of took charge of Coronado Island. You know, the military base? There might be hope for that city yet. Most homes even have running water again. No electricity, but there are teams working on it."

"Man, that's more organizing than we can hope for." Unibrow gestured toward buildings within sight near Whittier. "Gangs and guns run everything around here. You shoot first, and ask who you shot later. You know what I mean?"

"These are hard times." Wes nodded, his nerves beginning to settle. "Some guys on bikes chased me all the way to Anaheim yesterday, so I know exactly what you mean."

"Yeah, I know those guys. They're just trying to get fed, like the rest of us. So, what you got in your pack?"

Wes groaned internally. He thought he'd bonded sufficiently with the gang lord, hoping the man's nature could be reasoned with.

"Survival gear."

"Yeah, you said that." Unibrow sucked on his bottom lip. "Your gear is too fancy not to have something that tastes good in there."

His companions shifted a little closer. Wes could sense their hunger. How they'd survived this long wasn't something he wanted to imagine. How they'd survive until tomorrow seemed to have his own supplies on their menu.

"I have enough to get me to where I'm going, just one man's rations." Wes glanced over the side of the overpass. "You guys must've stashed what canned goods you could find, right? You must have something in reserve."

"Man, people's eating rats all over the city. Disgusting!" Unibrow spit. "I swore I'd never eat a rat, and I never will. So, what's a rich man carry in his fancy pack, San Diego?"

Wes's breath came in shallow pants. He felt his nerves twitch. Six men was a lot to shoot it out with, especially when half of them were still aiming their weapons at him. He could dive clumsily off his bike, and maybe roll over behind the cover of the nearest vehicle, but his heavy pack would surely hinder him until he wrestled out of the straps. Maybe if he used Unibrow as a human shield, or took a few rounds in the pack by turning his back to the bandits . . .

"I have a long road ahead of me." Wes was done being friendly. Now, the bandits were trying his patience. People headed to the mountains needed him. His wife was about to have a baby. He couldn't miss that. "I should get going."

Wes made a move to put his foot on one pedal, but Unibrow raised his free hand and gripped the handlebars.

"Whoa, whoa, whoa, San Diego. We just want a peek inside your pack. You owe us that much, right?"

Wes's jaw was clenched, but he still managed to smile. He hadn't lived as the CIA's Pacific Rim lead agent without having a sense of humor, and he hadn't climbed up the ladder to become the president's liaison for COIL without having the skills to best the common criminal. But six men? It was asking a lot.

"Owe you?" Wes asked. Using his left hand, he slowly reached up to his left eye, then turned up the blue patch that covered his socket. The subtle misdirection caused the six to lean closer with curiosity. With his right hand, he drew his sidearm in a flash, and held it against Unibrow's cheekbone. "I don't think I owe you anything, friend. I'm traveling along on a public highway here, minding my own business, and you've delayed me long enough. If anything, you owe me. Now, we can part friends, as long as I and everything in my tightly-sealed pack of gear continues on the way. Or, we can join the millions of others in this wild land who've turned on each other over a scrap of food. Friends or enemies? It's your choice."

"You must be crazy, old man!" Unibrow froze, not moving his shotgun from his shoulder. "I bet you don't even have bullets!"

"Wait a minute," said one of the other bandits on Wes's right. "He looks serious, guys. He's not like the others. Nobody do anything!"

"You better pull that trigger, old man!" Unibrow cursed and swore, but then seemed to agree with his partner—or maybe he noticed the resolution in Wes's face. "Easy, now. I just wanted to see what you have. Ever since you said how you lost your eye, I knew you were good people. I got a little brother to take care of. Dying today isn't part of my plan. Not out here. Not like this. Look, you can just go on your way, all right? Just go!"

Wes narrowed his eye.

"So, you're saying we're friends?" Wes asked.

"Not right now, you lunatic! You got that gun in my face!" Unibrow's nostrils flared, but he seemed to reconsider his temper again when Wes's hand remained steady. "Yes, we're friends. You're cool, all right? He's cool, guys. Be cool. Everyone, just chill out! We don't need this guy's food. We're all friends here, see?"

The rest of the bandits hesitantly obeyed their leader, and lowered their guns.

"Sometimes good friends just need to know where each other's boundaries are, right?" Wes carefully eased the hammer forward on his weapon. "Don't mistake me for being someone courageous. I'm just committed to catching up to my people."

"Courageous?" Unibrow rubbed the cheekbone where the muzzle had been pressed. "That's not the word I'd use for you, San Diego. Cold-hearted is the right word. You was gonna shoot me in cold blood just like that? Now, can we see what you're carrying all the way from San Diego or what?"

Wes frowned, wondering if they were going to have round two of the stand-off. But then he realized Unibrow was serious about peeking into the pack. None of the others had raised their weapons again. Although Wes had lowered his gun, he wasn't about to holster it.

"I suppose a quick look won't hurt." Wes backed off his bike, leaving the handlebars in Unibrow's grip. A few steps away, still facing the men, Wes eased out of one shoulder strap, then the other, but kept his weapon loosely ready to raise and use. With his free hand, he set the heavy pack on the pavement and backed farther away. The pack stood upright on its own, almost four feet high. "Go ahead. Take a look."

They didn't need to be told twice. Like jackals on mutton, they loosed the top covering and started pulling gear out. A crossbow with titanium inserts, tarp, sleeping bag, folding game saw, cans and pouches of food, a fishing pole, and finally the battle rifle with scope attachment.

"Look at this!" They passed the rifle around, having set their own weapons aside. "It's so short!"

Next, they admired the food, licking their lips as they eyed the labels on the food pouches. Unibrow was the first to step away and approach Wes.

"You're some crazy fool, old man, to be traveling alone with all this stuff." The man held out his hand, which wasn't usually done since the Meridia Virus was suspected of transmission through touch. "But you're all right. They call me Bone."

"Wes Trimble." He shook the bandit's hand. Wes knew the virus was transmitted only through bodily fluids, and these men bore no visible symptoms. "If you guys were half as aggressive at catching food as you are at trying to ambush travelers, you'd make pretty good hunters to feed your neighborhood."

"Catching food?" Bone scoffed. "What do I look like, Robin Hood?"

"No, seriously. You have bird guns." Wes pointed at their shotguns. "You haven't sawed off the barrels of all your shotguns, have you?"

"Sure, we've still got some originals. What's your point?"

"You have wildlife moving back into some of these deserted neighborhoods. Even some deer. Wherever there's water, you'll find ducks and geese. That's good food, Bone. Think about how many a single deer could feed. Several families for a week or two. You want to do right by your people and feed your brother, right? This highway robbery business is going to get you killed. I'm not confusing you for being Robin Hood or anything. Hunting game is serious work. It's stealthy work. You've got to be an inventive predator to go after wild game. You'll reclaim your dignity, Bone, and the neighborhood will take note of you in a different way. That's the kind of man God made you to be."

"You might be on to something." Bone wagged his finger at Wes. "Next, you're going to tell me to go fly-fishing, and then I'll know you're messing with me."

Wes frowned, then caught the personal joke about his eye. He roared with laughter, even throwing out his left hand to balance himself on Bone's thick shoulder. The five other bandits barely noticed as they continued to inventory Wes's pack.

As a friend, and not as an enemy, Wes left Bone and his friends with a pouch of ground beef and gravy—compliments of Titus Casperlein's stash of supplies from before Pan-Day.

"You come through here again, Wes Trimble, and you ask for Bone." The man thumped his chest, his unibrow scowl returning. "Everybody knows Bone!"

Wes pedaled away, a prayer of both relief and thanks to God on his lips.

One day later, Wes huddled under his tarp as sheets of rain pummeled the interstate. Tejon Pass, commonly called the Grapevine, lay ahead of him a few miles—leg-cramping miles of uphill pedaling. The pavement was so steep where he was crouching that the highway ran like a shallow river past him. All the snow had melted, and if the temperature dropped any lower, the mountain would be an icy mess by dawn.

Beside him, he'd placed his pack on top of his bike, with his bike on its side, so his gears didn't get soaked from the falling and streaming water. With night closing at four thousand feet elevation, he barely remembered his joy from the day before when God had preserved him from the highway bandits. Now, he prepared for a long night with no trees or overpasses in sight, and no cover that he could—

Chuckling to himself, he realized there was plenty of cover to find shelter from the freezing rain, if he was willing to leave his bike outside. There were several cars and trucks scattered along the freeway! Since he wasn't interested in getting any wetter than he already was, he approached the nearest four-door Ford with the driver's window broken, and opened the door. Glass littered the front seat, so he unlocked the back door and threw his pack inside. On the far side of the car, where the pavement ended at a median, he laid his bike, then placed the tarp over it to protect the gears from the weather.

Inside the car, he closed the doors and rubbed his hands together. Much better! And relatively safer than huddling under the tarp in the middle of the interstate. The clouds to the west were visibly darker, so the storm wasn't ending any time soon. He could have continued to cycle uphill under his weatherproof gear, but his legs were done-in from climbing the slope for hours already.

He relaxed his head against the back seat and closed his eyes. Privately, he counseled himself that the delay to help Titus Caspertein squash a settlement dispute outside San Diego was worth sending Wynter ahead without him. She was with Chevy, so she would be safe. Wes had volunteered to help Titus and other COIL agents who'd remained in San Diego, but he didn't like being separated from his wife of one year. Wynter was eight months pregnant, and he wasn't at her side! But the needs up north had warranted their early departure, along with fifty other refugees who were seeking safer regions as well.

Chevy had been willing to go north by himself to help the survivors of Pan-Day settle up in the mountains, even though he didn't have the expertise that Wes had at mountain survival. Of course, Wynter had grown up in the woodlands of Arkansas, and her outdoor skills were as dependable as her brother's. Thus, Wes had volunteered his family's skills and thrown in with Chevy.

Marrying into the Caspertein family had been an adventure all on its own, besides facing the collapse of America. The Casperteins were a dedicated family who worked hard and played hard. Titus' casual amusement toward life was contagious, and Wes would miss the aging operative's rowdy banter with Oleg Saratov, his Russian partner. Of course, Levi Caspertein was never far from his father's side, either. The boy was twenty years old now, and in a few years, his frame would fill out. He'd be the same stock as his father, maybe even bigger, Wes guessed, and with the same zeal and courage as all the Casperteins had.

His reflections of what he'd left back in San Diego made Wes think of all those he'd parted ways with during Pan-Day. Corban Dowler, COIL's founder and director, had set up a relief compound somewhere in New York, and although Wes had known Corban much longer than he'd known Titus, Wes had chosen to stay on the West Coast instead. Wynter had come to trust her enterprising brother more than anyone else, and Wes wasn't about to separate his new bride from her extended family.

Many other COIL agents had chosen to stay with Corban in the east. Chloe Azmaveth lived in New York with her husband, Zvi. Nathan "Eagle Eyes" Isaacson, Bruno, Scooter, and Luigi had all opted to remain at Corban's side. Wes had heard that Fred "Memphis" Nelson had taken his wife, June, back to Memphis, Arizona, where he'd once been a Phys Ed teacher. The whole old COIL team seemed to be scattered, but wherever they were, Wes knew they'd continue to be used by God. COIL wasn't gone, only reassigned for domestic work. They were still saving lives, protecting the afflicted, and sharing the love of Christ wherever the Lord had planted them.

As he blinked awake, Wes's eyes widened. It was dark and rain was still pelting the roof, but he knew to trust his senses—something had startled him awake. He drew his sidearm and held it close to his chest, taking account of his situation. His bike was outside the car door, even though it was too dark to see it. The driver's window was broken and missing, so he could hear the rain cascading down the pavement. Yes, he decided, an unnatural sound had alerted him, heard through the open window.

His ears strained for some indication as he prayed for calm. Any number of villains could've snuck up on him, using the rain to cover their advance. Like Bone had said, people were just trying to get fed. Some had turned even to cannibalism, no doubt, because so few had the skills to fend for themselves, or to grow food that didn't require a microwave or drive-through.

Ten minutes passed and nothing happened, but Wes hadn't remained alive through countless Middle East and Pacific Rim conflicts by being hasty. His hand began to cramp, so he lowered his firearm to rest on his lap, but otherwise, he remained alert, playing out dozens of scenarios as his eye and ears reached for some glimmer of light or a hint of noise. Someone from Los Angeles may have been trailing him, although he was miles beyond the city itself. Neighborhoods lined the freeway in some sections, although the interstate had been particularly desolate the last week since it could only be accessed by the rare on-off ramps. Basic necessities had long since been stripped from the abandoned vehicles, so the locals probably found little reason to move along the many lanes of scattered and still vehicles.

The rain stopped before dawn, and as gray shapes began to form in the morning light, Wes's first concern was to check out the right-hand window. His tarp, which covered his bike, seemed undisturbed, except by the rain. At least no one had stolen his wheels. He still had hundreds of miles to cycle to reach even the base of the Sierra Nevada Mountains. Hiking that far didn't sound very appealing.

Then, Wes saw the movement he'd been waiting for. He licked his lips and re-gripped his handgun. Three cars ahead of him, someone else had found refuge from the rain as well. It was too much to hope that it was Wynter and Chevy, or even anyone from the fifty-person band with whom they'd left San Diego. Now he understood: he'd probably heard someone slam a door in the night, maybe running out for a bathroom break, or throwing something out of the car. But were they friends or enemies? And were they traveling north or south?

He slid farther down in the seat, peering over the dash with his only eye. From his pocket, he drew the binoculars and held up one side to his eye for a better view of the vehicle ahead. One, then two people emerged from the car, then moved as if they were putting on coats—stretching arms to fit into coat sleeves, and donning caps. Wes lowered his field glasses and briefly studied the whole freeway. Two people all alone? There could be others nearby, traveling in the same party, having all slept in different vehicles. Nobody in their right mind traveled alone—unless they were as armed and resolute as Wes felt he was to catch up to his wife.

The two people moved away from him, carrying nothing that he could see, not even backpacks. One of the people was a smaller adult, or maybe an older child. The other was certainly an adult. Having no backpacks meant they were probably locals and not actual long-distance travelers at all. Neither had a rifle, but that didn't rule out that they could be carrying one or two handguns in front of them.

Wes raised his head enough to gaze out the back window for a full minute, waiting for movement. He didn't mind facing conflict, but at that moment, an aggressor would have him at a disadvantage, since he was immobile and half-blinded by the interior of the car he'd chosen. Cycling on the open freeway, he'd been able to see people coming from far off, and avoid them or pass them cautiously, as he'd done for the past week. But he felt disabled inside the car. It was time to move, and to get back on the road.

But the two travelers in front of him were going his direction, up to Tejon Pass. He'd have to pass them at some point soon, and hopefully not get shot in the back while doing so. By some act of God, no doubt, he'd traveled through and escaped Los Angeles without losing anything he hadn't been willing to give away. The hunger of others might not be as easy to work around as Bone's had been.

Outside the car, he shook out the tarp while keeping a wary eye on the nearby cars. Two lone travelers? It was unlikely. A crowd of travelers made sense, since it was safer for a group. He tucked the tarp into a pack strap so the covering could dry out, and he shrugged into the shoulder straps. The morning air was brisk, but his parka was warm enough with its fleece liner to keep the front unzipped. He could draw the pistol from his shoulder holster faster than he could draw the sidearm from his hip under the bottom of his parka.

He began to pedal his bike in the lowest gear up the mountain slope. Any snow that had fallen at that elevation in weeks past had been washed away by the night's rain, but it was cold enough to snow again. Tejon Pass was just a hill compared to the Sierras where he was going. Those peaks were over ten thousand feet, and snow lay year-round, but this pass was a worthy test of his gears and strength.

Since the two travelers had set out on foot only fifteen minutes before Wes, they came into view far ahead after he rounded a bend. Now that he could see them up an empty lane of freeway and not through the glass of several cars, he felt certain the smaller person was a child. And by the walk and frame of the adult, that person was probably a woman. A woman and child were traveling alone in such dangerous times and places? Foolishness!

And his next thought was more foolishness, he scolded himself. His thought was to get them to safety, even at the expense of his own plans.

"Not foolishness," he whispered. "Just being neighborly."

It could mean missing the birth of his son or daughter, if he accepted the detour to help others. But it would be better to live with missing the birth of a child than to live with the knowledge that he'd abandoned two unprotected and needy strangers to face certain danger. After all, he wouldn't want anyone to leave his wife and child alone, if they were his.

His cycling rhythm didn't change as he swiftly approached the two strangers on foot.

Chapter 2

Wes Trimble passed the two travelers on the steep uphill grade of the Grapevine. Since he'd chosen the far left lane to peddle up, and the travelers were on the far right shoulder, he was ahead of them when he noticed that they froze at the sight of him. He came to a stop and planted his feet on either side of the bicycle. From a holder on his bike frame, he drew his canteen of water and took a few swallows, allowing them to observe him. Out of the corner of his eye, he watched as the two backed slowly away, perhaps hoping they hadn't been noticed. However, there was nowhere for them to hide.

He turned toward them and waved casually, but neither waved back. The woman was a blond, and the girl was a teenager, a smaller version of who was probably her mother. As he'd noticed that morning, they had no packs, only bulky coats. But now he could see that the mother held a handgun in one hand, while with her other hand, she reached out to pull her daughter behind her.

"I hope you ladies have a reason for being out here all alone," Wes called. "It's not safe to be traveling without an armed escort nowadays."

"We're fine!" the woman snapped. "Just keep going."

Wes understood they were afraid. Everyone those days was afraid. Many predators were about.

"How far north are you going?" Wes frowned. "I hope it's not far. You won't survive without provisions."

The teen peered from behind her mother, holding her carefully in front of her.

"Just go on, now." The woman shifted her feet nervously and whispered something to her daughter, who glanced left and right, maybe looking for cover. Perhaps they were preparing to run away. "We're doing just fine on our own."

"Okay, okay." Wes raised his hand, not wanting to push them further. "You two continue on your own, then. I'll just be on my way. I'm trying to catch up to my wife in a caravan a few days ahead. Maybe you saw about fifty people moving up the highway here?"

"We don't want any trouble." The mother turned her handgun sideways and looked at it, as if checking to see if the safety was off. "Don't make me shoot you!"

Wes doubted she could hit him at that distance, and chances were, she didn't have bullets. Most people in San Diego had run out of bullets in the first weeks after Pan-Day, protecting their property from thieves and looters.

He gazed ahead and up the highway with a frustrated sigh. It was just plain ignorant of them to be alone, and it was far from chivalrous to leave them in their current state. But he couldn't make them receive his help. On foot, they'd be walking through cold temperatures for days, if they were headed to the San Joaquin Valley. And without sleeping bags or a tent, they were probably counting on sleeping in cars along the way, but Wes guessed on the far side of the mountain, cars would probably be fewer, since drivers would've coasted down the long northern slope from Tejon Pass. The pair would have nowhere to get out of the cold.

Taking his pack off his back, he opened the top. What could he leave them? He'd packed so carefully from Titus Caspertein's stores of gear. Helping so many suffering refugees reach the mountains could take a year, and he didn't want to short himself. Nevertheless, he drew out a long-sleeved thermal and a pouch of dried meat. From the pouch, he took a fistful of about half and stuffed it into his own coat pocket.

"Maybe this'll help a little," he said, and wrapped the pouch of meat in the thermal top, then tossed it closer to them. "It'll be tough on you, but it would be safer to travel at night and sleep during the day, since you're determined to travel alone."

The mother didn't respond, but the girl's hunger was apparent as she stared at the food and shirt.

There seemed nothing more to say, so Wes shook his head and pushed off. In low gear, he continued the slow crawl up the mountain lanes. Far ahead, he stopped again and looked back. He didn't like leaving them behind. The freeways were already scarce of abandoned cars. Survival, even with a little food and an extra shirt, seemed unlikely for the pair. Against what his conscience was comfortable doing, he kept going.

About noon, he reached the summit, icy ridges above him keeping the freeway in shade, and buildings nearby appeared abandoned. Pulling over to the shoulder, he leaned his bike against the guardrail to stretch his tired legs. He would've been in worse shape if he hadn't been active since Pan-Day. For a year, he'd been marching or biking alongside Titus and Oleg around San Diego, cleaning up the city, settling disputes, and rebuilding what they could. Hundreds of civilians had remained along the city's coast rather than join the thousands who had fled inland. Many of those who had remained owed their lives to Titus' vigilance and creativity to keep people fed, safe, and busy.

But now, the many who had fled inland needed to be helped. Wes and Wynter had waited for a caravan to leave for the Central Valley, since travel would be safer in a crowd. And Wynter could have their child in the mountains. With Chevy beside them, the growing family hoped to build a new community of Pan-Day survivors at an abandoned ski resort called Lune Lake. But there were many unknowns, and Lune Lake was far away.

Walking away from his bike, Wes noticed movement on the hillside two hundred yards away. Something light brown moved against the brush. He used his binoculars to study a grazing deer picking at dead grass now visible since the rain had washed away the snow. There were so many starving people in America, but here was a deer that could feed a family for several weeks. For a moment, he considered leaving the deer alone. After all, he had a pack full of provisions. However, it seemed that God was offering him the deer for a reason that had nothing to do with himself.

Setting aside his pack, Wes drew out the stubby battle rifle and checked the thirty-round magazine. He had only three magazines—two with gel-tranqs for tranquilizing a human enemy, and one with regular .308 rounds for hunting game. By the time he exchanged the non-lethal magazine for the live rounds, he figured the deer would be gone, and he could continue on his way.

Peering through the rifle scope, he saw the deer was still there. He knelt on the pavement and rested the rifle muzzle over the highway median to steady his aim. Although he was a trained marksman, he didn't have the skill of Titus or even Titus' son, Levi, when it came to using the bullpup with proficiency. After gauging for distance and slope, knowing he didn't want to waste ammunition—he fired. The deer dropped where it had stood.

"Now what?" he asked God directly. "I don't know anyone around here. What am I doing here, Lord?"

He returned to his bike and lifted it over the guardrail to hide it from passersby, and did the same with his pack. With the rifle on its sling over his shoulder, he left the highway, passed a burned-down restaurant and its empty parking lot, and climbed the hill to the deer. From that elevation, standing on rain-soaked grass, he studied the landscape. The buildings within sight seemed abandoned, and the houses were all dark. *Wait!*

Without moving anything but his eye, he watched a curtain in one window of a two-story house behind the restaurant. No doubt, anyone who was on the mountaintop would've heard his gunshot. It would've signaled danger for most people. Everyone those days seemed to want to be left alone, except Wes had learned with Titus and Oleg that those barriers of fear needed to be broken down. After all, Jesus had taught that being neighborly meant looking for folks to treat as neighbors, even if people didn't at first want to be recognized as such.

Wes dressed the small spike using a thin-handled skinning knife. His thoughts about being neighborly brought to mind the two travelers behind him on the freeway. Maybe he hadn't tried hard enough to help them, or maybe his worry for them was needless, since they weren't traveling that far. The woman clearly wasn't familiar with firearms, and if they came upon trouble, they would be otherwise defenseless.

With a grunt, Wes took hold of the little buck's antlers and dragged it off the ridge. He angled toward the house where he'd seen the curtain move. At first, he'd been uncertain about God's intention with the buck, but now he was certain that God wanted to accomplish something special at Tejon Pass.

Across an access road and down to the back of the house, he dragged the deer. Fresh boot tracks in the mud led to and from the backdoor, out of sight from the highway. Someone was living in hiding, and Wes didn't want to interfere too much, but he couldn't walk away after God had clearly directed him to the deer.

"You can split the deer with me," Wes shouted at the house. "I just need your help, please. Come on, I saw you looking out your window twenty minutes ago."

He kept his eye on the two windows in sight, wondering if he'd need to dodge a shotgun blast if he pressed the residents too hard.

"Go away!" a man's gravelly voice yelled back.

"That's not happening, friend. Don't mistake me for a trouble-maker. I've got a whole deer out here to barter with. I need a few things, minor things, then I'll be going on my way."

The back door cracked. Sure enough, a twelve-gauge shotgun barrel emerged first, paused, then extended farther as the door opened more. An elderly man in long johns and an unzipped coat elbowed the door all the way open and stood in the doorway.

"Move away from the deer," the old man ordered. His hair was white, and his eyes squinted as he blinked rapidly at the bright day. "You left it. Now get on your way."

"No, that's not the way friends barter. I'll give you three-quarters of the deer, but I need your help with a few things first. I'm a traveler. Look at me. I have no use for a whole deer, so it's yours, I assure you. You want to hear me out, or turn me into a spaghetti strainer?"

"I should shoot you." The man snarled, or maybe he was just squinting more. "But you might be honest. Hard to tell between the two these days."

"I know what you mean. Listen, I have a couple of lady friends coming up the road, and they could use some supplies. Do you have a backpack and some extra clothes or anything to offer these travelers?"

"There wasn't much left in this house when I came here last spring." He lowered his rifle. "I was like you, traveling through, but my eyes got so bad. I'm afraid that deer won't be much help to me since I can't see even to butcher it. There's a kid here who's too young to do it. How soon do you have to move on?"

Wes rested his hands on his hips, then adjusted his eye patch like he did when he didn't know what to say. He guessed Wynter and the baby would just have to wait.

"I can butcher the deer for you, but I need to be heading out by morning. My two friends should be caught up with us by then. Do you have a smokehouse?"

"No, just a fireplace where I cooked some bird meat a couple weeks ago. My eyes haven't been good enough to do much more lately."

A child in stocking feet, stained jeans, and shaggy hair pushed around the old man. He couldn't have been older than three years old, and Hispanic by the look of him. Wes figured he probably wasn't a relative of the old man.

"He wandered in a few weeks ago," the man said. "Doesn't eat much. Doesn't cry or talk."

Wes smiled. God's ways were sometimes hard to discern at times, but once they started unfolding, it was easy to see where to go, like now. These two survivors needed his help.

"Let's get this deer hung up so I can butcher it, and I'll build you a small smokehouse. It'll be simple, but it'll do the job. This much meat should hold you for the next few weeks."

Before he got started, Wes fetched his bike and pack from the highway, and set his belongings behind the house. The man had relaxed considerably, and the shotgun was nowhere in sight as Wes hung the deer from the awning of a little shed. The boy squatted next to the deer's head and poked with a finger at the animal's pink tongue. The old man tore boards off the walls of the shed and laid them on the wet ground. Without waiting to be asked, the stranger told his story while Wes worked.

His name was Ivory White, a name his merchant father had bestowed on him after he'd retired from his illegal trade dealings with Africa.

"He was a hard man," Ivory said, rubbing his half-shaven face. It looked as if he'd started with a razor a week earlier, then had given up. "I can't think of anything I got from him that I liked—not my name, and especially not my eyesight. As luck would have it, my own kids were no better than he was. They put me in an old folk's home the minute I told them my eyes were going. But I busted out a year later and continued to run a delivery business for a few more years, then a tourist shop in Ventura, usually barely scraping by. During Pan-Day, I knew I was finished since my eyes were going so quickly. I wanted to reach the Sierras, but my legs were finished coming up that mountain. I guess my eyes aren't the only thing giving out.

Been here ever since, starving most days, unless I can find some roots to boil, or mice to trap and eat."

"It's funny how life works." Wes laid one quarter of the deer on newspapers. "You thought this place was your final destination, it sounds like. But I think it'll be a point of salvation instead—for you and for others."

"What others? You? I don't believe you need salvation. My eyes aren't that good, mister, but a man who shoots like you do doesn't need any help from someone like me."

"Maybe I don't, but my two friends on their way here, they'll need you. Friendly people are hard to find nowadays. They've come upon hard times, I think, maybe harder than others, and they'll need somewhere to stay. They'll help you stay alive."

"What do you mean, *you think?* I thought they were your friends. You don't know what they've been through? Are they with you or not?"

"A woman and her kid are hiking this way up the freeway. They don't have anything but their coats. I think they need help, but they're too afraid to accept it."

"Nobody wants to be a victim."

Wes finished cutting steaks off the deer an hour before sundown. Though he wanted to start building a smokehouse for preserving the meat, he didn't want the two travelers to pass by without him having another opportunity to help them. Carrying his rifle, which was now loaded with gel-tranqs, he hiked back to the highway, then up to the eastern ridge that overlooked the southwest stretch of freeway.

Sitting down against the base of a rotting billboard sign, he watched the road and admired the setting sun. Maybe Wynter was looking at the same sunset, praying for him to catch up to her soon. She and Chevy knew a few people in the fifty-person caravan, but most in the group were strangers from Mexico—Americans who'd been trapped south of the border before Pan-Day. Now, they were trying to reach what was left of their homes, or trying to find refuge in the mountains. Some of the families in Wynter's caravan, Wes had learned when they'd passed through San Diego, were traveling by foot farther to the east. Millions had perished, and those who'd survived seemed desperate to return to family and familiar places.

The sun touched the horizon. He could almost see the ocean. Sometimes he wondered how other nations were faring with the Meridia Virus, but there was no news. Maybe the virus hadn't spread beyond North America at all, as if God were calling for repentance in the United States alone, whose might and wealth had made her complacent, proud, and wicked.

Finally, the two travelers came around a distant bend as they walked up one of the inside lanes of the freeway. Wes held the rifle scope to his eye to see if he could tell how weary they seemed. Depending on how tired they were, he might be able to convince the woman to let him help them. Exhaustion had a way of breaking the will, and Wes hoped his resolve to help them was stronger than theirs to reject his hand.

But on the edges of his scope view, a flicker of color drew his attention to the foreground. He studied two abandoned vehicles in the fading light before he spotted a crouching man. Then he started to see more shapes. Like jackals, several men darted from cover to cover, closing in around the two female travelers. Ignorant of the ambush quickly tightening around them, the two travelers were dragging their heels as they plodded uphill.

The ambushers were poised to attack when Wes flipped off the safety on his rifle and fired into the back of a bandit nearest to the travelers. The bandit leaped upright, then fell as if dead across the hood of a car. Eight others shifted their attention toward Wes, but he didn't bother to look for cover. He was nearly three hundred yards uphill, and that was a long shot for the likes of these few, only two of whom had long rifles. The rest had handguns or shotguns, but they were no threat to him, only to the woman and child.

Two bandits made a desperate lunge toward the two travelers, perhaps to use them as human shields or hostages, but Wes shot one of them with a tranq before he reached the woman. The second man changed his mind and scrambled up the opposite ridge. The others in their party did the same. Wes fired twice more to send them on their way, but didn't manage to hit any more of the moving targets.

In the last of the light that evening, Wes stood upright so the woman and child could see him in the red rays of the setting sun. He watched them hesitate, maybe not recognizing him yet, since they'd seen him for only a few minutes on this bike earlier that day. But finally, they seemed to reason out the alternative of spending the night alone with the bandits prowling nearby. They continued up the freeway to the top of the hill, where it gradually began to arc down toward the north.

As darkness closed over the pass, and a cold wind with it, Wes traversed down the ridge to reach the interstate. The woman and child shied away from him, shivering and clutching one another. The woman held her handgun aimed at Wes's feet as if she wasn't sure whether she should shoot her savior or not.

"It looked like you two were about to have some company tonight." Wes slung the rifle onto his back and blew on his cold hands. "Thanks to God, He introduced me to someone safe where you two can stay as long as you want. Come on."

He didn't force them to accept his words. The cold would do that, along with their weariness, he guessed. After a few steps toward the demolished restaurant, he heard them hustling behind him, whispering to one another.

"Come on in. Get next to the fire." Ivory White welcomed them in his gruff way, opening the door for his three guests. "All right, Wes. What are their names?"

Wes set his rifle on top of the fridge where no one else could reach it easily. The boy played on the floor in front of the fire, the two little antlers from the buck in his hands. The mother and daughter slowly took in the small living room, the old squinting man, and Wes, who crossed his arms and stood casually against the wall. He knew that his eye patch sometimes gave the impression that he was a pirate, so he intentionally smiled to offset their uneasiness.

"I'm Jill," the mother said. She studied the room, as if she expected other house guests or enemies to jump out. She was pretty and looked to be about 40 years old, with lines starting to show around her mouth and eyes. Her daughter glared boldly from her mother's shoulder. "And this is Dalia."

Cautiously, they accepted Ivory's invitation to the fire where he gave them blankets.

Wes borrowed one of the three lanterns Ivory had placed on the kitchen counter, and returned to the back yard where he began to construct a small smokehouse, using spare boards torn from the shed. If smoked over several days with a little seasoning, the meat would be preserved for weeks and ready for cooking and eating down the road. Although Wes wasn't planning to wait around to smoke the meat, he'd picked out a couple choice steaks for that evening's meal. After strenuous biking for a week now, he noticed he wasn't filling out his clothes as much, although Wynter had teased him that summer for having gained a few pounds. He still had a little weight to fall back on, if times got tougher.

Working in the lantern's dim lighting, Wes managed to build a four-foot-cubed smokehouse. As he dug underneath it, where firewood could be placed to burn, he thought back to the nine bandits he'd intercepted that evening. That confrontation had happened only a quarter-mile away from Ivory's house. With the right breeze, the crooks could have already smelled the smoke Ivory was making by cooking inside at the fireplace.

After an hour, the two who'd been tranqed would have woken drowsily, realizing they hadn't been killed after all. Although COIL's non-lethal weaponry had been designed to show mercy—to encourage an enemy to think twice about their choices—Wes knew that some saw the mercy of Christians as weakness. Realizing they wouldn't be killed during an attack, the bandits might try to attack with renewed aggressiveness. But Wes knew they'd find a surprise if they attacked the blind man, Ivory. The old man's shotgun didn't have tranquilizers, but buckshot, which could tear a man in two up close.

At the smell of the meat cooking inside, Wes's stomach growled. He wiped his muddy feet at the back door, and stepped inside. Jill and Dalia were devouring their food, using their fingers. The boy was gnawing on a charred steak, held with one hand, while the other hand still clutched one of the spike antlers. He watched Wes with wide eyes as Wes bent down and picked up Jill's nine-millimeter she'd set on the floor. When she lunged to take it back, he grabbed her wrist and held her back with ease.

"Relax. I'm just going to load it, then give it back to you."

"It is loaded," she said.

Sure enough, Wes slid out the magazine and found three brass cartridges, but nothing was in the chamber. It seemed she needed to learn how to chamber a round. Walking over to his pack, Wes emptied her gun of lethal rounds, then dug out a magazine-worth of nine-millimeter gel-tranqs, which he kept for the Desert Eagle on his ankle. Back at the fire, he sat next to her and loaded the weapon where she could watch. After he slammed the magazine back into place, he held it up in the light of the fire.

"You need to put a bullet in the barrel like this." He pulled back the slide and let it chamber loudly, making everyone flinch. "Now, it's ready to shoot. Don't carry it if it's not ready to shoot. You try it."

He ejected the chambered round, fed it into the magazine, and gave her the weapon. Apparently, it was her first time chambering a round, and she did so with difficulty. But when the gun was sufficiently ready for use, she smiled weakly, almost apologetically.

"Thank you." She stuffed the weapon into the waist of her jeans, then returned to her food.

"Before you came in," Ivory said, "we were talking about their plans. I'd like you guys to take the boy with you when you leave tomorrow."

Wes raised his eyebrows.

"I brought them to keep you company, Ivory, not to keep me company."

"I can't take care of anyone anymore, Wes." The old man frowned. "The boy needs an adult who can watch after him. He needs a mother."

"I'm not his mother!" Jill blurted.

"She's Jill Austin!" the teen said, as if defending her mother.

"Dalia!" Jill glanced at Wes and Ivory with fear on her face. "That's no one's business."

"It's no secret, Mom. People are going to figure out who you are sometime."

Wes heard Dalia's tone and recognized the voice of a spoiled child who was probably torn between rebelling against her mother's authority and appreciating the safety of her protection—like most teenagers.

"Is Jill Austin someone I should know?" Ivory asked, his weak eyes aimed toward Wes. "I couldn't recognize my own hand in front of my face right now."

"She's been in, like, nine blockbuster movies!" Dalia reported. "She's a millionaire!"

"Dalia!" Jill slapped her daughter's leg. "Too much information, little girl!"

"I'm not a little girl, Mom!"

"Maybe it would help if we did have some information about you," Wes said. "I don't recognize you or your name. Sorry to disappoint. And having millions of dollars hardly matters anymore, Dalia. I've seen people burn stacks of hundreds to cook food when they were starving. We're all the same now, all of us needing God to show us His peace in our broken lives."

"The boy needs a name," Ivory said after a moment. "Something besides Boy, which I've been calling him."

"I once had a Mexican friend named Elio." Wes nodded, savoring a mouthful of steak. "It's a good name. A strong name. What do you think, Jill? Will Elio do?"

"Me?" The mother lowered her head. "I can barely take care of my own child. I'm not his mother."

"I like Elio." Dalia reached across her mother and tickled the boy's knee. "Hey, little cutie. I always wanted a little brother."

"I'm not adopting that kid!" Jill gasped. "Look at me. I'm in no shape to help anyone. I'm still shaking from those guys who tried to kill us tonight."

"It's true," Ivory said to Wes. "They won't be safe here. I'm in no condition to travel, and you need to get moving tomorrow. I feel it in my bones, Wes. I probably won't last the winter."

"We could find a trailer for my bike. You could ride in that."

"Ivory White isn't going to sit in no bike buggy!" The old man threw down a fire poker, making sparks fly up the chimney. "You all got somewhere to be, but not me. This is as far as I go."

"We can go with you?" Jill cautiously asked Wes. "My brother was murdered at Castaic Lake, and my husband died from the virus a few months ago. We ran out of food at our house, so we have to go somewhere. We don't have anyone. We just want to be safe. You have a wife, you said earlier."

Wes stared at the fire before he responded. He remembered his conversation with God that morning. If necessary, he'd agreed to put off his plans to catch up to his wife's caravan if these two travelers needed his help. Now, he knew they needed him.

"There are a few houses up this canyon," Wes said. "Maybe we can find some bicycles for you two to ride. We can cover twice the distance on wheels than we can on foot, until we get up to where the snow is."

"I never learned to ride a bike." Dalia scowled at her mother. "No one ever taught me."

"But you're not a child, right?" Wes said, reminding her. "So, you'll learn tomorrow morning. If you're going with me, that's the way we're traveling."

"Well, I want a gun, too," Dalia demanded. "Everyone else has a gun, so I should have one, too."

"You may have to put that one over your knee before your journey's end, Wes." Ivory chuckled. "A few good swats like the old days would do wonders."

Jill tried not to show her own amusement at her daughter's expense, but the mother seemed pleased that someone could correct her pouting, mouthy teen.

"On a serious note," Wes said, "I need to say something. We could've all died today, if those bandits would've attacked instead of fled. We could die tomorrow just as easily. And Ivory, I'm not leaving you behind to die without telling you all about what has brought me peace about dying. That day will come for each of us, and we need to be ready. Maybe before Pan-Day, none of us were too concerned about what eternity holds, but we've seen a lot of death this past year. The whole country stinks of it. Believe me when I tell you, true hope still exists, even when facing death. A lot of people don't understand why

Jesus Christ had to die, but I assure you—He died for us. And if you believe it, it'll change your life, and change the course of your eternal destination."

As the fire crackled, Wes told the story of the Bible. Long after Elio yawned and went to sleep in Dalia's arms, Wes shared the gospel, and how they didn't need to face death with fear. He told them that their loving God had come in the flesh and had overcome death. Now, He waited to receive repentant sinners.

While Wes spoke, Jill pulled a drawing pad out of her coat and used a pencil to sketch something Wes couldn't quite see. Ivory listened without interrupting, but Wes saw him shake his head several times, like he thought the whole record of Scripture was crazy. It would take time to win their hearts, Wes knew, but it all began with sharing the truth. God would work out the rest.

Chapter 3

Wes's eye flashed open, and his body was instantly alert. The fire crackled softly in the hearth. For a moment, he wondered if he'd woken merely to the sound of the wood settling in the fireplace. But no, like the morning before, he needed to trust his instincts, now honed to the dangerous world they lived in. As soon as he made sure no one dangerous was in the living room, he slipped from under his blanket and stood against the wall, his elbow at the edge of the hearth. Flickering shadows danced across the room, but adjacent to the fireplace, he was in darkness.

The sidearm from his shoulder holster slid lightly into his right hand. Then he reached across his torso with his left and drew his other Desert Eagle. Softly, as quietly as the fire popped, he drew back the hammer on both weapons.

Below him, Dalia slept on an old rug, her arm over Elio. Jill slept on the far side of the room, facing the back door. And Ivory White, in the corner to Wes's right, snored lightly, his head cocked back farther than seemed comfortable.

When danger was present, waiting had always been easy for Wes. From reading old Western dime novels as a kid, he'd learned that the difference between a living cowboy and a dead cowboy, where Indians were concerned, was simply a matter of patience. He knew that when a threat existed, the first one to move without all the information is usually the first cowboy to die.

Then he heard it—a rattle, as if someone was testing a doorknob. It was coming from the kitchen, or the front door. Wes's heart pounded against his ribs. Although the fire was low and the curtains were partially drawn, someone could've seen from afar the glow and flicker of the fire through the window, or smelled the smoke. It could even be the nine highway bandits from the previous evening.

Wes reprimanded himself for not being more vigilant by checking the security of the house after everyone had fallen asleep. Even in San Diego, where a semblance of security had returned to the city, marauders were known to lurk on the streets until they were caught by vigilant citizens or civil volunteers. Sharing an apartment complex with Titus and other COIL personnel had had its advantages, since all of them were weathered combatants from hundreds of conflicts. But now, he was alone, and these lives were his responsibility.

He had to assume the prowler or prowlers were about to make their entrance. His head snapped to the left as a new sound reached his ears. *Someone was on the roof!* Ivory White may have locked the front and back doors, but had he locked the windows upstairs? Were there windows that could be accessed by the roof?

The room was empty of old furniture. Ivory White had burned everything that could burn, even tearing open some of the walls to pull out the wood studs. But the fire mantle was synthetic marble and felt sturdy. Wes seemed to be standing in the safest place if a gun battle was about to take place.

A floorboard upstairs creaked, and Jill rolled over. Wes stretched out both arms, aiming one weapon at the stairway, and the other at the window. Still as a statue, he waited. They were coming. Gunfire was about to startle his new friends awake. He just hoped they didn't leap up into his line of fire. They would remain relatively safe as long as he was still alive and able to fire at the enemy.

Jill lifted her head, and Wes saw the glint of firelight in her open eyes. She stared at him, but Wes didn't want to make a sound, in case the enemy was already close. In his peripheral vision, he saw Jill moving her hands under her blanket. He guessed she was preparing her pistol for use. The celebrity actress had some maternal courage after all.

Wes glanced at Ivory White, who still hadn't stirred. The man's shotgun was leaning against the corner near him. Somehow, the old man had survived alone without much vigilance. After staying up late, talking and enjoying the warmth of the fire, the poor guy was exhausted.

The sound of soft whispering came from the stairway. More than two men, Wes concluded, were approaching from the stairs. But more were moving around outside. Still, his arms held steady, his head motionless, his pulse pounding. For years, he had protected Americans from dangers outside her borders. Now, it only felt natural to protect Americans within her borders.

The leg of a man appeared on the highest visible step. In the flickering light, nothing was especially obvious, but then another foot stepped farther down. A man crouched low, easing down the stairs, followed by another man urging him to descend faster. They seemed focused on the sleeping forms in front of the fire, but Wes knew it was just a matter of time before they recognized the shadowy stillness of his own figure against the wall—and the empty sleeping bag on the floor.

He dared to glance at Jill, then returned his gaze to the predators. Jill lay perfectly still, her eyes on him, perhaps waiting for him to make the first move.

A third man appeared on the stairs as the first man reached the bottom step. If Wes could have given Jill an order, he would've told her to roll over right then and shoot up at the nearest man, whose feet were two yards from her head. But she was just a civilian, barely surviving, fortunate to be alive since she had no gear or experience.

A fourth man crowded the others on the steps, and the first man stepped around Jill's head.

Wes couldn't wait any longer for more enemies to arrive. He couldn't be sure if these were the same nine from the evening before, but he wasn't waiting for the other five to file into the room.

Since no one seemed to be coming in through the window, Wes swiveled his right arm to parallel his left, extended straight out in front of him. He fired with both guns simultaneously, and worked his way to the right, toward the fourth man, whose body wasn't completely exposed yet from the stairway. One advantage with the gel-tranqs was that they didn't need a body shot to incapacitate a person. The tranqs could put a man to sleep through any exposure to the blood stream. Shooting the fourth man in the leg put him down two heartbeats after the first man fell on top of Jill.

Jill screamed and fired her gun as the unconscious man smothered her, but Wes ignored her wrestling match as he stepped over the other three, who now lay unconscious. Almost too late, he noticed two faces at the window. He fired four times through the glass, shattering the window, and sending two armed figures retreating in haste from the house.

Arriving at the window, he put his shoulder against the wall and tried to discern shapes in the darkness. At least one man outside had been hit; he could see a man's leg as he lay on the cold ground about eight feet from the window.

Wes licked his lips and contemplated reloading in the sudden silence. Jill had stopped screaming. After throwing off her unconscious attacker, she'd risen to her knees, and held her handgun with both hands to sweep the room back and forth. Ivory White sat wide-eyed against the wall. His shotgun remained within arm's reach, but the action was already over. Wes was glad the half-blind man hadn't grabbed the long gun and started blasting away. He might've hit him or one of the other three in their party.

Elio didn't make a sound as he clung to Dalia, who was now sitting up, clutching her new little brother in return. The fire popped, making Jill flinch, but otherwise, she was steady, waiting, and listening with Wes.

Wes grinned. The prowlers hadn't expected such a response from those they probably thought would be easy prey. They hadn't even gotten one shot off in response. After holstering one gun, Wes leaned out the broken window.

"Come on, you jackals!" he shouted. "We've got more where that came from!"

The sound of several running feet could be heard in the distance. If it was the men from the night before, Wes guessed they now knew he was firing tranqs, but maybe they didn't know for sure it was him. For a few seconds, the house had been filled with terror, and to anyone who had been outside, it would've sounded like a terrible battle.

Little Elio began to cry quietly in Dalia's arms when Wes stepped from the window. He stoked the fire while he contemplated what was best for the small band of travelers.

"What do we do with these clowns?" Ivory White asked, gesturing at the four unconscious attackers. "I don't see any blood."

"I shot one of them," Jill reported quickly, then bolder. "I shot one of them!"

Wes laid the poker aside and rose to his feet. He gently took Jill's firearm from her hand and walked to his pack where he reloaded her gun.

"Nobody killed anyone," he said. "This is non-lethal ammunition. Jill, you did well, protecting everyone. Let's hope we don't need to do something like that ever again."

"That's unlikely in this country." Ivory scoffed.

"Mom, you shot one of them?" Dalia asked, admiration in the teen's eyes.

"I was . . . so afraid." Jill mumbled. The poor woman seemed to be going into shock.

"There's no jail to put these boys in." Wes faced Ivory directly. "Once they wake up in about an hour, they'll be angry. It won't be safe for anyone to stay here, not now. I'm a Christian. It's not in me to kill them all. Dawn is coming, and I think it's time we find some way to bring you along with us, old man."

"I told you, I'm not riding in no bike buggy!"

"You don't have a choice." Wes took the shotgun from the corner, checked the load, and set it beside his pack. "I'm not leaving you behind to blindly shoot anyone, or to get yourself shot. Come on. Let's pack up and find some bikes."

For good measure, Wes used some old extension cords from upstairs to tie up the bandits before they woke and tried something else. As dawn peeked through the broken window, Wes noticed how young the bandits really were. They were barely older than Dalia, most without any hint of facial hair.

Outside, Wes spoke to Ivory about cooking as much of the deer meat in the time they had left, and leaving the rest behind.

"What a waste." Ivory cursed, then apologized. "All that meat gone to waste."

"It won't be wasted." Wes nodded at the house. "Once those guys come around after we're gone, they'll struggle loose and take the meat for themselves. We didn't shoot them to kill them, and we're leaving them half a deer so they don't starve through the rest of the winter. This is the kind of grace God shows us, which is what I was talking about last night. This kind of grace has the power to change lives, if those lives receive it with a right heart. We may never know how leaving the meat for those men may affect the world, but it's the right thing to do."

"Well, you've got a better heart than I do!" Ivory grumbled as he knelt over the smokehouse to take the meat back inside to cook.

Wes jogged up the street, away from the freeway, toward several houses on either side of the canyon lane. He slowed to a walk as he eyed garages next to homes that had been visibly vandalized and looted. The doors appeared to have been smashed in by sledge hammers. The twisted metal had been damaged enough for thieves to climb inside. But now this property was owned by no one. Sadly, all these homeowners were probably dead, or at least never coming back. So, it was Wes's turn to climb through the broken garage door of the first home and see if he could salvage anything.

In the first garage, he found an assortment of tools worth a fortune, but he couldn't carry the weight. In the second garage, he found one bicycle that was a little rusted, but workable, if he fixed one flat tire. He rooted around a workbench until he found a patch kit. In the third garage, someone or something had died recently, and the odor of rotting flesh forced him to hold his breath to peek into the garage. A large family must've lived there at one time, because he spotted five bikes against the back wall, and two more hanging on hooks on the side wall.

Since the odor was coming from inside the house to the garage, he closed the door leading into the house, and forced opened the twelve-foot garage door a little more to vent the space. These bikes were in excellent condition. The only problem was, all the bikes were adult mountain bikes, male and female. With Elio too young and Ivory too blind, something would have to be built to accommodate them for travel.

Outside, Wes found a lawn trailer, a four-wheeled cart meant for leaves, and brought it into the garage. Using tools from the previous garage, he took off the trailer's two front wheels so when the handle was tethered to his bike, it would roll on the back wheels. He found no rope, but more extension cords would work just as well.

It took him two trips to and from the garage to bring two bikes and the trailer to his waiting companions, who were gathered outside.

"They're awake," Jill reported. Her sidearm was tucked into the waist of her pants. "You want me to shoot them again?"

"No, let's leave them be." He studied each one in his party. They had hardly any gear amongst them. Ivory had shared what little he had with Jill and Dalia, but that had been only the blankets and meat. "Okay, we're ready to go. Dalia, it's time to learn how to ride a bike. This one's yours. You're responsible for taking care of it. Hop on. You'll learn in no time."

"Is that supposed to be a trailer for me?" Ivory asked Jill, but she only shrugged and looked skeptically at Wes, as if she knew it would be a challenge to make the old man ride in the trailer.

Wes guided Dalia up and down the street for ten minutes before she got the balance of the bike. Her steering was a little wobbly, but Wes felt comfortable moving out.

"You'll be an expert by the end of the day," he assured the teen, "even if you take a couple of spills along the way. It's all part of learning."

Dalia was beaming when she returned to Ivory and her mother.

"I always wanted a horse," she told her mother, awkwardly jumping off her new bike. "But Wes got me something even better. I'll clean it up and it'll be just like new!"

Wes left his travel companions to inspect their various road-worthy vehicles, and went back into Ivory's house. The bandits were struggling against their binds until he knelt among them. They immediately stopped pulling at the cords and hid their faces in shame.

"I wonder what kind of hearts you have." Wes drew one sidearm and tapped it on his knee. The young men were shaking. "How dark does a heart have to be to prey on women and children and old men?"

"We weren't going to—" one man began to say.

"Quiet!" Wes didn't like to speak harshly to anyone, but he'd rubbed shoulders with hard military men his whole life, and he knew how to command a room when he needed to. "You have no right to speak. You deserve to die, and that's the path you're on right now. I promise you, there are people all over California who won't hesitate to kill you. You're not even that good at what you do. Look at me. I'm a one-eyed, middle-aged guy, and I took you down twice in the same night. You should find something honorable to do with your lives. Next time I come this way, I may not be so gracious. If you were wise, you'd find a Bible and beg God to forgive you. Otherwise, you're headed toward a pitiful death without mercy."

One of the young men wept softly, his head lying on the floor near the window.

"There's some deer meat by the door." Wes gestured at the back entrance. "You're only getting it because you're such bad criminals. I hope it'll spare some innocent victims from shooting you in the belly. Take your food and go home. If you don't have a home, then build one. Learn to survive. Work together to do something that helps others instead of harming others. God made you for so much more than the embarrassment you've become."

Wes loosened the wrist binds of the young man who was weeping openly, and left the living room.

Outside, Ivory had found an adequate position in the trailer behind Wes's bike, and Dalia was trying to convince Elio to join the old man, although Elio seemed to be resisting. The trailer was no place for a child and an old man—but for that day, Wes didn't see any way around it.

"We can fashion a kid's seat on your bike at our stop tonight, Dalia, but he's got to ride in there today."

"Come here, tiger." Ivory growled, taking the boy in his arms. "We're old friends, see? Neither of us wants to ride in this animal cart, but the alternative is much worse, believe it or not. Come on. We'll make Wes do all the hard work for us."

Wes needed to walk his bike a ways to get the trailer rolling, then he hopped on. He was thanking the Lord he'd already reached the summit of Tejon Pass, and most of the day they would be heading downhill into the San Joaquin Valley. If the snow hadn't melted from the rain, traveling would've been more complicated for the group.

"You should've let me carry my shotgun back here," Ivory grumbled. "Even a stagecoach in the old days had someone riding shotgun."

"You're liable to shoot one of us before you hit anything contrary," Wes joked, but he was partly serious. The shotgun was lashed across his handlebars, from where he could draw it if he spotted a grouse or pheasant. "Besides, Jill's proven herself more than capable at defending us, so you can just sit back and tell Elio some tall tale."

"I don't know if this kid even knows any English," Ivory said, but he began to share a story from his youth, anyway.

"You think anyone will attack us again?" Jill asked as she rode parallel with Wes.

They reached the freeway and spread out across the lanes, ready to weave through the occasional abandoned car.

"It's a little less likely now." Wes smiled to reassure her. "But we'll remain vigilant."

"Yeah," the woman agreed, her face more resolute than the night before. A corner of her drawing pad was visible under her coat, sticking up near her neck. "We'll be more alert."

Nearly twenty miles later, Wes stopped for a break at the California Aqueduct. As Jill and her daughter went below the bridge to see if the water was drinkable, Wes inspected the trailer wheels. Ivory crouched beside him, squinting at the trailer.

"We picked up some pretty good speed coming off that mountain." Wes clucked his tongue. "This old leaf wagon wasn't made for that kind of speed or anything more than a little weight. I hope it limps along the rest of the day, and we can find something else soon."

"We're coming up on Bakersfield." Ivory scratched his head. "How far away do you think we are from the city limits?"

"About thirty miles or so. Maybe a little less." Wes checked the sun. "I'd like to reach the city by nightfall. It'd give us a chance to—"

He stopped speaking as he noticed movement on the freeway behind them.

"What is it?" Ivory turned to the south. "What do you see? Is it another deer? You want me to get your rifle from your pack? Or the shotgun?"

"No, it's someone on a bike, coming down the hill after us." Wes stepped away from the bikes and moved toward the approaching rider. As he walked, he drew the sidearm from his hip and held it at his side. If he'd been alone, he might've welcomed some riding company, but he had women and children to think about now. And this was no casual rider. He cupped his hand to his mouth to yell. "What do you want?"

The rider braked and stopped thirty yards away, far enough where they would need to yell to communicate, but not far enough where Wes couldn't fire his weapon and tranq his target. The man on the bike wore a rifle across his back. It was one of the bandits who'd attacked them overnight—the weeper from that morning.

"I'm . . . on my own, now," the young man yelled back. He fidgeted, then spoke too quietly for Wes to hear.

"Speak up!" Wes took a few steps closer. He was keenly aware that this type of situation could've been a setup for an ambush, but it would be hard for an enemy party to approach without being seen across the empty fields. Besides, Wes and his band had just flown down a mountain highway, separating themselves from the aggressors from the night before. Although this young man had recovered one of the bikes from the neighboring garage as well, Wes knew there weren't enough bikes for all the bandits, unless they had their own rides stashed somewhere.

"I said, I want to go with you!"

Wes clenched his teeth, wishing he could read the young man's mind. From his years in the CIA, he knew better than to trust anyone in this kind of situation, especially with young Dalia and her mother at risk. But from his years with COIL, he knew that the compassion that a Christian shows the undeserving has a way of piercing the hardest of hearts.

"Why should we take you with us?" Wes waved his arm. "Get out of here. We have no use for highway bandits!"

"I'm not a bandit, anymore. I never wanted to be. I just..."

Wes sighed and glanced at the sky. Was God serious right now? The bandit had a rifle on his back, but no pack at all, only a water bottle fastened to his bike frame. Without gear or supplies, he would probably return to his old ways, unless Wes took him in. Maybe the stranger just needed some guidance, or a father figure.

"Well? Why would we want you with us?" Wes walked closer, until they were only ten feet apart. "What do you have to offer? How do we know you won't cut our throats in the night and take off with our gear, or hurt my lady friends?"

The young man searched for words.

"Look, I've done some really bad things." The bandit's voice broke.

"No kidding!" Wes wasn't about to make this easy for him.

"I've been a bad person. I want to change. My dad taught me to hunt when I was younger. I can hunt for you."

"What's your name?"

"Royce. I mean, Roy. Roy Mallinger."

"How old are you, Roy Mallinger?"

"Eighteen."

"Eighteen? Where are your parents?"

"Everyone's gone." He looked down and to the left, which told Wes that he was hiding something. Maybe his family wasn't really dead, just gone. "It's just me now."

"Where are your people from?"

"Escondido."

"What are you running from, Roy?" Wes moved directly in front of Roy's front wheel. He holstered his sidearm, realizing the young man couldn't take his rifle off his back faster than he could reach out and grab him. "What's haunting you from your past, son?"

"I'm not running from anything. I mean, I'm running from my past. And from death. I just want . . ." He looked as if he were going to start crying again as he'd done that morning. His shaggy brown hair needed a trim. Otherwise, he appeared strong and healthy. "You remind me of my dad. He was the tough-love kind of guy. You spoke to us in the house like my dad would have. I think that's what I need right now."

"I don't know." Wes rested his hands on his hips. "You're not telling me something, but maybe that's your own business. You tell me when you're ready, all right?"

"Okay. I mean, I will. Yes, sir."

"And you're going to have to prove yourself, to prove you're not up to anything sinister."

"I'm not up to anything sinister."

"Your actions will speak louder than your words, Roy. I don't want you riding with us until I know you can be trusted." Wes watched the young man's reaction very closely. He saw disappointment, but not anger. "For now, I want you to ride point, way out in front of us. Use your hunting skills to look for danger, then report back to me anything and everything ahead. You can start by riding into Bakersfield on Highway 99 and finding us a place to stay the night. Something out of this cold would be nice."

"Okay, I can do that."

"Your bike is in good shape?"

"Yeah, I think so." He shrugged. "It's a bike. I don't know."

"The minute I see that you're a threat to me or my people, I'll shoot you and leave you behind, Roy."

"I'm not a threat. I mean, yes, sir. I'll be on my best behavior." His face brightened. "You want me to start for Bakersfield right now?"

"Unless you have other plans I don't know about." Wes moved aside.

Roy stood on his bike pedals for a few yards as he started off, then sped to the north. Jill emerged from the river at the side of the road and saw the stranger coming. She drew her sidearm, then looked to Wes, who held up his hand. Jill watched as the ex-bandit passed them without slowing.

"That guy looked like one of the men from last night!" Jill gasped as Wes walked up to the bikes. "We're just going to let him go?"

"I talked to him for a few minutes. His name is Roy. He's just a lost boy. He left his gang and wants to fly straight. That's the whole point of shooting people with tranqs. You never know how God might reach into their hearts and bring about some change."

"Just like that?" Jill turned in a circle, waving her gun still in her hand. "You're going to let a murderer and a bandit just fly by us, and not do anything? What about the kids?"

"I'm not a kid, Mother!" Dalia snapped as she fastened her canteen to her bike. "Elio's a kid."

"I've forgiven Roy," Wes stated, "but forgiveness doesn't come with blind trust. He's going to have to prove himself to us. He'll show that he can keep us safe, or we'll leave him behind. He knows those are the conditions. Besides, Ivory and I could use another man's hands in our band so we can relax at night."

"Speak for yourself!" Ivory grumbled. "If I had my eyes, I wouldn't be relaxing! I'm getting enough relaxing in this fool trailer. And I wouldn't be letting criminals off the hook, either! Letting them ride on by? That's just plain ignorant of you, Wes. People don't change. You have no idea what that man's done to other travelers."

"Oh, I have an idea. And it's nothing pleasant, I'm sure." Wes looked after Roy, now far ahead. "I'll take responsibility for him. Believe me, I'll be keeping him so busy, he'll be too exhausted to do anything else but ride that bike, hunt game, and sleep. Mount up. We want to be in Bakersfield before dark."

Chapter 4

After a breakdown with the trailer, Wes pedaled wearily toward Bakersfield far behind schedule. As the sun set, he noticed a lone figure on a bike approaching them from the north.

"I would've been better off back at the pass!" Ivory grumbled. "And warmer!"

Wes didn't respond as he eased his bike to the shoulder. Jill and Dalia drifted to a stop as well. The buildings on the outskirts of Bakersfield lined both sides of the highway, but none of the residences in sight seemed inhabited.

Elio must've been as tired of the trailer as Ivory, for the boy climbed off Ivory's lap and hustled to Dalia's side before Wes could plant his kickstand.

"Wes?" Jill called, and nodded her head at the approaching cyclist. She rested her right hand on the butt of her handgun while still straddling her bike.

"Easy, Jill." Wes held up his hand. "It's just Roy. Let's see what he found up ahead for us."

Ivory continued to complain under his breath as he adjusted his position in the trailer. Wes moved ahead of his small band to intercept Roy and speak to him alone.

Roy was winded as he applied his brakes and slowed to a halt in front of Wes. The young man's cheeks were flushed from the cool air and his eyes were wide from the exhilarating ride.

"There's a barricade across the road, right in the middle of the city." Roy took a drink from his bottle. "There must be a hundred guys up there. They saw me coming, and everyone aimed their rifles at me."

"Does the barricade stretch beyond the sides of the highway?" Wes gazed past Roy to the north, trying to envision the next hurdle in their way to his wife and the safety of the mountains. Somehow, his wife's caravan had gotten through the barricade. Her painted marks still appeared on the roadway every couple miles. "Maybe we can go around?"

"No, they thought of that, I think. There's a lot of people in this city, and they don't look too friendly. We'll have to find another way north."

"Good recon, Roy." Wes pointed a thumb at the bikes. "Top off your water bottle and take a breather. I need to figure this out."

Wes walked farther ahead of his companions and drew out the map to hold up to the fading light in the sky. They could back-track to Route 223, but that was a half-day's ride. And what if that highway was blocked by some other group of survivors? Because of the trailer and Ivory's condition, not to mention Elio, they couldn't go cross-country on foot. Besides, Wes wasn't interested in leaving the bikes behind, not when they were still so far away from the mountains. And if he left the path that his wife was on, he might miss her sign if she turned off.

He prayed as he walked back to his band and stowed his map in his pocket.

"I'm going up there to talk to the people of Bakersfield." Wes set his pack against the guardrail, and uncoupled his bike from the trailer. "It's too far and it'll take too long to go around Bakersfield. And this trailer won't hold up for more than a couple more miles. We need to find something else for Ivory while we're here."

"I'm going with you," Jill said. "We're all going with you."

"No, you're staying here. Look, I'm leaving my pack behind. I'll return as soon as I know a little more about what we're dealing with."

"You're not leaving us here with him, Wes!" Jill nodded her head at Roy, who was still quenching his thirst from the water bottle. "You know what he is!"

"Roy, you'll be on your best behavior, right?" Wes said. "Or Jill, you shoot him."

"Hey, what'd I do?" Roy capped his bottle. "I thought that was in the past, Wes."

"Give me twenty minutes." Wes climbed onto his bike. "If you hear gunfire, get out of here. Find another way north and catch up to the group my wife is with."

As Wes peddled away, he glanced back. Roy had seated himself against the guardrail, and Jill stood protectively near her daughter and Elio. Dalia was helping the boy into another layer of clothing to ward off the growing cold.

It felt good for Wes to stretch his legs peddling at full speed, which he hadn't done all afternoon. The trailer seemed to require agonizingly slow speeds, but only because he'd pushed it past its limits coming down the Grapevine.

In minutes, the barricade came into sight, not far from where Highway 58 met with the 99. Sure enough, as Wes coasted up to the barricade, a wall of school buses came alive with shooters along the bus rooftops. He guessed the rusting yellow buses were just the front of the barrier, and that there was more piled junk heaped behind the buses.

He stopped his bike forty yards from the barricade, just close enough to be heard if he yelled. But he wanted a closer look, especially as dusk settled. Laying his bike on its side, he walked closer on foot, wondering if he should've brought the battle rifle. But no, he decided. A shootout was a bad idea being this outnumbered. As Roy had said, the barrier overflowed the highway and stretched into the broad streets of downtown Bakersfield. The dark windows of nearby buildings could hold other shooters, he considered, and the red stains on the pavement at his feet probably weren't old gasoline stains, either.

"That's far enough!" a man yelled from atop one of the buses.

Wes stopped twenty feet from the center bus. He hoped it wasn't too obvious that he was studying everything about the barricade. Underneath the buses, he could see twisted metal and scavenged vehicle parts to block bullets if a battle occurred.

The bus in the middle moved backwards as it was drawn aside on flat tires. The sound of screeching metal made Wes flinch as a gap opened in the barricade wall, just wide enough for a broad-shouldered man to walk through. The man who appeared was burdened with so many rifles and pistols that Wes wondered if he could move well enough to fire the mini-gun he held in one hand. He wore black, and as intimidating as all of his weapons were, his face was even more startling. It was covered in faded green tattoos, from his forehead, down his cheeks and nose, all the way to his chin. On one of his hands, he wore a glove. The other hand was bare, although it was evident the tattoo gun had made its mark there as well.

"What do you want?" Tattoo asked.

Wes acknowledged the shooters scrambling closer on the bus roofs, looking almost straight down at him. This was the most established barricade that Wes had seen since Pan-Day, and Wes had seen plenty. He'd accompanied Titus and Oleg to the east side of San Diego to deal with hoarders who had established a bunker system. Titus had had a way of fixing things with a mixture of humor, force, and bluntness, which wasn't normally Wes's style, especially since he was all alone. But he needed to get through the barricade one way or another.

"I'm just traveling through, hoping to catch up to my family." Wes was careful with what he did with his hands, so he hooked his thumbs on his belt, near his sidearms, which were visible to all. "They must've come through here a few days ago, right? I'm with them."

"You don't look like you're with them. You look like you're all alone."

"Yes, it may seem that way. You apparently let them pass, though, huh?"

Wes said nothing about the spray paint on the pavement nearby that indicated his wife had moved through the barrier.

"You can pass, too." The man sneered. "But everyone pays. We search everyone."

"I figured as much." Wes smiled patiently, but inside he felt his hackles rise. He didn't have enough gear for his band as it was, and Jill and Dalia had nothing that he hadn't given them or that they hadn't gotten from Ivory's house. He wasn't about to submit to the greedy hands of this bunch. "I know some of the people in the caravan ahead of me. I don't think they would've paid you."

"They paid their respects."

"Ah, I see. You mean they showed you their guns, and you weren't about to get into a fight with a group that size."

"You have a smart mouth on you, man. For that, you'll pay double."

"Double?" Wes chuckled. "Double what? I have nothing."

"Those double pistols will let you through. I was just going to take one from you, but now I think the pair would look nice on my belt."

Wes studied the other men. They were a motley crew, for sure. A few women were among them as well, and they appeared as rugged and sinister as their men. Somehow, even in their winter coats, they managed to appear intimidating and fierce.

"I think maybe I'll find free passage through here a little later."

"There is no later, man." The man laughed like he'd just told a joke. "We're up all night. Nobody gets through unless we allow it. This is my city. You pay, or you die. Unless I'm feeling merciful, in which case I'll just take your other eye, and leave you to wander wherever you like."

"Nah, I'll make my own way." Wes nodded. "Have a nice evening, y'all."

He turned his back to the road crew and walked straight back to his bike. But as he walked, he browsed the horizon, searching for a line of sight far away that he could use as a shooting platform. Far off to the left, he noticed a building that might work for his idea, but it was risky. This wasn't a familiar area to him. This was Tattoo's city, and Wes wondered if they'd even allow him to reach his bike without shooting him in the back. Wynter could become a widow before she reached the mountains or had their baby.

But he climbed onto his bike and turned south without being shot. He pedaled slowly away, as if out for a summer's ride, checking the streets to the left and right of the highway. They were cluttered with abandoned cars and debris looters had left behind, like most city streets he'd seen. There were plenty of hiding places in which to lurk in the dark, if he could take his time to move through them. Of course, having the diverse group that he had would take some extra care, but he imagined there was a way through the blockade.

If it came to it, Wes had the battle rifle, and nothing in Tattoo's arsenal had looked like it would be able to stand up to that weapon!

As he rode back down the highway, night settled over the valley. Wes struggled with the lack of depth perception of his one eye to swerve around objects that still littered the lanes. When he reached the point where he thought he'd left his travel companions, he stopped to look around and listen to the night, but no one was there. For a moment, he doubted he'd gone far enough. But no, this was the location where he'd left his friends and pack.

He quickly gauged the distance from there to the barricade. It wasn't more than a half-mile. Without strain, he would've heard a gunshot if his friends had been accosted, and Jill, if not Roy, would've gotten off a shot if someone had tried to abduct them.

A whistle drew his attention to the northeast. He went to the guardrail and stared out into the darkness, only to hear the whistle again. Although he wasn't comfortable with others making decisions without consulting him, it seemed that his friends had found somewhere to go, which wasn't altogether unwise since they couldn't rightly stay all night on the highway.

Now pushing his bike, he back-tracked through the night to the previous off-ramp, and waded through blowing newspapers to angle along the streets to the source of the whistle. Much to his surprise, he came upon an RV lot where dozens of new and used motorhomes sat just as they'd been left one year earlier.

"This one hasn't been vandalized," Roy whispered hoarsely from behind a thirty-seven-foot Sunova motorhome. "Well, at least until I jimmied the door and got inside."

Wes walked around the vehicle with Roy, inspecting its exterior. He could tell the paint was chipped, but it seemed in good shape, otherwise. At the front, he looked up at the windshield and saw Jill waving at him from inside. It was the type of wave that demanded he come and talk to her.

"It'll do for the night," Wes told Roy, then moved to the side door. He was about to step into the motorhome when Jill emerged. "Is something wrong?"

She glared at Roy until he sensed her aggravation. The young man hopped into the vehicle, giving Jill the privacy she was demanding.

"That boy!" Jill guided Wes by the arm farther away from the motorhome's door. "You're putting us in danger by keeping him around us. My daughter, Wes, is still a child, remember?"

"Dalia's not the child you think she is." Wes took off his wool cap and ran his fingers through his hair. Roy wasn't the only one needing a trim. "And Roy's not a boy, either. He's a young man who's been needing someone to guide him right. That's all."

"And you're that someone? Have you seen the way he looks at my daughter?"

"What do you want me to do, Jill? Throw everyone away who has picked up some baggage in the last year? I'd have to leave you behind, too, if that's the case. Or maybe you want me to abandon Roy to the likes of the people of this city?" He tugged his cap back onto his head and adjusted his eye patch. He had better things to do than soothe the paranoia of the ex-actress. "I'll keep an eye on him. Will that satisfy you?"

Even in the dark where only the stars and moon shinned on the lot, he saw Jill's narrow finger wagging in his face.

"I don't want him around us! You think of a way to drop him off somewhere, or we're going off on our own again!"

Wes started to protest that bad idea, but Jill turned away and re-entered the motorhome. Roy leaped out as if she'd pushed him aside.

"Wow, what's her problem?" Roy asked.

"I think you and I had better lay low tonight," Wes said. "The roof on this baby is pretty high. I wonder how the view of the roadway is from on top."

From the back of the Sunova, they climbed onto the roof, lay prone side-by-side, and studied the lights up the freeway.

"Torches and burning barrels," Wes announced as he gazed through his binoculars, his elbows resting on the roof. "There's plenty of trash to burn around the city. Looks like they've lit a couple bonfires, too. Tomorrow night, I figure we can find a way around the barricade. They don't look too vigilant."

"Why not tonight?"

"Because we need to find Ivory some new wheels in the daylight tomorrow." Wes turned his ear to listen to the high-pitched arguing between Jill and Dalia. Something about Dalia not being a child, and Jill insisting that she was. "Is Ivory in there with them?"

"Where else would he go?" Roy sat upright and faced the northern skyline. "I don't think that woman likes me too much."

"You need to settle in and let them see that you're trustworthy now. Maybe you haven't been around many pretty women, Roy, but you can't be gawking at them. You need to treat them with respect and let them know they're important and valuable."

"I'm trying, but I know she's Jill Austin, right?" Roy sighed. "Any guy would love to be around her. I saw all her movies."

"You recognize her?"

"Yeah, don't you? Sure, she looks different in person, without all the makeup and lighting, but it's her. And Dalia is going to look just like her mom, someday."

"We're responsible for their lives." Wes scoped farther to the west, trying to trace a possible street entrance past the barricade. "Men of dignity hold certain thoughts captive. We don't allow our imaginations to wander, because we live our lives based on the facts. And the facts right now, Roy, are that you're still on probation in our little band here. Last night, you and a bunch of mad men attacked us. Jill remembers that very clearly, and you won't earn her respect by gawking at her or her daughter. You need to show her you're a good man."

"Yeah, trustworthy, like you said." Roy groaned. "But how do I do that? We live in an eat-or-be-eaten world now. I don't know anything about dignity or trust or women."

"A lot of people don't have good role models in their lives, but that doesn't excuse them from living like animals. We still have the Bible. I carry one with me. You want to be a man of dignity? Now, there's a book you should read. It'll teach you to live like a real man—a hero. God will change you from the inside, Roy. And when you trust Him with your life, things will fall into place—and you'll really see His hand in this world."

"Even now? I mean, this world's in chaos!"

"The world has been in chaos before, and we can look back and see that God wasn't missing from the equation even then."

"But why trust God? I don't know anything about Him. What do I have to do with Him, and what does He have to do with me? Honestly, Wes, it sounds like a bunch of pointless religious stuff."

"A lot of people think that. But let's look at one little thing, all right?" Wes spoke as he kept his eye on the distant barricade. "Let's consider your conscience. Describe your conscience to me right now. It's just you and me out here. Man to man, tell me about your conscience."

"My conscience?" Roy scoffed, as if he'd never been asked such a ridiculous question before. "I guess, I never really thought about it."

"Do you have a clear conscience?"

"Of course not. Does anyone?"

"Some people do."

"Yeah, maybe perfect people. But I'm not perfect, Wes. Even you know that."

"No one's perfect, Roy. But it's possible to have a clear conscience and live the rest of your life knowing that you're right with God."

"What are you talking about?" Roy's voice was softer. "You really have a clear conscience?"

"I do. You know how I got it?" Wes asked. When Roy didn't answer, he continued. "God made us with a conscience, Roy, so we can discern our right and wrong actions and thoughts. We know we are guilty of so much, if we're truly honest with ourselves. None of us deserves anything but judgement for all the bad thoughts and bad things we've committed. And when we die, God would throw us all into hell because that's where we belong. Your filthy, burdened conscience knows it, you just said. But God provided a way for our consciences to be made clean, and for our sins to be forgiven. He sent Jesus to die for us, so we don't have to experience the penalty we deserve. When we place our trust in Jesus for dying on the cross for us, God applies His forgiveness to our lives. When you believe that, Roy, you live with a clear conscience."

"A clear conscience . . ." Roy turned around and lay on his back, his hands under his head. "I've never had that. Now that you point it out, it would be pretty nice. Forgiveness? So, that's the whole point of God and Jesus? They give us a clear conscience?"

"God the Father gives us a clear conscience if we believe what God the Son has sacrificed for us. Then, God the Holy Spirit is sent to live within the one who believes, comforting and helping us. They are one God, three in one, Roy. The Holy Spirit becomes your companion and teaches you how to live according to His will, rather than by your own. You want to be accepted by normal people again? You're not going to do it on your own. You'll need the help of God. He'll need to be the influence and power behind your new life. I'm telling you that you need to be saved from your own sin nature, and He's the only One who can do that for you. Jesus Himself said we must be born again, Roy."

"Born again. And then I'll be like you? I'd have a clear conscience, and people would depend on me?"

"Your relation to people would be a product of getting right with God, Roy. It will take time to prove yourself to people, but trusting in God is an instantaneous reality. When you listen to the Holy Spirit inside you, you learn to discern His voice separate from your own imagination. Usually, the way the Holy Spirit speaks to us is real softly, and you know it's Him when He's encouraging you to be like Jesus."

"What was Jesus like?"

"Bold, loving, courageous, patient, sacrificial. Maybe we can find you a Bible tomorrow when we're looking around the city for some new wheels for Ivory."

"Sacrificial, huh?" Roy thought about that a moment. "I could be sacrificial."

"Sometimes being sacrificial is just an attitude, especially the attitude that you and I need to have for a journey like this. We need to keep the others safe before we think about our own safety. We need to make sure they have water to drink before we get water for ourselves. The Lord will guide you, once you take the leap of faith."

"What's the leap of faith? I've heard that phrase before, but I never really understood it."

"In this case, the leap of faith is trusting that Jesus really is God, and He died to set you free from guilt before God Almighty. He loves you, and you trust Him with your life. That's a leap into what might seem like a void, but it's the best leap in the world."

"What do I have to do? Like, is there a ceremony?"

"No, it's about your heart, Roy. God sees your heart. What does God see in your heart right now?"

"Embarrassment, I think. I've never known any of this. You believe God did all this for you?"

"With all my heart. I live for Jesus Christ, and some day, I may have to die for Him. But it won't matter much. An instant after death, I'll be in the presence of God Himself. That's the advantage of giving your life to Him. He owns you for eternity."

"I don't want anyone to own me."

"But remember, God already came in the flesh to show you that He has nothing but your well-being in mind. He created us, and His ownership of us is the most secure reality we'll ever know. I would say that's real freedom—remaining in the security of His protection. He showed us on the cross how much He loves us, so it's not a gamble."

"Yeah, I guess so. So, you're not afraid of death?"

Wes smiled in the night, understanding that Roy was certainly one reason why God had directed him to the north. The young man needed to hear the true gospel.

"No, I'm not afraid of death, Roy. See, once you believe—"

"Listen!" Roy flipped over and rose to his knees. "Hear that?"

The soft staccato of gunfire rapidly grew in succession and volume far away.

"I do now." Wes rose from his belly to his knees as well, and through the binoculars he viewed the torchlight of Tattoo's barricade on the highway. "Oh, something big is going down. That's not celebration gunfire. Someone is attacking them from the north!"

Wes described what he could see for Roy as they listened to a few gunshots quickly turn into a full-fledged battle that spanned the length of the barricade itself. Torches were thrown, and at least one RPG was firing grenades at the barricade as fast as the shooter could reload. Since the motorhome was so far away, they couldn't hear the screams and shouts that Wes knew would be accompanying the war zone.

"They look like they're coming this way!" Roy said. "Are they?"

Using his field glasses, Wes gauged the distance. Fires flickered and rifle barrels blasted steadily.

"I think you're right. Our friends at the barricade are retreating towards us! Yes, they're definitely coming this way! Hop down and grab my pack and rifle." Wes jumped to his feet and tore open a sun roof covering, then helped Roy drop straight into the Sunova. "Everyone stay inside! Lock the doors! We're about to have company!"

"What's happening?" Jill cried.

"It's one thing after another with you, Wes!" Ivory cursed.

Roy handed the battle rifle up to Wes, followed by his pack, which contained his extra ammunition. Then Roy held out his hand for Wes to take, but Wes hesitated.

"No, stay down there, Roy. It's safer."

"I'm not here to be safe, Wes. I'm here to be sacrificial. That's what you said."

"We should all just hide inside!" Jill yelled. "If we're quiet, they won't even notice us, and we'll be safe!"

"Quiet, Jill!" Wes ordered. "Get everyone in the back room and keep quiet." He held his empty hand down to Roy, who grasped it firmly. "You may regret this, son."

Struggling, Wes lifted the young man up through the hole, then the two lay again on their bellies to observe the approaching battle. Torches bounced in the night as people ran in different directions. Muzzles flashed north and south, and now the sound of the wounded and frightened men and women reached Wes's ears. It was an awful sound of suffering and terror. Any anger that Wes had had toward Tattoo and those at the barricade melted away at the slaughter he envisioned taking place in the dark of night.

"Here, you might need this." Wes drew his nine-millimeter from his ankle and handed it to Roy. "If you have to fire it, hold it steady with both hands, and don't fire too quickly. We engage only if we are engaged."

"Whoa!" Roy gasped as wildly-fired bullets pinged into the motorhome and peppered across the other RVs on the lot.

Wes settled his cheek against the short stock of the bullpup and peered through the scope. With the scene now magnified, he started to pick out shapes in the distance, even in the darkness. The little flashes of light, the burning fires, and the torches that people were using to escape the battle gave him a good indication of where people were at. Tattoo was losing the fight. An enemy force was steadily advancing in a line. They'd reached the highway, poured over and under it, and were now in pursuit of Tattoo's fighting forces, which seemed to be fleeing eastward, while civilians fled to the south.

"We're about to be overrun," Wes stated calmly to Roy. "I don't want to expose our position, but we're looking at a slaughter unless we help somehow."

"It's not our fight, Wes!" Roy was so close that Wes could feel him shaking. "What can we do? We're only two men!"

"With a battle rifle and God on our side? We can do a lot." Wes looked back at the sun roof. "When I start firing, we're going to be noticed. We're going to draw more fire. And people."

"People?"

"The people from the Bakersfield barricade and other parts of the city are fleeing the fight right toward us. When I start shooting, they'll think we're on their side, and they'll come straight here for safety."

"But are we really on their side?"

"The only side we're on is God's side, and right now that means that we do what we can to bring peace instead of slaughter." Wes flipped off the safety on his rifle. "It's about to get bad around here, and you're not armed for staying on the roof with me. I'm going to need you down on the ground, son, directing traffic."

"What do you want me to do?" Roy jumped to his feet, then crouched. "You want me down there?"

"There'll be wounded, and a lot of blood." Wes took a deep breath, steadying his own breathing. "Are you ready for this?"

"Sometimes men have to do hard things, right? If I die, I'll be okay?"

"You will be if you believe that you need God to save you from your sins. Do you believe Jesus died for you?"

"Yeah. I mean, you're sure He did, right?"

"I'm absolutely sure He died for us. You need to be sure too. Now, get down there, open up the nearby RVs, and get the wounded inside." Wes leaned into the hole in the roof. "Jill, you and Dalia help the wounded!"

"What?" her muffled voice yelled back. "I'm not doing—"

"Do it!" Wes slapped Roy on the shoulder. "God is with us, Roy. Get to it. I'll hold them off, somehow."

Roy dropped through the hole and landed with a grunt. Wes settled onto his belly once again and licked his lips. He sighted on the offensive line of flashing muzzles, now within a quarter-mile.

"Lord, You helped David beat Goliath," he prayed to the night sky. "We're looking for . . . another miracle here."

Chapter 5

As a former agent and the deputy director for the CIA's Pacific Rim Security, Wes had seen his share of action, even before he had joined Corban Dowler and Titus Caspertein to help COIL impact the world for Jesus Christ. He knew that the fastest way to defeat an enemy was to divide them, confuse them, and overwhelm them. Although he was just one man, the battle rifle had a range that bested what sounded like .223 rifles popping in the distance. Tattoo's people needed cover fire against a stronger force, so Wes hoped to provide that cover fire, and provide the sanctuary the civilians sought.

He fired his first shot into the middle of the advancing line of aggressors. In the motorhome, Dalia screamed and Elio started crying loudly, but those were sounds that Wes could push to the back of his mind, and he fired again. Another soldier fell in the center of the line.

From his vantage point, and since the offensive line had little cover, Wes fired in rapid succession, and tranquilized a dozen more of the attacking fighters before he paused to reload. He'd been noticed now, he guessed, but he couldn't see enough in the dark to determine how the enemy or Tattoo's group were responding to another shooter inserting himself into their battle. A few more bullets lobbed into the RV lot, but Wes knew he was still out of effective range of the close-combat weapons the assaulters were using. Of course, the RPG launcher was a concern, but that person was steadily attacking the barricade up on the highway, almost a half-mile away.

The offensive line—missing about a quarter of its attackers—was now broken into at least two divisions with more scattering by the minute, yet they kept advancing, shooting on the run. Breaking up their coordinated attack was a good start, Wes decided, but now the hard part: targeting isolated enemies. It was a sniper's skills he needed, which he didn't have. However, the closer the enemy came, the better he was at hitting his targets.

Shapes moved in the darkness in front of the motorhome. Two people helping a wounded man were met by Roy. Wes fired over their heads at the enemy combatants as Roy welcomed others into the lot.

"Wes!" Jill screamed from inside the motorhome. The ex-actress sounded panicked. "Roy went outside! He unlocked the door!"

"Help him, Jill!" Wes shouted over his shoulder. "Roll up your sleeves and get busy!"

More defenders from Tattoo's forces walked, ran, or stumbled into the RV lot. Wes focused on the battle, firing with timely precision as the fighting drew closer and closer. Soon, the enemy's rifles would be able to reach him, and then he'd be in trouble—they'd all be in trouble.

Judging by occasional muzzle flashes, Tattoo's main defensive force seemed to be gathering to the east, perhaps preparing for a counterattack. But Wes was most concerned about the violence that kept inching toward the motorhome.

The wounded were crowding together on the pavement next to the vehicle, and Wes heard Dalia asking far too politely where someone was wounded. Roy directed people toward other RVs nearby as they continued to arrive from the darkness.

"Get them back!" Wes ordered the crowd, hoping some of the people below weren't wounded too badly and could help the others. "Get them inside if you can. The fighting has almost reached us!"

He ducked his head as bullets in close succession crashed through the motorhome's windshield right below his elbows. Firing more desperately now, he aimed at muzzles that were spitting fire directly at him. The wounded and fearful below were crying and groaning, and it seemed that Roy hadn't succeeded in moving many of them inside, or they were too wounded to be moved any farther.

The fighting was within one hundred yards when Tattoo's fighting force launched their counterattack, pouring into the east flank of the scattered offensive. But it wasn't soon enough. Other enemies had prowled closer than Wes had first detected. They came into sight twenty yards to his left, four heavily-armed fighters making their way straight for the Sunova.

The bullpup was useless for up-close fighting, so he set it aside and lunged to his knees, drawing both Desert Eagles from their holsters. Firing the handguns was more his kind of fighting, so he confidently tranqed the four aggressors below before they could fire a shot at the wounded or at himself. But others kept coming. Two more snuck behind the motorhome, and Wes caught them just in time. He guessed he might happen to shoot one of Tattoo's soldiers by accident, but the gel-tranqs were harmless. The only threat of real injury was a deep bruise or falling wrongly once the target was unconscious.

Three more attackers fired at the wounded, and before Wes could direct his own gunfire, someone from within the RV lot fired a pistol in response. Nevertheless, people below were screaming and calling out for help. Wes ignored them and reloaded both handguns, then held them ready to fire, all while standing on top of the vehicle roof like a warrior protecting his village. He could smell the blood and the gunpowder in the air, and it sickened him, but those in his care needed to be protected.

Tattoo's counterassault was working, and the battle shifted back to the west, crossed the highway, and pushed it further. Wes saw no more reason to pick up the bullpup now that the fighting had moved away, but he remained ready in case other enemies approached.

After another ten minutes, the gunfire dwindled, then ceased altogether. Now, Wes could hear children crying, and it wasn't Elio or Dalia. Whole families had found refuge below Wes's motorhome. He didn't know what the dynamics of the conflict were, or who the enemy was, but he wasn't sorry he'd joined the fight to defend women and children from being slaughtered, even if they were the families of the rogue highwaymen of Bakersfield.

"Hold your fire!" a commanding voice ordered from the darkness. "We're coming in."

Thirty or forty men approached the motorhome. Wes recognized Tattoo's voice, though he couldn't pick out which of the men he was. Two soldiers climbed up the back of the Sunova and joined Wes.

"Who are you?" one of them asked. "We thought you were with us."

"This is my motorhome," Wes stated. "Who are you?"

The men hesitated in their confusion.

"We're with Novak. We're here to spell you. You've been defending this position for a while. Take a break."

Wes took a moment to consider the offer and saw no harm in it. Although he'd inserted himself, the matter wasn't really his fight. He probably wasn't going to stop a feud between two gangs, but he hoped he'd stopped the slaughter before it had become too horrible.

He collected his rifle, dropped his pack through the hole into the motorhome, and climbed down the back of the vehicle. For a moment, he stood in shock as he took in the sea of frightened, wounded, and dying people. In his estimate, there were close to two hundred lying on the ground and leaning against the nearby RVs. A couple lanterns were lit, and the anguish from the wounded seemed to intensify.

"You!" Tattoo approached, a shotgun in one hand and five heavily-armed men at his side. Wes guessed this was the one the two others had called Novak. He stomped up to Wes. "What're you doing here? If you had anything to do with what just happened, I swear I'll—"

"Novak!" someone called from the roof. "Look at his rifle. He's the one."

Novak's eyes settled on the battle rifle in Wes's hands, then the man's face lit up.

"You were the one helping us?" The tattooed man browsed the scene, as if seeing it all through different eyes. "You and who else?"

"Just me, and a few with me who are helping your wounded." Wes shrugged. "You and I had words earlier today about my good eye. You still want to try to take it?"

Novak rested his shotgun over his shoulder.

"No, all that's forgotten now. I don't say this often, but thank you. My family is here, too."

"Then let's see to them." Wes shifted his rifle to his left hand and held out his right. "But tomorrow, I'll assume I can travel north without being troubled further."

"Yeah." Novak grinned. "Hey, man, you can have your run of my city for saving our necks!"

They shook hands.

"Wes!" Jill called. "Wes, get over here!"

Wes skirted dozens of wounded to reach Jill where she held a bleeding man in her lap. The man's chest, as best as Wes could see by the lamplight, wasn't moving. A crimson stain had spread across the young man's collar. It was Roy.

"They killed him!" Jill sobbed, rocking back and forth with Roy's head held close. "He died for us, Wes. He . . . stood in front of Dalia when those last killers shot at us."

Wes knelt next to her leg, sorrow making him realize his exhaustion. He felt his shoulders sag and his eye water.

"He sacrificed his life." Wes nodded and rested a hand on the young man's arm. "I think Roy Mallinger learned something tonight."

"I was so mean to him!" Jill wept. "He died for us, and I didn't even say a kind word to him. He died thinking I hated him, Wes! What do I do? How could I be so cruel?"

Wes didn't have answers for her right then. His heart was heavy as well, although he hoped Roy had indeed placed his faith in the God of the Bible and the forgiveness from Jesus Christ.

Rising to his feet, he placed his hand on Jill's head for a few seconds, trying to comfort the torn woman, then he moved off to another familiar figure. Dalia was using torn clothing to wrap a woman's head. The woman held an infant in her arms.

"You okay here, Dalia?" Wes asked.

"Yeah." The teen's face appeared empty, but she was doing what needed to be done. "I'm okay. But, Roy died."

"I saw. But he wasn't alone. He was just following the example of Jesus Christ by being sacrificial."

"I'm ready to leave this city."

"Me, too."

He found Ivory White and Elio inside the motorhome, sitting in the back room with two wounded men on the bed. One looked like he'd passed away, but Ivory was holding a bottle of water to the lips of the other.

"This place is cursed, Wes," Ivory said quietly. "There's nothing to help these people. What are we supposed to do?"

"Pray, Ivory. We need to pray. Only God can cure the mess mankind has made of this world."

In the night, the tranquilized enemy had woken and slipped out of the city. Wes had learned they were a criminal band of raiders called the Diablos. Once daylight broke, the only thing left to do for Bakersfield was to bury their own dead. Roy was buried in a mass grave with Novak's other deceased—men, women, and children. Novak had spoken words of heroism and honor over the grave, then asked if Wes had anything he wanted to say, since one of his own had died helping the innocent. Wes had drawn out his pocket Bible—one that Titus Caspertein had made sure all COIL personnel carried throughout and after Pan-Day.

Over the open grave, and for Novak's people to hear, Wes read the first eight verses from Revelation Chapter 21, then he prayed aloud for them all, that everyone listening would find security in the arms of the God who had sent Jesus to bring peace to the world.

Before noon, Wes, Jill, Dalia, and Elio prepared their bikes for departure from Bakersfield. Ivory White had approached Wes at dawn, having slept only an hour, and told Wes that Bakersfield was the end of the road for him.

"These aren't my kind of people," the old man had said, "but because of you, I'm welcome here. A blind man has no business on the road, and I know the journey for you will only get more difficult as you get closer to the mountains. I told Jill the same, but she'd rather go with you."

"It seems the Lord brought us together at the right time, old friend," Wes had responded. "I won't forget you, and I hope you won't forget about what Jesus Christ did for all of us."

"If you're ever back in Bakersfield, Wes," Novak said as he approached to shake hands again, "just know you have a friend here."

"I may come back." Wes surveyed the RV lot and the blood-stained ground. "But even if I don't, there'll be others who'll travel this highway. If you're my friend, Novak, and if I'm your friend, then you won't cause any reason for me to return here because you've harmed someone I know."

"That sounds like a threat." The tattooed man's frame stiffened. "Nobody threatens me."

"Think of it more like a covenant of peace." Wes smiled. "Unless you rule Bakersfield with wisdom and grace, like a good shepherd should, there will be more nights like last night."

"I wonder who you were before Pan-Day." Novak narrowed his eyes. "I've never heard of anyone tranquilizing the enemy like you. Or talking like you. What I would give for ten men with your kind of skills."

"I'm not worth knowing, Novak." Wes climbed onto his bike. "But those words I spoke about Jesus Christ—He's worth knowing. Get your hands on a Bible and look into that."

One-eyed Wes Trimble and his travel companions pedaled north on the highway. Catching up to his wife before she and Chevy reached the mountain snow seemed unlikely now, but Wes wasn't worried about things that were out of his hands. He was simply remaining obedient throughout America's last days, and leaving the details to God.

~ End of RESOLUTION Book One ~

RESOLUTION BOOK TWO

America's Last Days

D.I. Telbat

~*~

To those who feel alone, yet know God's presence;
To those who seem lost, yet cling to God's promises.

D.I. Telbat

Book Two, Prologue

Journal Entry:
   The Diablos grow more restless around me. They haven't been content with the raids against farms and small settlements. They pressure me for plans to attack travelers on the roads. "Torrey," they demand, "our children are starving! We have more guns than everyone else. Who cares who we kill if we stay alive? We have families!"

   Their cold hearts make me shiver. We have already taken in numerous orphans, and many of the men have kidnapped more women than they know what to do with. I fear that if we do what they want, and we begin to attack travelers on the highways, then the dread of the Diablos will reach farther than we know. As if in a vision, I have imagined a force coming to punish us if we range too far from our bases, or attack the unarmed caravans on the highway.

   My own family has tripled in size since Pan-Day struck California. The children I have adopted were never mine, and many of the children in my compound are the offspring of my victims. Looking at their faces, I remember their parents' cries, and I am forced to realize that I'm being torn apart inside. I am expected to be a great, merciless leader, since I was leading a ruthless gang in prison. But now, I'm just growing old. My wounds pain me. The foolishness and greed around me cause great weariness. I'm constantly looking to the west, toward Salinas, where I grew up.

   I'm afraid of a stronger force than our own coming to check our violence against innocent people, and I'm afraid of my own army as they grow stronger and more vicious.

Some of my lieutenants have even shown me disrespect, yet I didn't put them in check immediately. My weakness is beginning to show. But my own fear traps me from doing anything different. We have to survive, so we must continue to raid people. And if that means we attack travelers, then so be it.

Whatever force is out there waiting to shatter the Diablos to pieces, I hope it will see my own reluctance to continue this life. I, Torrey of the Diablos, am a man trapped between starvation and slaughter. Perhaps in the afterlife, I will be shown mercy since my heart isn't truly in this bloodshed. But somehow, I doubt my situation is known at all. How else could such evil as the Diablos run so rampant?

If I die before my next journal entry, I hope whoever reads this is wiser and stronger than I have been, and is able to lead the Diablos to a gentler life, and one without war.

I so hate myself and what I've become . . . —*Torrey*

Chapter 1

Panting, one-eyed Wes Trimble fell to his knees at the sight and stench of the massacre in front of him. A caravan of refugees had been attacked by someone, and no one seemed to have survived.

On the highway next to him, his travel companions, Jill Austin and her daughter, Dalia, climbed off their bikes. Dalia wailed aloud at the landscape, as if she herself had been physically injured. The teen's cries startled young Elio, and he began to weep from his seat in the jogging stroller Wes had managed to connect to the back of his mountain bike.

Jill dropped her bike and stumbled several steps before she fell to her knees beside Wes. Unlike her daughter, Jill was silent as tears rolled down her cheeks. And then she vomited.

"What kind of world do we live in?" Wes gasped as his heart broke. "My wife was with them! And Chevy..."

He struggled to his feet, swaying from the heartache of what he was afraid he would find. His pregnant wife, Wynter, had been traveling several days ahead of him, accompanied by Avery "Chevy" Hewitt, the last of the Kindred of Nails operatives who had once infiltrated North Korea. In his mind, Wes wanted to hope that this was a different caravan, but how many columns of refugees would there really be coming up from San Diego at this time and on this trail?

Two days earlier, Wes's small party had left Bakersfield, and Wes had been thankful to continue their journey with nothing more than a few bruises and some weight loss after what they'd experienced. He had hoped to reach the Sierra Nevada Mountains where other refugees had probably also fled the violence that seemed to saturate the San Joaquin Valley. There would be safety in the elevation and snow. But, the violence had sprung upon these poor people before they'd found sanctuary. And if he hadn't stayed behind in San Diego for a few extra days to help Titus Caspertein, he would've been among these dead as well.

From the highway, Wes crossed the ditch into a trampled lettuce field where the refugees had gathered, apparently trying to defend themselves against an oncoming foe. Not even the thugs guarding Bakersfield had attacked the caravan of fifty men, women, and children. But someone else had targeted them, and it must've been a sizeable force since the caravan had had about twenty armed men amongst them.

Stepping over bodies, Wes prayed for strength from God like he'd never prayed before. How could he survive if he found his wife of only a year, pregnant and left for the crows? It would take a miracle, he decided, and he pled for God to spare him that experience, and kill him right then. He couldn't bear the pain, that burden of loss.

He found the outlying defensive line on the northwest side of the group of women and children. A dozen riflemen had been killed where they'd lain prone behind a makeshift barrier of gear and backpacks. They'd been overwhelmed by a superior force. That much was obvious, but who had such firepower to catch so many fighters out in the open, unprepared? Unless it had been an ambush, or maybe the enemy had approached under a facade of friendliness, then attacked.

Standing on red ground among the bodies where the defenders lay, Wes surveyed each person. The winter day was cold, and the dead stared with frozen eyes at the blue sky. Wynter, even late in her pregnancy, would've fought shoulder to shoulder with the defenders. She and Chevy would've handed out their spare battle rifles, the .308 bullpups, and they would've stood for the innocents, as

COIL operatives had been doing ever since Corban Dowler had founded the organization. The collapse of America hadn't brought an end to COIL's work. No, since they weren't able to help overseas, then they'd help right here at home, inside America's borders.

Maybe Chevy and Wynter had defended the women and children in their final moments. Wes searched farther back, where the women and older children had huddled before they were murdered. But he didn't find Chevy or Wynter among the dead there, either.

"Dalia," Wes said to the blond teen, "you should go back up to stay with Elio."

For once, the girl didn't respond. She simply turned from where she'd followed him into the field, and returned to the highway. Jill, however, continued to stagger among the dead, ringing her hands, her blond hair blowing in the breeze and sticking to her wet face.

For a second time, Wes walked through the bodies and the baggage, searching for the two people he knew were with this caravan, but finally, he was certain. They hadn't died there. He used his sleeve to wipe his face, then crouched to analyze the scene like the CIA agent he'd once been. Enough emotion, he told himself. He needed to look at this situation objectively. Wynter and Chevy had escaped, he considered. Or, they had been taken captive.

He turned his head as a cold realization spread down his spine. The raiders had taken the youngest children, and maybe the pregnant ones, too. Wynter had been one of two visibly pregnant women in the caravan, if he remembered right. Where was the other pregnant mother? And there really were no children under the age of about ten. So, some had been spared. His wife was still alive, somehow, somewhere. And for some reason, Chevy had been spared as well.

"What are you doing, Lord?" he mumbled at the scene. "Why my family, but no one else's?"

Jill picked up a canteen from the ground, then tossed it aside when it leaked water from a bullet hole. The majority of the baggage the refugees had been carrying had been torn open and looted. All the assault rifles had been taken, but a few hunting rifles still lay beside the defenders.

Wes choked through a sob, and shook his head at the perseverance of Wynter. It was just like her to survive, too. She'd traveled the world as an archaeologist, and survived a hundred close calls. And now this.

Then he saw them, and knew they didn't belong. Sure enough, three men, lying at various angles amongst the dead, didn't belong with the group. And they had black armbands on their right arms.

Before Chevy and Wynter had left with the caravan from San Diego, Wes had met the families and shook the hands of many of the men with whom his wife would be traveling. Although Wes had only one eye, his memory was sharp, and he would've remembered men with black armbands. These men weren't with the caravan. They were some of the attackers, men who had died attempting to raid the refugees.

"They're organized," Wes concluded, beginning to profile them in his mind. He'd hunted killers before, across the Pacific Rim. If he could learn a little about them, he could gain an edge, predict what they might be doing, or where they were going. They had Wynter. For him to go on without her was out of the question.

"Come on, Jill. Back up to the road." Wes kicked at a crow as he headed back to the two-lane highway. "We're leaving."

"Hey, guys?" Dalia called from where the bikes lay. "I think I hear something."

"But we can't just leave them like this!" Jill joined Wes, stepping over the dead. "Shouldn't we do something?"

"We are doing something," Wes said, and stomped his boots on the pavement, freeing them of the red dirt. "I'm getting you three somewhere safe, then I'm going after them. They have my wife."

"They have Wynter?" Fresh horror swept across Jill's face. "Are you sure?"

"She was with them, but she's not here. The only explanation is that she was taken. She and Chevy, for some reason. And the youngest children." Wes climbed onto his bike. "Families lost a lot of kids during the Meridia Virus outbreak. One way to continue your family line is by stealing other kids and making them your own. Kids, and women who can bear children. We saw it in San Diego until Titus and Galt Brogdon put a stop to it, but it's probably the new norm in this crazy world."

"Guys, I'm serious!" Dalia repeated. "I hear something!"

Wes glanced back at the young woman and read real concern on her face, not just a teen's whining. His hand went to the primary sidearm on his hip as he browsed the horizon for movement.

"What is it?" He saw nothing but the annoying crows settling on the field once again. "What, Dalia?"

Dalia walked away from the bikes and crossed the ditch, moving back into the blood and gore.

"We don't have time for this," Wes said to Jill, who shrugged. "I'm serious. We need to get some place safe, and I need to get on their trail."

"Yeah, it's over here!" Dalia bent over and stared intently at one of the dead where most of the women and children had gathered. "Wes, come here! I think it's an animal, or a puppy."

Grumbling under his breath, Wes joined Jill as they walked back to the middle of the killing field. Arriving next to Dalia, he heard the noise as well—sounds of muffled crying.

He gently pushed Dalia away and grabbed the shoulders of a young woman who lay partially on top of another adult. Laying them both aside, he uncovered a small car seat with an infant inside—a very young baby, almost a newborn. It was so small. Wes rested his hands on his hips as he stared at his find.

"The only survivor, so far." Wes shook his head. "The mother must've carried the baby down here, and used her own body to shield it from the gunfire."

"What should we do with it?" Dalia asked.

"What do you mean, what should we do with it?" Wes chuckled, his hope returning with the discovery of life in the midst of so much death. "What do you think we're going to do with it?"

"Don't look at me." Jill backed away. "I didn't even raise you, Dalia. The nanny raised you. I've never even changed a diaper!"

"First Elio," Wes said, kneeling down and unbuckling the infant, "and now, this little one. You're turning into quite the mother, Dalia. We need to get food into this little one soon."

Searching the area, Wes found a diaper bag tucked underneath the car seat, and in a side pocket he found packets of powdered baby formula.

"I don't see any bottles." Jill crouched next to Wes. "I don't think babies can drink from our water bottles, can they?"

"Probably not." Wes opened a packet of formula and sniffed it. "Even if this one could, the water's too cold. This baby needs warm fluids. And the sooner the better."

"You want me to start a fire?" Dalia asked, a lighter already in her fingers.

"No, it's not safe for that. Besides, this is more of an emergency." Wes handed the baby formula to Dalia, then cradled the baby's head as he picked it up. The child's weak whimper quieted, but Wes knew they didn't have much time to save its life. "Come on. Back to the bikes."

At his bike, he handed Dalia her own water bottle.

"Hold some water in your mouth to warm it up," he told the teen, "then when it's warm, sprinkle some formula into your mouth, mix it up by swishing it some, and then dribble it into the baby's mouth. Go ahead. We can't move on until this baby starts to recover. A little sustenance will go a long way."

"*Seriously?*" Dalia held her water bottle in one hand and the baby formula in her other. "Mom?"

"What are you waiting for?" Jill took the baby from Wes, suddenly seeming to forget her aversion to motherhood. "Here, I'll hold it for you. Nod when the water's warm then I'll stroke its chin to get it to open its mouth. The poor little thing has to be dehydrated."

Wes returned to the field and tugged the diaper bag loose from the car seat. When he came back to the highway, Dalia was trickling formula into the infant's mouth. Between whimpers, the baby seemed to be sucking down more fluid than it was spitting out.

After a few minutes, Wes gauged from Dalia's water bottle how much they'd fed the baby.

"That's probably enough for now," he said. "But we need to stop every couple of hours to feed it again. Babies this young need a lot of feedings."

Dalia took the baby from her mother and expertly patted the infant on the back.

"What do I do with it?" Dalia held her cheek to the baby's cheek. "Its face is so cold. No wonder it keeps crying."

"It's probably crying for other reasons, too." Wes hung the diaper bag strap on Dalia's shoulder. "Go ahead. We can wait for this. Do the honors, Dalia. Find out what it is so we can stop calling this little one an *it*."

"What?" Dalia looked from Wes's face to her mother's face, then at the diaper bag. "What? What am I supposed to do? What's the *honors?*"

"I'll let you two ladies figure this out together." He nodded at the highway. "The men will be waiting over here."

Wes sat down next to the bikes to keep Elio company where he was still strapped inside the jogging stroller. Even trying a little Spanish with the child, who seemed to be about four years old, produced no response from the boy who still hadn't spoken. But he did accept a stick of dried deer meat from Wes's hand.

A few yards away, Jill and Dalia laid out a blanket and tried to shield the tiny baby from the breeze as they cleaned and changed it. If Wes had to guess, he figured the massacre had happened two days earlier. The infant would slow them down even more, with the feeding and changing, and they'd need to figure out a temporary fix to carry their new little passenger on a bike.

The raiders had a two-day head start, but they were a big group, and Wes was alone. He could move almost twice as fast on the bike. If he left the bike behind, he could hike cross-country, then intercept them somewhere where they'd be vulnerable. Wynter would be having their baby soon herself. He had to get to her before she bore a child in the company of killers!

"It's a girl!" Dalia reported with a grin.

"Great," Wes scoffed to Elio, who didn't stop gnawing on the meat. "More women to boss us around, little man."

From the caravan's debris, Wes found two semi-clean blankets, and created a small cradle beside Elio in the stroller, then strapped the bundle in place with the boy.

"She's so small," Jill commented, seeing both Elio and the infant together. "Just think. We found her. She's alive because of us."

"The Lord must have big plans for that little one." Wes signaled at the bikes. "Hop on. Let's get going while it's still light out."

Wes took the lead as Jill and Dalia rode behind, admiring their new find as if they'd given birth to the child themselves. But Wes's mind was on the hunt, on another child, and on a woman he'd fallen in love with. His fury was monstrous, and he struggled to submit it to the Lord. Vengeance wanted to rise up. It was the old Wes way, the old Wes who had taken life, before he had understood he was to love his enemies, before he'd begun to substitute tranquilizers into his Desert Eagle handguns.

They pedaled up Highway 65 for two hours before they saw the glimmer of a fire in the fading light. According to his map, Wes thought this might be Sandburg, but for some reason, the signs along the highway had been removed. Maybe people were using the metal signs as frying pans like others had done, he thought, or maybe they were making weapons. Then he guessed the road signs had been removed to discourage or mislead strangers passing by. Not many wanted company in those days.

"Who goes there?" someone shouted from the darkness as the travelers rode up the middle of the road. A lantern illuminated a barrier of garbage and several vehicles blocked the street ahead. "Go ahead. You can speak. Tell us who you are."

Wes planted his feet on the blacktop, straddling his bike.

"We were trying to catch up to a caravan from Mexico and San Diego, but they were slaughtered about two hours south of here." Wes felt the weariness of the day settle in his bones. Somehow, he needed to find the energy to press on after the raiders. "We just need a safe place to stay for the night. I'd like to leave my lady friends and two kids here while I try to recover some friends the raiders kidnapped."

"There's no recovering anyone from the Diablos." The man moved from behind the barrier, and Wes noticed several other silhouettes beside him. All the men were armed. "Come on in. We'll get you warmed up and bedded down. Can't say we have much for food, but we have plenty of firewood."

Part of the barrier was wheeled out of the way, and the cyclists walked their bikes through.

"I understand you have to do this," Jill whispered to Wes as they entered the makeshift fort, "but don't leave us with just anyone!"

More lanterns, burning some sort of fuel, lit up more of the street, which was further blocked on cross-avenues for entry or exit. The few men Wes noticed crossing the street, moving from building to building, carried rifles, and he suddenly felt like he should be carrying the bullpup. He wasn't interested in drawing attention to the powerful weapon, but he seemed to have stumbled into a reality where everyone remained armed and ready. Even Jill's right hand rested on the pistol in the waistband of her jeans.

"We get travelers every few days," the first man wearing a cowboy hat said. He pointed them toward what looked like a sporting goods store. "You'll find lodging over there."

"If you get so many people, where is everyone?" Wes asked. "Is there more to your fort than I can see?"

"No, this is it." The man pushed his hat farther back on his head. Two men behind him rolled the gate back across the barrier. "People stay here a few days, but the threat of attack from the Diablos pushes people on. It's bad all over, buddy. We try to help as many people as we can, but nobody has much."

"Thank you." Wes held out his hand to shake the friendly man's hand.

"Whoa, we don't do that here." He backed away a step. "The virus could still be sneaking around. Even your friends will need to keep their distance from people until they've shown for a couple weeks that they aren't infected."

"Of course." Wes dropped his hand. Not everyone had returned to civilized greetings or understood the virus as well as those in San Diego. It felt like the Central Valley was the Wild West. "We'll head on in. Thanks for your hospitality."

Wes walked with his party to the sporting goods store and parked their bikes against the curb where cars had once parked. A few other bikes were leaning against the wall of the store, so Wes figured leaving their bikes unattended for a little while wouldn't matter. But he wasn't leaving his pack behind.

"Go on in," he told Jill and Dalia, who rescued Elio and the baby from the stroller. "Keep your eyes open for a place to spend the night. I'll be right behind you."

The store's bell jungled when they opened the front door, and then his friends were gone. Wes turned in a circle to admire what the survivors of Sandburg had done with their town. If he wasn't mistaken, he saw damage on some of the building fronts from bullets or grenades. The town was on a new frontier now.

"Where you from, stranger?" a man asked in passing. He carried an armful of firewood.

"San Diego."

"Rough down there?"

"Coronado Island is setting up a new government, but it's rough everywhere."

"I hear you. The earthquake is the big news up here, not counting the Diablos, of course."

"What earthquake?" Wes asked.

"Shook us something fierce about a week ago. I heard it was worse to the east."

"The mountains are to the east. Any news?"

"Haven't heard any more. Later."

The man moved on, but Wes contemplated the facts as he would've done in his previous job. He would've given his case workers data to plug into their computers, working with the Pentagon to coordinate a strike somewhere overseas. But now there would be a strike here at home, where evil men roamed free and unchecked. They wore black armbands and went by the name of Diablos. *Devils*—it seemed fitting.

When the street seemed relatively clear, Wes opened his pack and slid out the compact COIL NL-X2 battle rifle. It fired a .308 cartridge, accurate up to six hundred yards, and fired three types of ammunition: standard cartridge, gel tranquilizer, and a phosphorus round.

The phosphorus round had been designed by Titus to disable vehicles, utilizing the acid's corrosive properties, which ate anything it touched. In the early days, right after Pan-Day, Titus and Oleg had used the phosphorus rounds on armored vehicles to put a stop to several civilians rampaging through the outskirts of the City of San Diego. Wes had seen the acid work, and he was glad he'd allowed Titus to talk him into taking ninety rounds with him. It was more than enough to stop an army, if that army had heavy artillery.

He loaded the bullpup with gel-tranqs, then hung it on the sling over his shoulder. Over his other shoulder, he hung his heavy pack, not willing to leave it outside where he didn't know the townspeople yet.

When he pushed through the door of the sporting goods store, he was hit in the face with a blast of warm air and the smell of a wood stove. Except for a brief night of warmth at Tejon Pass, he'd been waking and sleeping in the cold air since leaving San Diego. So this felt good.

Instead of finding empty shelves or racks in the store, the place had been gutted to accommodate sleeping bags and campers in stocking feet. Kids were playing a board game in one corner, and a number of women sat at the store counter, which had been transformed into a tea and gossip counter, it seemed. Dozens of people were already climbing into their sleeping bags on the left side of the store, many of them bearded men. Instinctively, Wes looked for black armbands, but he saw none. Not in this place, of course.

"Wes!" Jill tried to call discreetly from across the building where she and Dalia stood speaking to an official-looking hefty woman in a down vest. When he reached her, she tugged on the arm that held his rifle sling. "This is Nicole. She says we can stay here if we help with the chores. I think it'll be okay. There are good people here."

"Okay." Wes sized up the large woman in front of him, who gazed back skeptically as well. She wore a revolver on her belt. "What happens if the Diablos attack?"

"They've attacked before." Nicole's eyes narrowed. "That's why every adult here is packing."

"Oh, I'm packing, too," Jill happily announced, and patted the handgun Wes had loaded with gel-tranqs days earlier.

"How strong was their force?" Wes asked Nicole.

"About eighty. We know they were testing our defenses. They'll be back, and we'll be ready."

"How many shooters do you have here?"

"About fifty." She looked at him sideways. "Why so many questions?"

"Because I'm going after them."

"They took his wife," Jill informed softly.

"Another guy had a rifle like yours." Nicole stepped closer. "What's that supposed to be, anyway? Some sort of military gun? I've never seen anything like it, except with that other fellow."

"Someone else had a weapon like this?" Wes felt his pulse quicken. The only way someone could have a bullpup was if they'd taken it from Chevy or Wynter, and neither would have given such a valuable weapon away. "Is that person still here? Is he in this room?"

"Nah, he's staying down on the other end of town. We have two lodges, see? To cover both ends of town."

"Stay here." Wes set his pack at Jill's feet. "Watch my stuff. I'll be back."

He marched out of the sporting goods store and flipped his rifle into his hands. Someone from the Diablos was in town if there were indeed other rifles like his about.

Instead of marching down the middle of the street like a gunslinger, he moved against the storefronts on the right-hand sidewalk, searching for the other lodge. Even now, the Diablos could be organizing, planning an attack from inside Sandburg itself.

At every intersection, he looked left and right. Barriers at least a story high had been stacked to ward off attackers. Sandburg had been reduced to a one-street frontier town.

On the east end of town, only five blocks from where the first lodge was stationed, Wes came upon the second lodge, which had been fashioned from a school gymnasium. Like other parts of the town that Wes had seen from a distance, the school buildings themselves had been burned down. He chambered a round in the bullpup and prepared himself for action. Although he'd been a high-ranking agent for the last ten years, even as a liaison for the president, COIL, and the Pentagon, he'd often preferred to handle the bad guys on his own. And he was no stranger to being outnumbered.

A man with a rifle stepped away from the shadows around the front door of the gym. The night sky was clear and the moon was out, so no one had lit any lanterns at this end of town.

"Wes?" a familiar voice called when he was still several yards away.

Wes slowed but kept walking, processing what it meant to hear this man call his name.

"Chevy? Thank God!" Wes flipped his rifle onto his shoulder and rushed the last few steps to embrace Chevy. Chevy was a few years younger and thinner, but he was as tough as any COIL agent Wes had worked with. "I thought the worst when I found the caravan. I was ready to saddle up and go after the Diablos myself!"

"Wynter went into labor early, Wes." Chevy's voice sounded grim. Wes wasn't seeing the friendly man's usual toothy smile that he felt the occasion called for. "We left the caravan three days ago. When they never arrived, I went back yesterday and found what you apparently found."

"But you survived!" Wes held out his hands. "What? What's wrong?"

"Wynter was in labor for a long time. She bled a lot, Wes. A doctor here was with her the whole time, but they're not sure she's going to make it. I'm sorry, Wes, but . . . they lost the baby. It was a boy. I buried him yesterday."

"But . . . Wynter's okay, right? I mean, you guys escaped death at the hands of the Diablos. You made it. We're here." Wes gritted his teeth and turned away. He'd been ready for battle, and now this. The emotional roller coaster of the last day was too much. "Is Wynter awake? She's inside?"

"She's inside, but she hasn't been awake. I've been praying non-stop at her side. There were no meds to give her, so she felt the whole labor, almost twenty hours long. The doctor says she may not remember much, like even losing the baby, when she comes to."

Wes bowed his head under the starry sky, reaching with his whole soul for God's help, His comfort for Wynter, His healing hand. She'd lost the baby. *A boy!* He could've been holding his baby boy right now, but it wasn't meant to be. Tears ran down his cheeks. One minute, he was finding a baby girl in a field of blood, and the next minute he was losing a son.

After several minutes of grieving and praying, he lifted his head and turned back to Chevy.

"Can you go to the first lodge, Chevy, and find a teen named Dalia. She has a newborn. Tell her that my wife lost her child, and to bring the baby girl to us. I'm going in to see my wife."

"All right, Wes." Chevy walked away, then called to him from a distance. "I'm sorry, Wes. You trusted me with Wynter, and here she is."

"It's not you, Chevy. You brought her to safety. You did your job. Thank you, friend."

Wes dried his face and took a deep breath, then opened the gymnasium door.

Much like the first lodge, there was a socializing area as well as a sleeping section inside the gym. A few families mingled in the living area, which had probably been carpeted to reduce noise, and several sleeping bags and cots were occupied, since night had fallen.

"The pregnant woman?" Wes asked a man in a western shirt and stocking cap. "I'm looking for Wynter Trimble. I'm Wes Trimble. Do you know where my wife is?"

Without saying anything, the man pointed to the far corner of the gym. Wes imagined everyone knew about the pregnancy and the difficult labor. Wynter had probably screamed her lungs out for hours, giving no one any sleep. She was a Caspertein, though, and a fighter. He prayed she would pull through. He couldn't bear to lose her.

An older woman sat with a lamp on a chair beside a sleeping Wynter. The nurse looked up when Wes drew near.

"I'm Wes Trimble, her husband." He knelt beside the military cot and took Wynter's limp hand in his. "How's she doing?"

"We got some fluids into her by IV, but she needs to wake up now." She frowned at Wynter. "The longer she's in a coma, the more unlikely . . . well, you know. I'll leave you two alone."

"Thank you."

The woman left her chair, but Wes didn't sit in it. Instead, he bowed over his wife and prayed. He was still praying and holding her hand when someone touched his shoulder. When he looked up, he saw Dalia with the newborn baby girl, with Chevy right behind her.

"I heard." Dalia held out the infant. "She wasn't really mine, anyway, but I was starting to think of names."

"What was your favorite name?" Wes received the baby and held her to his chest, the same way he had earlier that day when he'd picked her up from the massacre. "You found her, Dalia. Maybe you should pick her name."

"For some reason, I really liked Mia." Dalia shrugged. "I don't know why. It's just simple, but it's pretty."

"Mia. Mia Trimble." Wes laughed. "It is pretty. I like it. It's a good name."

"Do you think your wife will take her? I mean, it's not really her baby."

"If I know Wynter, there won't be any problem," Chevy assured Dalia.

"Mia." Wes held the infant up to look at her face closer. "My daughter."

Chapter 2

Three days passed before Wynter woke, and Wes was at her side with the baby when she moved her hand. The elderly woman had continued to nurse the ailing mother, but Wes hadn't left her side for three days.

"I was afraid I'd lost you." Wes leaned over Wynter and kissed her forehead. "Everyone in Sandburg has been checking on you, wondering if the lady who screams really loud is ever going to scream again."

"Oh, Wes." Wynter tenderly touched his face. She squinted her eyes as if trying to remember something, or maybe to forget. "Did I—? Is the baby—?"

"She's right here." Wes gingerly lifted the infant from a crib someone had found in one of the houses nearby. "Tiny little thing. You and I never really talked about names. We sort of picked one out already."

"She?" Wynter sat up with effort and took the baby in her arms. "Hi, there, little one. Wes? Things are a bit fuzzy for me, but I was awake for the delivery. The doctor said they were trying to get control of the bleeding. But I thought . . . I mean, a little girl is a blessing, but I thought I had a boy. That's what I remember the nurse saying."

"Sweetie, you remember right." He focused on her so intently with his one eye that she seemed to understand that she was to give him her full attention. "I talked to the doctor. There was a little boy."

"Oh, no, Wes . . ." She shook her head, her face twisting in pain, tears running down her cheeks. "No . . ."

"So much went wrong, I guess, honey. He just never started breathing. Chevy buried him outside the barrier. He told me where. We can go there together when you're feeling better."

"Oh, Wes, our baby?" She looked down, suddenly remembering that she was holding another infant. "Whose is this one?"

"I don't remember her name, but you probably knew her in the caravan. There was another pregnant woman. She was killed, Wynter. This one is only about a week old."

"Yes, I was there. I remember when she had it." Wynter nodded slowly. "Victoria. They'd gotten stuck down in Mexico on vacation, she and her husband. They were going back up to Washington. This is her baby?"

"This is Mia. Mia Trimble."

"I'm pretty sure you're supposed to wait for the mother to help pick out the name of the child, Wes!" She cast him an annoyed look. "I don't recall Victoria having a name for her yet. It was a bit of a joke in the whole caravan. Everyone had a different name for her. How'd you come up with Mia?"

"It's quite a story of its own. I'll tell you sometime."

"Mia Trimble. It's a good name. Hello, Mia. Oh, I think I see a little smile!"

With Wynter conscious and beginning to move around, Wes was free to go see the townspeople without them all coming by to see how he and Wynter were doing. Chevy had had almost a week to visit with the people and to find out how Sandburg was situated, so Wes received a tour from him.

"Directly east of us is Sequoia National Park, all along that snow line up there." Chevy swept his hand at the Sierra Nevada Mountains as the two men stood alone on the roof of the gym. There were provisions already on the gym roof as a final sanctuary, if the rest of the town was overrun by invaders. "Now, on the north side of Sequoia is Kings Canyon National Park. We're talking about some old forest up there, giant trees, snow as deep as this roof. I've talked to some hunters who won't even go up that high, and they're from this area."

"But where's Lune Lake?" Wes asked.

"There's a mountain peak about right there. It's hard to make out from this distance, even on a clear day like today. That's Mount Ritter, at thirteen thousand feet. Lune Lake is on the other side of that, on the other side of the Pacific Crest Trail."

"So, we're too late? There's too much snow?" Wes adjusted his eye patch, trying to hide his frustration. "What about all the people up there who are waiting on us? We know there were people running up there to get away from the violence here in the valley."

"Wes, that's what I'm saying. We'd have to travel up the San Joaquin River Gorge, which you can't even see from here, and that's packed with more snow than you and I have probably ever seen. It's been that way since December. No one's gone up there, and if they are up there, we can't get to them until spring. That's what Hoxborn said."

"Which one's Hoxborn again?"

"The cowboy hat and fancy western shirts."

"Do you think he owns other shirts, or he just likes those fancy designs?"

"Wes, I'm trying to tell you something serious here." Chevy chuckled. "Look, it gets worse. I don't think anyone's been reaching the mountains like we thought. There's the Diablos. They're killing and pillaging everyone and everything. People can't travel safely. Even if we were up at Lune Lake right now, no one would be on their way. They'd be killed by the Diablos, or freeze to death in the snow. And that's not even to mention the avalanches. Hoxborn says that whole roads have been wiped out from that earthquake a few days ago."

"So, what'd we come up here for? Do we go back to San Diego?" Wes walked closer to the edge of the gym roof and looked down at the few pedestrians. "This is no way for these people to live, Chevy. We've come all this way, certain it was for a reason, to be used by God to help people. Bad weather and bad people can't get in our way!"

"I agree with you. We came all this way. We may as well do something."

"You know what Corban Dowler would do?" Wes groaned and shook his head. "Scratch that. You know what Corban and Titus would do together? They'd take on the Diablos."

"There's hundreds of them, Wes, between two camps—Isabella Lake and Twitchell Reservoir."

"Yeah, well, there's two of us. And we have five more battle rifles to put into the hands of others once we recruit more people."

"No one will sign on for something like that. They're good people, but they aren't fighters or people of faith."

"We could make the valley safe again for people to move about," Wes said. "We'll still get to Lune Lake. And we'll make sure others can, too, if they want to."

"We're not peacekeepers, Wes. We're COIL operatives. We learned how to survive in San Diego, and we came up here to share the gospel and to teach others how to survive."

"A lot of what we did in San Diego involved peacekeeping."

"Let's say we catch some Diablos," Chevy said. "What do we do with them? There's no authority structure anywhere. Not even San Diego was taking in prisoners. Criswell and Brogdon were just executing people."

"We can figure out something. I don't have it all figured out, but I can envision it. It's a COIL mission. It's no crazier than you going into North Korea last year for a woman about to be executed."

"We need to bring Wynter into this conversation. She thinks a lot like Titus." Chevy threw his hands up. "But I still think it's a little wild, even for us."

The two men stood shoulder to shoulder for a moment, observing the town. Several people carried armfuls of what Wes thought were belongings, until they threw them onto the nearest barrier blocking one of the avenues. Garbage. They were hemmed in by garbage on the inside, and by murderers on the outside.

"We'd need to target the leadership of the Diablos," Wes stated.

"Is that CIA training you're voicing?" Chevy elbowed his friend. "Like you and Titus were strategizing a few months ago—divide and conquer, exploit the enemy's weaknesses, remain more mobile and supplied than anyone else."

"Titus was the muscle. I was just the brains, although Wynter might tell you I was less than half the brains."

"She is your better half—I'd have to agree with her!"

"Careful," Wes warned. "If I shove you off this roof, you'll land in that garbage heap!"

The men laughed together, almost as if death didn't surround them, almost as if they weren't planning to risk their lives for the safety of people who would never know it.

"It's insane!" Wynter shouted in the gym where Wes, Dalia, Jill, Elio, and Chevy had partitioned off a small corner. She touched her mouth and lowered her voice after a glance at the crib where Mia lay sleeping. "Who are we to go after people like the Diablos? We would need an army!"

"Or a couple sharpshooters," Wes said. "And we have those."

"The Diablos have mortars, RPGs, and sniper rifles of their own." Wynter raised her eyebrows. "What about that?"

"They don't know how to use them." Wes crossed his arms, looked at Chevy, then continued. "Of all the gear they have, they're not trained to use it. They broke into an army depot and raided it like they've raided everything else. We can take care of any armored unit with the phosphorus rounds. All their rifles and small arms—we have them beat by distance and marksmanship."

"We can't help these locals," Chevy said, "unless we first show them that the roads are safe to travel again. Massacring entire caravans of refugees like the Diablos did is totally unacceptable. No one else is equipped to handle something of this magnitude. I think we can do it in a peaceful way. Wes has a plan. We might even lead some Diablos to Christ."

"We're going to make Mia an orphan?" Wynter pressed with a sharp tone. "For a second time?"

"Wes and I can recon to start with," Chevy said. "The valley is massive but flat. As long as we work as a pair and keep our distance from the enemy, we should be able to see anyone coming for miles around. Hoxborn says the Diablos always work in packs, rarely less than ten or twenty in a unit. We can handle that many."

"Two against twenty?" Jill glanced up from her sleeping bag where she sat drawing clothing designs on her notepad. The corners of her tablet were curled from being carried over many miles, but the woman's skill was remarkable. "Isn't that—what do you call it—being presumptuous?"

"It would be presumptuous if it wasn't what COIL operatives have done regularly," Wes said. "God's people have always been outnumbered. With God's help, we could do this, especially on the psychological warfare front."

"Oh, this should be good." Wynter checked on Mia, then returned to face the two men. Below her in the close quarters, playing on one of the sleeping mats, Dalia had found a card game that Elio was responding to. "Psychological warfare, Wes? Seriously? This I've got to hear."

"Well, Chevy and I were praying. We know we can't march these Diablos into the nearest town to be held in a jail. The citizens would kill them immediately. There's no law. No government. And even if there was, I doubt there would be justice. Regardless, we're Christians. As challenging as it is sometimes, we're called to forgive sooner than we condemn."

"Get this, Wynter." Chevy stepped up, his face showing his amusement. "We tranquilize these bandits, then we let them go."

"Let them go?" Wynter scoffed. "That's your psychological impact on them?"

"Not just let them go." Wes held up his pocket Bible. "We disarm them of their weapons. That's a start. That will begin to impact them down the road, especially with their leaders. Then, Jill sketches their portraits, so we have them on file. We begin to profile these criminals."

"Tell her the best part, Wes!" Chevy urged.

"Wait, what am I doing?" Jill set aside her notebook and stood next to Wynter. "Wait, start over. I was only half listening."

"Then we post their portraits up where we know the Diablos frequent," Wes said. "Underneath their portraits, we write something like—'Because you are loved, we did not kill you. Consider your life precious, and the lives of your victims as sacred before God. Turn from this evil and humble yourself before the cross of Jesus Christ.' Something like that."

"So, after letting these Diablos go, you're going to give them a picture of themselves and a Bible verse?" Wynter's face showed her skepticism. "And that's supposed to do what?"

"They'll mock it, we know that." Chevy nodded. "But it'll get under their skin in time. And we'll be praying for each individual we catch."

"Not just under their skin." Wes pinched his fingers together to emphasize his point. "It'll get into their hearts. The Holy Spirit will do something. I know it!"

"Wicked killers are just going to lay down their rifles and stop killing people because you've drawn their pictures and told them to repent?"

"History is full of Christians who've remained passive," Chevy said, "and they've won over just the right people. I've read about persecuted Christians bringing their jailers or torturers to Christ, simply by their testimony. If we look at this in a worldly way, yeah, it seems weak."

"But look at it from God's perspective." Wes held up his Bible again. "It's really all about strength. Trusting God to tear down the impossible! Maybe just a man or two at first, but it'll send a message. And we're not weak, are we? Trusting in Egypt was weak for Israel, in the Bible. But trusting in God was true strength."

"And it's not that we're weak," Wynter said. "I mean, with the bullpups, we have a shooting advantage."

"Who am I supposed to sketch?" Jill asked again. She rested her hand on her sidearm. "You want me to help, right?"

"Yes, we want you to help." Chevy set a hand on the actress's shoulder. "You play a vital role here. God's going to transform this valley for Christ, and He's going to use us."

"The Kindred of Nails lives again?" Wynter laughed. "I can't believe I'm buying into this ridiculous plan!"

The next day, Wes and Chevy set off together from the east end of Sandburg. Hoxborn and the other riflemen within the town had been told only that the two new men in town were going hunting. The fact that they had headed toward the east probably hadn't raised any alarms for anyone. However, before they were beyond the burnt outskirts of the town of Sandburg, they turned directly south through the orange groves. They carried light packs, enough supplies for three days, and two canteens apiece.

By heading south from Sandburg, they were approaching Isabella Lake directly, which was forty-five miles away cross-country. Wes didn't need to tell Chevy to stay sharp, since they'd already discussed and prayed the night before about the probability of meeting a party of Diablos long before reaching the lake. However, they—and Wynter—had agreed that recon was their objective at this point. They needed to know more about their enemy, even if it meant taking a couple of prisoners.

The fields south of Sandburg, like the rest of the valley, had once been used for agriculture. Now, the land had a frostbitten look to it, which was evidence that it had been abandoned for at least a year. Crops that had once relied on constant cultivation to thrive now grew without care, or the fields were completely barren and unplanted.

The morning of the second day, the pair crossed the White River using a small county bridge. The farmhouses scattered throughout the fields were dark and quiet. Since the two travelers anticipated they would reach Highway 155 by noon, their gait was steady as their legs were getting used to movement once again after a week of inactivity.

Suddenly, Chevy slapped Wes's shoulder, and the two dropped to their knees in the middle of a field. They watched together as two people on mountain bikes sped west on a dirt road. The strangers were a quarter-mile away, too far to be of any danger, but Wes and Chevy remained motionless in the field as a precaution.

"I can't tell if they have black armbands or not," Chevy said, using a small pair of field glasses. "We should've brought a better scope for better recon. But they definitely have rifles on their backs."

"They could be scouts," Wes guessed, "looking for more caravans to ambush. They'd waste too many resources if their whole fighting force marched all over the fields and roads. Maybe they send out just two scouts at a time like this."

"It blows Hoxborn's theory out of the water that they travel only in packs of ten or twenty." Chevy stuffed his gloves into his breast pocket where he kept his Bible. "What if we target their scouting teams? We'll force them to start fielding larger scouting forces, and that'll use up more resources. See? Now I'm starting to think like you."

"Lose one of your eyes, and you'll be as handsome as me, too." Wes reached for his pack strap. "Here, I've even got an extra eye patch for you."

"No thanks!" Chevy pointed across the landscape. "Come on. They're out of sight. Let's move up and see if we can figure out why they're on this road."

With caution, Wes and Chevy avoided the dirt road, but followed it at a distance on the south side as it led east. Two miles later, it turned south toward Isabella Lake.

"It's a back access road to Kernville, maybe." Chevy tossed a couple oranges to Wes. Citrus groves were still plentiful around Sandburg, even though they lacked care. "Discovering this route isn't much for our first recon, but it's something."

"We need to think about how Sandburg could be blamed for anything the Kindred of Nails does." Wes used his binoculars to check to the west. "You and I sneaking around like this could get us into trouble with everyone, not just the Diablos."

"It makes me nervous," Chevy said, finishing his orange, "but maybe we should think about doing a little more than just recon right now."

"Yeah?"

"Two more scouts are coming from the south. Look!" Chevy pointed. "And they definitely have black patches on their arms. What do you think?"

"It's risky without a solid plan " Wes swept his glasses across the landscape. "It's clear in this direction. Yours?"

"No one for miles."

Wes jogged west one hundred yards, then lay on his belly in the crop field where the two scouts would be facing him once they went around the bend. Chevy remained to Wes's right, where he'd be shooting broadside at the scouts. As Wes piled dirt in front of himself for the off-chance that there was a firefight, he prayed about all that was about to happen. No one had confronted the Diablos in a meaningful way, but God had already trained the COIL men to be both peacekeepers and evangelists. With his heart racing, Wes aimed his rifle.

When the two scouts made the curve, they sped abreast toward Wes. Chevy would be shooting at the scout nearest him, so Wes aimed at the rider on the left, and waited for him to come within one hundred and fifty yards before he fired.

Since Wes fired first, the second scout flinched at both the collapse of his companion as well as the gunshot. Chevy's first shot missed, but his second round caught the scout in the side.

Neither Wes nor Chevy were quick to run up to their downed targets. Wes scoped to the west again and Chevy did the same in his direction, searching for movement over the crops and weeds of the fields. Finally, they rose to their feet and jogged up to the unconscious men.

"You know," Wes said as he approached the fallen, "these could be some of the same men who massacred those refugees."

"They probably are." Chevy's voice was low. "That idea will just help us pray for them more. I was like them once, Wes. There's still hope for them, too."

Each man carried a scout over his shoulder far off the road and into the near-dry bed of an irrigation ditch. The two bandits appeared to be in their twenties. As Chevy ran back for the scouts' bikes, Wes began to sketch the men's faces in the back, blank pages of his Bible. When Chevy returned, he jumped up and down on the bike frames, doing his best to damage the two Diablos' method of transportation. Finally, he opted to removing the bike seats from both of them, and slashed all the tires. He threw the bike seats into the darkest mud the irrigation ditch offered.

"Take off their armbands, too," Wes suggested, then he pocketed his Bible and pencil, and shouldered the men's assault rifles. "As much as I'd like to beg them to change their lives, we should leave them here before they wake up."

"I hope they realize what a break we're giving them." Chevy rifled through their small packs and held up a map. "Look at this."

"More intel." Wes studied the materials briefly. "Take it, and let's get out of here. We'll leave tracks going west to throw them off. We'll hit Highway 65 tonight and tomorrow we'll follow it back into Sandburg."

The two jogged away, their extra gear jostling for a mile, then Wes threw the two extra assault rifles into a drainage pool.

"So, everyone in Sandburg is saying Jill is somebody famous," Chevy said as they continued at a fast walk. "You ever heard of her?"

"Stars and starlets from Hollywood never caught my eye."

"Your eye, funny. I'm serious. She was someone?"

"Dalia said she'd been in some movies. I didn't pry. I try not to encourage people to live in the past, or as the person they used to be, you know?"

"I was talking to her about God's Word because I saw her reading Wynter's Bible yesterday, but she said she's not a believer."

"Yet." Wes smiled. "Since she's been shown her need for a Savior, it's just a matter of time, I'd say. Just remember, if you scoop up that one, you've got a teenage daughter to deal with."

"*Scoop up*— What are you talking about?"

"What? Jill's a beautiful woman. I'm just saying, after she's in the fold, and you start praying more seriously about matrimony, don't forget you have a temperamental teenager on your hands. Dalia's not bad, just argumentative with her mother. But you'd get two for the price of one."

"I am not— You can be so— Wes! I'm not talking to you anymore about this!"

Wes roared with laughter as Chevy walked ahead.

Chapter 3

The second time Wes and Chevy went on recon, they distanced themselves from Sandburg by two days. On a small mound of earth, they set up a blind overlooking Highway 43 and an intersection west of Earlimart, a town that had been decimated and abandoned.

"Just don't ruin their bikes this time," Wes suggested. "We can use two of them to get back to town."

"We might need to take some of their food, too." Chevy picked through his pack, taking inventory of the extra gear they'd brought. "Depending on how long we're sitting here waiting for a scouting party, we might need to be resupplied from their own stores."

They used bushes and plants to camouflage their blind eighty yards from the intersection, then set up a watch schedule, taking turns day and night. Both men had Bibles to read privately or quietly, while the other kept an eye on the three stretches of roadway. But after two days of praying and waiting, they started to discuss other locations. Though they were about a day west of where Wynter's caravan had been slaughtered, there hadn't been a single hint of traffic in that area where cotton fields had gone unharvested for a second season.

Chevy voiced the possibility that there were more frequented routes the Diablos were using between their two bases, when Wes interrupted.

"Here they come!" Wes gazed directly east. "This isn't good. I think we bit off more than we're comfortable with this time."

Using a telescope, Chevy peered down the two-lane highway.

"I count twenty. They're all Diablos, too."

"Yep. I say we log them down and don't tangle with this bunch right now."

"They could be on their way to raid someone, Wes. They're packing some heavy equipment, too. Two of them in the rear are towing trailers. Could just be water or tents, but it could be mortar tubes and firing platforms."

"But still, twenty is a little steep for our beginning efforts to impact the lives of the Diablos." Wes considered letting them pass, and continuing their dull waiting and watching behind their blind. "Unless they turn to the north at the intersection. Then, their backs will be to us. If we wait for them to travel three hundred yards, we could open fire."

"We'll need to keep count. There's cover for them in the cotton shrubs on the east side of the road. But they'll have no approach to our position."

"And we're elevated." Wes checked the shadows of the blind. "The sun will be in their eyes. We'll be here close to sundown disarming them and sketching their faces."

"This is what we came for." Chevy set aside the powerful scope and cautiously picked up his rifle, careful not to disturb the foliage of the blind. "Let's give Jill something to re-draw."

"Re-draw?" Wes scoffed jokingly. "You mean duplicate. What's with you bringing up Jill in every serious conversation, anyway?"

"Get serious, will you?" Chevy smiled. "Do you want me to tell Wynter about your lame attempts at matchmaking when our lives are on the line?"

Wes muffled his laughter, appreciating the operative's humor—knowing that the man's attraction to Jill wasn't really causing him to be biased about her artistic skills. She had a gift, and she'd taken Wes's rough drawings of the first two scouts and turned them into masterpieces that their own mothers would've recognized. And she hadn't even seen either man!

The party of soldiers indeed turned north at the intersection, and Wes's lightheartedness all but vanished as he calculated his shots. Either he would die in the next ten minutes, or he'd soon be walking amongst the tranquilized. Twenty men was too many for just the two of them, he realized, but the situation in the valley was desperate, and desperate measures were called for. Wes hoped their elevation, positioning, rifle range, and surprise would make the difference.

"I'll go left," Wes reminded, even though it was a given that since he was on the left, he would naturally fire at the soldiers on the left. And when on foot, he'd move to the left.

"Copy that," Chevy said softly, his cheek against the bullpup. "Two hundred and fifty yards. You ready?"

"I'm ready. A little farther . . ."

This time, Chevy fired first. Wes was an instant later, hitting the back of one of the cyclists who towed a trailer of gear. The soldiers didn't react too quickly, so Wes fired rapidly up the left side of their perfect line of formation. He'd dropped four by the time half of the men lunged from their bikes into the shallow ditch. Since they were using sound suppressors on the bullpups, the muzzle sound was distributed outward instead of toward the target. It was certain to disorient the men as they searched in the daylight for a muzzle flash, but that was useless.

Six men in Wes's charge waited in the ditch, perfectly still, but completely in his view. Wes took an instant to check Chevy's progress. He'd tranqed one more man than Wes, but the rest of Chevy's men had crawled into the overgrown and neglected cotton plants on the right side of the road.

Wes targeted his six men who hid in plain sight in the ditch, starting with the one farthest from him. The last two were confused, and in their inability to locate the shooters, they made a charge back to their bikes. One, Wes shot as he reached his bike. The last, he shot in the back as he made his escape down the highway.

"Want to give me a hand here?" Chevy asked. "I've got four sneakers about thirty yards from the road. See that tall clump of bushes?"

"They've figured out where we are." Wes glanced left and right. "They're making plans, so we need to, too, before they flank us. I'll draw their fire. Cover me!"

Charging to the left out of the blind, Wes stumbled into a run, then caught his footing an instant before he started to slide down the slope to the ditch next to the road. He heard Chevy's gunfire behind him, and from the enemy in front of him, but he didn't stop. With his head low, he ran straight north down the ditch toward the six men he'd tranqed minutes earlier. Chevy was a decent marksman, but the man hadn't spent his whole adult life hunting international criminals and chasing fugitives like Wes had. Although Wes knew he was older and not as agile as Chevy, he was at home on the move, creeping down a ditch like this, seeking an edge against an otherwise superior force.

When he reached the bikes and the first men they'd tranqed at three hundred yards, Wes looked back at Chevy. The gunfire had ceased. It would've been a good time to have walkie-talkies, but Wes knew Chevy had been trained by Titus and Oleg, and no one knew flanking and assault procedures better than those two.

Wes waved his hand in a flagging motion once, twice, then three times. With that, he ran up the ditch and leveled his rifle when he reached the road. Sure enough, two soldiers were caught by surprise behind their rows of cotton plants they'd used for cover, which Wes had now flanked. He fired quickly at them before they could fire back.

A rifle blasted at him from the right, and he felt the heat sear across his belly. He dove to the ground, breathing heavily and wincing at the pain in his gut.

Where were the final two men? Had Chevy gotten one of them? They needed to coordinate their signals better if they were going to take on a force this size!

He rolled over once and leaped back to his feet to sprint up the row of vegetation. After hurdling the two he'd just tranqed, he dove back to the ground and listened. The one or two left were sandwiched between Chevy and himself. There was no hope for the soldiers.

"Come out with your hands up!" Wes yelled. "You're boxed in. We've got you covered on both sides. There's nowhere to go."

Two men's voices could be heard from a few rows away, perhaps discussing their decision. Wes waited, praying they didn't think they needed to fight to the death.

"You won't be harmed!" Wes assured them. "Throw down your weapons and show us your hands!"

"We'll surrender with conditions!" one man called back.

"Conditions?" Wes shook his head. The stranger's voice sounded young, far too young to be demanding conditions. "You're in no position to ask for anything but mercy. Come out or we come in!"

There was more discussion.

"We're coming out! Don't shoot!"

Wes hesitantly raised his head, hoping Chevy didn't mistake his wool cap for the head of one of the Diablos. A gel-tranq to the skull, even against a wool cap, wouldn't kill him, but it would rattle his brain.

Two men rose from the bushes, their empty hands held high. Chevy fired at one, and Wes, guessing Chevy hadn't heard their pleas to surrender, fired through the bushes at the other. Both men went down. They had indeed been surrendering, but Chevy couldn't have known or heard, and it was safer to have them unconscious for the next part of their plan.

Wes checked his watch as he jogged back to the highway, counting the men as he went. It had been twelve minutes since the first man had been tranqed. That left about forty-eight minutes before the first of them started to wake up.

When he reached the intersection, Wes cupped his hand around his mouth to yell.

"We have forty-five minutes to get this done. Is the road clear?"

"We're clear," Chevy said, then left the blind to join Wes on the road. Together, they jogged back to the bikes.

"You confiscate equipment after we get them tied up," Wes instructed. "Load up those trailers with their rifles and gear. We'll leave them stranded with nothing but their canteens."

"This just means they'll have to start scouting the valley in groups of fifty."

"That's too many for us, Chevy. Don't even think about it!"

"Hey, you're bleeding." Chevy gestured to Wes's belly.

Wes checked his wound. It burned like hot lava, but it didn't go deep.

"Just a graze. It was close, but the Lord doesn't want to take me home just yet, I guess."

"I think He wants you to practice your drawing a little more."

Wes let the wisecrack go as they split up and started to group and tie up the men. Using whatever they had on them, they bound their wrists behind them, then their ankles. Once that was done, they had twenty minutes left before the tranquilizers started to wear off. Both men fashioned bandanas over their faces so they couldn't be recognized once the men woke, and they continued working. Chevy ran back and forth, fetching rifles and carrying them to the bikes with trailers. Wes found a pair of sunglasses on one of the men, and put them on to hide his missing eye.

As the first men began to stir, Wes was getting started on only the third man's portrait. He sketched quickly, hoping the likenesses were close enough to be recognizable later, or for Jill to perfect.

At first, the men blinked in puzzlement at their situation, saying nothing. They didn't fight their binds or struggle to stand since Chevy stood stoically next to Wes.

The defiance of the twenty began when Wes shifted to draw the face of the fifth man, and the man turned his face away. Wes and Chevy glanced at one another, not wanting to openly communicate since they didn't want the raiders to know any more about them than they had to know, like whether they spoke English or Spanish. But their plan hinged on the portraits, so Wes drew his sidearm and shot the defiant one point-blank in the chest. He lay again on his back, and Wes drew him without further annoyance.

But then the others started to protest.

"Hey, you can't treat us this way!"

"Yeah, my shoulders have arthritis. Loosen my wrists, homey, huh?"

"Hey, I can't feel my fingers. These ropes are too tight!"

"Hey, old man. Yeah, you!" One of the Diablos cursed at Wes. "I see you looking at me. Why don't you let me up and see who's a real man, huh?"

Wes continued to draw, committing one page for each individual. He'd come with notebook paper this time.

Some of the men spoke Spanish, trying to get Chevy or Wes to react, but neither operative showed any weakness, and no one else turned their face from Wes's intentions.

After another hour, he was done. He folded the pages and stuffed them into his shirt. He and Chevy moved a distance away from the twenty to speak in whispers.

"I'm seeing a lot of prison tattoos on these men," Chevy said softly. "And the way they're talking, I'd say we're dealing mostly with gangsters, some sort of hybrid between the Northern and Southern Hispanics, but there are whites mixed in there, too."

"So, they're ex-cons?" Wes asked through his bandana. "Is that significant? What am I missing?"

"Not *ex*-cons. *Escaped* cons. You know how many prisons are within two hundred miles of where we're standing? The Corcoran Complex isn't far away. That's fifteen thousand inmates. The two Kern Valley prisons held another eight thousand. Then you've got Avenal, Coalinga, Wasco, and more. We're talking thousands upon thousands of inmates who may have survived Pan-Day, were able to get out of their prison cells, and now they're showing society some payback. You were trying to make sense of the slaughter of the caravan in the lettuce field. Here's your reason: these weren't civilians who suddenly turned violent to survive. These were already experienced predators—the worst of society—and now they're just having their kind of fun. This world is now a playground for them. They thrive on this sort of chaos. Remember, I did twenty years with these kinds of men. Maybe even some of these here today."

"Society's castaways." Wes looked back at the lot of them. "They're watching us now, trying to figure out who we are or what we're going to do next. They don't realize we're here hoping to impact their lives for eternity."

"What we need to do next is get on a couple of those bikes and get out of here." Chevy moved closer to Wes. "We should take the road south, then dump the bikes and gear we don't need anymore, then lay low while it's daylight. We should travel only at night while heading back to Sandburg. Look at their faces."

"Yeah, we've stirred the hornets' nest enough for one day." From his pocket, Wes pulled the two portraits of the first two scouts they'd abducted. "Let's wrap this up."

The two of them returned to the twenty tied men and the bikes. Chevy climbed onto one of the bikes with the attached trailer while Wes wrestled one of the smaller Diablos to his feet, then threw him over his shoulder.

"Put me down! Where are you taking me? What are you doing?"

Wes walked the screamer across the road and dumped him onto the ground. He held up the two portraits of the scouts, each portrait with text at the bottom and signed by the Kindred of Nails, then stuffed them into the man's jacket.

"Hey, what do I want with those? What are you doing?"

Aiming his pistol at the man, Wes shot him in the chest. The mouthy man fell over unconscious, then Wes loosened his binds. In a civilized world, he would've turned such criminals over to the court system. But this wasn't a civilized world, and there was no more court system. He tried not to imagine that these very men had been involved in the slaughter of so many just thirty miles to the east.

Emerging from the ditch, Wes nodded at Chevy, then climbed onto the second bike connected to the trailer of gear.

"Hey, you can't leave us here like this!" one of the Diablos yelled. "Hey, at least untie us! It could be days before someone else comes this way! We could die out here!"

Wes ignored their pleas, knowing that in an hour, when the screamer woke, he'd find his binds loose and he would free his buddies.

Chevy had removed the chains from the other eighteen bikes, confiscated all their firearms, and piled as much gear onto the trailers they could burden, so peddling away to the south was a slow venture for both men. It took one hundred yards for Wes to get his speed up, then they flew down an otherwise empty road.

"They'll be hunting for us now," Wes said, switching to a higher gear. "They may not recognize our faces, but our rifles and methods will be known from now on. They won't be afraid of us any longer; they'll know we won't kill them."

For several miles they rode south, then turned west on a paved road, intent on leaving no trail for anyone to follow. Soon, though, they'd have to leave the pavement and start on foot. Wes contemplated how best to do it, knowing trackers might be sent on their backtrail, on both sides of the road, looking for their prints.

Miles later, they found an irrigation pond where the access road was paved up to several small structures. They parked the bikes behind the shed and unloaded the gear from the trailers.

"Two RPG launchers?" Wes gasped as Chevy smiled and held up the short tubes. "They're going to miss those. Let's bring them with us."

They threw what gear they weren't taking with them into the pond, unhooked the trailers, and sped away on their new bikes—now with only their own packs and an RPG launcher apiece. Cycling farther west, they searched for a good place to abandon their bikes. This time, they decided to simply hide them, with the chains removed but hidden nearby, to perhaps use the bikes again another day.

At a road that cut through a farmer's strawberry field, Chevy stepped on packed earth to reach the field without leaving too many prints. For both of them, he carried the bikes to deposit them out of sight. When he came back to the pavement, Wes wiped away Chevy's few boot prints from the ground.

"It's the rainy season." Wes smiled and picked up his pack. "The next rain will wash away whatever sign we're not concealing."

They hiked a little farther on foot, then left the pavement with just as much care to leave no tracks behind. With dusk closing, they hustled south, looking for a place to hide and spend the night. It would be a long, dangerous trek back to Sandburg.

Five days later, Wes rose early from his sleeping bag in the corner of the gym, grabbed his rifle, and left his wife and friends undisturbed. As he tugged on his boots at the door of the partitioned room, he looked back at the people God had brought into his life. Jill and Dalia slept nearest him, with Elio between them. The young boy's arm was tossed over Dalia, his adopted mother. The teen hadn't seemed to mind the child's extra attention at all.

Tiny Mia slept peacefully in the crib next to Wynter's cot, next to his own place on the floor. Mia, fortunately for the occupants of the gym, wasn't a big fusser, or they would've needed to find a new residence where they didn't disturb the whole lodge.

Chevy snored lightly, face down on his sleeping mat. Wes yawned and thanked the Lord for the godly man the Lord had given him to serve with, even though Chevy's muddy boots had tracked debris into their makeshift living quarters. Even after all the suffering Chevy had witnessed, it was refreshing to Wes to have a partner who was more interested in showing mercy rather than harm.

Wynter's old nurse was a sort of den mother for the gym lodge, and she had risen earlier than Wes to put water on the wood stove. Someone had fashioned a chimney that angled up and exited the wall a couple feet away. Wes mumbled his thanks to the elderly woman as he held a mug and sipped the scalding chicory-flavored water. It wasn't coffee, but it was something to warm his insides.

Outside the gym, he held the mug in one hand and climbed the access ladder to the roof—one of his favorite hangouts when he wasn't busy with chores in the small town. He and Chevy had already commandeered chairs from outside the barrier and towed them up to the roof by rope. It was here that Wes stretched and welcomed the dawn, then walked all around the gym roof, checking the town and the distant views for movement. Content that all was quiet and non-threatening around Sandburg, he sat in one of the chairs and huddled around his chicory water. On his lap, he opened his Bible and read from the Psalms, pausing often to consider a phrase or two, gazing up at the majestic Sierras while he thought of his amazing God. Even though America was in her last days, Wes knew God had much more planned for those who trusted in Him.

When he heard footsteps behind him, he reached over to the other chair and angled it toward the mountains as well. Guessing it was Chevy, Wes quickly thought of an early bird joke about the sunrise and fishing, but instead, Dalia sat in the chair.

"It's freezing up here!" The teen drew her hood over her head and curled her fists into her sleeves. "Why do you come up here all the time? Aren't you cold?"

"Yeah, but it's peaceful, isn't it?" Wes gestured at the mountains. "I hope to be going up there this summer. It's colder up there, but it'll be easier in some respects, to live off the land. Safer."

"A beach in Florida would be fine with me."

Wes nodded and closed his Bible, guessing that Dalia had come up to the cold roof for a reason. He waited for her to bring up whatever it was she wanted to talk about, but then he realized that some people needed to loosen up before getting to the point.

"They got you on dish duty again?" Wes asked.

"Nah, scavenger duty. You?"

"Firewood. You joined the scavenger crew? You don't mind going outside the barrier?"

"It's like a treasure hunt. I don't know." She shrugged. "It's sad going through people's houses, but you never know what you'll find. Of course, Hoxborn and Nicole give us a list of things to look for. I think it's safe as long as we stay together, right? There are others my age doing it, too. Everyone else is doing something useful. I'd go crazy if I had to do the pots and pans another day."

"I hear you on that one!" Wes chuckled. "It's good that you're—"

"Wes, do you think Roy is in heaven?" She looked up at him, as if searching his face for the truth. "He saved my life in Bakersfield, so I think God will let him into heaven, but you know Him better than I do."

It was an unexpected question, but Wes had been mentoring youth for many years, so he appreciated the unexpected.

"Well, I think the reason Roy gave his life for you is the same reason God will welcome him into heaven."

"What was that reason?"

"Roy had learned just that night that he needed forgiveness for all the rotten things he'd done in his life. He was born with a sinful heart, and he knew he didn't deserve God's best, but that he deserved God's wrath."

"So, what happened?"

"Roy heard the message I told him from the Bible, that God offers us forgiveness, but on His terms, not ours."

"What are God's terms?"

"That our forgiveness comes through God's own Son dying in our place. Roy learned that God was sacrificial for him, so Roy was willing to be sacrificial for others. You remember Novak and his people? Roy was running all over that motor home lot, trying to take care of everyone. He risked his life for all of them."

"So did you. And Mom did, too."

"And so did you, remember?"

"So . . . that's why Roy will go to heaven? Because he accepted God's forgiveness?"

"That's it. There's no other way to enter heaven, Dalia. We must be forgiven. That's what the whole Bible is about. We all need God's forgiveness because, if we're honest, we know we're each selfish and cruel, if we live our own way."

"Mom said Roy was a wicked person, but she cried for him after he died. You think Mom's accepted God's forgiveness? She's been reading Wynter's Bible a lot. She needs forgiveness, too. She was a bad mother my whole life."

Wes leaned back in his chair, trying to follow the rapid-fire thoughts of Dalia's young mind, and not wanting to mislead her in regard to her relationship with her mother.

"I think you know that your mother has struggled to find her place in this world, like we all have. Your mother's not the only one who depended on the society that collapsed last year. It shakes a person up, but she'll be all right now. Like you said, she's reading the Bible and getting to know about God."

"But you don't seem shaken up. And Chevy is always joking around like you guys aren't afraid of anything."

"Well, we're not shaken, Dalia, because our world hasn't collapsed. Our world, or our perspective for living, is still the same as before Pan-Day. Chevy and I have been following Christ for many years now. God hasn't changed just because America collapsed. God is our foundation, so our sense of humor and our focus is no different. But we're still struggling to deal with the situation today, like everyone."

"Do you think Chevy and my mom will fall in love?"

Wes couldn't hold back a chuckle as he admired the mountains.

"I'm not getting in the middle of that one, young lady." He rose to his feet. "If the Lord directs their hearts, and they find that they'll be good Christians together, then there's no reason why they couldn't get married. Come on. Let's go see if there's any breakfast on the stove yet."

"I wouldn't be caught dead eating all these potatoes and deer meat back home. It's so unhealthy and greasy. Nicole said there's a whole lemon orchard outside the wall that will be ripe in five months."

"You should bring that up to the town council. They might put you on garden duty next."

"No way! Scavenger is way better than digging in the cold dirt all day! Picking weeds? Or fruit? No thanks!"

A shrill whistle sounded from up the street. Wes tensed and tossed the remainder of his drink off the side of the gym.

"Get below!" he ordered Dalia. "Keep all the kids safe and calm. You're in charge, Dalia!"

She disappeared down the ladder. He wasn't sure why he'd told her she was in charge, except to let her know he was counting on her role as a teen to keep the younger children calm while the adults manned the perimeter.

Wes jogged to the street-side corner of the gym roof and swung his rifle into his arms. The whistle had come from the west end of town, so someone on watch had spotted something. Kneeling, Wes peered through his rifle scope at the distant barrier across the street, which was less than three hundred yards. Even from his position inside the barrier, his rifle could reach well beyond anything within Sandburg, and he was far down the street.

Other whistles blew as the alarm was passed, and people hustled from their morning duties with hunting rifles in their arms. Everyone had an assigned position on the perimeter to occupy in an emergency, and Wes was already at his.

"What do you see?" Chevy asked as he reached the roof.

"Nothing yet!" Wes yelled over his shoulder. "Cover the south side!"

Wes studied the street beyond the barrier to the west. Then he saw them—dozens of Diablos on bikes. But it was nowhere near the number that Wes guessed they had in reserves, not if their gang was hundreds strong, as he'd heard.

"I've got about forty Diablos at the west gate!" Wes yelled to Chevy. "Nothing aggressive yet. They're trying to engage someone. Hoxborn's getting on the wall. You see any movement? This could be a diversion for others to sneak up on another side."

"Nothing on this side," Chevy reported. "I'm holding."

Wes watched but couldn't hear Hoxborn in his cowboy hat, shouting back and forth to several Diablos who'd approached closer than the others on their bikes. It was a show of force on the part of the Diablos, but Sandburg could probably repel that many without too much strain. The Diablos certainly knew it, since they'd tried before to take Sandburg, and had kept their distance since.

"This has to do with the Kindred," Chevy voiced from the far side. "How do you want to play this? They're hunting for us, you know."

"We stay on script," Wes said. "There's just a few of us who know what we've been doing."

"Word will get out soon. What then?"

"Hopefully by then, God will have made enough of an impact to save our necks from Sandburg's citizens. Hopefully."

Hoxborn finished at the wall, and the Diablos turned their bikes around and pedaled away. No one on any of the walls moved, and Wes knew they wouldn't, not until Hoxborn himself called an all-clear for people to relax. But no doubt an extra sentry would be posted on every side of the town for the next few days.

Wes waited as Hoxborn walked down the street, speaking to people along the way. Finally, the leader of Sandburg reached the gym. He used his hat to shade his eyes as he looked up at Wes.

"You and Chevy both up there?" the man hollered.

"Yep. All seems clear. Chevy has the south side covered. What was that all about?"

"They're looking for someone. Beats me who. Someone fool enough to pick a fight with the Diablos."

"That's it?"

"They threatened to attack us if it was us, but I told them it wasn't us, that we were just fine keeping the peace between us and them. Then they left. Why don't you and Chevy stay up there for an hour and keep a lookout, then come find me, all right? I want to talk to you two—about your rifles."

"You got it."

Hoxborn turned away, but a knot twisted inside Wes's gut. So, it hadn't been an innocent exchange after all. The Diablos had asked about two men with their kind of guns. It was all the raiders could identify them by. And Hoxborn seemed to be keeping it quiet, not raising any alarms. But Wes guessed everyone at the western barrier within earshot must've heard the warning, too. They'd been exposed, but it sounded like Hoxborn wasn't giving them up. At least, not until he'd spoken to them.

Wes walked over to Chevy to speak privately.

"I think we'd better prepare to pack our bags, my friend. Hoxborn knows it's us. The Diablos identified us by our rifles."

Chapter 4

Wes and Chevy filed into a back office of the sporting goods lodge where Hoxborn sat behind a large metal desk. It was as if he were a high school principal about to lecture two unruly youths. For once, his cowboy hat hung on a wall hook. Nicole, in her down vest, had propped her hefty frame against the wall behind Hoxborn, and crossed her arms.

Seating themselves, Wes glanced at Chevy and noticed the man was trying unsuccessfully to hide his smile. Apparently, Chevy sensed the same feeling about a principal and unruly youths as Wes did.

"It took me all of ten seconds to realize the Diablos were looking for you two." Hoxborn's face reddened visibly in the light of the window. "No two hunters hunt more than you two, and repeatedly come back with nothing—unless they're not hunters at all. You two are the most unlucky deer hunters we've ever had, but the way you carry yourselves—like cats—you should be bringing in more game than anyone. So, would you care to explain? Wes, you seem to be in charge of your little group in the gym. Let's start with you."

"We're provisional peacekeepers," Wes admitted.

"I knew it." Nicole turned her back to the room, then faced them again. "I knew it! You're putting all of us at risk. Think of the children!"

"Why don't you think of the children growing up?" Chevy said, then looked at Wes. "Sorry. I'll keep my trap shut."

"Chevy's right." Wes decided to stand up and lean against the wall. "It'll be dangerous for us for a little while, but someone has to accept responsibility and put the Diablos out of business."

"And you picked us?" Hoxborn asked. "Don't we get a say?"

"You've already had your say. You've already let the Diablos know that you won't be pushed around. When Chevy and I arrived here, we saw a town from which we could strike back. Hundreds and hundreds are being slaughtered up and down this valley. Sandburg volunteered to help the people who are still alive when you guys built your first barrier across the street. The Diablos attacked, but you held, and now they come humbly to your wall."

"Not for long." Hoxborn took a deep breath. "They threatened to burn us out. It wouldn't take much to start a fire."

"We'd all burn, then!" Nicole hissed. "For your crimes!"

"What are our crimes?" Wes asked. "You said it, Nicole. So, what are our crimes? Speak up. We're a provisional peacekeeping force, sanctioned by the president before Pan-Day to operate worldwide under the COIL Charter. I helped write it, and I stood in the Oval Office when the president signed it. We're here to save lives and fight evil in a day of wickedness, *and you accuse us of crimes?* We are here to confront mass murderers. Those evil men have pushed up against you, and you call us criminals? Tell us, Nicole, whose side are you on?"

Nicole's mouth gaped. Her eyes went from Wes to Hoxborn, then she turned toward the window without responding.

"We didn't know you had actual authority." Hoxborn sat up straighter. "The president's involved?"

"The president sanctioned the Commission of International Laborers before Pan-Day to operate inside and outside the borders of the United States. I was his liaison with the CIA, with an office in the Pentagon to also work with the Department of Defense. COIL personnel like Chevy, my wife, and I are specially trained for guerrilla warfare of this type. We're aware of the need to take care of the civilians in this situation. That's why Sandburg is central to our plan working. Civilians across the valley will hear that there is a heroic town that's standing up to the Diablos, and that peacekeepers have stepped up to deal with the threat of bandits. People will flock here, more than they already are, and we can prepare them to survive in the mountains or to put down roots right here."

"But right now, we're facing a pretty daunting Diablos problem." Hoxborn rubbed his jaw, which needed a shave. "What's your plan? I mean, what should we do?"

"Keep Operation Kindred quiet. Play innocent. Keep brushing the Diablos off, even if they apply more pressure. We'll continue to protect Sandburg when we're outside, and you protect Sandburg from the inside."

"Operation Kindred?" Hoxborn leaned forward. "It even has a name? This is all way over my head. I'm just a high school janitor."

"A janitor?" Chevy asked. "I thought you were the principal."

"So did I." Wes smiled.

"My sister was the lunch lady." Hoxborn jabbed a thumb at Nicole. "People just came to us, so we did our best to organize them."

"You've done remarkable." Wes nodded. "I couldn't have done it better, and I've managed entire military campaigns for generals and sea captains. Keep doing what you're doing. Although, if there's a threat of fire and future attacks, I'd expand Sandburg's barriers to include a couple more streets, then clear about two blocks outward. Flatten everything for two hundred yards for a clear field of fire."

"That's a good idea." Hoxborn tapped his knuckles on his desk. "It'll be hard to start a fire from two hundred yards away. They won't have any cover, right?"

"Right. And change the schedules for the hunters and woodsmen every couple days. Their routines shouldn't be predictable."

"Got it. I like that."

"I don't!" Nicole complained from the window, her back still to them.

"The Diablos will fall, or splinter into other factions," Wes said. "It's what happens in these kinds of situations. They last for a while, then the good people who stand strong keep rebuilding. Sandburg has the opportunity to lead in that rebuilding process. People with the best skills and the most to offer will come here first, and Sandburg will thrive."

"But first," Chevy added, "things are going to get rough."

"It's okay to send us anyone in town who wants to help," Wes said. "Nicole, you can send us people, too. Operation Kindred will be a success based upon the coordination of a lot of elements. We're all afraid of the worst happening, but that's why we can't let fear dictate our lives. COIL field agents are God's people, and we don't operate on the basis of what might happen. Whatever the cost, we have to trust God and do the right thing."

"There was some talk that you guys were Christians." Hoxborn shook his head, but his face showed amusement. "Christian peacekeepers. With rifles. A one-eyed Christian sheriff. Hah!"

"This guy's got my kind of humor." Chevy laughed. "I bet deep down, Nicole thinks there's something funny about a one-eyed sheriff, too. Eh, Nicole?"

Everyone waited for the woman to respond. When she turned around, she was hiding a smile, but still not making eye contact.

"Maybe you guys can make this work in the long run," she said. "I mean, we're in this together, right?"

"Yes, we are." Wes offered his hand to Hoxborn, who stood and shook it heartily. "Anything that Chevy and I can do to support you two, just let us know. From here on, we'll run things quietly by you before we do something, that way you can have everyone ready if things start to jump."

"That'd be great!" Hoxborn said.

Chevy's sense of humor won Nicole over enough for a half-hug before they left the office.

"Well, that could've gone worse." Chevy breathed a sigh as they headed toward the front door. "They could've kicked us out. Nice bit about the presidential authority."

"It was true." Wes shrugged. "The last presidential policy I received was that COIL had a right to operate here. Until I hear otherwise, we'll use it."

"And even when some government does pop up and tell us to shut down?"

"We're COIL." Wes opened the door for Chevy to step outside into the sunlight. "We'll just go underground and continue with business as usual. God will provide the means and the people. We'll just stay on our knees about it all."

"These two families are Christians," Wynter said one day in the gym as Wes and Chevy came back from firewood duty. "Isn't this nice? Hoxborn sent them over."

Wes offered his hand to the two men with small families. He needed to clean pitch from his hands, but he shook anyway.

"Christians, huh?" He glanced at Chevy. "We were praying for help . . . You ready for recruits, Chevy?"

"Recruits for what?" one of the men asked. "Are you guys Christians, too? That Nicole gal said we'd be welcomed here, that you had some work for us or something? We just came into town yesterday, so we're not sure how things run around here."

"Yes, we're Christians," Wes said, "and as Christians, we have a special calling in this valley. Have either of you fired rifles before?"

They were the Lander and McHugh families, and before Wes and Chevy took them out to practice shooting, they wanted to hear both families' stories. Melvin and Trisha Lander, with their two little girls, were from Lemoore, a town about forty miles northwest of Sandburg. Melvin had been in forestry management with the Parks and Rec Department, but he'd remained in the valley through Pan-Day, rather than heading into the mountains because he knew the hard winters in the Sierras would be difficult on his girls. He was short and stocky, with thinning blond hair. His ready smile made up for any shyness he had, and Trisha, his wife, was already doting over little Mia.

Wade and Natalie McHugh were also from Lemoore, although they'd only recently met the Landers while Lemoore was being evacuated due to lack of water.

"We've been praying for a safe place to raise our families," Wade said, looking up at the interior of the gym. "This place seems sturdy enough."

The dark-haired man was a carpenter by trade, and once Wes asked him a few questions to see if he possessed real experience, the man wouldn't stop talking about the homes he'd built up and down the valley. Natalie, his wife, was exactly opposite—shy and blushing—though direct with their two young boys who had already devised a game of chase with other children in the gym.

Melvin and Trisha had been believers since their youth, and they'd remained committed through the challenges of Pan-Day. Wade and Natalie admitted they'd both been lukewarm Christians before Pan-Day, but the catastrophe had humbled them to repentance, and they now regularly sought God's hand in their family.

"From Lemoore, we'd seen the bandits on the road," Wade shared, "but neither of us are killers, so we made a decision to leave our rifles in Lemoore rather than tempt a conflict with the Diablos."

"But if you want us to do some hunting for you," Melvin volunteered, "we can both shoot, to answer your earlier question. We just need a couple of rifles."

Within hours, Wynter and Jill had enlarged their gym corner habitat to include the two new families, and Melvin, Wade, Chevy, and Wes went to the roof to discuss more serious matters. Dalia was finished with her chores and insisted on listening in. Melvin and Wade listened closely to Wes's explanation of their operation against the Diablos, and their Christian stance of faith while dealing with the bandits.

"Tranquilizer guns to put a stop to criminals?" Wade shook his head. "I've never heard of such a thing. Is it working? Have they stopped killing?"

"We've only just begun," Chevy said. "We've been waiting for you guys. With you two, we can work in pairs, putting someone out in the field every week, while the other pair rests."

"Two Christians are worth twenty Diablos," Dalia stated proudly, then lowered her head when Wes glanced at her. "Sorry, but they are."

"You guys have taken down that many Diablos already?" Melvin's smile was hard to miss. He seemed to love the idea. "These rifles of yours really are able to cover that kind of distance? Six hundred yards?"

"If you've got the eye for it." Wes touched his patch. "Obviously, I'm at about fifty percent, so Chevy handles the precision business."

"We've never hunted anything but deer around the fields of Lemoore," Wade said, "but if you have a range, we could give it a try. I like the idea of bicycles. My feet are still sore from the last two days of walking!"

Within a day, Melvin and Wade were outfitted with one of the five spare bullpups Chevy and Wynter had brought with them in the caravan. They would share the rifle, depending on who was in the field each week. Since both men were Christians, they immediately saw the value before God of preserving life, but they were still skeptical about how their tactics of mercy would actually impact the hardened Diablos. To them it seemed that all the Diablos would need to do was return to one of their bases, pick up more rifles, and keep killing. But Chevy encouraged them to give God time to work it all out.

Wes teamed up with quiet Melvin for the next operation abroad. Chevy and Wade registered their hunting abilities with Hoxborn, who was thrilled to find two more food-gatherers in town. The two new wives also joined Nicole's kitchen and laundry brigades, keeping Sandburg residents healthy, fed, cleaned and scrubbed.

Taking the bikes, Wes and Melvin ranged northwest, past Lemoore, and came upon refugees from Fresno, Merced, and Sacramento—around forty of them. Although Wes wanted to push on, there was hardly a shooter amongst the forty civilians. With all their possessions, they were moving too slow, which would make them prime targets for the Diablos.

"I don't know of anywhere else to take them but to Sandburg," Wes said to Melvin, who agreed. "Hoxborn will just have to expand the barriers of the town sooner rather than later."

Wes escorted the caravan from the front, and Melvin from the rear. The group was spread out along the highway for a quarter-mile. Near Tulare, Wes spotted a band of Diablos crossing the field from the east to get a closer look at their caravan. They came within three hundred yards. Wes could've taken a shot at them, but the five bandits were just scouts. Without a full army, the thugs weren't about to tackle such a large party.

They camped that night on the open field, and Wes and Melvin prayed specifically for God's safekeeping in the night. However, for the scouts to race back to Isabella Lake, and for an army to mobilize by dawn would've been pretty difficult.

Daylight broke upon the valley. Wes rubbed his eyes, having not slept for twenty-four hours, and they still had a full day of escorting to reach Sandburg. But the highway east and south remained clear throughout the day, and Hoxborn opened the barrier to welcome the people once he saw Wes leading them.

The following week, through heavy rain, Chevy and Wade spent five days across the valley, and tranquilized fifteen Diablos. Wade was a fair sketch artist and brought back more portraits for Jill to enhance and copy.

The next week, Wes and Melvin rode southwest, with the recent fifteen portraits in their pockets to leave somewhere that the other Diablos would find them. They reached as far as Lost Hills, then turned north toward Kettleman City for the return trip. On the narrow Highway 41, they came upon a small band of travelers on bicycles. At first, Wes and Melvin prepared for battle, but then realized there were women and children in the bunch. Melvin stayed back fifty yards to cover Wes as he went out to speak to the travelers on the road.

As he drew close and stopped his bike in the center of the highway, he counted only three adult men and three women, but there were several teenagers and about a dozen younger children. He stepped away from his bike and stood with his rifle cradled lightly in his right arm. All three men shifted assault rifles in their own hands, and glanced at one another as they stopped twenty yards in front of Wes. At their mothers' commands, the children huddled together in the back.

"Where are you coming from?" Wes asked, thinking it strange that they were heading west instead of east toward the only safe town known around the valley.

"From the east, near the mountains," one man said. He bowed his head a little, and Wes recognized that the man was trying to hide his face beneath the bill of his hat. "Just taking our families over to the Salinas River area."

"Yeah? Nice range over there." Wes studied the band closer. Their assault rifles made him suspicious. Most civilians carried hunting rifles or shotguns for hunting deer or water fowl. Assault rifles were generally for killers. "You're a pretty small group to be traveling on such dangerous roads. If you came from the east near the mountains, you must've come across the Diablos."

"Yeah, we saw those guys from a long ways away," another man said, looking at his companions as if he wanted them to back up his statement. "But they left us alone. I think they already had their hands full."

"Uh-huh." Wes frowned, and raised his rifle a little. "You there, with the hat—where do I know you from?"

All the men suddenly shuffled backwards. Their suspicious behavior quickly became dangerous, and Wes leveled his battle rifle, sighting down the barrel with a steady pose at the man with the hat.

"Nobody move!" Wes yelled, ignoring the cries of the women and children. "You lift those rifles, any one of you, and we'll take you down! Now, who are you? And don't give me any nonsense about the Diablos ignoring you. A group your size, with only three men, is just what the Diablos like to attack. Start talking!"

"It's me, all right?" The man with the cap took it off and sighed. "You drew my picture a few weeks ago after you shot me over by Colonel Allensworth State Park."

Wes thought back. He was one of the twenty he and Chevy had taken down at the beginning of Operation Kindred.

"Lay your rifles on the ground. Do it now!" Wes stepped closer, threateningly, as the men complied. "How do you know it was me?"

"I have my family right here!" The man shook his head. "Please, you let me live, right? Just let us go. We're done with the Diablos. We're done, you hear me?"

"I asked you, how do you know it was me?"

"Well, I recognize the gun." The man pointed at Wes's midsection. "And I think I did that to you."

Wes put his hand on his belly where his jacket hadn't been fully patched from the bullet that had grazed him. It had scarred him for life.

"You're the one who shot me?" Wes turned his head slightly, sensing Melvin was moving closer on his right side. "Speak!"

"Yes. I'm sorry. You came into the cotton bushes after me. I didn't know you weren't trying to kill us. Please, I would take it all back if I could. We'll take our families west, and you'll never hear from us again. The poster of my face, it said that Jesus Christ cares for me, right? Please . . ."

"I remember you." Wes lowered his weapon, then waved with his left hand. "Come here. Step forward. Let me look at you."

The traveler took a couple of small steps, then seemed to relent and walked right up to Wes. Wes studied the man's face from a couple different angles, and remembered drawing it, especially the little bump on the man's nose.

"I guess God's been merciful to both of us, young man. I let you live a few weeks ago. And because you're not a very good marksman, I'm not dead."

"Yes, sir." The traveler shuffled his hat in his hands. "I'm sorry about that. The poster you drew of me got me to thinking about it all, you know? Me and some others have been going our own ways. I think it's all right to tell you that I thought I'd die in prison."

"You were an inmate?"

"Yeah. But we got out, me and these two. We've started families since Pan-Day, but I guess we just threw in with the wrong crowd."

"How'd you start families since Pan-Day, but you've got all these children already?"

The man looked back at the group.

"There's no easy way to answer that. But you know what the Diablos have been doing, I think, better than most."

"The kids are orphans?" Wes took a deep breath, remembering all of the young children who seemed to be missing from Wynter's slaughtered caravan. "They're not yours. You've kidnapped them."

"Well, it was either leave them at Isabella Lake, or bring them with us. We figure between the three of us, we can support the mouths we brought with us."

"And these are your wives?" Wes stepped up to the man to stand beside him. The women and children still grimaced in fear and held onto one another. "They're kidnapped as well?"

"Two of them are, but now they're with us because they have no one else. I met my wife about eight months ago. She was a lady of the night, if you know what I mean. But she's changed, too. Both of us are done with our past lives."

"God has given you a second chance." Wes faced the man, his heart aching. "You can't leave Him out of what you now realize must start anew."

"I won't. I know there's a God, sir."

"You need to look for a Bible. There'll be places to search between here and Salinas. You need to find out who Jesus Christ is and what He's really done for you, what He's provided for you. You need to lead your new family right, even if you've had a rough start."

"Yes, sir." The man bowed his head, his eyes welling. "It's going to be hard, isn't it?"

"Yes, it'll be hard. But it'll be good. And one day, Jesus Christ will return, and He'll look upon you with joy because you've turned to trust in Him to give you a new heart and a renewed mind."

"Man, where were you months ago when I needed some guidance then?" The man chuckled through a sob and wiped his eyes. "Look at me now. Homeless and crying like a baby."

"God is just breaking you down to rebuild you from the bottom up." Wes smiled. "You're going to be okay. What's your name?"

"They call me Torrey."

"I'm Wes Trimble. I'm with the Kindred of Nails, a division of COIL."

"Kindred. That's like a brotherhood?"

"Something like that. Let me shake your hand, Torrey." Wes shook the man's hand and drew him into a quick embrace and slap on the back. "If you're ever on the east side of the valley again, just ask for One-eyed Wes Trimble. I'm one of the Kindred. I won't forget you, Torrey. I never forget the people who shoot me."

Torrey laughed and together they gazed upon the three families. The people had settled down considerably since they'd seen Wes and Torrey acting more friendly toward one another.

For a few more minutes, Melvin and Wes met the rest of the adults in the group. To some degree, Wes wanted to get a feel from the women if they were indeed traveling on their own free will. And they truly did seem to be. The women expressed happiness and relief that they were safe to continue their journey, and Wes took that as a good indication that they were families brought together through tragedy, each one of them. Somehow, God would reshape them, if they really turned to Him.

Then, the three families pedaled away.

"How does a kid grow up in a family like that?" Melvin asked about the orphaned children with Torrey. "Knowing you live with some of the people who killed your family?"

"When you have nothing else, Melvin, I think you figure out where you fit in best." Wes waved at the travelers as they departed. "We can't expect the Diablos to abandon all the women and kids they've kidnapped. If they're able to care for them, then maybe they'll heal and grow together."

"So, are the Diablos falling apart?"

"A few at a time, it seems. We'll keep praying every night for the portraits we have copies of. The Lord will do the rest. But some of the Diablos have apparently realized their stampede across this valley is over."

"We need to get back to Sandburg and tell everyone." Melvin shook his head. "This is amazing. God did this. You just hugged a man who shot you! Is that what I understood?"

"Mel, I can't explain the wonders of God." Wes put his hand on Melvin's shoulder as the two walked back to their bikes. "What I do know is, we've got about two more months of winter until the snow melts up in those mountains, and that means you and I have at least two more months of bandit-patrolling to do. If we can meet more ex-Diablos like this, I'd be willing to be grazed by a bullet for each one of them."

"Maybe just not across the belly." Melvin laughed. "That seems like it would hurt!"

"You're right. Maybe a graze across the arm or something not so sensitive. I'll see if I can manage that!"

The men laughed together and climbed onto their bikes, their hearts light from experiencing God's providence.

Chapter 5

The Kindred patrols for Diablos met with two more conflicts over the next two weeks. Melvin got in his first firefight and took down two Diablos while Wes captured four. Another time, Chevy and Wade captured fifteen—and walked away with enough gear to equip thirty men.

On a sunny winter day, as Wes was butchering a buck he'd shot the day before, the Sandburg alarm sounded, and the whistle drifted up and down the street until everyone was running intently for their posts. The barrier around the town had been expanded to hold many more people who had come to Sandburg in hopes of staying there until the snow melted up in the mountains. Hoxborn had said he liked having the extra hands on deck, and now he was concerned he'd be short-handed once everyone left for the mountains in the springtime. Melvin and Wade had assured him that their families wouldn't leave, but Wes and Chevy had made no such guarantee.

Since Wes was closer to the front gate of the town than he was to the roof, he ran to join Hoxborn at the western barrier.

"Wes!" Hoxborn saw the Kindred peacekeeper running to him. "Make room, everyone. Wes is here. Looks like ten Diablos out there. What do you think?"

Resting his rifle over the barrier of debris, Wes peered through his scope. He didn't mind Hoxborn's dependence on him, especially since it meant that Christ's values would be influencing Hoxborn's decisions for the town.

"I don't know. Someone with a more powerful scope needs to look. Anybody see black armbands?"

"Not from my angle," a rifleman called back. "They're just wearing those heavy parkas."

"Maybe the Diablos stopped wearing their armbands," Hoxborn said. "What do you think?"

"It's unlikely." Wes kept his scope on the strangers. "They need to identify one another from a distance, and it's a sort of pride thing with them now. The black armbands cause fear in people. Not in us, but some people. That's what they like—to cause fear."

"So, who are these folks?"

Wes looked back up the street of Sandburg and saw Melvin had made his way to the roof of the gym to stand on the corner. Wes signaled to his partner.

"I'll go out there. Melvin will cover me. Nobody fire. Hold your fire, everyone!"

The gate was pulled back, and Wes stepped outside. The ten men were about three hundred yards away, and they started to approach when they saw Wes walking toward them. They were all on foot, with no bikes in sight, and they carried packs and hunting rifles, though a few of them had assault rifles.

Both sides walked toward one another until they were within talking distance, then stopped. Now so close, Wes realized none of them were men at all, except one bushy-bearded man. The nine were just boys in their teens.

"Is that Sandburg there?" the bushy-bearded man asked, pointing with a strong-looking hand.

"Yep, Sandburg." Wes cradled his rifle across his body, but he didn't think he'd need it with this lot. "They're some nice folks, even though everyone is up in arms right now. Can't be too careful with all the bandits running around."

"We crossed some the day before yesterday." The man hooked a thumb at his companions. "My boys and I dispatched them without much effort."

"We've been working on that ourselves." Wes nodded. "Glad to see you're all fine."

"We heard Sandburg has some sort of civility and organization." The man stepped a little closer. "Are you someone who might have some information for me?"

"Could be. I've been working with the people of Sandburg for a few weeks, but I'm not from here."

"I'm looking for one of my sons. We had words about five months ago, and he left our home in Escondido. We found some dumb kids he was hanging around with up on the Grapevine. They said he came this way."

"A lot of people are getting out of the valley, not coming into the valley. The Diablos were attacking everyone in sight up until about a month and a half ago. What's your son's name?"

"Royce Mallinger. We're the Mallingers. Well, there's some others back home, but these are my oldest boys. Except for Royce. He's my eldest. He's not a bad kid, just has a mind of his own. I might've gotten too firm with him one night. He needs to know we all want him back home."

Wes took a couple steps closer, until they were only three paces apart.

"Yeah, I knew Roy," Wes said. "That's what we called him. He caught up to us on this side of the Grapevine, like you said. You know how things are today. People pull together like family when things get tough, even in a short time."

"So, you know where he is?" The father smiled and glanced at his sons. "We're really on his trail, boys!"

"One night, we ran into some trouble in Bakersfield." Wes licked his lips, and cringed at having to be the bearer of such bad news. "We took a stand to help the city. Didn't know it was a bit of a war zone."

"Yeah, we went around that place. Then what?"

"There were a lot of wounded falling back to us, and Roy and a couple of women with me were seeing to them. A young woman was about to be shot, and Roy took a bullet for her. Her name was Dalia. Roy died in the arms of her mother, whose name is Jill. Jill and Dalia are alive and well, living here in Sandburg now, thanks to Roy."

"My boy's dead?" The big man choked on his words. "He's gone?"

"He died a man, and he was with friends. Earlier that night, he and I had talked about sacrifice and having our hearts right with God because of what Jesus Christ did for us. If you're a Christian man, you'll be pleased to know that I believe Roy gave his life because he was inspired by Jesus Christ's own sacrifice."

"And you buried him in Bakersfield?" The man shook his head. "We can't even see where you laid him, not in that mess of gunfighting."

"Not true. Because Roy died helping the people of the city, they buried him with honor. You tell them you're Roy's father and family, and they'll be hospitable to you. And you tell them One-eyed Wes Trimble sent you. Tell them you're friends with me, too. When you get there, ask for Novak. He looks something fierce with all his tattoos, but he won't hesitate to welcome you."

"Your brother's dead, boys." The father gathered his sons around him, several of them crying. "But we're still a family. We'll go see where they buried him. He died a hero at least. That's something, right?"

"You'd be welcome in Sandburg, if you want to come in for the evening before you head back. We've got fresh deer meat, and the ladies are working on some new cabbage stew recipe that smells promising."

"No. No, we'll be heading back now." The big man dried his eyes. "We got what we came for, and I've got these other boys to raise now in this cursed land. You say you're One-eyed Wes Trimble?"

"That's right. I'm with COIL, Kindred Division, based out of Sandburg right now. We have a whole peacekeeping force patrolling this region. You let people know as you cross them—Sandburg is a safe zone. The Kindred are keeping these roads safe."

"We'll let people know." He offered his hand, which seemed twice the size of Wes's own. "People don't shake hands enough nowadays, but I don't care. My name's Sebastian. Sebastian Mallinger from Escondido."

"It's a pleasure, Mr. Mallinger. Safe journey back to Escondido. Don't forget to keep your heart open for what God may be doing still, even in this fallen world. He touched your son's heart, and he was a better man for it."

"Maybe next time." The man smiled politely. "You never know what the future holds. Come on, boys. Shake Mr. Trimble's hand so we can move on out of here."

"Isn't this amazing?" Dalia asked Wynter as she finally reached the top of the ladder and planted a foot on the roof of the gym. "You can see the whole world from up here!"

Wes turned with Chevy, Melvin, and Wade to see Wynter and Dalia make their way over to their chairs. Surrendering his chair to his wife, he positioned it so she could look up at the mountains above them.

"Oh, it's breezy up here!" Wynter buttoned her top button. "This is what all the excitement is about? All this cold?"

She plopped down in the chair as Dalia continued the tour, pointing up at the Sierras.

"Forget the cold for a minute and look out there. Follow my finger. First, you locate Kings River Canyon. Follow it up to Wishon Reservoir, and Courtright Reservoir. Now go farther north, you have the South Fork of the San Joaquin River. That's where we're going this summer. Wes says that Lune Lake and the resort is on the other side of all the stuff I named."

"Why would I want to go up there when I'm already cold down here?" Wynter winked at Wes. "It's probably way colder up there."

"Have you ever worn snowshoes?" Dalia asked Wynter. "It's these things you put on your boots, and you can walk on top of, like, feet and feet of snow. You'd trade that for all this?"

Wes and the men chuckled, but he knew Wynter was just playing with the girl. Wynter had explored the world, searching for treasures for museums long before Dalia was even born.

As Melvin was coaxed by Dalia to explain how snowshoes were made, Wes wandered off to the side of the roof and looked down at the town. Hoxborn was there, at the front barrier, visiting with one of the new defenders of the town, keeping everyone's spirits high, and teaching them the town's history. Wes had heard the history of the town just recently from Nicole's own mouth. Down at the sporting goods lodge, she hadn't seen him come in, and she was telling the story to a group of ladies who'd gathered to gossip and drink tea. The story was about a simple few blocks of the town that she and her brother had pulled together. But then the Kindred had come with their non-lethal rifles, and the Diablos were being kept at bay, even shattering their ranks. Now, as Nicole had recited, Sandburg was becoming known as the headquarters for the Kindred of Nails, and they were all there that day because the Kindred had made it possible.

If Wes had told the story, he would've included the help of God's mighty hand along the way, but Nicole had come a long ways from the woman whose arms had been crossed at the thought of facing the Diablos at all.

"Oh, thank You, Lord, for everything You've done," Wes whispered. "And for everything You're about to do with us . . ."

~ End of RESOLUTION Book Two ~

D.I. Telbat

RESOLUTION BOOK THREE

America's Last Days

D.I. Telbat

~*~

To those who have grown weary,
but know the journey is its own reward.
Onward for Christ!

Book Three, Prologue

If someone finds this, it probably means that I'm dead. My name is Bill Jevans, and I remained behind in Lune Lake when all others left. The virus killed most of our community around the Loop, because we lived so close to one another before Pan-Day. Those who survived buried their dead, then chose to leave the area rather than stay where their loved ones were laid to rest. Since I have had no one before or after Pan-Day, and nowhere else to go, I have remained here alone.

But, since I am now nearly dead, it's obvious that by remaining alone, I have welcomed my own death. If others had been near, or someone could have heard my calls for help, maybe I could recover with their help, but my fall was a bad one. My back is broken. My food is gone, and my water will be gone soon as well. As I write this, I may have three more days left of water, then I'll die of starvation and thirst.

But I'm not writing this to beg for your pity, stranger. I believe that someday people may return to this place. It's the reason I have done my best to maintain the lodges, cabins, and apartments the last six months, and boarded up as many hotels as I could. Should you find me, please know that the structures around me are yours. They once belonged to landowners, and I buried them one at a time. Now, I leave the buildings to you.

If it's not too much trouble, bury me beside one of the lakes nearby. This has been a paradise for me as long as I was custodian over several of the lodges. Now, though, I'm not sure paradise awaits me at all, for I've not lived a good life. If my legs still worked, I might try to find a Bible in one of the buildings so I could find out what the hereafter might hold for someone like me. But maybe I'm better off not knowing until I meet God face to face, since I'm afraid it's going to be bad news for me.

Maybe if I'd lived a better life, I wouldn't be dying like this. I don't know. Maybe it's some consolation that I've cared for the houses nearby, after everyone else abandoned them to the elements. Now, in the years to come, they will serve the needs of others who arrive. I hope so. Farewell, *Bill*

Chapter 1

One-eyed Wes Trimble balanced carefully on the log that crossed the raging river below. Its bark was slippery as the muddy winter runoff surged against the fallen tree's underbelly.

"Hang on, Chevy!" Wes shouted, his voice trembling as much as his knees. "I'm coming!"

Avery "Chevy" Hewitt clung to another log in the middle of a fifty-tree log jam that choked the river gorge. His muscled arms tried to pull his body back up to the precarious natural bridge across the eighty-foot-wide river, but the surging water was tugging him down. The pressure of the water had already stripped the bark off most of the bottom trees, and it was seconds from stripping Chevy from his grip as well.

Wes wore army surplus combat boots with all-purpose tread, but he needed cleats to have any traction on the slippery logs. He was twenty feet from Chevy when Wes leaped from one log to another, and his foot slipped. He landed on his belly, and his legs were immediately pulled with unforgiving force by the rapids below him.

"Wes!" Chevy's strength was exhausted. One of his arms slid from the log to which he clung. Limply, he tried to fling his arm back up, but he had no strength left. By one arm now, he inched downward. "I can't . . ."

"Chevy!" Wes screamed, furious at his own inability to recover fast enough from his own fall. "No! Hang on! I'm coming!"

But Wes wasn't able to regain his own position atop the logs. Angry tears mixed with frothing water as he kicked and fought for better leverage to hoist himself up. The thought of a watery death, his body caught in the tree branches below, terrified him enough to give him a surge of adrenalin. To his left, he hooked his elbow around a broken-off branch and pulled himself up a few inches. It was enough to throw one leg onto the log as he prayed it didn't roll and pin him further.

Like a seal on a beach, Wes rocked his body and scooted back on top. His weary arms and legs begged for rest. But there was no time to rest. Now, he crawled toward Chevy, unable to even stand. However, when he arrived to where he thought Chevy was, his Kindred of Nails partner and brother in Christ wasn't there.

Thinking he'd miscalculated somehow, Wes shakily stood and looked around. Chevy couldn't hang on much longer. Where was he?

Then he realized that he hadn't misjudged where Chevy had been. He'd not been able to hang on any longer, and Wes hadn't gotten to him in time.

"Noooo!" Wes screamed and leaped precariously down the log jam, endangering his own life as he searched between the logs, looking for some hint of his scouting partner in the blinding spray of angry water. But there was no sign. "Please, God!"

He slipped again, and cracked his knee against a tree knot. The pain shocked him back to reality. If he wasn't careful, he'd join Chevy in the unknown depths of the raging river. With a heavy heart, he crouched low and steadied his nerves, then studied the logs for a safe route back to dry land. Their packs and rifles remained on the bank of the river, but now there was only one man returning to claim them.

With much more care going back to the bank than when he'd tried to rescue Chevy, Wes finally reached the bank and collapsed. His elbows rested on his knees, and his hands held his head as he scowled at the logjam. It stretched for thirty yards downriver—an unforgiving tangle of branches and logs and even some boulders. The earthquake from weeks earlier may have shaken the mountains above and sent the debris downriver to lodge there. Anything alive that went through or under those rapids wasn't coming out alive. One thousand tree boughs, like deadly spikes, combed the water for anything trying to pass through. If Chevy hadn't been impaled immediately, then he would've drowned from being trapped beneath the logs. Having already been exhausted, Chevy would never be able to climb back out.

Wes thought of Jill Austin, the actress back in Sandburg who'd recently come to Christ. Chevy had begun to court her. She would take the news hard. The whole town of Sandburg would grieve since Chevy had accompanied the other Kindred to bring peace to the Central Valley. In fact, Chevy had been the last, true, living Kindred of Nails, of the original COIL operatives who'd risked their lives to rescue Christians in North Korea. All that had been before the Meridia Virus had decimated the population of the United States. Now, one hundred million deaths later, Chevy would be counted amongst the deceased. But there would be no body to bury this time, Wes guessed. If anyone ever did find it, it would be too torn and decomposed to identify.

Taking a deep breath, Wes climbed to his feet and checked his cuts and scrapes. The logs had soundly beat him up, but he would live. His sores were nothing serious, so he ignored them and left the blood to trickle. He shivered from the cold water saturating his clothes, and he was reminded that it was only early spring in the Sierras. Just because the sun was shining and the snow was melting didn't mean he wouldn't die of hypothermia come nightfall.

Picking up both packs and rifles, he moved into the forest toward the road he and Chevy had left as they had scouted a route up the mountain. There were many who would soon come after them, if Wes could stay alive long enough to discover a route and return to Sandburg. Lune Lake was many miles away, and as yet, Wes and Chevy hadn't found a road northeast that hadn't been blocked by ruined bridges, or by the previous winter's avalanches and earthquake. To make matters worse, all of the road signs had been removed, and the hundreds of twisting forest roads that snaked through the mountains seemed to look the same. Wes guessed that mountain residents had removed the signs themselves to discourage valley people from venturing up there at all. Like the Greeks who'd built their towns intentionally as mazes to discourage invaders, Californian mountain dwellers were leaving their fellow citizens lost and confused by all the unlabeled roads.

On the road, Wes looked to the right first. He could go back down the mountain to Sandburg and tell his wife, Wynter, and the others of their loss. It would set them far behind their plans to find safe passage up to Lune Lake if he abandoned his mission. The bandit presence in the valley had been checked, but still, the only safe towns were those that were heavily fortified. That was no way to raise a family, although some were choosing to do so.

Instead, Wes had resolved himself to finding a way to Lune Lake, where a massive ski lodge and resort was rumored to be uninhabited. It could house several hundred families on the eastern slope of the Sierra Nevadas, as the people migrated out of the west and moved to safer altitudes. More civilians would need to be taught how to live in the mountains, as Wes and Chevy had already taught countless others the previous year in San Diego and the surrounding hills. Thousands owed the Kindred their lives.

Wes turned and looked to the left, up the mountain gorge. He needed to keep going, he decided. There was no point returning to Sandburg with only bad news. He may as well go on alone, and hope to find a way over the river—which had been one of a dozen they had crossed one way or another. Although they hadn't found safe passage of any kind over this river, they could've counted their journey a success so far since they knew not to come this way. It was the rivers that continued to thwart their progress, emphasized now by Chevy's own death.

Weary and mournful, Wes traipsed up the road, hoping it didn't lead to another bridge ruined by logs and water. The earthquake and flooding upriver was the source of the damage, carrying all sorts of debris with the water. Someday, maybe when the dams upriver broke, the logjam that had killed Chevy would break as well, and it would cause fresh havoc downstream. Wes figured that with a couple sticks of dynamite he could create a controlled purge of the gorge. But this time he was carrying a light pack with only the essentials for the scouting trip.

A wind blew through the treetops, making the giant pines groan along with his heart. The lonely sound reminded him of his plight, and he walked off the road to search for a campsite. He was done hiking for the evening. He needed to get out of his wet clothes and curl up around a blazing fire. His sorrow wouldn't let him think about tomorrow—he could only think about the loss of the tragic day.

The next morning, Wes woke after dawn to scramble to his low-burning fire where, through the night, his pants, arranged on two tree boughs, had leaned too close to the flames. He slapped the smoking cloth until it stopped sizzling, then stood there in only his shorts, admiring the new hole he'd managed to burn in the backside of his trousers. He dropped the pants on the ground next to his tarp and pack, then raised his hands to the sky and screamed a guttural cry. Finally, he fell to his knees, asking God for fresh strength to face the day, to deal with his anguish, and to remain safe, for the sake of his family and friends who were counting on him.

"And thank You, Lord, for dry clothes," He chuckled as he tugged on the pants. Though he had another pair in his pack, he saw no reason why he couldn't wear a perfectly good pair of leggings, even if part of his backside was exposed to the elements. People seemed to be rare or evasive in the mountains, and he guessed some of their clothes were probably in no better shape after this kind of rough living.

With sadness, Wes consolidated his gear by emptying Chevy's pack into his own, then rolled up Chevy's backpack and stuffed it into a side pocket. Good packs were hard to find. Although he now had enough gear on his back for two men traveling lightly, the residents of Sandburg had worked hard to send them up into the mountains, and Wes wasn't about to leave behind valuable supplies for the bears.

Slinging a battle rifle over each shoulder, he returned to the road. With somberness, he nodded at the part of the forest that separated him from the roar of the river where Chevy had died. It seemed unfair that Chevy should survive twenty years of prison, a dangerous mission to North Korea, a year of the Meridia Virus, and all the violence from the Diablos in the valley—only to die by drowning in the mountains.

"I'll see you again, old friend," Wes said, knowing the Bible promised a blessed reunion in heaven with loved ones who were in the faith.

For two hours, he climbed the mountain road, which was flooded in some spots by the nearby river. He skirted the flood waters and pressed on, ignoring side roads that led south as he searched for a safe way to cross the river to the north. He knew he was too far south to find a good road to Lune Lake, but all that could change if he could only cross the wild river!

The forest cleared up ahead. To the right, Wes came upon a mining town that was one hundred years old or more. He'd been told by some of the Sandburg hunters that there were mining towns sprinkled all over the mountains, abandoned since the gold had dried up, or the government had run out the miners. Whole settlements lay still, as if frozen for decades, falling apart from the heavy snow and freeze inflicted upon the buildings each winter. Some of the towns, like this one, had doubled as timber outlets for the great Sequoia pines. A saw blade, rusty and as tall as two stories, stood leaning against the rafters of a half-collapsed, barn-sized structure.

Then, Wes spotted chimney smoke wafting up from one of the buildings on the far side of the ghost town. He hustled off the road to use the forest as cover. Behind the safety of a small pine, he studied the ramshackle buildings. It was a good place to rebuild, although most of the wood was rotten. Someone had preferred to stop there rather than travel farther away from the valley's horrors and bloodlust. At that point, they were only four days of hard hiking from the Friant-Kern Canal, which ran north-to-south from Millerton Reservoir at the base of the mountains. Wes preferred to be much farther away from the valley, but not everyone had the capability or drive to press on.

More people would be leaving the coastal cities, and that meant bandits would be taking advantage of them. Sandburg had vowed to maintain a Kindred peacekeeping force using COIL's non-lethal weaponry. But Wes felt it was his calling to help refugees survive above the snowline, where they would indeed be safe from most violence. Although no one would be safe, it seemed, from the natural elements. Chevy could attest to that.

From his vantage point, Wes couldn't see the camp or cabin that was burning wood, but he felt a need to make some sort of contact. If he did bring the refugees through here one day soon, having friendly people at a four-day way-station could be established right now.

He picked his way through the forgotten buildings, which seemed to have popped up without any particular order, and approached the smoke. It was behind the sawmill, closest to where the mill itself had been powered by a water wheel, close to perhaps a smaller tributary of the nearby raging river.

He rounded the sawmill building and paused to see a pleasant homestead before him. It made him smile. A young woman in her late twenties was hanging clothes on a clothesline. A boy of about ten was trying to chop firewood, using a man-sized axe. His efforts were guided by a much younger boy, probably his brother, on how to swing the axe more effectively. They all seemed so normal, as if they knew nothing about the rest of the nation being ravaged by a pandemic mixed with panic across a society that had imploded. Of course, they wouldn't have been living four days away from civilization if they hadn't known there was danger everywhere else, but Wes liked to think that there were still peaceful spots in the world, and there were people who hadn't been affected by the trauma.

Stepping away from the sawmill, Wes walked toward them.

"Hi there!" He waved, hoping to connect with the less-dangerous members of this family before he met the man who probably wielded the axe with force. "I was just hiking up from—"

The boys scattered and the woman dropped her remaining clothes. She yelled to someone. Wes stopped in the open as a man with a bolt-action hunting rifle emerged from behind the house. His sleeves were rolled up and his hands were bloody up to the wrists. He was bearded with a deeply furrowed brow, and the rifle was aimed at Wes before Wes could say another word. A bullet whistled past his head—a sound that he knew well from other close calls during his operative days.

Wes's own rifle from his right shoulder flipped with ease into his hands. He leveled the bullpup and shot the man in the chest before he could fire another shot—before the man could send Wes to join Chevy in paradise sooner than expected.

The .308 round knocked the man backwards, and the rifle fell from his hands as he settled on his back. Wes growled at himself for acting so rashly, even if he was firing only gelatin tranquilizers. He should've greeted the family with more caution, maybe from the cover of the sawmill. But still, did he appear especially dangerous? Probably so, he guessed, since he carried two rifles—and part of the seat of his pants was missing.

Wes approached the homestead with more caution now, but no more gunshots were fired at him. Anyone within miles would've heard the smaller deer rifle the man had fired, followed by the cannon noise that the battle rifle had made. He knelt beside the sleeping man and gently touched the center of the bearded man's chest where the gel-tranq had smashed like putty, but probably felt like a steam freighter.

"Take what you want and leave!" the woman shouted from inside the house. The door wasn't just missing, it had been removed, it seemed, maybe for repairs. It was leaning against the support of the porch roof, in desperate need of some new hinges.

One of the boys whimpered as Wes stepped onto the porch, then she hushed her son to silence. Cautiously, in case the woman or the older boy wielded another gun, Wes peeked through the doorway. By the looks of things, they'd been there through the winter. A number of pieces of furniture had been made recently, probably as projects that had filled the long winter days. Even a few books were arranged on the shelf near a short-legged, twin-sized bed. A ratty army surplus blanket hung on hooks to separate the living space of the one-room cabin, almost giving it a two-room feel.

"Your husband's fine, ma'am," Wes said. "Come on out and we'll talk. I won't hurt you or your boys. Your husband will be awake in a few minutes and we can all start over. I'll be waiting out here with him."

Wes went to the woodpile and selected a block of wood to sit on beside the fallen man. He picked up the dropped hunting rifle and checked it for damage, then inspected the chamber. It was well-greased and cared for. From this angle in the front yard, he could see where the man had been skinning or butchering a deer hanging from a tri-pole on the shady side of the cabin.

"You killed him!" The woman stood in the doorway. Her sons peered past her on either side. "He was a good man! You murderer! Look at you, gloating!"

"He's still a good man, ma'am, and I'm not gloating." Wes rolled his one eye. "Wait there, if you want to, if you don't feel safe. You'll watch him wake up in . . . forty-eight minutes or less. Come here. Check his pulse. Look, he's not even bleeding. I just shot him with a tranquilizer. It seems we were both a little quick on the trigger."

She eased out of the doorway and off the porch. Her boys were just as curious, although not so bold as to leave the defenses of their mother's protection. Creeping closely, watching Wes for any sudden movement, the woman touched her husband's hand, then felt his wrist.

"He still has a pulse," she said, then seemed to reconsider all kinds of disastrous thoughts she'd had moments earlier. She stood tall, flipped her brown hair, and wiped her hands on her jeans. "So, he's okay, you say. You should probably leave. He won't be happy to find you here when he wakes up. Others have been here before, and it didn't go well."

"I can imagine. But whether he's happy or not, I'm not a man to run away from conflict." Wes rested the deer rifle on his knees. "I came to talk to you both, and I'm resolved to do just that. As a man of God, I trust in His guidance, so I'm stubborn about not turning away from something that seems to be His leading."

"Oh." She frowned, then glanced at the boys. "You two get back in the house!"

They spun around and bolted for the door like she'd chased them with a whip. Her hands were thrust halfway in her pockets, appearing now much more casual than she had minutes earlier.

"It's a nice place." Wes nodded. "Good location. Is that a creek out back?"

"To be honest, I'm not comfortable speaking to you any longer until my husband can join us."

"I respect that. I'll just sit here then." He crossed his arms, then decided to change his eye patch. After all, it was Wednesday, if he remembered right. That called for a gray patch. "One for every day of the week."

He noticed her grimace as he pulled off his Tuesday patch, tucked it into his breast pocket, and fit his Wednesday patch over his head.

"You look like a pirate," she said.

"You've seen a lot of one-eyed pirates in your day?" Wes chuckled. "What are you, about twenty-five?"

"It's not polite to ask a woman her age." But her bite had disappeared from her voice, it seemed, with his pirate retort. "But you're close. What are you, about sixty?"

"No, but I guess I deserved that." He laughed. "I thought you were done talking to me."

"How much longer until he wakes up?"

Forty minutes later, the bearded man stirred and rubbed his head, then touched his chest. He sat up with a groan, and his wife was immediately at his side. Slowly, he gathered his senses, and Wes remained seated and silent as the man and his wife whispered a few things about Wes's presence and why everyone was still alive.

"Seems I should've shot a little straighter with my first shot." The man, not much older than his wife, lumbered over to Wes and stopped a few paces away. He was taller and broader, but since his chest was probably still throbbing from the bruising, he didn't appear too sturdy. "That'll be the last time I give anyone a warning shot around here."

"If that was a warning shot, it was a little close." Wes stood and offered the man his rifle. "Nice weapon. I respect a man who takes care of his firearms like you do."

"My father taught me." He shrugged, his guard evaporating with his rifle back in his hands. "They're dead—Mom and Dad. I came up here a lot as a kid, hunting with Dad, prospecting. This seemed like a good place to hide out and start over with my own family."

"It's a good location." Wes surveyed the nearby buildings, then smiled. "A good fixer-upper."

"Yeah—ten-year's worth." The man's hard exterior was gone. "What's that you're shooting with there? Felt like a horse kicked me."

They talked the morning away, and his wife served them lunch as the boys ran into the forest to play. Wes rolled up his own sleeves to help butcher the deer at the side of the house. The two seemed to need the other's conversation for different reasons. Wes told him about losing Chevy the evening before, which had left a pit in his heart, and the man admitted that he hadn't spoken to another person outside his family for months. He was happy to hear some news about conditions in the valley, even if those conditions weren't good.

Their names were Anthony—or Ant, as his friends called him—and Liana Bartlik. They'd escaped the valley the summer before, realizing that a horde of unknowns was about to be unleashed from the Grapevine to Redding. They were high school sweethearts, growing up in a rural community east of Red Bluff. When Pan-Day had struck, they'd taken their young son and run into the mountains. Along the way, they'd found the older boy wandering the countryside, so they'd adopted him.

"It's hard living away from everyone," Ant said as he leaned into the carcass, trusting Wes to steady the ribcage, "but we trade loneliness for safety."

"Well, you understand that there are hundreds of people just waiting to roar up this mountainside, so you'd better brace yourself for the company."

"But, we came up here to get away from the people." The man stepped away from the deer and wiped his brow with the back of his forearm. "Do you think we should go up higher? The winters are bad enough this high up."

"Other people are trying to get away from the violence and danger as well, Ant. What we're looking at here may be an opportunity for you. You and Liana can be host and hostess to people passing through. These people aren't criminals. They're family people, civilians looking for a better home out in the woods and mountains. This place could become a station for resupplying them with gear, and you and Liana and the boys would have your pick of whatever people are willing to trade."

"When you put it like that, it doesn't sound so bad. Maybe like a trading post. There are some things we just haven't wanted to go back down to the valley to get. I don't want to leave Liana and the boys here alone."

"That's understandable." Wes pointed at a nearby structure. "That shed looks pretty sturdy. What's in there?"

"Just some firewood I've been stacking. I only use about a quarter of the space."

"Imagine the rest of that space filled up with hiking supplies and hunting gear. This could become an important hub for people to survive as they head over the mountain, even into Nevada, if they're going that far."

"Now a trading post is starting to sound like too much for one man and woman with a couple of boys."

"Nah, you wouldn't do it alone." Wes shook his finger at the younger man. "I've got dozens of families who would love to take part in something like this. We'd want you to have at least one good worker, and maybe a tradesman or two. You might need to train some of them to live in the outdoors like this, but we have people right now in Sandburg who could help make this work. This is an important first location for travelers."

"Food is something everyone on the move will need." Ant tapped his knife on the carcass. "Yeah, I'd need at least one other hunter up here. If he's got a family, we could use the help of our wives to keep things running smoothly, too."

They made plans into the afternoon, and some of the melancholy Wes felt about losing Chevy was tempered. Ant also had some knowledge about the route ahead and to the north that Wes sought, so it seemed that tremendous progress was made even though he'd lost a day of hiking by remaining there.

"The only thing to figure out now is what to call this place," Wes said as he bedded down on the floor next to where the boys slept, but they could hear each other across the room behind the partition. "People need to know where they're going and what they're passing through. It needs to be a name that means something to you guys as well as to people making a stop here."

"Supply Town," one of the boys suggested.

"No, call it Bartlik, like our name," the other boy said.

"Well," Wes chuckled, "you can work on the name. But when I pass back down this way, headed back to Sandburg, it would be good to tell me what you decide on so I can let folks know."

Chapter 2

Wes was being followed. He hadn't been sure the first two days after leaving Anthony Bartlik's homestead, but now he was certain. Birds had been startled numerous times from behind him, drawing his attention. On a high meadow where flowers of every color were waking up after a long winter, he'd waited with his rifle and scoped the tree line. Sure enough, he saw movement. It was a man, but Wes hadn't waited around to see if there were more than one.

Now knowing for certain that he was being tracked, Wes looked ahead and up a ravine for a shortcut up the mountain. The road cut wide around the ravine, but if Wes entered the gorge, which was full of trees, he could get far ahead of anyone on the road behind him.

Wes jogged through the rocky ravine, cutting through giant pines to avoid the long curve of the road he'd been following. The shortcut would save him twenty minutes. Twenty minutes closer to Lune Lake. Twenty minutes farther ahead of whoever was behind him. It could only be an enemy, he decided. Ant had already said he'd never leave Liana and the boys to go anywhere, so it wasn't him. No one from Sandburg would've caught up to him so soon, even if someone in town had left the day after he and Chevy had left. They'd ridden their bikes hard up Highway 168 as far as they could, and Wes couldn't imagine anyone out-hiking them as they'd followed the river those first days.

Since Wes was on a mission that hundreds were depending on, he wanted no further delays. To move even faster, he'd entrusted Ant with Chevy's battle rifle, a weight Wes didn't want to carry, but he'd pick it up on his way back down the mountain.

As he quickly climbed the next ridge, he pushed on his knees with his hands, straining for greater distance between himself and whoever was tracking him. For months, even while living in San Diego, he'd remained active, and although he was over fifty now, he'd never felt he'd had such endurance. He'd even heard Chevy sigh from exhaustion occasionally at the pace he'd set for them on some days.

The day was warm, and perspiration wet his hairline, but the warmth also meant the rivers were higher as the snow melted faster. Higher water meant fewer bridges. But higher waters also meant dams would be threatened up and down the San Joaquin River. If one dam broke, the next one would fail, and it could wipe out half of Fresno downriver. Wes had heard there were still people struggling to live in the city, but they had no idea how precarious the situation was up in these mountains.

At the top of the ridge, Wes found the road. He knelt and swung his rifle up to his eye. Behind him, a lone man jogged up the mountain road. This guy was relentless! Wes turned and gazed up at the higher passes where he still needed to climb. Roads were limited up there, but he'd find trails that led over the upper ridges. The question was, did he want to travel at his own pace, or travel while wondering when he was going to be shot in the back? His adversary could've been after the bullpup. It was a coveted rifle. Even Ant had admired the compact stock, which had a barrel long enough to drop a target at six hundred yards.

Wes made his decision on how to deal with the tail. He climbed the embankment above the road and cut through the trees to set up an ambush. His heart rate quickened at the possibility of conflict, but he prayed that his temperament remained Christ-like. Even though he was losing valuable time dealing with a stranger, he didn't know how God might use even this interaction.

One hundred yards later, hidden in the trees overlooking the road, he gently lay on his belly and scoped the farthest bend. His stalker had to approach that way. After all, Wes had just seen him jogging up the road.

But the longer he waited, the minutes ticked by, and he began to doubt himself. Maybe the man had left the highway to cut through the ravine as well. Or, maybe he'd seen Wes climb into the trees to ambush him. Or, maybe Wes was going insane, mistaking a homesteader for a stalker!

He licked his lips. Too much time had passed. The stranger should've come into view by now. This was no homesteader. Someone was intentionally tracking him and now avoiding his ambush. Wes's eye twitched as he lowered his rifle. What was the stalker doing? How would he try to attack him?

An instant before he rose to run higher into the mountains, he heard a branch break behind him and to his left. He remained perfectly still, trying to remember if he had any bright colors on his pack. With a snarl, he realized the only thing on him that wasn't earth tone was where his pants were burned away to expose his shorts on his backside. White shorts in a brown and green environment would stand out to even a novice woodsman! Somehow, this predator had gotten the jump on him, and Wes was feeling like anything but the veteran he was. Closing his eye, he prayed for invisibility, hoping his stalker passed him by.

Footsteps drew nearer, too near to miss him. He turned his head, wondering why he hadn't been shot yet.

The form of a man hovered over him, closer than Wes had suspected. He turned further and looked up at . . . a dead man—or a man he'd thought was dead!

"Who's out there?" Chevy asked in a whisper, his bullpup in his hands, as he gazed through the trees at the road below. "Is it more than one person?"

"How did you—?" Wes rose to his feet, and gasped, abandoning his rifle altogether. "I'm . . . looking at you, but . . . *I can't believe my eyes!* You're the one I thought was following me?"

"I *was* following you, but you weren't making it easy, since I had to make up a whole day!"

"But . . . *you're alive!* How is this possible?" Wes grasped the man by the shoulders and shook him. *"I can't believe this!* I was dreading going back to Sandburg and telling Jill about your death, and here I was running from you for the last couple days! Why didn't you fire a shot or something? If I knew how to dance, I'd dance around you right now!"

"And scare all the forest creatures?" Chevy laughed. "I think they're already scared enough from your fanny hanging out of that hole in your britches! What happened here? Playing with matches?"

"Nothing like waving a white flag for you to follow, huh?" Wes kicked Chevy in the seat, and the two laughed breathlessly.

They embraced and slapped each other on the backs. Wes couldn't remember being more pleased ever—except when he'd married Wynter.

"I figured you'd keep heading upriver," Chevy said, "so I tried to catch up. I came across Ant's home and spent a night recovering there, then he gave me my rifle. You've recruited a nice family there."

"But I saw you go under the logs!"

"I couldn't hang on forever, and you were going to kill yourself trying to help me." Chevy shook his head. "The water just swept me through all those logs and branches. I keep playing it back in my head, Wes. There's no reason I should've survived, except by God's miraculous hand. I'm just meant to slow you down on this trip, I guess."

They slid down the embankment to the road and continued walking.

"The river carried me down about two miles before I could get hold of something to drag myself out. I barely escaped before another log jam! Of course I laid there on the river bank for an hour, bruised all over my body."

"I should've gone downriver!" Wes made a fist. "Even if surviving that was so unlikely, I should've checked on you. You could've been injured."

"When I saw you slip off the log, I thought maybe you'd died, too." Chevy laughed. "I didn't know for sure until I found Ant and his family. You've been busy, lining things up. He says they've decided on a name, by the way. They're going to call their way-station *Ant's Place*. His boys liked it especially, because it sounds like a bunch of bugs crawling all over the place."

"Any name with a story behind it will mean something to people later on." Wes nodded. "I like it. It'll do. Now, is there a reason we're walking so slow?"

"Well, yeah. I've been running for days trying to catch up to you!"

A modern bridge had been placed over the river before the South Fork merged with the larger river. With care, in case there were people guarding the bridge, the men crossed the bridge one at a time, Wes first. The bridge stood high over the river below, and there seemed to be no structural damage from the flooding and trees ramming into the pilings.

"That's an important bridge for us," Chevy said as he caught up to Wes. "This is definitely our route, I'd say, although we have yet to see what the rivers ahead may be like."

The next morning, they were hiking toward Mount Ritter in the distance, when Chevy chanced a shot at a small deer. They needed the meat, and what meat they couldn't carry with them, there were plenty of natural predators like bears and coyotes around to finish off the carcass. In minutes, the deer was gutted, and with two of them working together, they'd quartered the back haunches to wrap up and carry with them.

"Tonight, when we camp," Wes said, "we'll cut the meat into strips and smoke it overnight. That'll keep it from spoiling for a few more days."

"Speaking of spoiling," Chevy gestured to the east, "those boys might be spoiling our fun."

Wes had just shouldered his pack, but he slipped it to the ground when he saw three men with hunting rifles at the edge of the timber.

"How do you want to play this?" Chevy asked. "They must've heard my shot."

"Well, we were planning on feeding the local wildlife with the rest of this deer." Wes adjusted his eye patch, then checked his rifle. "Maybe we can feed the local residents instead."

Although his rifle was ready to fire, Wes flipped it over his shoulder on the sling, and approached the three men standing across the meadow. Chevy walked beside him, his own bullpup over his shoulder, moving through the grass, stumps, and flowers that covered the clearing.

"Maybe you should've patched up your pants last night," Chevy said, teasing. "We're out in public now you know, Wes. What would Wynter say?

"How about we focus on something besides my system of ventilation?" Wes growled softly, but he appreciated his partner's light-heartedness at such a tense moment.

A distance away, the three men still hadn't moved, so Wes paused as well, wary since the strangers hadn't made their intentions known one way or another. They were almost within shouting distance, but drawing any closer seemed unwise to Wes.

"Maybe this is one of those situations that we don't need to confront the people directly," Wes said. "We can just walk away."

"And what happens when people from Sandburg start to run through here?" Chevy shrugged. "I don't like it any more than you do, but we need to make contact here, Wes."

Wes looked back at the deer, really wishing they could continue on their way.

"You're a better shot than me," Wes said, "so I'll approach them. That'll be better than both of us going forward. I'll move to my left to stay out of your line of fire, in case you need one."

"It would be nice to sort this out without shooting it out." Chevy hooked his thumb under his sling. "Maybe they know what lies ahead to the east."

With a prayer for guidance, Wes walked away from Chevy, easing to the left as he went. As soon as he was within talking distance, he waved his hand.

"Hi there." A few steps farther, he stopped. They were twenty feet apart. The men hadn't raised their rifles, but they hadn't offered a greeting, either. "We were just bagging a deer on our way through God's good country here. We have more meat than we can carry with us, if you want half."

They shifted on their feet. It was understandable that they were hesitant. If they'd come to the mountains directly after Pan-Day over a year earlier, then the last thing they would've heard of was death, carnage, and tragedy in every city and on every road. For all they knew, Wes could've had the Meridia Virus.

"As long as you really are just passing through," one man finally said loudly. He wore a stocking cap over a shaggy head of hair. "We have families, and we don't want strangers settling around here."

Wes took a deep breath, remembering Chevy's words. They needed to prepare the way for the refugees coming through from Sandburg.

"I'm just a scout for a larger party that'll begin traveling through here from Sandburg. We're headed for Lune Lake."

"How many people are we talking about?" Stocking Cap asked, his brow furrowed.

"A couple hundred probably at first, and more as others hear what it's like on the east slope of the Sierras."

"That means they'll be hunting our deer like you are," one of the other men said, then spit on the grass. "A couple hunters passing through is okay, but a whole crowd is too much. We're not welcoming any crowds up in these mountains. You should know that."

"Anyone who harasses these travelers will have a swift and decisive confrontation with my rifle here." Wes still hadn't swung it off his back. "I'm just a scout, me and Chevy there. But we're part of a whole fighting force. Several of us are ex-military or combat-trained. Now, I've told you they're traveling through, and you've told me that's unacceptable. How do you figure we should solve this matter?"

"There's no need to get unfriendly!" Stocking Cap shouted.

"Unfriendly? No, I'm your friend." Wes smiled. "Don't let my eye patch fool you. Only a friend would warn another friend of a line that shouldn't be crossed because there's danger across that line. The people we're bringing through here in a few weeks are families as well, people who are fed up with the violence down in the valleys. They're not interested in living way up here in the mountains. That's why I'm assuring you that we'll be passing through. I'd like to tell them that they'll be passing through the hunting land of friendly people, so they shouldn't overstay their welcome on your property, but I can just as easily tell them to keep alert for an enemy up here. Which are you?"

The three glanced at one another and seemed to agree on something.

"We'll be neighborly," Stocking Cap said. "You can tell your people we'll leave them alone, and they can leave us alone."

"If you're willing to take that step," Wes said, "why not take another step and make yourselves available to travelers, so they have someone to trade with along their route? They'll be bringing all kinds of stuff with them from the valley, and some of them will be willing to trade it off for supplies, rather than carry unnecessary weight the rest of the way. Come on. Why don't you meet Chevy and we can talk about it as you come get your half of the deer."

Wes turned his back to them and smiled his praise to God. He liked to draw the line with tough hearts, then unbalance them with grace and friendliness. It was definitely God's way of doing things.

Chevy matched Wes's enthusiasm to meet the three woodsmen, and in minutes, the three strangers heard the full story about the Kindred and what had happened in the Central Valley with the Diablos. The three men agreed that there was some value after all in the frequenting of well-meaning people through their back yard, as long as the Kindred were around to keep the peace.

They parted ways as friends, although they didn't shake hands since the mountain dwellers were skittish about contact, but Wes was undaunted. Making contact with the mountain dwellers hadn't been the same as setting up a trading post like *Ant's Place* would become, but it was a healthy step to a new beginning along the route.

Two days later, when Wes and Chevy were climbing a steep section of road, a man on horseback trotted up the pathway. He carried a sidearm and two axes, but no rifle. Without hesitation, he introduced himself as Frank Rorick. Chevy split their meat and sliced several smoked portions for Frank as he told his story.

He'd once been an engineer on the Pine Flat Reservoir over on the Kings River, far to the southwest.

Though he'd lost his wife and son to the virus, he'd stayed on at the dam when everyone else had left. After opening up the flood gates at Pine Flat the summer before, he'd guessed that the other dams deeper in the mountains also needed to be tended to, especially with winter and another thaw, and maybe more earthquakes, on the way. Although he was just one man, he'd been doing his best to keep even Mammoth Pool Reservoir maintained, so what bridges still remained, as well as all the civilians downriver, were kept safe and sound.

"Wherever I go," Frank explained, gesturing to his axes, "I try to keep the roads clear of fallen trees, too. Maybe things will get better someday, and people will drive up here again."

Wes doubted anyone would be driving up in the Sierras anytime soon, but he didn't discourage the older man from doing what he thought was useful. Chevy shared with the man how they were scouting for a larger party, and that his road-clearing work would be valuable to those with wagons and carts in the coming weeks.

Happy for the meat and the brief conversation, Frank and his horse continued in the other direction, as Wes and Chevy praised God for His goodness at meeting just the right people along the way.

A week later, the two men looked down at Lune Lake from the heights of the Sierra Nevada Mountains. Surrounded by Lodgepole Pine and Red Fir trees, they noticed Ponderosa and Jeffrey Pine trees that crowded the scattered resort community at an elevation of over seven thousand feet.

"It looks so peaceful and still," Chevy said, spying on the few visible buildings through his high-powered telescope. "There's some haze down there, but I don't see anything human moving around. I'm not seeing any smoke from cook fires, either. It appears to be everything we've been praying about for the people."

Wes used his weaker binoculars to survey the desert highways far to the east and south, imagining cars once zooming up and down the roadways.

"Half the highways out there are covered by sand since there's been no cars for over a year." He tucked his binoculars into his jacket. "Another decade of this kind of existence, and those highways will be lost forever."

Together, they started the descent toward Lune Lake, pausing on occasional bluffs to study the area below. Wes didn't want a repeat of surprising any woodsman, and Chevy was concerned about a violent welcome from citizens who were still afraid of the Meridia Virus. The closer they drew, the more visible Lune Lake Loop became, which was the road that connected the resort community in a five-mile loop off Highway 395.

When the two men finally walked into the horseshoe-shaped canyon that connected four lakes, they held their rifles ready to fire. They found trails and roads along the way, and a few abandoned and isolated houses. They crossed streams and passed meadows that would've been worth admiring, but they were scouting for a lodge or property that could host an untold number of people. They didn't have time to appreciate anything more than what was practical.

"Which lake is this?" Chevy asked Wes as they reached a pine-littered highway that rimmed a glassy lake. Log cabins peeked through the trees nearby, and several abandoned cars along the shoulder had been left in sight of a gas station. "Can you tell?"

"I think it's Silver Lake." Wes folded up his map and stowed it in a pocket. "Lune Lake is a little farther up the Loop to the east. I'm interested in those lodges north and east. Shall we?"

The two men walked up the middle of the two-lane highway surrounded by creaking pines and chattering squirrels. Wes kept sniffing the air for some sign of wood smoke that would indicate residents, but there was none.

"Nothing's burned or looted," Chevy said as they separated to inspect different cabins. "There was nothing back in the Central Valley that hadn't been ransacked or burned. But now, this place seems eerie. Look, some windows are even boarded up, and the glass is still in them."

Wes tried the front door of a cottage and found it locked. He wiped at dust on the window to peer inside.

"Fully furnished," he yelled over his shoulder. "It's like everyone closed up for the season and went back to Vegas or somewhere."

"This is better than we expected." Chevy joined Wes again on the highway and they continued to approach more buildings, including a modern hotel. "Is this place so isolated that no one has been here for a whole year? Since Pan-Day?"

"It's got miles of desert on one side and steep mountains on the other." Wes shook his head. "I don't know for sure, but maybe we're the first ones to return to this place. If it's really been abandoned like this around the whole Loop, there could be shelter here for thousands of people. *Listen!*"

Both men jogged to the west side of the road and knelt, their rifles against their shoulders. Turning their heads, they tried to discern from which direction a noise was coming.

"It's knocking in a rhythm," Chevy said. "That's manmade! Three knocks, a pause, and three more."

"It's an SOS!" Wes lunged to his feet and ran away from the road, straight into the forest. Twenty yards later, he intercepted a dirt road that cut through the trees. "This way!"

He heard Chevy charging after him, but Wes focused on a cabin against the canyon wall. A pickup truck was parked in the carport, and firewood was stacked under the awning, which looked like it had been split within the last few weeks.

The knocking grew louder as Wes stepped up to a narrow doorway and tried the door handle. It was unlocked and the door swung inward. The knocking stopped.

"We heard your SOS!" Wes called into the cabin, but didn't step inside yet. "Are you hurt? We're here to help you if you need us. My name is Wes Trimble, and I'm here with a friend named Chevy. Are you able to speak?"

Winded, Chevy stopped next to the porch, his eyes wide and his rifle leveled. Wes held out his hand to Chevy for silence, so the younger man managed his breathing.

"Yes!" a man's weak voice yelled. It sounded muffled. "Please, I'm in the back room! Help me!"

Wes stuck his head through the door, suspicious by nature after the past year of conflict. Someone could ambush the two of them, especially if people were in hiding and they thought that killing two strangers would keep their location a secret. But the living room of the small cabin seemed empty except for a little furniture and a rustic kitchen in the far corner.

"We're coming in!" Wes called, and stepped inside. He gestured for Chevy to hold back. "Let me check it out first."

Across the living room, Wes edged up to a bedroom door partly open. He glanced inside and saw a man lying awkwardly on a twin-sized bed. At first, Wes thought the man held a rifle, but then he saw it was a canoe paddle. He was bearded and in his 50's, but his teeth gleamed brightly as he smiled at Wes.

"I thought I would die alone." The man's smile left his face, and a frown now tugged at his mouth. He dropped the canoe paddle, which he'd apparently been using to knock on the wall. "I didn't think anyone was around for miles."

Wes edged closer to the bed, noticing more about the man's position. For one, he wasn't sitting upright, and his legs lay at a strange angle. Food wrappers and empty water containers littered the floor. A notebook and pen lay on the night stand within reach.

"Two of us came over the mountains," Wes said. "The San Joaquin Valley is in chaos. People need somewhere safe to raise their families until the violence stops, if it ever does. We were hoping to find some shelters here, but what we saw down at the lake is a little unexpected. No one's here. Except you. Everything is still intact."

"Come here." The man waved his hand. "Are you real? I thought I was a goner, for sure."

Shifting his rifle into his left hand, Wes stepped closer, realizing the man was crying. He held out his right hand. Any fear the Lune Lake resident might have had about the Meridia Virus was long gone as this man clasped Wes's hand in a strong grip.

"You're okay now," Wes said. "We're here. Just tell me what happened."

"I fell out back. Slipped on a wet log, then landed below on the rocks. Broke my back. It took me two days to crawl back in here. My food's been gone for several days. Water, too. I was just hitting the wall, wondering if someone might happen by. It was a long shot. I haven't seen anyone around here in months. You said your name is Wes? I'm Bill. Bill Jevans. I was a caretaker of the big lodge through the woods. I just stayed on after everyone else left—the people who survived the virus, I mean."

Wes called Chevy into the back room and they assessed the situation together, after getting the man a drink of water. Bill was paralyzed, and he needed immediate help. Although he might have been as strong as a lumberjack until recently, he'd been diminished to a cripple who could now only drag himself across the floor. He would've been dead within days, starved or eaten by wild animals, if he'd tried to drag himself through the woods to another dwelling.

It took Wes and Chevy together to get a fire going and heat a basin of water to clean the man up and change his soiled clothes. Between expressions of gratitude, Bill was talkative, telling the two explorers all about Lune Lake.

The virus had indeed wiped-out half of the community the winter before. Since most people had been part-time residents of the neighborhood, they had banded together after burying their loved ones, and set off the previous spring toward Las Vegas, Carson City, or Reno.

"Neither of the groups that went north or south on foot," Bill said as Wes dressed him in clean clothes, "ever returned. They either died on the road or they made it. I think returning here would've been too depressing or dangerous for most, since the first few weeks after Pan-Day, all we did was bury people. I don't have anyone out there, so I stayed back to take care of the buildings. I figured someday someone would come back and I'd be their host. Now, it looks like I'm going to be a burden, not a host."

"Nope," Wes said. "You're still the host. Maybe you can't walk any longer, but we're going to need you to help us get set up here this summer."

"We have nurses and doctors in Sandburg," Chevy said. "They'll be able to take better care of you than we can, maybe even get you walking again."

"That's unlikely." Bill looked at his limp feet, now inside clean wool socks. "It's been two weeks since I fell. I've heard that neurosurgeons can do amazing things if a spinal break is caught early-on, but we're nowhere near a trauma center. I'm done-in, and I know it. But at least you guys can bury me proper and I won't lay around stinking."

Wes encouraged Bill to tell them more about the Loop rather than dwell on his own disability, and after two more hours, the shadow of night fell across the forest. After a light stew for the man who'd been starving to death, Bill fell asleep, and the two travelers made up their own beds in the living room.

"We can't leave him behind," Chevy said as he climbed into his sleeping bag.

"Well, we can't carry him back to Sandburg." Wes chuckled. "What do you expect? To carry him on a pole between us?"

"He'll die without us, and we need to get back to Sandburg quickly."

Wes lay on his back and closed his eyes.

"One of us will have to stay with him, and the other will have to return to Sandburg."

"The one who stays could scout around here better," Chevy said, "and get things ready for the people."

Opening his eyes, Wes turned his head toward Chevy.

"It sounds like you're volunteering."

"If you don't mind going back alone. I'm tired of falling in rivers, anyway."

"I don't mind. Now that we know the route, I'll mark it as I go back. I should make good time."

"Still, it'll be a month before you get back here." Chevy sighed. "But there's lots to do. Jill will be worried."

"Don't worry." Wes rolled over. "I'll make sure she's moving up the mountain in the first wave. Maybe by then you'll have found a wheelchair around this place for Bill."

"Just put on your other pants before you walk into Sandburg, will you?" Chevy snickered under his breath. "As Titus might've said—it ain't easy following a man wearing burnt britches!"

The next morning, Bill suggested a better route up the mountain for Wes to leave, by using Lune Mountain's Canyon Trail ski run, which switch-backed twice before a wide ridge offered a straight path into the wilderness.

From the ridge, Wes set his eyes on the Pacific Crest Trail. The sun was at his back and Mammoth Lake was on his left as he ascended the eastern slope. He didn't mind being the one to return to Sandburg, even if it was over one hundred miles back to the town. Wynter would be waiting for him, and in her arms would be their new baby girl, Mia. It would be nice to see his family again!

Chapter 3

Four days later, Wes had reached his mountain bike and was cycling swiftly southward on the highway when the reflection of the sun glinted off glass in a nearby field. In that instant, Wes realized the reflection had to have come from a rifle scope. But he imagined God wouldn't allow him to be shot since he was on a mission for His people. However, a breath later, it seemed that the impact of a truck had smashed into his lower body.

Since he'd been racing down the highway at over twenty miles an hour, trying to reach Sandburg, the wreck that followed spread for thirty yards. Bicycle parts, contents from his backpack, and Wes's body all flailed and slid across the road. When he came to rest, he found himself lying on his back at the edge of the road, with a deep irrigation ditch at his shoulder.

When he caught his breath moments later, the pain coursed up both legs, and he knew he was badly wounded. How cruel of God, he thought. To be so close to his destination and for God to allow such a catastrophe! How could God allow something so tragic when half of Sandburg was relying on him? This wasn't fair!

He cringed as he felt more aches and bruises up and down his body. When he lifted his head, he noticed his bike was in several pieces, and one of the wheels was bent in half. The bike frame had been strong, so how could it have broken during a mere wreck?

But it hadn't been a mere wreck. The memory of the sun reflection struck him afresh. He'd been shot, but how badly? Both legs burned like fire so badly that he couldn't pinpoint the exact location of the injury. Struggling to get his arm under him, he wrestled against the battle rifle on his back. While sitting up halfway, he looked down at blood-soaked cargo pants. Using his other hand, he gently prodded his thighs. A bullet had passed through the meat of both legs, tearing the flesh wide open, before the bullet had exited his body. Between his legs, the bullet must've shattered through the aluminum bike frame, warping the bullet even more, because his right thigh was more mangled than his left.

A short burst of gunfire nearby bewildered him. Gravel peppered his arm as bullets slammed into the ground. Didn't they see he was already down?

He looked both ways, then, from a seated position, he dove off the road into the canal. From a year of neglect and unrestrained water runoff, the canal had eroded to become deeper than normal. Wes tensed as he fell and landed ten feet later on his right shoulder. The soft ground sloped toward the small stream, so he rolled with his momentum, but he almost lost consciousness from the pain in his legs and shoulder.

When he stopped moving, his face was laying in the shallow water. He pushed away, coughing, and remembered that someone was still trying to kill him. The Diablos had to be responsible! And there would be more than one.

His legs needed to be tended to, but not yet. Somehow, he needed to stay alive! The people of Sandburg were counting on him. Thousands needed to know about the safe route out of the valley and into the mountains. Lune Lake was waiting for the refugees, but if he died, others might wander the mountains needlessly for weeks, and never find their way over the mountains and across the dangerous rivers.

Doing his best to ignore the pain, Wes dragged his body across the stream and under the eroding bank of the canal. There, in the shade where plant roots were tickling his head, he held his breath and took hold of his rifle. He surveyed the weapon briefly, and found it to be in one piece. That was all the time he had, for three men ran into sight above him. He raised the rifle and fired frantically at the opposite bank of the canal. Mentally, he prayed he'd changed his ammunition back to gel-tranqs rather than lethal rounds, since he'd been hunting deer earlier that morning.

Wes saw a gel-tranq smack into the chest of the first man, and he tumbled into the canal nearby. The second man received a round to the belly. Too late, Wes realized this man's hand was raised with a frag grenade in his fist, the pin already pulled! There was nothing Wes could do but drop his rifle and use his arms to cover his face and neck. The man fell unconscious, and the grenade rolled from his limp hand.

The blast of shrapnel pelted Wes on the torso and the back of his arms, but he knew the two men still on the canal wall couldn't have survived such an explosion.

Seconds later, the dust settled, and Wes lowered his arms. He felt the blood trickle from a dozen different wounds, besides his legs, but his eye settled first on the broken bodies across the stream. Only the first man Wes had tranqed seemed unhurt by the grenade, since he'd tumbled into the canal a breath before the grenade had detonated.

All three men wore black armbands. They were indeed Diablos.

Wes had the sense to check his watch. In one hour, it would be dark. And in one hour, the first man would wake from the tranq toxin. The other two Diablos were dead, their bodies torn asunder. And Wes would have been in similar state, but God . . .

Setting his rifle aside, Wes gritted his teeth to sit up and examine his legs again more carefully. His other injuries would have to wait. Right now, he needed to stop the bleeding of his legs. He couldn't simply wrap a tight tourniquet on them and hope an EMT took care of the rest. No, he was miles from Sandburg still. There were no

EMTs. And there was no help coming. He was stranded without a bike now, alone, and seemingly abandoned by God.

Tears streamed from his eyes as he felt his leg wounds. Blood seeped with every heartbeat. His tears were partly from the pain and partly from his accusing thoughts against God. It was extremely difficult to see God's goodness, kindness, and watchcare in this moment! But he had to try. After all, he'd counseled many others over the years to accept the bad with the good, and trust God through even the uncomfortable situations. Now, he was the one who needed that counsel. All things didn't seem as if they could possibly work out for good in that instant, but Wes pushed the doubt from his heart and pleaded with God to help him trust through the pain and hopelessness, even the unbelief.

The evenings in the valley hadn't been dropping into the forties lately, so Wes hoped he wouldn't freeze when he stripped off his jacket. Using the knife from his hip sheath, he cut the jacket into strips and tied knotted bandages over his entry and exit wounds, with the knots resting over the wounds themselves for added pressure. He needed to stitch his injuries closed, but that wasn't happening without his medical kit, which was somewhere above in his torn backpack. His water containers were also up with his bike, although in a pinch, he guessed he could drink the muddy canal water.

Exhausted from his pain and wound tending, he lay back on the soft dirt of the canal. The sky was darkening more by the moment. Sandburg didn't know to expect him that evening, and Chevy certainly wasn't able to help him. Even if he were above the canal, his situation would still seem hopeless, but here he was, stuck deep in the canal, with no way to climb out.

His injuries continued to bleed, and with frustration, he knew he needed to tend to himself more, or else getting out of the canal would be the least of his problems.

Forcing himself away from the dry ground, he dragged himself back through the shallow water toward the two deceased and one sleeping man. Although he needed to help himself, he couldn't avoid the urge to move the unconscious man's head and one arm to a more comfortable position. Then, he took the man's rifle and threw it into the water where it couldn't be seen.

Next, he moved farther toward the deceased men, their clothes torn and at least one of the packs strewn across the ground, ripped open from the blast. In the last light from the sky, Wes rifled through the contents of the pack and found a small first aid kit. There was no needle and thread for stitching himself closed, but there was a roll of elastic tape that would help close his wounds up nearly as well.

It was just medical tape, but Wes felt a tinge of hope. Maybe, even after being shot in both legs and being slashed by grenade bits, he wasn't entirely abandoned by God after all. Maybe he would survive. Maybe God still had something else for him to do.

Chapter 4

Wes closed his eyes as he sat in the middle of the canal stream, allowing the cold water to run over his thighs. The sensation was filled with burning and freezing at the same time, but he knew his wounds needed to be washed before he applied the tape to the torn flesh.

Finally, he was ready to tape up his legs, and it wouldn't be comfortable or proper medical attention, but it would be better than the knotted strips of jacket he'd already applied. After removing the strips, he wound the tape over his pants, which closed the wounds considerably, although sutures would've been ideal. Once tape encircled his thighs, he tied his torn jacket strips over the tape. It was all he could do.

The unconscious man across the stream moved. He was awake. Wes's mouth gaped at the mistake he'd made. He'd left his rifle several yards away, under the canal wall! But he didn't need his rifle, he reminded himself. His sidearm from his hip would work just as well, especially at close range.

The enemy sat up and looked around. He was ten yards away. Wes didn't say anything, but just sat and looked back. In the darkness, they couldn't be recognized, but Wes knew the man's silence would last only so long.

"Who are you?" he asked Wes, perhaps trying to discern if he was one of his friends or a foe.

Wes got the impression that the man was feeling around with his hand, probably trying to locate his rifle or another weapon.

"My name's Wes Trimble." He glanced at the top of the canal wall, a few feet up, wondering how far away the man's other Diablo friends might be. "This seems awfully extreme on God's part, but we're apparently supposed to meet, you and I."

The man was silent for a moment, and in the silence, Wes prayed. Of course, he thought. God would put him through all of this just to meet one person whom he would never meet any other way.

"We shot you. What did you do to the others? I smell blood."

"One of your buddies held a grenade when I tranquilized him. He dropped the grenade and killed himself and the third guy who was with you."

"That's what you shot me with? A tranquilizer? That's why my chest hurts. You're one of them. You're one of those Kindred."

"Yep, that's right." Wes smiled, feeling a peace in the night, even though his pain was extreme. "We believe life is precious. I could've fatally shot you, but I tranqed you instead."

"You didn't tranq my friends. They're dead because of you. How's that for your conscience? I thought you were a Christian."

"I'm not responsible for things outside my control," Wes declared firmly. "I meant to keep your friends alive. The grenade one of them had, that's what killed them. That's on them."

"And what, you stuck around until I woke up so you could torture me with your religious drivel?"

"No, I stuck around because you shot me, and I can't get out of the canal on my own."

"You can't move?" The man rose to his knees. "You don't have your rifle anymore?"

"No." Wes frowned. "No, my rifle is out of my reach right now."

"We've been trying to capture one of you Kindred alive for weeks." The Diablo climbed to his feet. He was just a shadow in the night, but Wes could still make out his shape in the darkness. "It looks like my lucky day after all. You don't have your rifle? That's going to cost you."

The man splashed across the stream toward Wes. But Wes raised his handgun and fired point blank at the man's body."

"Just because I don't have my rifle," Wes said, "doesn't mean I don't have other weapons."

The bandit slumped unconsciously one pace away from Wes. He holstered his firearm and grabbed at the man to roll him out of the water, lest he drown.

Wes didn't want to move any more than he had to, especially with his leg wounds, but he needed to put distance between himself and the bandit. Again, he dragged himself downstream, back to where he'd left his rifle against the west canal wall. He could see the moon from this vantage point, and again, he checked his watch to keep track of his enemy's waking time. It was going to be a long night if he had to tranq his adversary every hour. Somehow, he needed to make peace with this man, and send him to get help.

The thought made him chuckle. Only God could orchestrate something so unlikely as an enemy becoming a friend to the point of aiding him. At least, that was what Wes was trying to envision, since anything less than receiving this man's help would result in his death. With no food, Wes doubted he would survive in the canal more than a week. And if the Diablo didn't change his ways, Wes would run out of tranquilizers within a couple days!

His situation was desperate, and so his prayers were desperate. His prayers were focused on two things: Wes needed God's supernatural physical rescue, and the bandit needed God's supernatural spiritual rescue. Without the bandit, Wes guessed he would die from his injuries. But without Wes, he guessed the bandit would die in his sins. So, they needed each other.

The hour passed without Wes moving much at all. His legs continue to throb, and he worried some about the bones or tendons being damaged, but like he'd told the bandit, he couldn't focus on things outside his control. As much as he knew how to do, he'd patched up his legs. Now, he had to remain as immobile as possible to let the blood clot and the skin heal. The inner tissues would take days if not weeks to heal, but the outside was a priority—to keep infection out, and the blood in.

The unconscious man stirred again, and with a groan, he rolled to a seated position. With a curse, he rung out his wet clothes.

"You shot me again!" He grumbled more, but remained seated where Wes had dragged him. "Those bullets you use hurt more than you think."

"I can always swap them out for hollow points, if you'd prefer."

"No." The man was still for some time before he spoke again. "How about we stop shooting each other?"

"Sounds good to me." Wes chuckled. He didn't feel too jovial, but he needed to be agreeable, for both of their sakes. "I can agree to that."

"I don't know which is worse—getting shot by your rifle, or getting shot by whatever pistol you have there."

"It's a Desert Eagle .45." Wes scoffed. "I wouldn't want to feel the impact of either of them, so I don't blame you for feeling a little bruised. But I assure you, what you guys have done to me is ten times worse."

"How bad is it?" The man's voice was gentler than earlier.

"The bullet passed through both my legs. Then, when your friend's grenade went off, I got pelted with about a dozen pieces of shrapnel. Every time I move my arms, the shrapnel that's sticking out of my skin feels like fish hooks pulling on my nerves."

"Sorry." The bandit climbed to his feet where he stood and swayed, as if the tranquilizer effects were still clouding his mind. "We saw your pack and thought we could get something to eat. Then when you drew closer, we saw your rifle, and we knew you were one of the Kindred."

"You know, we would gladly give you food to eat and gear to use if you'd just ask us. We're here to help the survivors of Pan-Day. We all have families, right? It's all about sharing so we can survive for years, not about taking so we can make it for just a day or two."

"Yeah." The man sniffed. "Well, when you've done it one way for so long, taking just comes natural."

"I told you my name is Wes. Who do I have the pleasure of meeting?"

"Pleasure?" The man laughed loudly. "You've got a strange way of thinking about things, Wes. But, whatever. My name's Valles. I'd shake your hand, but I think you might shoot me again. Two times is enough for me."

Valles hopped across the stream and sat down in the dirt on the east side of the canal.

"You're not going to leave?" Wes asked.

"I'm a scout for the Diablos, which you probably already know." Valles sneered. "These two guys are dead by our own grenade. The boss won't be happy unless I bring him something."

"Something? Me?"

"If you're shot up as bad as you say you are, then I only have to wait you out. I don't mind waiting for you to die. I've sat with others who needed to talk before they died."

"Oh, I'm sorry to disappoint you, but I won't be dying. I've been shot before, and I need to get back to my people to share with them an important message, so I don't think the Lord wants to take me home quite yet."

"The Lord?" Valles cursed. "You really are a Christian, aren't you?"

"That's why I think you and I have met for a reason. I've made friends with others who were my enemies before tonight."

"You and I aren't friends, pal. I'm waiting for you to die, then I'm taking your rifle to the boss."

"I'm not going to die, and we are too friends. It's not up to you to decide whether we're friends or not. You need a friend like me, so here we are."

"I need you?" Valles swore. "No, it's the other way around. You need me. I could carry you out of here, you know. But I won't."

"That's fine with me." Wes laid back against the canal wall, but kept his right hand near his sidearm. "You still need me more than I need you."

"There's nothing I need that I can't get by taking it from anywhere I go."

"Yeah, if you say so. We both know that's not true, but tell yourself whatever you want."

Wes took a deep breath, smiled, and waited for his words to take effect.

"What do you think I need?" Valles asked a moment later. "Name one thing that I can't get for myself in what's left of this world."

"One thing? No, I could name a dozen things. How about peace? Just the way you're talking, I can tell you don't know anything but conflict. You probably don't even know the definition of peace. Peace is something that God gives you, something deep inside your heart that lets you know you're all right with Him because He loves you. And joy. I bet you haven't ever known true joy. Maybe you get drunk or high once in a while, right? You might feel great for a few hours, but then you come down, and what do you have? More misery."

"Shut your mouth. You don't know what you're talking about."

"Then, there's love. I've met enough Diablos the past few months to know that love is missing in your ranks. Love isn't something that's forced upon people. Love is the product of grace, and you don't know about grace, either, because you only know how to take. You don't know about humbly receiving favor you don't deserve. Yeah, you definitely need grace. You need it more than I need your help."

"If I thought you wouldn't shoot me again, I'd come over there and choke you out. Nothing of what you say means anything to someone like me. I'm not some child who needs fantasies about an invisible man in the clouds to make me happy. I'm a real man. I know what I want and I get what I want. Period. Besides, you're no one to tell me anything. You're going to die down here, and I'm going to walk out and keep living, no matter how many times you tranquilize me."

"The way you live, you'll be dead in a year." Wes's voice was firm. "All your pride won't let you receive from God what you need most. So, you'll get in a shootout with some refugees, or your boss will get tired of your attitude and shoot you himself. Or, there are other Diablos you don't get along with. Yeah, that's usually how it happens, right? Men who think they're on top start turning on each other. Sure, I might die someday, and when I do, people will miss me. I have close friends, a wife and a little girl. Who do you have? People who want to kill you to take from you like you've taken from others? Who'll miss you when you die?"

"Shut up!"

"Come on, Valles. You've told yourself for so long that you're doing so well. Now that someone is giving it to you straight, the truth is hard to hear, isn't it?"

"I'm not listening to you anymore. You're twisting me up, and I'm about to come over there."

"Take care of it. I'm a dying man, you said. You know I won't kill you. Why don't you come over here and shut my mouth?"

"Quit taunting me, Wes!" The man threw a fistful of wet dirt at Wes. "I'm warning you!"

"Oh, stop it, Valles." Wes's voice softened. "You already know deep down I wouldn't be telling you these things about yourself unless I cared about your life. You're lost without God. You wouldn't be hurting so many people unless you were hurt yourself. That's the psychology behind criminals, by the way. Everyone but the criminals know it. People who are hurt, hurt others. It doesn't matter what happened to you in the past, or how angry you are about life being unfair. I don't know or care about your past. What matters is right now and every day after this. It's time for you to walk away from the Diablos. It's time to accept what you've known all these years. It's time to lift your head up and accept the straight and narrow. You know what I'm talking about."

"Straight and narrow." Valles cursed. "I've heard all that before."

"You've heard it, but you've never embraced the peace that comes through accepting what Jesus Christ did for you, my friend. It's time to walk away from a life of death and turn toward a life of forgiveness, which will stretch into eternity with God. It's time to stop resisting. Boy, I was angry earlier when I realized how shot up I am! But then I realized, there are no accidents with God. You've got to be the reason why we're here right now. It makes my getting shot okay, if it means one life is saved from continuing down the dark path. I'd die for this to happen, Valles—for your life to be better, for you to know how loved you are, for you to know that there are people who care for you not far away, people who also know God."

Minutes passed, and Wes felt the weariness of his journey and his wounds. His eyes drifted closed, but he opened them suddenly at the cry of a wild animal nearby, somewhere above the canal walls.

"Are you still alive?" Valles asked in the darkness.

"Still here." Wes sighed heavily. "I'm not doing well, but I'm hanging on."

"How far away are your friends?"

"Sandburg."

"Figures. That place is like a fortress. It's the only fortified town us Diablos won't go near anymore."

"That's wise. They have enough shooters behind that barrier to handle any force you throw at them. Some of them are sharp-shooters, too. They'll pick you off at six hundred yards."

"Six hundred yards?" Valles whistled. "There've been rumors about you guys, but no one's gotten their hands on your rifles to find out for sure what you're working with."

"It's not the rifle, necessarily," Wes said. "It's the hearts behind those rifles. They have a confidence in what they're protecting and promoting that's stronger than the confidence you have in what you're trying to destroy. That's one reason why evil doesn't stand before kindness."

"It's why you use tranquilizers? But a smarter person who wanted to really remove evil would kill the evil one."

"No, you're wrong. Killing people isn't really removing evil. That's just avoiding dealing with the evil. If you want to remove evil, you care for the person who's in bondage to that evil, and help that person turn from evil altogether. Oh, yeah. That's where evil is destroyed, when there's a reversal, a new birth. That's what Jesus taught, and it's what has decimated the Diablos through the winter. How many Diablos have walked away since January? And we didn't kill any of them. We drew pictures of you guys, and we told you that you're loved. That's all."

"Insanity."

"That's what some say, but you can't argue with the results." Wes chuckled. "One day, you'll look back on this night, and you'll know this is the truth. Maybe we'll both be alive, and we'll appreciate this memory, the two of us sitting here, talking about hope and peace in this broken world. Maybe we'll be friends, and we'll die at peace with one another in the company of families who love us. We'll die knowing that God has forgiven us, and that we're going to Him without guilt on our account."

"You don't know anything about guilt, Wes. The things I've seen and done . . ."

"You're right. I don't know what you've done or what you've seen. But like you said, I'm a dying man. There would be no point in misleading you now. That's why I'm speaking to you honestly. Maybe I feel that for my death to matter, you have to know that your life matters."

Again, there was silence for a time, and Wes struggled to keep his eyes open. He prayed now more for Valles than for himself. It was true that he could die, since he'd lost so much blood. Death would bring sorrow, but only for those he was leaving behind. Temporarily, Wynter would miss him. But death itself wouldn't be a great loss. After all, his eternal soul was in the hands of the One who had defeated death. There would be a resurrection.

Wes felt hands on his shoulders, shaking him awake. He clawed for the pistol that must have slipped from his fingers. Instead, he felt the cold steel of his Desert Eagle against his temple, and Valles' heavy hand on his arm.

"I caught you sleeping, Wes!" Valles breathed inches from his face. "Who needs who now?"

Wes could see Valles' shape only by the way his head blocked out the stars above. The bandit's fingers dug into his shoulder where shrapnel lay embedded in his skin.

"We need each other," Wes said. "You need me to teach you about the peace found only in Jesus Christ, and I need you to get me to Sandburg."

"They'd never let me into Sandburg."

"I'm Wes Trimble, the Kindred of Nails field operative. You'll be welcomed as my guest."

The muzzle of the handgun eased away from Wes's head, and Valles' grip on his shoulder lessened.

"No one's ever offered to do something like that." Valles completely let go of Wes. "I have a bike up in the meadow where we laid our ambush for you. One of the other guys had a trailer on his bike. We can put you on that, and I'll get you to Sandburg."

"Not so quick." Wes pointed toward the highway. "I had all kinds of gear in my pack."

"Yeah, I saw it. It's spread all over the highway."

"It's important gear, and I have a lot of tranquilizer ammunition. I need you to collect everything you can find. Lives depend on it."

"Do you want me to take you to Sandburg or not?"

"Yes, I do," Wes said, "and I'm thankful for your help, but we need to get that gear as well."

"You don't do anything the easy way, do you, Wes?"

In piggy-back fashion, Valles carried Wes down the bank of the canal until they came to a bridge two hundred yards later. Using the bridge, both men worked together to climb up to the valley floor. Their work would've been easier if Valles had been stronger, but Wes guessed the slender man hadn't been eating well through the winter. The Diablos had had a rough season.

Traipsing up the middle of the highway, Valles panted loudly as he carried Wes to the pavement, which was strewn with his gear. Here, Valles laid Wes on the road and went to fetch the bike, then he collected the gear. Wes was exhausted by the time Valles placed him into the trailer and piled the loose gear onto his lap. Wes held his rifle across his chest and sipped from a recovered canteen.

"Can we get going now?" Valles asked, standing over the trailer. "Or do you have more orders for me?"

"No more orders, Valles." Wes could hear his weakened voice. "Go ahead. Start us off. If you get tired, I'll take over and pedal the rest of the way."

"Very funny. I've never known anyone to crack jokes so much when they were on the edge of death."

As Wes rested in the bumpy, uncomfortable trailer, he gazed up at the starry sky. This was his God's work. He who was once an enemy was now his friend. Maybe, with a little more attention, he who was God's enemy would become a son!

Chapter 5

Wes was startled awake by the jostling of the trailer as it bounced over uneven terrain. His rifle had started to slide from his lap. He grabbed it with one hand and reached with his other hand to steady himself against the side of the trailer. Meanwhile, the agony of his wounds made him hold his breath until the trailer came to a stop in a hay field. The fact that pre-dawn light illuminated the landscape alerted Wes to the fear that something was terribly wrong.

"Where are we?" he asked Valles. "We should've reached Sandburg long before sunrise!"

Valles answered by wrapping his arms around Wes's torso and dragging him out of the trailer. The next instant, Wes lay in shock on the hard, broken ground of a wheat field. Pain had a way of paralyzing the senses, and several seconds passed before he could gather his wits to think. From his back, he saw Valles lying on his belly next to him, peeking his head over the low-growth wheat.

"Don't speak. Diablos are coming."

Wes's eyes darted from the brightening sky to the little cover they had. He was seeing Valles in the light for the first time. The man appeared to be much younger than Wes had first thought. Unlike other Diablos Wes had captured or known, Valles had no apparent tattoos. His face was broad and his eyes were wide with fear. Over one arm of his thin wind-breaker, Valles wore the black band of the Diablos.

"I think they saw us," Valles reported, suddenly lowering his head, pressing his cheek against the rough earth. Inches from Wes's face, Valles seemed to be studying Wes's appearance for the first time, too. "I missed the turn-off to Sandburg. I went too far. If the Diablos find us . . ."

"The Lord is with us both." Wes hoped his resolve showed on his face for his young friend, knowing that no matter what happened now, he'd spoken the gospel the previous evening to the man. "It'll be okay, even if we're caught."

"They'll kill us both."

"How many are there?"

"Five, I think." With a grimace, Valles raised his head, chanced a look, then ducked back down. "No, six."

"They're coming our way?"

"They're off their bikes, searching the field for us. They must've seen us from a distance like we saw them."

From the joy of making a friend out of the bandit to the disappointment of not waking up back at Sandburg, Wes felt like crying. He was exhausted, anxious, and numb from nerve-penetrating pain from his shrapnel and bullet wounds.

"How far away are they?" Wes asked.

"About as far away as I can throw a rock."

Wes closed his eyes. He didn't know God's plan, and he didn't know how God would help the citizens of Sandburg reach Lune Lake without him, but Wes knew what he had to do.

"You can save yourself," Wes stated, "if you turn me in. You captured me, and you can tell them that."

"But . . ." Valles' face twisted in dissatisfaction. "I was going to take you to Sandburg, and we were going to start a new life. That's what you said."

"But now the Diablos are here." Wes tried to express his faith, even in that hopeless moment, but he was afraid the young man sensed his doubt anyway. "We have to accept what it seems has been meant to be. Turn me in and save yourself."

"No, I—" Valles' inner battle was clear as he fought tears. "But you don't even know me. Maybe we can shoot it out with them."

"We'd die for sure, unless we could draw them in closer and I can tranq them when they're unsuspecting." Wes raised his eyebrows. "Otherwise, take me in as your captive, and get free another day. Go to Sandburg, Valles. Tell them to follow the paint, that Lune Lake is available. Sandburg will welcome you if you come in my name."

"Follow the paint? They'll know what that means?" Valles shook his head. "No, we can go there together. We'll fight!"

"There's no time. Look at me. I'm done-in."

"You would die for me—a killer you met in the dark last night? Yesterday, I tried to kill you!"

"Remember what I taught you about Jesus. You're not far from understanding what He did for all of us. Give me up and save yourself. Don't add any more deaths to your account, not to save me from their hands."

Valles' face showed that he didn't like the idea of Wes saving his life with his own. The only alternative was that Valles would die with Wes, and that was certainly more unsettling.

"I'll try to find a way to save you." Valles rose to his hands and knees.

"It's okay, Valles." Wes nodded, a slight movement, but one that still hurt. "I'm at peace."

The young man rose to his feet and waved his arms.

"Over here! Hey! It's me, Valles! I didn't know who you were, so I was hiding. Wait till you see what I've got for you!"

Wes braced himself for what would follow. There would be a lot of pain, regardless of how they decided to kill him. Any movement of his body hurt him, and the loss of never seeing Wynter and Mia again would penetrate to his very core. But he would see them again in heaven, he knew. Even in that seemingly impossible situation, where he couldn't walk or fight, he sensed God's peace. He was sacrificing himself for Valles. Maybe Valles would eventually come to faith in Christ from it all.

Valles took Wes's rifle and drew his sidearms to hold them up for the men who were jogging across the field.

"Look! I got one of the Kindreds and his rifle!"

"Where's Spike and Cisco?" one of the men asked. They surrounded Wes, all heavily-armed men, and looked down at him. "Wow, you must've tortured this guy. Is he even alive?"

Someone kicked Wes lightly in the shoulder with his foot.

"Spike and Cisco were killed," Valles said. "It was Cisco, actually. He dropped the grenade and killed them both. I captured this guy a minute afterward."

Wes passively acknowledged the men standing over him. They spoke about him as if he were already dead. Valles held his weapons, and the six others each carried at least two weapons apiece.

As they discussed how to get Wes back to the Diablos' base at Lake Isabella, Wes prayed for strength for Wynter to endure his death. It might be days before Valles could get away from the Diablos and reach Sandburg. If he didn't, Wynter would never know what happened to him. Chevy would be forced to stay at Lune Lake indefinitely, taking care of Bill Jevans in his crippled state. Everything had gone wrong. Everything had—

Wes's heart surged faster when he suddenly realized he wasn't completely defenseless. In haste, Valles had disarmed him of his two sidearms and the rifle, but the nine-millimeter Baby Eagle was still holstered on Wes's right ankle.

Roughly, Valles and two other Diablos lifted him up from the ground and draped him across the trailer. Under him and around the trailer were the loose supplies that Valles had gathered in the dark for Wes, but now it all seemed useless. The bandits studied several items that had been in Wes's pack—a crossbow, and a hand-crank lantern. For a moment, the six were distracted, yet close together. In another minute, they would scatter to fetch their own bikes, and an attempted shootout would be impossible to win.

Steeling his nerves against the agony of moving, Wes took a deep breath and held it. From a reclining position in the trailer, his point of view of his enemy wasn't ideal. His breath nearly escaped his lips as a scream when he raised his right knee up to his chest, and used both hands to grasp for his backup pistol. His left hand drew up his blood-spattered pant leg, and his other hand drew the firearm.

He fired upward in a circle, pulling the trigger rapidly, only loosely aiming at the chests of the men around him. Two staggered away and tried to bring their own weapons up, but Wes rose halfway from the trailer to aim with purpose.

The instant it was over, his breath escaped his body, and he fell out of the trailer. His firearm, now empty, slid from his fingers as he crumbled to the ground next to Valles. In Wes's haste, he'd accidentally or blindly shot Valles as well.

He had nothing left in his being, but Wes struggled to remain conscious. By lying limply on his left side, he could reach Valles, but there was no waking up the young man, his only ally within miles. In an hour, Valles and the others would wake up, and Wes would have achieved nothing but angering an already predatory foe. The Diablos, who still wore the black armbands, had made the Kindred their archenemy, as Valles had indicated, so Wes expected no mercy from this band.

But Wes remained conscious, and as the minutes ticked by, he began to wonder if he could tranquilize each of the Diablos once more, while he waited for Valles to regain consciousness. It was unlikely that Valles would wake up first, since there were other men present who had a greater body mass, and the tranq toxin would be metabolized by them faster than Valles would.

Although his handgun was empty, Wes was close enough to Valles that he could see his other two sidearms not far away. And the bullpup must've been near also, Wes thought, since Valles had held it in his hands before Wes had opened fire.

With a whimper, Wes pushed himself from his position on the ground, and rolled over partway toward Valles. Neither of his loaded sidearms were within reach yet, but he was closer. However, he didn't see a way to reach the nearest one without sitting up. That would require strain that could cause him to faint.

But he had to act now. He hadn't looked at his watch when he'd shot the seven men around him, so he wasn't sure how long he'd been lying on the ground, fighting unconsciousness. They could begin to wake up any minute, and Wes had nothing in his hands!

Now with a growl, he worked his right elbow underneath his body, then flung his left arm over Valles. At the same time, he fell on top of the young man, but now the nearest sidearm was only a couple of inches beyond his fingers.

The largest of the Diablos twitched, and the man's leg moved. Wes panted, trying to hyperventilate, which he knew would help numb his nerves against the pain. He lunged for the pistol, failed to reach it, and rocked back for another try.

The waking bandit sat up and blinked with bewilderment on his face. Wes stared at him, hoping the man would lay back down and sleep off his drowsiness. Instead, he turned his head and looked straight at Wes. Wes couldn't wait another breath. He lunged again, and his fingers grasped the barrel of the weapon. As his body slid sideways, he flipped the weapon and gripped it tightly, a feel he knew as well as his own hand.

While awkwardly leaning across Valles' body, Wes shot the waking Diablo in the chest. Anger first swept over the man's face, but then his jaw slackened, and he fell over.

Now with care, Wes eased himself over to lie flat on his back again, a position from which he could watch for any other Diablo to wake before Valles. As he lay there, waiting, he felt blood trickle past the tape on his thigh wounds. He'd lost so much blood. His clothes were soaked and smelly, and he knew if he didn't receive actual treatment within a few hours, he'd die.

Another Diablo woke, and when he managed to find his feet, Wes raised his weapon and fired. He did the same to two others before Valles stirred.

"Thank You, Lord," Wes mumbled when Valles sat up next to him.

"Again?" Valles groaned, tenderly feeling his chest. "I think you broke a rib with that one. You were so close."

"Sorry." Wes's voice was barely more than a breath. "Desperate. Couldn't take time to aim. Let's go, yeah?"

"You could've let me know your plan." Valles dusted off his clothes in the morning sunlight. "I had your guns. I could've helped."

"Still can. If they wake up, be ready." Wes felt tears roll from his eyes. "I'm spent, pal. Can we get to Sandburg now?"

"Yeah, I know where we are." Valles gently lifted Wes into the trailer. "We're about thirty minutes away, I think. You good?"

Wes tried to respond, but he had nothing left. So close to reaching Sandburg, he hoped he wasn't actually about to die. His eyes closed. The pain ebbed, as if his body was too tired to feel any longer. And he slept.

Wes blinked awake. The noise of children playing nearby wasn't an unwelcome sound. *He was alive!* The familiarity of the gym lodge made him smile. When he turned his head, he saw Mia's baby crib, but she wasn't in it. While unconscious, he'd been placed on Wynter's cot in the corner, where he'd once held vigil over her when she'd been close to death.

He lifted his bare arm to see an IV in his forearm, and sutures covering a shrapnel wound on his biceps. Judging by the pink appearance of the sore, he'd been asleep for three or four days.

With difficulty, he shifted his legs off the side of the cot and sat up. The floor, usually covered by sleeping bags, was picked up at the moment, so it was daytime. The sleeping bags were piled against the wall, and the partition that separated the Kindred of Nails' area from the rest of Sandburg's citizens concealed the rest of the gym's activities.

When he drew a blanket aside, he found that he wore no pants, and his wounds on both sides of his thighs had been stitched. The muscles had been torn worse in his right leg, where the deformed bullet had ripped at tissue, but whoever had doctored him seemed to have known their business.

"This is the first I've ever seen you lay around," a woman said as she approached. It was the den mother of the gym, the woman who'd acted as nurse for Wynter during and after her pregnancy.

Wes covered himself with the blanket and accepted a cup of tea from the woman.

"It's not by choice, I assure you." He smiled. "Is Wynter around?"

"She's seeing off the second wave of people heading up into the mountains. Ever since you and that Diablo came back, we've known the way was ready for everyone to start for Lune Lake. Jill is beside herself, though, that Chevy has died. Dalia's been talking about him as her father, moping around here like her life is over."

"Chevy's not dead!" Wes lifted his head from sipping the tea. "I left him in Lune Lake. We found someone who needed help, so I came back alone to let everyone know we found a good route."

"He's alive? Well, wait here!" The woman hustled away and out of sight beyond the partition.

Wes laughed at her words, wondering where she thought he would possibly go. It would be a week at least, he figured, before his legs would be strong enough to walk on.

Minutes later, Wynter ran into the gym with Mia in her arms, followed by Jill, Dalia, and Hoxborn, who still wore his faded cowboy hat. After several painful embraces, through which he suffered in silence, he told them the story of the adventure into the mountains and down into Lune Lake, and then his trek back alone, marking the trail as he returned.

"We've been suspicious of that kid called Valles," Hoxborn said, "because he brought you to us, wearing that black armband. But it's good to hear that he's trustworthy. He brought you back, after all, and he told us your message about the way being marked."

"As usual," Wynter said, holding his hand, "you've saved countless lives."

"You think Chevy will be okay until we get there?" Jill asked. "I wasn't even going to go if he had died on the way through the mountains."

"Yes, he'll be fine. He's getting the cabins ready for everyone to arrive." Wes smiled. "Imagine that! No more community lodges. A cabin for every family!"

"It'll be a month before you're ready to move around," Wynter said, placing Mia in her crib. "Will there be a place even left for us after all the others get there before us?"

"Chevy will save a cabin for us, I'm sure." Wes winked at Jill. "And he'll probably be looking around the resort for a chapel, too!"

"A chapel?" Dalia frowned. "What do we need a chapel for? I like the Bible studies we do without having to go anywhere."

"We can study the Bible anywhere we are," Wynter said with a smile, "but I think Wes is referring to a proper wedding."

Jill blushed, and Dalia immediately caught the implication. The father she thought she'd lost would soon be married to her mother. It would be final, and Wes chuckled as the three women quickly started to plan the whole ceremony. As they arranged the wedding and moved a little away from Wes's cot, Hoxborn stepped closer.

"I didn't know Chevy had even asked Jill to marry him," the man said. "We all figured he was going to, but I thought he left without asking her."

"He did leave without asking her." Wes laughed. "But now he *has* to!"

~ End of RESOLUTION Book Three ~

Bonus Chapter - Valles

Hernan Valles wiped at his teary eyes and chastised himself for being so weepy lately. It had started a month earlier, when he'd experienced Christ's forgiveness from sin. After ten years of shedding not a single tear, now it was almost a daily occurrence while praying or doing chores. He understood that Jesus Christ was softening his new heart, just like One-eyed Wes Trimble had promised—but this was ridiculous!

Far above the mountain homestead called Ant's Place, Hernan stood on a rocky cliff and gazed down at the weathered buildings. He didn't feel like he belonged anywhere now. Once, he'd been a murderous Diablo down in the valley, but God had given him this new heart. And after volunteering to help Anthony "Ant" Bartlik at their way-station in the Sierras, Hernan wasn't feeling like he belonged there, either.

"I was better off as a Diablo," he said to the blue sky. But the words were like poison from his lips, and he regretted them the next instant. "Help me, God. I don't belong in the valley anymore, and I'm a stranger up on this mountain. How do I fit into Your master plan that Wes was talking about?"

Hernan sat down on the cliff and watched the sun set. Wes was his only friend now, but Wes was still back in Sandburg, healing from being shot by none other than Hernan himself. It was too weird to Hernan that the man whom he'd shot had forgiven him—so much so that Hernan believed only God Himself could have managed such a friendship. Almost overnight, Wes had become like a father figure to him.

Arriving two days earlier at Ant's Place had been like arriving on a strange planet. Hernan could shoot a rifle to hunt deer and swing an axe to chop firewood, but he'd lived in the valley his whole life. The mountains and the forest were so strange. Ant and his wife, Liana, were already established in their cabin with their two boys. And what was Hernan? A somber bachelor, living in the tack shed next to the old saw mill.

With the last bit of light in the sky, Hernan decided he'd better head back to the cabin. He rose from the cliff and skirted the ridge to descend to the mill. Ant and Liana were hospitable, even cooking meals for him, but they weren't Christians yet, so Hernan had been reading his Bible privately, still learning what it meant to be a follower of God who had come in the flesh. He could hardly wait for Wes to come up the mountain after he healed up, and pass through Ant's Place. Hernan hoped the one-eyed man would stay at the way-station for a week to visit and answer questions about the Bible, before Wes and his family continued on to Lune Lake.

With only the moon to light his way through the forest, Hernan arrived at the old mining settlement in the dark, looking forward to whatever dinner Liana had planned. Chopping firewood in front of the house had been exhausting!

Praying to God up on the ridge had helped him sort through his emotions somewhat. Ant and Liana had lived up on the mountain for months, so of course they seemed to fit in better than he did. In time, he hoped he would feel welcome and useful, rather than just a stranger to whom Ant had to explain everything that needed to be done around the homestead.

Hernan stepped onto the porch of the little cabin in which the family of four lived. It overlooked the old saw mill, with a creek out back, and the road winding up the mountain on the opposite edge of the clearing.

The front door swung open, and Liana stepped outside as she dried her hands on a dish towel. Ant had fixed up a tank outside, which offered running water for the cabin.

"Oh, I thought you were Ant," she said, disappointment in her voice.

"I just came to pick up my plate." He leaned his rifle against the outside wall of the cabin. "I'll eat down in the shed tonight, so you guys can eat together for a change."

"But Ant's not back yet." Her face turned to the west. "I thought he might be with you, cutting wood for that new trough he wants to build."

Hernan followed her gaze. The forest seemed especially dark in that direction.

"Does he stay out late to work sometimes?" Hernan walked to the end of the porch, straining his ears for the sound of an axe in the distance. "I don't hear anything. It's too dark out there to be swinging an axe."

"Something's wrong." Liana glanced at his rifle. "He would never stay out like this. He said there's been signs of mountain lions and bears around. Do you think—?"

The two boys appeared behind their mother, and Hernan held up his hand to stop her.

"He was talking about a pine he's been working on across the creek." Hernan picked up his rifle. "Don't worry. I'm sure he's already on his way back. I'll find him."

He leaped off the porch, his stomach growling for food, but he was thankful he could offer his assistance to a family who seemed to have everything already. Wes had sent him up there to help Ant prepare the station for more refugees who were escaping the valley. Ant was so independent, but maybe that night, God meant to show how Hernan really did have a place on the mountain.

Anticipation more than dread filled Hernan's heart as he reached the creek. This was it! This was God already answering his prayer on the cliff. He could actually be of some use, even if it was just offering Ant a hand perhaps in dragging a deer back to the house.

After following the creek for a short way, he paused to listen to the forest. The pines creaked in the breeze, and the wind swished with a haunting sound he'd never heard down in the valley. And somewhere out there, bears and mountain lions lurked? Goosebumps swept over his skin.

"Hello!" Hernan called, partially for Ant, and partially to make enough noise to ward off any predators. "Anthony, are you out here? Anthony? Hello!"

He heard nothing but the wind and trees.

Pushing himself farther up the creek on his tired legs, he wondered how far away Ant had chosen to chop at intervals on a thick pine. Some trees were so thick, they would take a month or two for a single man to chop through, working a little each day.

Again, he stopped and yelled. This time, he could hear a dull thumping in the distance, like wood clapping against wood. The noise stopped, then started again.

"I'm coming!" Hernan shouted, and he splashed across the creek toward the sound. He ran almost carelessly in the dark, holding one hand out in front, and his rifle pointing ahead, charging through bushes and past tree branches that scratched at his face. "Hang on, Ant! Keep knocking! Tell me where you are!"

He stopped and listened, heard the noise closer, then ran to his left to a giant pine tree that lay across several rotting logs. He followed the tree down, feeling with his hand. After setting down his rifle, he used both hands.

Suddenly, his fingers brushed over fabric. He felt the long-john top Ant wore, then Ant's hand that was grasping a tree branch. Apparently, the noise had come from Ant hitting the tree with the club-like piece of wood. Ant let go of the branch and grasped at Hernan. Hernan climbed down into a crevice amongst earth, rotting logs, and the monstrous pine. Only when he felt Ant's face did Hernan know exactly where the rest of his body was positioned, and he put his head next to Ant's head.

"Pinned," Ant whispered. "Can't . . . breathe!"

Hernan needed to hear no more. Only by God's grace was the man still alive. The rotting logs had certainly cushioned the giant pine from crushing Ant, but if the tree settled any more, the little bit of life that remained would be . . .

Digging frantically, Hernan clawed all around Ant's upper body. Down in the gap below the pine, there was no moonlight, but he didn't need light to tear at rotten logs and moss and earth. His fingernails broke and splinters gouged his hands, but Hernan wasn't bothered by these minor wounds. He'd come to the mountain to help Ant, and if he hadn't been especially useful so far, all that was changing now. Failing this family wasn't an option. Maybe, he thought, this was God's whole point of Wes leading him to Christ and offering him the position at the homestead—to save Ant's life!

After digging around Ant's upper body, he made room for his hands to swipe at the earth and crumbling wood underneath Ant. The bark of the tree was pressing upon Ant's belly and lower ribs, hindering his breathing. Another hour in such a position, the man would've surely suffocated. Hernan couldn't allow that!

Under Ant's spine, Hernan tore at roots and soil, then shoveled rotting wood away from under Ant's hips. Finally, feeling all around and under Ant, there seemed to be enough room for an evacuation. Standing above the woodsman, Hernan took both of Ant's hands in his own and pulled, dragging his limp body out from under the pine.

But he didn't stop there. Hernan pulled the man clear of the pine, away from the torn ground, and closer to the bank of the creek. There, Hernan collapsed next to Ant, moonlight peeking through tree boughs as they panted together. Slowly, they recovered and both crawled to the creek where they could slurp at the water.

"I thought for sure I was a goner," Ant said, his voice hoarse as he sat on a grassy patch. "Thank you. I don't know what else to say right now."

"You would've done the same for me," Hernan said, shrugging.

"I'd be honored to do the same for you. If you wouldn't have been here, Liana couldn't have done what you just did. Another minute, I would've blacked out."

"Hey, maybe I'll fall a tree on myself someday, right?" he chuckled. "Then we'll call it even."

But Hernan realized Ant wasn't laughing at his joke, and his feeling of not belonging around the homestead returned.

"When I was lying under that tree," Ant said quietly, "I kept thinking about how Wes Trimble has tried to talk to me about God and life after death. And now you're here with your own Bible, and then you just saved me. It really makes you wonder, doesn't it?"

"About what?" Hernan was confused.

"What would've happened if I would've died just now?" He cleared his throat. "It makes me wonder if it's all true, like maybe you're even here according to God's plan."

"I'm only here because I became a Christian," Hernan admitted, "and because I wasn't feeling especially welcome back in Sandburg, since I used to be a Diablo bandit."

"Well, I probably haven't made you feel especially welcome here, either. It's strange having another man around. All that changes now." Ant offered his hand. "Come on. I think I can walk again."

Hernan took the man's hand, and they rose to their feet together.

"Nothing's broken? Your ribs?"

"No, just my ego. I should've been more careful."

They crossed the creek and angled toward the house, its light visible through one window beyond the trees.

"We should've been working together," Hernan said. "That's what I came here to do, not run off alone like I did when my chores were finished."

"Hey, from now on," Ant said, "we'll do these chores together. We'll get them done in half the time. Besides, it'll be safer having someone else nearby."

"I wouldn't mind that. It gets lonely chopping firewood all day."

"Well, by working together, you can tell me what you're learning in that Bible."

"Really? You want to hear?"

"I didn't think I did, but now I do. I need to know. There could be other trees, you know!"

They reached the porch, and Ant allowed Hernan to approach the door first. Long gone were any of his feelings of not belonging.

"I see what you mean now." Hernan placed his hand on the door knob, but didn't open it. "Wes has said that everything God allows to happen is for a reason. That tree on top of you gave me a chance to save your life, and it gave you a chance to think about God."

"You're right." Ant laughed. "It'll be hard to deny there's a God after tonight!

The two went into the cabin together, and Hernan now knew he had a purpose on that mountain. He finally belonged somewhere.

~ End of Bonus Chapter – Valles ~

D.I. Telbat

RESOLUTION BOOK FOUR

America's Last Days

D.I. Telbat

~*~

To those who remain,
even through the sacrifices.
The end is near!

Book Four, Prologue

Avery "Chevy" Hewitt frowned as the refugees poured through the trees and passed him at the Lune Lake Resort and Campground. After a two-week trek through the rugged Sierra Nevada Mountains, they'd finally arrived at the four lakes that made up the refuge. Instead of relief on their faces, Chevy saw mostly selfishness.

"Gently!" he called after several families who ran to the north toward a cracked highway along the pristine lake. "There are enough homes for everyone!"

"I don't think they're listening," Bill Jevans said from where he sat in his all-terrain wheelchair off the side of the trail. "What are we—invisible?"

The adults continued to jostle past one another, even elbowing each other as they sprinted for the choicest cabins, the number of which spanned for miles around. Of course, the families emerging from the mountain trail couldn't see anything but what lay within their sight, and those cabins were already claimed.

Two men threw punches as they moved beyond Chevy.

"Hey, take it easy, guys!" Chevy gasped, ran up to the refugees, and pulled them apart. "Your families are right here. What are you fighting for?"

"Back off, Chevy!" one of the men ordered, and shoved Chevy backward. "You may have called the shots back in the valley, but this is our home now."

"Fine, but there's no need to fight over the cabins." Chevy raised his empty hands to the men, hoping to show he meant them no harm, even though he carried his rifle on his back. "Bill and I have been getting all the homes ready for you guys. There are hundreds of cabins, houses, and apartments from here all the way up to the north end of Lune Lake."

The conversation was broken off as one of the fighting men turned and sprinted away, apparently hoping to get a jump on the next cabin before the others.

"Everyone's forgetting why we came here," Chevy said to Bill, moving out of the way as more families descended the mountain. "We've brought them here to get away from the violence in the valley. But it seems they've all brought it with them!"

"Not everyone," said a man named Rick Lusis, who offered his hand and a smile to Chevy. Chevy remembered the young man as a smart aleck back in Sandburg. He was barely in his twenties. "This place looks promising, huh? Plenty of hunting and fishing to get to?"

"It's good to see you, Rick." Chevy pumped the young man's hand, grateful to meet a friendly face. "What's with all the madness? Where's Wes Trimble?"

"He got into a scrape with the Diablos." Rick frowned, "But he's healing up, and he'll be bringing his family over the mountains soon. He left us a good trail marked the whole way."

"Well, go on and find yourselves a place to live," Chevy said to those who had stopped to listen to their conversation. "There's plenty of room for hundreds."

"Many of us would like to settle close to where you and Wes are living." Rick gestured to several other families at the back of the procession. "We've been talking about it while coming over the trail. Any cabins near you guys?"

"Really? You don't want a lakeside view like the rest of the people?" Chevy raised his eyebrows. "Wes and I and Bill here have chosen to stay back in the woods off to the south a little, and leave the lakeside places for you guys."

"We'd rather live near the Kindred," a stout young man added, whose wife was carrying an infant on her back. "Even if it means we're out in the forest a little ways."

Chevy couldn't remember all their names as they stepped closer, but he was thankful for their friendliness.

"Then head off to your right here." Chevy pointed south. "Move through the forest there, and you'll come across all kinds of cabins that are still open. We'd be glad to have good neighbors who care about each other."

The rest of the refugees coming off the mountain had the same notion, and they greeted Chevy and Bill with joy rather than bitterness.

"What a contrast!" Bill said once the last refugee had passed into the trees. "The first ones down the mountain didn't care at all what we've been doing for them, but the last ones down seemed to understand you've been busy for days preparing their homes for them."

"There's a spiritual lesson here, Bill. Come on." Chevy waved at Bill, and Bill carefully navigated his wheelchair down the bumpy trail. After recently breaking his back, the man was quickly growing accustomed to his new form of transportation. "Those who think only of themselves rush headlong forward, and they miss what's important. But those who take their time and humbly proceed will find what's really valuable."

"And what's really valuable nowadays?" Bill asked.

"Well, in this case, good neighbors!" Chevy chuckled. "Those who came down first with greed and anger will finish last when it comes to finding good neighbors. But those who came down last with gratitude and consideration for others, they'll finish first."

"I see. You're talking about a Bible lesson. The last will be first." Bill laughed. "See? I'm reading that Bible, too. Now, why couldn't I have figured out that principle from what just happened?"

"You will in time, especially once Wes returns." Chevy held back a tree branch for Bill to pass. "His cabin isn't far from yours. His insight into God's wisdom for everyday life will rub off on you naturally. That's what having good neighbors is all about."

Bill moved down the trail in front of Chevy, but Chevy paused and looked back at the mountain, a little sadness piercing his heart. He'd hoped to see Wes with the refugees. Chevy didn't mind serving the new residents of Lune Lake, but Wes was the one who had a sense of authority and management that was apparently needed to keep the peace in the new community.

There were certain to be struggles ahead, and the refugees didn't seem like they were off to a good start. Well, some of them were, he reflected. That was something to build on. A few good neighbors in that day and age needed to be appreciated!

Chapter 1

One-eyed Wes Trimble ran with his axe down the wooded trail, Avery "Chevy" Hewitt a few steps behind him. Their afternoon of cutting firewood had been interrupted by gunfire. It was common to hear an occasional gunshot around the Lune Lake Resort community since several hunters kept the people fed with deer in the area. But these gunshots hadn't come from the wooded mountainside. They had come from the inhabited area along Lune Lake Loop.

The summer was nearly finished on the east slope of the Sierra Nevada Mountains. After healing from bullet and shrapnel wounds in Sandburg, Wes had hiked the mountain roads and passes with Wynter to reach Lune Lake, the wilderness refuge that he and Chevy had discovered months earlier. Since finding a safe route through the mountains, over two hundred men, women, and children had made the trek, settling in the dozens of cabins, lodges, and campgrounds around two of the four lakes.

"Let me take point, Wes," Chevy urged as he jogged past Wes on the trail.

Wes didn't argue with him. Chevy was clutching a battle rifle, while Wes only carried one sidearm on his belt. Since they'd been out in the woods cutting firewood for a harsh winter ahead, they hadn't been prepared for any kind of gun battle.

Chevy easily outdistanced Wes as they drew closer to Yost Creek Trailhead. Although Wes's injuries had healed, the strength in his legs hadn't returned completely. Daily, Wes was reminded of the hard life he'd lived, often punishing his body for the safety of others.

Skirting a small meadow, Wes paused to locate Chevy ahead. He found him against a thick pine tree, peeking at the cluster of two-room cabins along the Lune Lake Loop. Chevy's bullpup was aimed toward the cabins, but Wes saw nothing moving ahead. As he eased up behind Chevy, he rested a hand on the younger man's shoulder.

"Anything?" Wes whispered, trying to catch his breath.

"No movement. The girls are at home, right?"

"Yeah, doing laundry, trying out that new washboard."

Wes moved to the other side of the tree and watched the adjacent cabins that he and Chevy had moved into with their families. Since Chevy had married Jill, he lived in one cabin with her and teenager, Dalia, and young Elio. Next door, Wes had made a pleasant home with Wynter and their seven-month-old baby, Mia. The rest of the cabins nearest theirs had been occupied by other Christian families, specifically the five Kindred of Nails foresters and riflemen.

"They weren't rifle shots," Wes said. "And I know the sound of a pistol. Two shots, and if my ears aren't playing tricks on me, I'd say the shots came from farther to the east, near the old ticket office."

"Okay, let's go," Chevy said. "I'll lead."

Like the selfless man Chevy had become, he moved into the clearing around the cabins, apparently willing to risk his life before he allowed Wes to risk his own. Wes jogged to the left, his sidearm held with both hands, ready to cover Chevy. Movement at his cabin brought Wes to a stop, but Chevy kept moving to the east. Wynter, standing against the door, signaled him with a nod. She held up a battle rifle for Wes to grab as he continued past her. When he glanced back, she had leveled another bullpup toward the highway, but was remaining at the cabin. Someone had to stay around the cabins to watch over the Kindred women and children. And she knew how to use the specialized guns.

As Wes hustled to catch up to Chevy, the other Kindred men materialized from their own cabins—five experienced shooters who were prepared to defend the community from danger as well. The five men were younger, but they had expressed their zeal for Christ in prayer meetings and fellowships since arriving in Lune Lake. Three other Kindred men and their families had volunteered to remain in Sandburg as peacekeepers and guides between Lune Lake and Sandburg, where families continued to arrive from the Central Valley. Soon, the snow would fall, and passage would be impossible over the mountains, but until then, the Kindred remained available to serve.

Wes crossed Lune Lake Loop, the two lanes of pavement littered from a year of neglect, and followed Chevy along the road toward Yosemite Gateway Chalet. A crowd was now visible through the sparse trees, and Wes signaled with two fingers to the other men he'd trained himself. The five split into two parties to set up a perimeter.

The crowd parted as Wes and Chevy pushed themselves through the group of familiar faces. But the familiar faces were anything but smiling and joyful that day, as they'd previously been since they'd found a safe home for their families. After all, Wes and Chevy had risked their lives to bring them there.

At the front of the group outside the chalet with a steeply-pitched roof, Wes came upon Matthias Seaver's frowning face. The man in his fifties held a firearm in his hand, and at the sight of Wes, he smiled and holstered the weapon in a polished holster.

"I knew a couple of gunshots would bring you all here!" Matthias Seaver said for the crowd. "I've come for a reason, so listen up!"

Wes and Chevy exchanged glances, and crossed their arms to listen. This wasn't the first time Matthias had inserted himself into community life there. He'd actively opposed Chevy's leadership role upon the arrival of the first refugees to Lune Lake. When Chevy had claimed the southern cabins for the Kindred, Matthias had led dozens of families farther north to the Village beyond the ski resort, to separate themselves from Chevy. Matthias hadn't hidden his disdain for Christians, and those who had accompanied him to settle around the Village and Lune Lake Hotel seemed to share similar sentiments.

"We should tranquilize him right now," Chevy mumbled under his breath to Wes. "Any time he comes down here to Reverse Creek, nothing good happens."

Wes didn't respond, but he did share Chevy's frustration. Matthias had tried to unite other settlers around himself—families that had sided with the Kindred through the dispute against them. But Matthias was a manipulator, and he knew how to draw crowds, as he had that day, and there was little Wes could do but to listen along with everyone else.

"An army that numbers in the thousands is on their way here!" Matthias yelled, which caused the crowd to murmur and shift their feet in uncertainty. A baby started to cry. "They've been spotted out on Highway 395. They're coming up from Las Vegas. You can imagine, it's been a long march for them through the desert. And they want what we've worked hard to build for ourselves all summer! They'll try to take what we've united to preserve. I will not allow it! You can't allow it! We must gather our arms and ambush them before they ambush us in our beds! We have rifles. We have handguns. Yes, there's not many of us, but we can get prepared, and we can catch them by surprise. If we strike them hard enough, they might just return to Vegas, and our lives will be spared!"

"How could we fight an army that's thousands strong, Matthias?" an older man asked. He'd shown interest in reading the Bible, and Wes had spoken to him weekly, sharing with him the truth of God's message. "We don't have more than fifty shooters among us, between you guys at the Village and us here on the south end. Most of us have never seen any kind of action. That's why we followed the Kindred here."

"We all came through Sandburg," Matthias continued. "You saw how Hoxborn organized that town and the Diablos left us alone. We all stood on the wall. We need to do that here. Each one of us needs to take up arms to defend what we have built. Lune Lake is ours now, and no one is going to threaten my family!"

The crowd nodded, shouted their agreement, and several raised their fists to show their assent.

"The only question is," Matthias glared firmly at Wes, "will you Kindred stop us from our right to protect ourselves? Listen to me, everyone! Anyone who doesn't stand with our families is against our families. Anyone who is afraid of destroying an enemy bent on destroying us—those people must leave Lune Lake right now, for they're worse than the invaders trying to slaughter us! If they want peace with the invaders, then they can go back to Sandburg. Let them know you'll have no more of their control over our lives! We need a firm hand today! Our families' lives are being threatened. Who will stand with me? Will you fight for your families? Will you help me attack the invaders, to protect what's ours? Who's with me?"

The people started to cheer, but Chevy elbowed away from the press of the people and turned around to face the crowd. Wes noticed a sinister smile on Matthias' face because he'd successfully stirred up the people that Wes called his neighbors, but Wes knew Chevy wouldn't allow the man's words to go unchallenged.

"Listen, listen, my friends!" Chevy raised both arms, like the street preacher Wes knew he'd been after leaving prison. "You know me as Chevy. I've chopped firewood for you. I've brought you meat and fish. I helped you settle into your new homes. Wes and I and the other Kindred have assured your safety over the mountains, and we've promised to help you remain safe while you live here. So far, between the Southern Loop and the Village community, we are only two hundred people. There are cabins, rooms, and campsites for several thousands of people up and down this canyon, all along the Loop. Why would we rush to slaughter additional settlers when we don't even know who they are yet?"

"Matthias said they're an army!" a man in the crowd responded. "We have to kill them before they kill us!"

"We don't have to kill anyone!" Chevy insisted, although the crowd's noise was beginning to grow. "They may just be families who are looking to settle peacefully next to us. There's lots of room here. The forests will provide wood to burn through the winter, and the wildlife and fishing—it can support an entire town, not just the few of us who've arrived first!"

"What if they're violent?" Matthias proposed, his hands on his hips. "What if they don't want to talk? What if they're angry about marching through the desert, and they want our cabins without discussion? What will we do then? Will we tranquilize them to sleep for a few minutes? That's what the Kindred want to do!"

"We can't make decisions on a bunch of what-ifs!" Chevy yelled to the crowd. "Don't make rash decisions based on your fear. Listen! Wes and I promise to go meet with whoever may be coming up the highway from Vegas, and we'll find out their intentions. We can let them know that we're a peaceful people, and we'd like to welcome others who are willing to live peacefully beside us."

"We can't risk our families!" Matthias turned on Chevy directly. "Would you risk our families for your religious nonsense, Chevy? Sure, you and Wes brought us over the mountains, but you're not in charge of us now. We need to protect ourselves against the threat that's swarming up the highway. They're as many as the locusts, I tell you! They'll rape the land and kill our children! Unless we push back right now! Today! We have to set off to meet them immediately, or we'll all suffer! Who will stand with me and defend our wives and daughters? Or will you welcome the devils from Vegas to become your neighbors? Because that's what Chevy is proposing for the Kindred! We have worked for what we have. Will we allow it to be stolen by strangers?"

The frenzy of the crowd turned after Matthias, and there seemed no further response that Chevy could give effectively. Wes guessed that Matthias had instigated the crowd to some degree before he and Chevy had arrived from the woods. It had been an ambush of sorts against the Kindred, against Christians, and ultimately against Jesus Christ.

"He's got them too worked up," Chevy said sadly when he and Wes moved away from the crowd. The other five Kindred walked up to join them. "You think we need to worry about our families?"

"Matthias is trying to set the people against us," Wes said, "but I don't think that's his most pressing move right now. He's got them focused on this band of Vegas travelers, if it's actually real. Afterward, he may try to turn on us personally, which won't go well for him."

"This is ridiculous," one of the other Kindred men said. "There's hardly a woodsman or hunter among them. They've been fishing from Lune and Gull Lakes since they came to the area. What do they think they'll do against an army coming from Vegas?"

"I doubt it's an army," Wes said. "They're probably just refugees looking for a safe place to raise their families, like the rest of us. But Matthias has them fearful now, because he's afraid, and people do strange things when they're afraid."

"I don't think my words helped anything," Chevy said, frowning.

"Sometimes we just need to take a stand," Wes said, "even when we know it won't change hearts on the spot."

"I volunteered us to go up the highway to see what all the fuss is about," Chevy said, raising his eyebrows. "Was that premature of me?"

"Finding out the truth of the situation is the wisest thing we can do for ourselves." Wes eyed each of the other Kindred. They were young, but he'd recruited them personally, and each man had professed their dependence upon Christ. Along with that profession, they'd become Kindred only by their understanding that, as Christians, they would carry a battle rifle to preserve life, not to take life, for the sake of Christ. "While we're gone, you five will need to continue gathering wood for the winter. Quite a few families still need more firewood stacked."

"You mean get firewood for the families who just turned their backs on us?" one Kindred man asked. His name was Rick Lusis, a red-headed young man whose tongue was a little loose while in private, but he seemed loyal to a biblical testimony of Jesus Christ.

"Yes, I mean exactly these families who've just rejected us," Wes stated, following his words with his one-eyed stare to enforce his words. "We don't push them away just because they've pushed us away. Our love for them isn't conditional upon their friendliness or cowardice. It's not even our job to be their governing body here in Lune Lake. It's our job to represent Christ here, and that means we look out for our neighbors, even when our neighbors are headed down a bad path. We'll keep them alive through the winter by hunting and chopping firewood, even if they keep hating us by the poisoned words of Matthias. The seven of us need to remember what we've all agreed to as Christians. Our faith in God transcends anything else happening right now. Agreed?"

Chevy nodded his approval, but the others affirmed verbally. And Wes saw in their faces certain resolve.

"Let's pray about this right now," one of the Kindred said. His name was Oliver Newlander, a close friend to Rick Lusis. Oliver liked to hike and climb the rugged mountains around Carson Peak. He started praying as the men gathered closer together, shoulder-to-shoulder in a tight circle, their rifles pointed at the ground.

His prayer was brief, but Wes knew the young man's words represented all of their hearts, and he was honored to stand beside them. Only their faith in God would carry them through the animosity from their neighbors and the potential persecution they were about to receive.

Oliver accepted Wes's commission to organize the other four Kindred into relay teams so they could continue to accomplish their work, though also remain ready to respond to a crisis. As the five set off to see to their duties, Wes and Chevy returned to their cabins to gear up for their hike south.

As Wes packed, Wynter questioned his hasty response to Matthias' seemingly baseless words.

"How do we know what he's saying is even true?" Wynter asked. "An army? How would he know that? We all know the Village community that has gathered around Matthias hardly even leaves their beach-front residences. And they're going to fight off some sort of attacking force?"

"I'm figuring a traveler or two might've arrived at Lune Lake." Wes loaded two battle rifle magazines with gel-tranqs. "Matthias wasn't too interested in sharing how he got his intel at his little meeting. He was more interested in turning public opinion against us, and slaughtering whoever is coming up the highway."

"What if we really do need the whole community to stand with us, though?" Wynter handed him a bundle with two days' worth of unleavened cakes. "We stood with the Town of Sandburg, and they had lethal weapons. We had to stand together or the Diablos would've overrun the town. How is this different?"

"I highly doubt we're dealing with the Diablos here, for one." Wes tested the weight of his pack. He hadn't carried a heavy pack since he'd come over the mountains four months earlier. "And for two, we never approved of the way Hoxborn wanted to kill the Diablos. We did our best to lead Sandburg in a way that would arrive at a peaceful resolution with the Diablos, and the townspeople saw us as an asset. Matthias is trying to snuff us out simply because we're interested in the peace of Jesus Christ. This is a spiritual war, and we need to proceed accordingly."

She embraced him, then held him at arm's length, looking him in the face. Tenderly, she tucked some of his hair under his eyepatch strap.

"Come back safely," she said softly, then smiled and patted his cheek. "If you don't come back, I won't know what to do with your extra eyepatches. There's no other one-eyed mountain men around here that would want them."

He laughed heartily, then covered his mouth when he realized he'd disturbed Mia's mid-morning nap. The baby fussed a moment before settling back to sleep. Wes turned his back to Wynter so she could help him into the pack straps.

"We shouldn't be more than two days, depending on how long it takes us to find whoever Matthias says is coming up the desert highway."

"I'll be praying night and day."

He kissed Wynter goodbye and stepped off the porch to find Chevy exiting his own cabin, with Jill wiping her eyes over his departure. Teenager Dalia was standing inside the doorway, a begging look on her face, having probably just asked to come with them. But Wes knew Chevy would've turned her down. A gunfight might be coming, and that was no place for a young woman.

Chevy carried his battle rifle across his chest and set a fast pace for them toward the east. From the pine needle-strewn road, Wes stopped and turned to look back at the cabins. Wynter stood on their porch. It was possibly the last time they ever looked upon one another—on earth, anyway. She waved and he waved back, then marched after Chevy.

Nearest the highway, Bill Jevans pushed his all-terrain wheelchair up to Wes's side, easily keeping pace.

"Anything you want me to take care of while you're gone?" asked the Lune Lake maintenance man. While Chevy had been alone with the injured man for a few weeks, they'd worked together to find an old wheelchair frame, then attached all-terrain bicycle wheels to the front and back tire rims. "It's getting a little late in the year to be receiving a bunch of visitors out here."

"What about all the cabins and lodges over by Silver Lake?" Wes asked.

Together, Wes and the wheelchair-bound man passed the cabin nearest the highway where a wheelchair ramp had been constructed to access the porch. Bill lived in the cabin alone, but an older Christian couple from Sandburg, who'd lost a son of their own, had made Bill their responsibility, looking in on him daily.

"Only a couple families have settled over there," Bill said. "You want me to get things ready for newcomers?"

"Would you please?" Wes shifted his rifle to his left hand and set his hand on Bill's shoulder. "We don't know exactly how many are coming, but it'd be good to have a Christian's friendly face here to welcome them, especially since Matthias is stirring up people against them."

"It's the least I could do. You guys opened my eyes to Christ. Why shouldn't I open the door for others, right?"

"God's made you a good man, Bill." Wes smiled down at the civilian Chevy had led to Christ months earlier. "God must have a sense of humor to use cripples like us to help others who think they've got it all together, huh?"

Bill chuckled and pushed his wheelchair around Wes.

"I'll make sure there's firewood ready for whoever shows up, Wes."

"See you soon!" Wes waved, then hustled to catch up to Chevy to share what Bill was doing for them. "Even in that wheelchair, he's still the most dependable man to get this place ready for newcomers."

"I explored the Silver Lake campgrounds while he and I were alone out here," Chevy said. "There are some sturdy buildings that Bill had boarded up in that area, just waiting for permanent residents. As far as I know, no one's even fishing in that lake or hunting the woods west of Rush Creek."

"Now, all we have to do is fill those places up." Wes nodded resolutely at Chevy, who scoffed.

"Yeah, easier said than done with Matthias rounding up everyone to keep new folks out."

"Come on. This isn't the first time the Kindred have been outnumbered and outgunned."

"You're right, but Matthias has his heart set on slaughtering a bunch of innocent people, and getting rid of us!"

"I've learned to enjoy it when God disappoints people who intend ill will towards us. Haven't you?"

As the two men walked down the Lune Lake Loop, they reached Gill Lake and the Golden Pine RV Park where abandoned vehicles had been inhabited by Sandburg residents. A general store sat beyond the RV Park, along with a hardware store, sport and tackle shops, automotive shops, and numerous houses, apartments, and cabins. In the months during which the approximate one hundred people had made the Village their home, two horses had been rounded up. It was these poor beasts that were now the object of Matthias' attention.

"They can carry more!" Matthias guided several men with packs in their arms. "They don't have to carry it far, just down to Lune Lake Junction. That's where we'll make our stand! Go ahead, put another pack onto each horse. We don't want to carry our own gear down there."

Wes intended to walk past the crowd gathering for the ambush against the Vegas travelers, but Matthias noticed the two Kindred men moving up the highway. The balding man adjusted his glasses, left the loading of ammunition and arms to his lieutenants, and walked briskly out to the highway. A few yards away, Matthias drew a handgun.

"Where do you two think you're going?" Matthias shouted. "Hey, I'm talking to you, Wes Trimble!"

Though they didn't slow their march, Wes saw that Chevy was adjusting the bullpup in his hands.

"You know what Titus would do in this situation," Chevy said.

"What?" Wes gasped. "You can't be serious! Don't do it, Chevy. I don't think Matthias would actually shoot us, do you?"

"Look at them! They're getting ready for war, Wes. We may as well slow him down for an hour."

"It's just asking for trouble," Wes said, raising his rifle. "But he's asking for it already."

Wes shot Matthias in the thigh. The man's face twisted into a snarl for an instant before he slumped unconsciously to the ground. His gun clattered across the pavement. The soldiers Matthias had gathered stared passively at the two Kindred. Chevy and Wes stood prepared for a heightened confrontation, but no one ran to Matthias' side.

"You're all so swift to draw blood," Wes called to the forty men. "You forget that when you were in need of a safe residence for your own families, others helped you. Now, at the moment others need that same welcome, you are listening to this man who wants to kill people who need you!"

A tall, slender man who was often at Matthias' side, stepped away from the others.

"You can't tranquilize all of us, Wes! We're just protecting our homes. If you get in our way again, I'll kill you myself!"

"Wes," Chevy said softly, "let's just go."

"I'm going." Wes walked away with Chevy, both men keeping their rifles ready until they'd passed beyond the lot. "It did feel good to shut Matthias' mouth for a little while, though."

"Maybe not everything Titus would do in our situation is going to work for us."

"You're right. We should focus more on aiding whoever's coming to us, instead of hindering whoever's against us."

"Now, you're sounding more like Corban Dowler," Chevy said.

"I'll take that as a compliment!" Wes laughed, trying to keep his heart light with optimism, but he felt a rising dread of conflict. It was hard to focus on doing right when so many were focused on doing evil.

Chapter 2

Long before Wes and Chevy reached Lune Lake Junction, they turned southeast to climb the rocky ridge, which was interspersed with a variety of pine trees. The ridge rose abruptly and steeply, but ascending took only thirty minutes. At the top of the bluff, they found a view of the east through the trees toward the White Mountains and the desert. Chevy used a powerful telescope to study Route 395.

"The shortest route from Vegas is to come up the 95," Wes said, rehearsing the map from memory, "then hooking over to the 395 at Big Pine."

"Big Pine's miles away," Chevy said, "but there's definitely something closer to us than Big Pine out there. And it's moving slowly up the highway. I can see colors—a stream of humanity, as wide as the highway. Definitely coming this way."

"ETA?" Wes asked.

"They won't reach this far by nightfall, I'm guessing." Chevy checked his watch, then the sun overhead. "I figure they'll reach the Junction before noon tomorrow."

"Okay, that means they'll be camping down there somewhere tonight. We have time to talk to them."

"Yeah, but it also gives Matthias time to dig in to fight it out around the Junction." Chevy surveyed the ridge. "We could bring the people up through here, over the ridge, and cut past the Junction altogether."

"Can you imagine women and children and elderly people climbing up those rocks?" Wes shook his head. "Even if we did side-step Matthias' ambush, there would still be a face-off, I'm afraid. No, there's no shortcut to avoid what we have to do. If these two sides don't want peace, there'll be war."

"Well, Matthias has overestimated his own forces." Chevy raised the scope to his eyes again. "Even if the guy does set a trap for these newcomers, I'm looking at about five hundred people, front to back, give or take a hundred."

"We know Matthias has no military background, so it's no wonder he doesn't understand what he's about to do with only forty men." Wes started down the southern slope. "Come on. The sooner we can talk to the travelers, the sooner we can give them time to think about how they can do their part to keep the peace."

"Are you thinking there might be a compromise?" Chevy followed Wes down, knocking small rocks loose that tumbled past Wes. "People have so little nowadays, they're usually not willing to give away anything that could be a peace offering. At least with the Diablos, we had a few weeks to instill some moral reflection. We have one day, no more, before the Junction becomes a battlefield. What do you think will work?"

"I don't know, yet." Wes stepped down the rocks carefully, his heavy pack making every movement more precarious. "If there are any Christians in that bunch, it'll make our job easier. But we won't know which direction to encourage them until we get a little more intel. It'll take a miracle, though. This isn't something you and I are going to be able to fashion."

"An act of God?" Chevy whistled. "I like the sound of that!"

"But even acts of God aren't without danger to His people. Peace is sometimes costly, as you know. And we'll be the ones who may have to pay that cost."

When the two men reached the valley floor, they walked up the highway side-by-side in silence. Wes didn't ask what Chevy was thinking about, but Wes was reviewing the Bible's record of God's feats through His people when challenges seemed unsurmountable for them. It gave Wes hope, even inspiration, to know how His God had moved powerfully in the face of opposition. Trials and tests weren't removed from the lives of Christians, Wes knew well enough. But God promised to remain in the midst of the test, molding and refining for the outcome He desired. It wasn't comfortable in the flesh to be walking toward hundreds of possibly armed people that afternoon, but on the spiritual side, Wes felt perfect peace. He wasn't alone. He wasn't powerless. He wasn't afraid.

Before sundown, the approaching caravan of travelers stopped and made camp. Wes and Chevy walked within two hundred yards and paused to study the people as they gathered desert twigs for fires, and erected tents and lean-tos. About half of the adults carried rifles, which came to be about two hundred and fifty armed fighters, by Wes's calculations. He shared his estimate with Chevy.

"I don't even have that much ammunition on me," Chevy said, perhaps intending it as a joke, but Wes was merely reminded that they had never faced a fighting force that strong. "Maybe they'll invite us to join them for dinner."

"Like I said earlier, let's pray there are some Christians in this bunch."

As they continued to walk closer, the travelers noticed them, and an armed band of twenty stern-faced riflemen positioned themselves across the road from one ditch to the other. The milling about of hundreds of family members in the back was hushed, and Wes felt all eyes upon himself and Chevy. They drew up within a dozen paces, very aware that too many gun muzzles were pointing at them to survive even a brief shootout.

A light-haired man in his forties took his stance in the center behind the wall of shooters. Wes recognized a leader when he saw one. The man held a hunting rifle with no scope, and he had steady eyes that didn't blink as long as Wes looked at him.

"Where are our men?" the stern man demanded, his gravelly voice matching his daring glare.

Wes was instantly unbalanced by the question, and he felt Chevy glance at him with uncertainty as well. In a second of reflection, Wes made sense of the situation. Matthias Seaver had known about the approaching travelers from Vegas because this man had sent scouts ahead, which apparently Matthias had abducted and held, maybe even tortured for information. Now these people wanted to know what had happened to their scouts.

"That's what we're here to talk to you about," Wes offered, and slung his rifle over his shoulder in an attempt to diffuse the tension. At his side, Chevy did likewise. "My name is Wes Trimble, and this is Chevy. We've come to welcome you to Lune Lake. There's plenty of housing available for everyone here, but we have unrest among our own people who don't want you here. If you'll allow Chevy and I to escort—"

"There will be no negotiations until our men are returned!" the stern man shouted, maybe intending his own people to hear his declaration more than Wes. "We've survived this far by standing together. And I assure you, Wes and Chevy, that we will stand again, even if we have to wipe out everyone at Lune Lake to win back our men."

"Chevy and I don't have your men," Wes stated. "Your ultimatums are wasted on us. Until this very second, we didn't realize the frightened people up at Lune Lake had taken captive of some of your people. How many did you send?"

"Two men, two of our best!" The leader passed smoothly through his line of shooters to draw closer to Wes. The man had a way of moving that reminded Wes of Titus—like a cat. "According to the map, we're just a couple hours from Lune Lake Loop. I suggest you take the night hours to return to your friends and bring us our men. If they aren't returned to us by the time we reach the lake, we won't expect hospitality, and you won't need to expect friendly visitors. We'll kill you all!"

Wes sighed with frustration, hearing the same attitude from this man as he had from Matthias.

"Can we lower our guns and speak about this like civilized men?" Wes asked. "We came out here to welcome you, sir, and to help you settle along the shores of—"

"Your welcome is a lie as long as you hold two of our men against their will!" the man accused.

"Stand down!" a loud voice boomed from the crowd of standing families. The wide frame of a dark-haired man shouldered past several riflemen and approached the defenders. "I said, stand down!"

Regardless of the tense moment, Wes smiled at the sight of a familiar face. It was Oleg Saratov! Chevy ignored the danger that faced him and went forward to embrace the big-shouldered Russian—Titus Caspertein's most loyal companion. They slapped each other on the back in the middle of the line of shooters, which seemed to cause the steely-eyed leader to question his aggressiveness.

"You know these men?" the leader asked Oleg.

Wes shook Oleg's hand, but the hearty COIL operative pulled Wes into a bear-hug.

"Yes, Kevin, I know these men. They are God's men, servants of Jesus Christ. Whatever the problem is, I'm sure we can figure it out. As a friend of mine would say, it ain't easy trusting new faces nowadays, but that doesn't mean it's impossible. Wes Trimble, meet Kevin Avon, trail master of this rabble."

Reluctantly, Kevin Avon accepted Oleg's word and agreed to sit on the highway pavement for a brief conversation that didn't require gun muzzles pointing at each other's faces. Briefly, Oleg shared with Wes and Chevy that he'd joined a small caravan from San Diego that was heading north on Interstate 15. Eventually, they'd joined the larger Vegas caravan that was led by Kevin Avon.

"I've got fifteen more battle rifles for you," Oleg stated in confidence to Wes, "and several thousand rounds of gel-tranqs. Titus figured you could use a little resupply, but I think he really sent me up here to find out how his sister, the baby, and you boys are making out."

Although the rifles had been lowered, Avon was flanked by three heavily-armed soldiers when he sat and faced Wes, who was flanked by Oleg and Chevy. Slowly, Wes explained the Lune Lake situation, how Lune Lake and Silver Lake areas were already settled, though only slightly, but that Grant Lake and Silver Lake campgrounds, lodges, and cabins were all available.

"My family, and the Kindred families I've described," Wes said, "will be your closest neighbors along the Lune Lake Loop Road, which is five miles end to end. If you would agree to settle on the far side of the canyon, we can meanwhile make peace with Matthias Seaver, as soon as he sees there's no threat from you all. There are plenty of resources for five times your number for years to come."

Avon had listened quietly and thoughtfully, and now it was his turn to respond. Wes prayed for sound reason from the man, who was certainly under pressure to recover his missing scouts.

"I'm not a Christian," Avon said. "I have nothing against you, but I'm not bound by any ideals regarding the moral or supernatural. Your friend Oleg has been an asset to our group since we left Vegas—hunting and helping. But he isn't one of us. My only objective is to preserve the lives of my people, and I will do that at any cost. This Matthias Seaver fellow has kidnapped two of our own. That can't be forgiven. It can't be allowed. Swift justice will follow, unless our two men are immediately returned unharmed. I have nothing against whatever few Kindred people you belong to, unless you get in our way while we're recovering our two men."

"Well," Wes said slowly, "would you at least accept my offer of the residential territory around Grant and Silver Lakes? It's the largest tract of land in the whole canyon area, and it's being prepared for your arrival as we speak."

"It sounds acceptable," Avon said, "if it's everything you say it is. But my people aren't willing to settle into new homes while our two men are still missing. I can't stress to you the willingness we all have to fight for their recovery. The mere fact that some people already in Lune Lake would kidnap strangers makes me want to remove them once and for all, anyway. I assure you: you may see families in our band here, but the men are hearty. We've survived hundreds of conflicts already, and we won't rest until all of our men are safely returned. Take that back to your Lune Lake community. My original statement stands. By tomorrow, when we reach Lune Lake, we either fight to the death, or we move into our new homes."

"Kevin," Oleg said, "I'd like to return to Lune Lake with these men tonight. I may be able to influence this Matthias character against further nonsense. And maybe with my help, we can recover the scouts you sent. I know them both, and they are good men."

"If you three fail to get them back," Avon said, his voice as firm as ever, "don't get in my way, Oleg. Don't defend them, or you'll be killed along with them."

Wes looked at Oleg, who had once been an Interpol agent, before joining COIL. The Russian had as much experience at high tension moments as Wes, but in that moment, Oleg visibly struggled to contain himself. Finally, he seemed to settle on the right words.

"I'm with the Kindred now," Oleg said in a low voice. "We don't take the side of one man's conflict over another. We take the side of Jesus Christ, and that means we're interested in preserving all life—yours and that of Matthias."

"Oleg speaks for us all," Wes said. "We're here to help resolve this situation, and to direct everyone to live peacefully. Ideally, we would remind you and your people that God Almighty is calling upon you to bring Him into your considerations, but we're all humbled in different ways and at different times to accept or reject His hand of care."

"Don't use this moment to try to convert me," Avon said coolly. "I'm from Vegas, and not the law-abiding quarter of the city. If your God knows about me, I assure you, He wants nothing to do with the likes of me. And I want nothing to do with the likes of Him. Oleg, I hope you're able to take care of this. Otherwise, stay out of my way tomorrow."

With that, Avon rose to his feet and walked away. His gunmen closed as a wall of fierceness, barring Wes, Chevy, and Oleg from mingling again with the caravan.

"For some reason," Wes said to his two companions, "I don't think we're camping here tonight."

"I suddenly regret packing such a heavy pack," Chevy said as he climbed to his feet, pulling Wes up with him.

"This is me." Oleg gestured to a trailer with two knobby bicycle tires attached to the back. "I pulled it behind my bicycle until my bike broke down. I can adjust the balance. Throw your packs on top and let's get going."

Wes didn't need to be told twice. Oleg's gear was contained in a soft-framed crate, which was large enough to carry fifteen bullpups, ammunition, and his own gear.

"Where was this invention when I pedaled out of San Diego last year?" Wes joked.

The three men started up the desert highway, pulling the trailer by hand in the dark, while behind them, Kevin Avon's caravan sat down at their campfires and war rallies. Wes passed out flat cakes to his two friends as Oleg shared the latest news from San Diego.

"Young Levi just keeps growing," Oleg said. "He and Titus have gone with Annette to the east side of the city to help settle new refugees from Arizona. I guess those people thought coming to the coast would be safer or calmer. It's safer in some respects, since the Brogdons have been using their military command to keep some law and order. There was another Meridia Virus outbreak in El Cajon over the winter after you two left, but we were able to contain it. Thirty people died, so the fear of the contagion started all over again."

Wes changed the subject to the challenge ahead, guessing they had two hours before they would reach the ridge and Lune Lake Junction.

"What are the chances that Matthias will give us the two scouts?" Chevy asked. "After we tranquilized him to shut him up earlier today, he probably won't be in a giving mood."

"I'm open to suggestions," Wes said, looking forward to the forest and the nearness of his family.

"If Matthias really is setting up an ambush at the Junction," Chevy said, "he probably isn't holding the two scouts there with him. I say we go get the scouts by covert force, and try to pacify Kevin Avon, who is clearly the more dangerous superpower in this struggle."

"I was thinking more of a head-on approach might work," Wes said, "but maybe some COIL stealth would be smarter. If we remove Matthias' bargaining chips, he'll have to deal with the Vegas troops more directly."

"But your Matthias friend doesn't sound that smart," Oleg said. "After all, you said he's put together a band of only forty men who are hardly familiar with a rifle. Why would we expect him to be reasonable after we take back the missing scouts—if we can even locate them?"

"If Matthias won't be reasonable," Chevy said, "then we have to pray that Kevin will be, after we return his people to him."

"That's a lot of *ifs*." Wes groaned. "We're going to need to inform the other Kindred of our plans before we initiate contact with the Village, but we don't have time to get the scouts and get down to the cabins to warn the Kindred to brace for impact."

"I don't feel comfortable with any conflict with this load of rifles on my tail, either," Oleg said. "I've been towing these babies around for a couple hundred miles, and it's only been by the protection of God that no one's found out what I'm carrying. We need to get this gear to a safe place before we make any moves."

"Then, we need to split up," Wes said.

"I'll take the gear back to the cabins, and warn the Kindred," Chevy volunteered, "if you two can promise not to ignite the entire Loop in an all-out war."

"I can't promise anything." Wes chuckled. "But I do have some ideas where they might be holding the two scouts. And they're probably not guarded too well, since Matthias wants all his best people out at the Junction for his idea of a slaughter."

"Yeah," Oleg said, "except the slaughter is going to be his own if he thinks he's going to take on five hundred people with his forty shooters! I've seen Kevin mobilize his soldiers. They're experienced—comparable to COIL's best, but without the superior weapons we have."

"If there's a fight, we'll need those extra guns," Chevy said, "and it won't be the Kindred against Matthias or Kevin. It'll be the Kindred against Matthias *and* Kevin."

"Hey, where's Titus when we need him?" Oleg laughed. "A wild and dangerous operation comes up, and he's nowhere to be found!"

"I'm sure he's having his own fun," Wes said. "You know—juggling the Meridia Virus and fighting off mountain raiders!"

Since the three men wanted to avoid Matthias' ambush troops at the Junction, Wes figured they needed to cut toward Lune Lake by once again climbing the ridge, this time by going north up the steep slope. With Oleg's two-hundred-pound wheeled resupply crate, made heavier by Wes and Chevy's packs, the three struggled uphill for two hours before they reached the top. As they caught their breaths and tightened their boot laces after the scrambling climb, Wes reviewed aloud for Oleg the layout before them.

"I know it's dark right now, Oleg, but you can see a few lamplights below. Those are all from the families who are living around the Village and Lune Lake."

"Matthias' people." Oleg nodded. "And where are the Kindred living?"

"Farther west." Chevy pointed in the darkness. "It's too far away to see through the forest, but there are seven Kindred families, including Wes's and mine, living in cabins at the bottom of Lune Lake Loop. There are almost one hundred people who live around us, but Matthias has scared a lot of those family men to fight against the Vegas arrivals."

"About where would you say is the Junction in this darkness?" Oleg asked.

"About right there." Wes pointed with his whole arm. "Unless Kevin Avon brings his whole caravan up the ridge that we just barely climbed up, the only reasonable path into the Lune Lake canyon is through Lune Lake Junction. If we can get the two scouts back to Kevin before he reaches the Junction, we just might avert a massacre on either side."

Chevy set off alone, angling toward the west, headed to find the rest of the Kindred. The original Kindred of Nails operative left his pack for Oleg and Wes to carry, since Chevy wanted to travel light and fast. Meanwhile, Wes guided the trailer from the side as Oleg anchored it from the rear for the descent from the ridge. It was as precarious going down as it was going up—all done in the half-light of the moon. More than once, Oleg's heels slipped on shale or pine needles, and Wes had to get in front of the heavy trailer to stop the gear from bouncing down the cliffs and dashing to pieces.

Finally, an hour after midnight, the two men reached the pavement of the highway. Both were winded and sweating in the summer air, and although Wes wanted desperately to visit more with Oleg, their night of stealth and intercession was only beginning.

At almost a jog, they pulled the trailer toward the Village, the residential area between Gull and Lune Lakes. Under the cover of darkness, their return to the community was much more covert than their departure in daylight when Wes had tranquilized Matthias. Wes directed Oleg to leave the trailer in the ditch on the south side of the road, then they crept together into the Village.

"Lead off." Oleg patted Wes's shoulder. "I'll cover."

Wes felt a surge of confidence to take point into the Village with Oleg watching his back. The wide-shouldered Russian had been partnered with Titus for years, and Wes didn't know a single soul who knew assault tactics better than Titus.

With his compact rifle leveled, Wes walked down what he knew from the map as Knoll Avenue. On his left, Lune Lake Village Motel stood, known for its rustic lodging from the 1920s. Towering pines rocked in the night breeze and a coyote yelped in the distance—oblivious of the violence that Matthias' hard heart waited to inflict upon hundreds.

Moving off the avenue, Wes didn't hesitate to approach a one-story duplex where a light was shining from one window. It was the middle of the night. He guessed the only people still awake in Lune Lake's Village would be those associated with all that Matthias had in mind for the Vegas refugees.

Below the window, Wes rested his back and surveyed what he could of the neighborhood. Oleg knelt twenty yards away, steadily aiming his rifle at the house. Nothing seemed to be moving.

With care not to make any sudden movements, Wes rose and spied through the window, seeing all with his one eye, then slowly lowered again. With his left hand, he held up two fingers to Oleg, indicating that he'd seen two men inside the room. Both were armed and one had appeared to be sleeping in a chair next to the hearth, but Wes knew they needed to invade the house with the assumption that both men were wide awake and ready—and other men could be nearby.

Wes allowed his rifle to hang on its sling as he drew his nine-millimeter, then screwed a short, black cylinder onto its muzzle to silence the inevitable shots. Although the bullpups could aptly tranquilize a foe, the battle rifle didn't have anything but a sound suppressor, which would disperse the sound of a gunshot but it would still be loud enough to be heard for miles around.

Oleg hustled closer as Wes approached the front door by way of the low porch in front of the duplex. The standard doorknob on the door was unlocked, and Wes turned it quietly but quickly. With the door cracked, he stepped briskly into the living room and the brightness of the fireplace. The building had often been used by Matthias as a type of headquarters for the Village, but they'd been so overconfident that they hadn't prepared for an organized assault.

Oddly, the two men weren't startled as Wes loomed over them, not even the one who was awake. Wes remembered them both from Sandburg. Hoxborn had had to load their own guns for them when they were required to man the walls, so Wes wasn't surprised they'd been left behind when battle seemed imminent. They weren't altogether dense men, both in their forties, but they'd simply grown up in an age of microwaves and push-button satisfaction, and had no desire to learn how to survive without electricity.

Not wanting to risk a struggle and a gunshot against the two men, Wes tranquilized them both where they sat, using his silenced handgun.

"Wes?" Oleg gestured to a back bedroom door that was closed. A length of frayed rope was tied to the doorknob, the other end being tied to an empty water pitcher balanced precariously on the kitchen counter. It was a poor man's alarm system, one that was easily disarmed by Wes as he carried the pitcher over to the door. He threw the door open and instantly recoiled into Oleg. The sight in the bedroom was too grizzly to accept at first glance. While turned away, he laid a hand on Oleg's chest.

"Go," he told the Russian. "Watch the front. I'll check them out."

Wes had been in the CIA for twenty years, and Oleg had been in Interpol for nearly as long, so either man could have inspected the crime scene adequately, but Wes was sparing his COIL friend the sadness. As Oleg returned to the front of the living room to watch for visitors, Wes eased into the bedroom to examine two men who lay bound and bloodied on the floor.

Gently, he touched each man's neck for a pulse. The first one was cold and still, certainly the result of bruising around the neck from being choked and battered. The second man's appearance was no better, but his body was warm and his pulse was strong enough to feel past Wes's own racing heartbeat. The second man's eyes opened to see Wes holding a skinning knife in front of his face. The man's eyes bulged, and Wes quickly covered the wounded man's mouth lest he scream an alarm for anyone nearby.

"I'm a friend of Avon's," Wes whispered "I'm taking you back to your people, if you're able to travel. We need to keep quiet."

The man obliged and didn't move as Wes cut his hands and feet free of rope. But once free, he still didn't move, and the misery on the man's face wasn't from being tied up, Wes realized. It was from his grave wounds.

"It's my ribs," the man moaned. "I can't move."

With his own hand, Wes wiped at blood on the poor man's cheek, realizing it had recently come from his mouth and not from an old wound.

"You probably have broken ribs, causing a punctured lung." Wes reached over the man and ripped a blanket and sheet off the bed. "We have a doctor a mile to the south, but we have to get you somewhere safe. We have to risk moving you."

"Take me to Avon," the man whispered, his pain gripping him to the point of breathlessness.

"You'd die before we ever got you over the ridge." Wes folded the sheet and blanket length-wise. "No, Avon will have to come to you instead. Come now. Lift up your arms. I'm going to wrap your ribs and torso real tight so we can move you. Don't worry. We'll carry you. Just do your best to keep silent. We have a little ways to go."

Wes wrapped the man with the blanket first, then tied the sheet around him to hold the blanket in place. Next, he took the last sheet from the bed and wrapped the dead man in it, from head to toe. It was immediately stained with blood, but Wes felt it necessary to respect the fallen for the sake of the peace he still intended to broker.

Out in the living room, he told Oleg the score: one dead man, and one nearly dead.

"Convincing Kevin Avon not to counterattack just became a lot more difficult for us," Oleg said. "I have no doubt that Kevin will break through Matthias' meager defenders at the Junction. The only question is, will he stop there, or slaughter everyone in Lune Lake for what's happened to his two scouts?"

Chapter 3

Wes stood in the light of the lamp hanging from the awning of his cabin on the south end of Lune Lake Loop. Chevy, Rick Lusis, Oliver Newlander, and the three other Kindred Christians gathered around him, their ammunition belts laden with gel-tranqs and their battle rifles in their hands. Other community citizens stood beyond the inner circle of men. They'd woken in the night to hear the latest on the local upheaval. Someone had fetched the doctor and brought him to Wes and Wynter's cabin where the wounded scout of Kevin Avon's lay on Wes's own bed. Wynter was inside the cabin with the doctor, but Jill and several other able women—wives of the Kindred—were armed with the additional battle rifles that Oleg had brought them. The result of arming the rest of the Christians with non-lethal weaponry gave them a total force of eighteen shooters, but Wes hoped they wouldn't need to fire a single shot.

Oleg was the only one absent from their group. Wes had sent him back to attempt to intercept Kevin Avon's advance, which would be difficult since Oleg carried news of the scouts' abduction and abuse, including one death.

"This isn't the way I wanted the Kindred of Nails to make their Christ-like presence known more broadly," Wes said loudly, "but if God has given us a vision to bring peace where there is no peace, then we must embrace the work of grace before us. One man has already died, and now we know why Matthias Seaver was so aggressively pushing everyone to cause a fight. He had kidnapped and tortured two men who were part of a crowd of refugees seeking sanctuary. His wickedness will be lost in the confusion of greater conflict, but our business as

Christians isn't to exact revenge, even though we may have the best vantage point of what has transpired. Our business is to offer ourselves sacrificially, hoping to resolve what has erupted within a community that we've helped found. We're responsible for these lives. Let's lead with Christ's love, and not put *being right* in front of *being Christ-like*.

"Oleg has gone before us to share the latest news with Kevin Avon. It's bad news that we have to give him about his two scouts, but now is not a time to hide the truth from him. By both Matthias and Kevin Avon knowing the truth of their need for peace, it's my prayer that we'll arrive at peace.

"Now, we've already shared the plan with you, so we have only to reach the Junction as a force of seven men. Seven probably isn't a very impressive force to the world, but we all know that just one man of faith with God backing him, is a force that can change the world. I can only imagine what seven godly men of faith can do, with their families beside them! Chevy, what we're about to do is already understood to be something in God's will, so pray for us—that our hearts and minds would be exclusively dedicated to Christ's glory. For some of us, this may be the most difficult night we've faced since Pan-Day."

Chevy prayed a brief prayer of dedication to the Lord, then family members embraced them and said their farewells to the Kindred men as they drew on light packs. Alone and off to one side, Wes watched the scene of God's special men and women. They cared deeply for one another, and yet the love of God for their neighbors was so pure and true that they were willing to sacrifice their lives for others to know that love.

With sadness, Wes realized he was the only one who had no one to wish him well in the night, but he didn't regret the demand that others had upon Wynter. As a Caspertein, God had brought Wynter through dozens of tragedies and circumstances. Now as a Trimble, God was using her to care for lives in a way that few others knew how to care. It was the reason they'd come to Lune Lake.

Wynter wasn't outside their cabin that night to say goodbye to him, but she was inside, helping save the life of the scout. It was that kind of dependency Wes knew he could have in Wynter that, when the night was over, he could bring his wounded back here. His wife would be waiting with the doctor, and there was no more comforting thought to him than what God had provided for him to carry on his work as a COIL-Kindred operative.

"Thank you for trusting me, Wes," Dalia said softly as she approached him. A battle rifle was slung over her shoulder, and although she wasn't yet twenty, she had matured the past year into a young woman of responsibility. "I won't let you or Dad down. I'll stay up all night and watch over the cabins here."

"Your father trained you to shoot." Wes gave her shoulder a squeeze. It meant something special to him that she was already referring to Chevy as her dad. "If he thinks you're ready for this, then I think you're ready, too. I know you'll represent what Christ wants you to on this night."

"I'm afraid." She smiled, her eyes close to tears, shimmering in the lantern light. "But I know you're going out to stand first, not to fight."

"A man you may never meet until eternity said something that applies to us right now." Wes raised his head, remembering the example of faithful Christians in times past. "If we die today, die well, because we'll be in the presence of the Lord the next moment."

"That's sort of exciting to think about, even though I'm a baby Christian." Dalia fidgeted. "I'll never forget what you did for us that first morning we met, Wes. I still have the thermal you gave Mom and me that day. We'd probably be dead if you hadn't helped us. I guess you've been saving our lives ever since."

"It's your father's fault," he joked, shouldering his light pack. "He's shown himself to be a hero for so many others that he encourages the rest of us to step up as well."

They laughed together. It was the kind of laugh Wes hoped he could one day share with his own daughter, Mia, when she was Dalia's age.

The seven Kindred men set off walking down the two-lane highway. As the lantern light faded and darkness embraced them, Wes's eyes adjusted to the bright starlight over the forest. Chevy walked beside him, and the five others walked in two columns, in almost military fashion behind them.

"Our departure took longer than intended," Wes said. "Let's double-time it, men, and we'll be there in fifteen minutes."

Although he and Chevy hadn't slept for over 24 hours, they led the men into the night, jogging with their rifles now in their hands, and their light packs jostling quietly on their backs. They carried only canteens, food for one day, first aid, and ammunition. Their mission of peace would be resolved, Wes guessed, within one day, or they'd be dead and they wouldn't need more than what they carried.

"Some might think we should leave well enough alone." Chevy spoke comfortably as he jogged. The man was in prime condition. "You know, let these two sides fight it out, and then we move in to help keep the peace."

"It would certainly be easier," Wes said, his breath coming more raggedly than that of his young soldiers. "And safer. But what's Christ-like isn't measured by what's easy or safe. We're hoping to save these men from themselves and what they think they need to do to defend their own rights and honor. We know that the outcome of their bloodshed will have long-lasting consequences for them. That's why we're doing this, even if they never understand. It's better to solve a dispute at our own risk than to allow a dispute to happen without check, just to avoid the personal trouble."

"That's a proverb America should've adopted before Pan-Day," Chevy said in a mournful voice.

Minutes later, the two short columns of Kindred jogged past the Village. From the look of the duplex, no one had discovered that the scouts were missing from Lune Lake Village Motel, or the two careless guards Wes and Chevy had left tied up in the back room.

"It's to our advantage they haven't been discovered yet," Chevy commented. "Matthias won't expect us."

"True, but sometimes even a wounded animal acts more unpredictable when you surprise it. He won't have time to prepare for us, but that also means we won't be able to anticipate how he'll react."

"Just know we've got your back, when you confront him."

"I never doubted it." Wes knew he could count on the sharp-shooting skills of Chevy and the others, more than he could count on his own sniper skills to watch over them. "Just promise me that if I start to make a mess of things, and Matthias reacts badly, tranquilize the guy with the eye patch first."

"Put you out of your misery?" Chevy laughed. "We may not succeed, Wes, but that doesn't mean failure, not if we're being obedient to the Lord. And I'm certainly not going to blame you if this doesn't work. But it's a good plan. We're all in agreement."

Lune Lake Junction came into sight, and as suspected, not a light was visible. Wes expected no less since Matthias was lying in wait, hoping to ambush the new arrivals before they reached the buildings up the canyon. The Junction was over two miles away from the Village, so there was plenty of distance for a battlefield to stretch across the rugged forest on either side of Lune Lake Loop.

The Junction, since it was on a major highway, had been burned and demolished by hooligans around Pan-Day, so instead of buildings, Matthias had debris to hide behind.

Without more than a whispered word, Chevy and the five other Kindred climbed the ridge south of the Junction, while Wes continued at a walk toward the forty shooters who were certainly hiding nearby. When he came within normal rifle range, he paused to allow the Kindred to get into position on the hill behind him. Although Matthias and his men had rifles that could accurately cover two hundred yards, the Kindred were fighting with the NL-X2, COIL's most advanced non-lethal weapon, able to fire a .308 gel-tranq cartridge up to six hundred yards.

A few minutes later, Wes started forward again, careful to keep a tree or two between him and the heart of the Junction, where he believed the ambushers were waiting, although they were certain to be focused on Highway 395 rather than the Lune Lake Loop highway. When he thought he was within one hundred yards, he knelt behind the last tree where the forest ended, and cupped his hand around his mouth.

"Matthias! Matthias!" He waited after hollering, knowing that his noise was sure to upset Matthias, since the ambush could only work if silence prevailed. "Matthias! I have news! It's Wes Trimble! I'm coming in to talk to you!"

But there was no answer, and Wes definitely wasn't stepping from behind the tree until he had some sort of assurance that he'd been heard and recognized.

"Matthias! It's Wes Trimble! I've got new information for you! We need to talk!"

Wes realized that he'd probably caught most of the ambushers dozing, since they were inexperienced and they'd surely grown sleepy through the long night of waiting. After all, Wes knew from his own intel that Kevin

Avon was a couple miles south of the ridge, camping across the span of the highway just north of Crestview.

"If I see you, Wes," a voice yelled back, "I'm shooting you, like you did me!"

Wes sighed and shook his head.

"I have new information that affects what you're doing! I'm coming in!"

"That's your gamble!" Matthias threatened back.

Wes prayed for wisdom in what to say next. He needed to bait Matthias just enough to give him an audience.

"I'm coming in! Kevin Avon knows you killed one of his scouts! You need to hear me out, before more people die! Over two hundred shooters will be here by dawn. You have to hear me out!"

After waiting a moment, Wes took a step of faith and came out from behind the tree. It wasn't such a dark night that one of the villagers couldn't see a little something move in the starlight.

He walked slowly, his boots hardly making a sound on the pavement strewn with pine needles. The wind blew gently from the north, a warm breeze slightly ruffling his hair, but not brisk enough that the long-distance shooters far above and behind him couldn't hit their intended targets.

The closer he drew, the more he recognized the signs of an actual ambush. On either side of the highway, foxholes had been dug, and pairs of men who'd awakened from the yelling pivoted in their shelters to watch him move past them. Finally, Wes reached what appeared to be a pile of railroad ties, and four forms rose to their feet. He guessed this was Matthias' command post over this tragic action. The rest of the fathers and young men Matthias had gathered were spread out in front of Matthias, but Wes had located only a few of their positions.

"Give me your rifle!" Matthias demanded, second from the right of the four men. "I can't believe you have the nerve to come here after you shot me earlier today!"

"I'm not the instigator," Wes corrected. "I'm the peacekeeper. You've already needlessly killed one man, and you're about to get a lot more killed today. It's almost dawn. By daylight, you won't have the element of surprise you think you do. So you built some foxholes. They'll be obvious in the sunlight, too."

"You said there's someone named Kevin who knows something?" Matthias cursed, and Wes thought the unbalanced man might shoot him then and there. "Hurry up! We're doing here what you don't have the spine to do. We're fighting back! Quit stalling and speak!"

"Your bargaining chips against who you think is the enemy are gone. The two scouts have been recovered—one is dead and the other beat nearly to death. A trained unit of snipers is sheltered up on the ridge behind me, and I assure you, they can see you, even though you can't see them. They're behind logs, rocks, and trees, and it would take a battalion to take that ridge. You're finished, Matthias."

The man took a half-step backward, as if he'd been shot already. The three men at his side glanced at one another. Even in the starlight, Wes could see their expressions were filled with fear. They'd killed a stranger and beaten another man. Their efforts to cover up the incident by a violent ambush and tough talk about invaders had been exposed.

"It's time to take responsibility, Matthias," Wes continued. "Let these men go home to their families. I'll be with you at your side, as we try to keep the peace with these newcomers. But there's no way you can win. You're about to get all of these men killed. Kevin Avon, the leader of the caravan from Las Vegas, has two hundred and fifty trained shooters about to come up that highway."

"I thought you said they were up on the ridge." Matthias' head tilted. "What are you playing at, Wes? Who's up on the ridge? Who recovered the two scouts?"

"He did!" one of the other men said, pointing at Wes. "He's bluffing. There's no one up on that ridge except maybe those cursed Kindred he's always brainwashing! We're not in any danger, Matthias. It's like you said, we're defending our homes and families!"

"There are two kinds of danger tonight, Wes," Matthias said, his voice low and hissing. "The danger that's from a known enemy, and the danger that's from an enemy who pretends to be a friend."

"I'm not a pretender," Wes defended. "Chevy and I found a route over the mountains from Sandburg to give you and your families a safe place to live. The shooters up on that ridge aren't a bluff. They are your neighbors, your friends, men who have cared for you by chopping firewood and bringing you deer meat. If one shot is fired in this darkness, it will alert the newcomers that there is conflict here. I'm not trying to escalate this moment, Matthias. I'm trying to save lives. Disperse the men, and I'll be your advocate when you face the people you've wronged. You killed a man in cold blood, Matthias. We, our whole community, needs to make this right, not cover it up with more bloodshed. If we don't, the cycle may never end."

"This is not the time for surrender, Wes!" Matthias argued. "Join us! Fight for your family! Or are you too much of a coward?"

"He's a coward, Matthias," another said, "and a turncoat. He's taken the scouts, and left us to take the blame!"

"You are to blame!" Wes shouted, not caring who else heard. "Walk away and let us find a resolution before it's too late! Imagine all of these men's families without men to lead them, and with winter coming on. It's not only folly to continue this, it's bad timing!"

"You're a coward and a traitor to your own people!" Matthias accused. "You're nothing but a—"

A shout from somewhere near cut Matthias' words short. Wes turned and crouched, his eye wide and focused on a distant point down the highway, trying to spot movement. Suddenly, a gunshot cracked through the night and rolled across the landscape like thunder. Wes crouched behind the railroad ties, doing his best to gauge the source of the gunshot. It hadn't been a .308 gunshot, but something smaller with a sharper sound. Maybe someone had accidentally fired a shot.

But, two more shots were fired, then a volley of automatic gunfire. Muzzles flashed in the night, and Wes could discern a line of shooters advancing on Matthias' position.

The men in foxholes opened fire, but they fired mostly bolt-action hunting rifles, and Wes predicted their demise since they were outgunned and outnumbered against the attackers. Apparently, Kevin Avon hadn't waited until daylight to approach Lune Lake. No doubt, Wes realized, once Oleg had informed Kevin Avon of the status of their two scouts, Kevin hadn't hesitated to storm the Junction with his full forces.

Wes waited behind the railroad wood only long enough to identify his next point of cover thirty yards away—an abandoned vehicle on the side of the highway. As he ran in a crouch, he realized he wasn't alone in fleeing Matthias' line. Three or four other shadows sprinted toward the west. One was cut down as he ran, but Wes couldn't see well enough while he was running to see what happened to the other two.

When he reached the vehicle, he looked back at Matthias, estimating the amount of gunfire in comparison to what Kevin Avon's troops were firing. Wes could see the attackers already among the ambushers, some shooting directly down into the foxholes as they swarmed Matthias' position. Kevin Avon's men had crept close much faster and quieter than even Wes had expected.

The next time Wes broke cover, he ran all the way into the safety of Lune Lake Loop, perpendicular to the Junction battlefield that raged with nonstop gunfire. Once he reached the trees, even starlight was choked out, and Wes stumbled off the pavement and crossed the ditch. With his free hand, he clawed his way up the slope as he attempted to join the Kindred on the ridge. The ridge height there was only about sixty feet above the road, but it was steep enough to break Wes's tired body into a sweat before he nearly trampled one of the Kindred lying in wait. As yet, he hadn't heard any of the Kindred fire into the confusion below.

They gathered around Wes and Chevy in the early morning dimness.

"Both sides are trying to kill each other," Chevy said in a hoarse whisper, "so we can't rightly attack one side over another, not that we can make out who's who, anyway. Not one of them is trying to defend himself. If we help one side, the other side will try to take advantage."

"It's a hard situation for us." Wes tried to drown out the gunfire three hundred yards away. "I can't imagine Matthias coming out of this well, but he wouldn't listen. Sadly, he's taking about three dozen families with him."

"That's what we might need to turn our attention to," Rick Lusis said, his young voice sounding eager. "We should protect the families of Matthias and the others."

"It's two miles away to the Village," Chevy said. "Wes, you think Kevin Avon will march on the Village? Killing innocents?"

"I'm sorry to say, he might, since he's so focused on recovering his two scouts." Wes pointed up. "Look at the sky. The sun will be up in about half an hour."

"What if we hold here?" Oliver Newlander asked, the adventurer offering what Wes thought was a sound plan.

"Kevin Avon won't be able to pass on the highway without crossing our field of vision."

"Okay, I like that," Wes said. "Let's shift our positions to aim northward, then, and anyone who's not retreating—which will be Matthias' men—we tranq."

"We need to think about what Kevin Avon has done with Oleg, too," Chevy said. "Obviously, whatever Oleg tried to do with the man, it failed. Oleg might be a prisoner of Kevin's now."

"For the time being, Oleg is going to have to endure that." Wes made a fist. "I don't like it, but we can't move on something we don't know about for sure. Oleg's been a prisoner of some pretty ruthless people before, much worse than Kevin Avon. He knows to just cooperate, if he's been abducted, until we can arrange for his release. We need to put everything we can into keeping Lune Lake safe now—and that's everyone, even people who've sworn to eradicate us. Spread out east to west. Look for firing paths through and over the treetops."

Wes hustled with Chevy to the end of the ridge where they had a vantage point of the Junction below. The gunfire had lessened, but muzzles still flashed sporadically, as if the winning side was exterminating even the wounded who lay helpless.

"How can people recover from something like this?" Chevy whispered at Wes's shoulder. "Unless people escaped, the men of almost forty families have just been erased from this earth."

"Sometimes, there's no positive or pleasant outcome," Wes said. "We just need to be available to the victors, I guess, to start over. Offenses and disproportionate responses have been done on both sides this day. There's no justice in war, not when everyone is killing each other in ignorance and selfishness."

"If we start to fire down on Kevin Avon," Chevy said, "it'll be interpreted as if we're against him. He won't stop until he wipes out even the Kindred."

"I can't believe God would allow that." Wes looked left and right, considering an idea. "In fact, I think He's just given me an idea that would ensure that doesn't happen, but it requires us talking some sense into Kevin Avon."

"Ha! He doesn't look like he's in the mood for conversation." Chevy scoffed.

"It's not his show, not anymore." Wes felt a smile of confidence creep onto his face. "For the first time in the last couple days, I know exactly what to do. We're taking his fighting force prisoner."

"Prisoner? You mean Kindred-Diablo style?"

"Exactly. As soon as they regroup at the Junction, I think Kevin Avon will leave a few troops at the Junction to help his wounded back to their families. The rest will probably explore the Lune Lake Loop. It won't take him long to come across our people."

"But we have to stop him before that. I don't think Jill would make a good prisoner."

"Neither would Wynter. Yes, we stop them. And we take them prisoner—all of them."

"That's a lot of people." Chevy whistled through his teeth. "Then what?"

"Then we force peace. Kevin Avon won't have a choice."

"So, we're in ambush mode ourselves now." Chevy rose to his feet. "I'll tell the others."

For a moment, Wes was alone, grimacing at the carnage below. They were close enough to hear the cries of the wounded. It was a sickening sound, a heartbreaking sound. This needed to end before it spread any further.

Chapter 4

As daylight touched the Lune Lake region, Wes repositioned the Kindred shooters farther up the ridge above the Lune Lake Loop Road. Kevin Avon would have to pass beneath them on the highway to reach the Village and the resort cabins, or travel north of the Junction five more miles to the other loop entrance. Avon's fighting men from Las Vegas couldn't travel south on Highway 395 without coming under fire from the Kindred. But from what Wes had noticed at the Junction, Avon was rallying his men to pour into Lune Lake as an invasion force.

Only Oliver Newlander, the most agile of the Kindred, was missing from their firing line that spanned the ridge, facing north. Wes placed himself on the extreme right end of the line, and Chevy went to the upper end to the left. They were spaced twenty yards apart with Wes being the lowest and closest to the road, at one hundred and fifty yards away. Chevy's position was over two hundred yards from the road, offering him the safest shooting position, since Avon's shooters carried mostly small caliber assault rifles for close fighting. The bullpups were worth three of the other rifles, but Wes wasn't kidding himself. Except for Chevy and Wes, the five other Kindred had never been in a firefight. They'd only been hunting, though they were schooled by Wes in battle tactics. Any of the younger men could panic under fire, and it could cost them all dearly.

Wes settled into a seated firing position, with one elbow resting on a knee. In front of him, a gnarled granite rock peeked through the brown grass, offering him cover from the immediate north. If the fight shifted, he could move around the rock as needed.

If he'd had a radio, he would've called Wynter to warn her of the coming attack. But he guessed she would know that something contrary was happening since the night had been filled with gunfire, and he hadn't returned home yet to their cabin. In moments, Wes guessed she and the other Kindred families would hear the coming gunfire, this time with the booming .308 COIL battle rifles, and Wynter would know that the Kindred had engaged.

"Pssst!" Oliver Newlander signaled as he bounded up the ridge toward Wes. The young Kindred defender picked his way up the rocky ridge at a pace that Wes remembered having when he was a youngster. Oliver reached Wes and crouched. "You said to let you know when they were coming, so I'm letting you know—they're coming. I counted one hundred and seventy. About forty are leaving, heading south back to their families, it looks like. What do you want to do?"

"The forty are probably the wounded from the overnight fight. We'll let them go." Wes sighted his rifle scope over the treetops below his position. "Tell the others the score, then settle into your position and wait for my first shot."

Oliver trotted away, skirting a lonely tree on top of the ridge, then continued to climb, sharing Wes's orders with the men along the way. Far up the ridge, Chevy would be hearing the number in a moment—*one hundred and thirty!* It was far more than any number the Kindred had taken at one time over in the Central Valley. But now they had seven shooters, and their elevated positions gave them a command of the highway below as well as the meadow opposite the highway where a thick forest grew five hundred yards away.

Wes felt a trickle of sweat run down his chest as he waited, still and focused. His palms were clammy and his mouth was dry. He wished he would've taken a drink from his canteen where it lay next to his pack behind him, but it was too late now. The first of Kevin Avon's troops were walking up the highway.

"Smart," Wes whispered, admiring the spread-out formation of their two columns.

But Wes had warned the Kindred men of the strategy the attackers might use. Thus, Wes had told them to hold their fire until Avon's men were all within firing range by one or more of their positions.

Oleg's whereabouts continued to nag at his thoughts, but Oleg would simply need to sit tight until the Vegas fighting force was neutralized, at least temporarily.

Wes estimated the count of passing soldiers below him. Through only a few trees obstructing his view, he had three alleys of fire: far left, center, and far right—almost all the way to the Junction itself.

The first one hundred men moved under him, and he started to grow concerned about the far front of the two columns moving out of Chevy's range. Avon really had spread his troops out! But then, far to the right, Wes saw the end of both columns, straggling behind with heavy packs, even a couple men who were bandaged. They'd probably insisted on joining the main force to clear out Lune Lake of any further "hostiles."

He took a deep breath and set his scope view on the back of the column. By tranquilizing both ends of the columns, Wes had strategized with Chevy that the rest of Avon's men would retreat into the middle, where they could be easily picked off. *Easily?* There was nothing easy about one hundred and thirty rifles shooting at them, but it was a plan.

The instant Wes fired, the rest of the Kindred followed suit. Wes dropped two men, checked his watch to time the tranquilizer toxin, then continued to fire. Ten seconds passed before anyone below figured out the gunshots were coming from the ridge, but Wes guessed they wouldn't realize for some time how far up the ridge the Kindred actually were. A foot assault up the steep ridge toward them would fail miserably, unless Avon had air support and mortars up his sleeve.

Wes experienced the same regret he always did during a firefight. He saw men's faces through his scope, faces that expressed a realization of certain death, even though they were only unknowingly being tranquilized. In the second it took for the toxin to course through their bodies, the brain would have plenty of time to communicate to the mind that they'd been shot. The gel-tranq, though gelatin, punched like a sledge hammer, and men tried to scream in their assumed deaths. Fear and panic covered the road, even among seasoned soldiers. Avon had attacked unseasoned men in the dark, Wes thought, but now these experienced troops found themselves out-maneuvered and out-gunned, at least ballistically. Avon's troops didn't know how to respond effectively.

A few of the soldiers below seemed to locate the position of the Kindred, and the word was passed down the highway, which was now strewn with unconscious men. Many tried to lunge over the ditch to hide behind a tree or rocky outcropping, but at least one of the Kindred could still see them from another angle. They had no cover.

Five minutes later, after half their number had been put down, the remaining soldiers decided to flee outright. They scattered in three directions: west toward Lune Lake, north across the meadow, and east toward the Junction. Their flights only further revealed them for the Kindred to fire free of any treetops below. Being the farthest to the right, Wes was responsible for those who fled toward the Junction, taking them out before they could escape range. Wes couldn't see all the way down the road to the west, but he heard the other Kindred firing steadily, reloading, and continuing. Men dropped all over the meadow, up and down the highway, and alongside both ditches.

Wes made rapid work of those within range on his end, and was about to shift to the left to help the others mop up their targets before they could reach cover, when he noticed movement on the ridge itself. Three men had somehow flanked him! They seemed to identify him the instant he pivoted ninety degrees and fired desperately. But only one round burst from his muzzle before he clicked on empty.

They fired from standing positions, hastily but far too close for Wes' comfort. He snatched up his ammo pouch and rolled downhill to get behind the rock that had protected him from shooters below.

"We're flanked!" Wes yelled to Rick Lusis twenty yards away.

As Wes reloaded behind the rock, he heard Rick engage the three flankers. A breath later, Wes had reloaded, and he leaped upright to find that Rick had tranquilized all three men—and he'd already turned back to the northern targets! Wes shook his head at his old, aching bones as he climbed back up to his original position. Through his confusion as to where the three flanking soldiers had come from, he suddenly realized that he already knew. They hadn't somehow avoided his detection from the front of the ridge. They'd come up the back of the ridge! The forty who were wounded and had supposedly been allowed to leave the Junction must've decided to engage after all. Apparently, they weren't as wounded as they'd seemed, or some who weren't wounded were helping those who were.

With that realization, Wes stepped across the crest of the ridge until he could see the highway to the south. The column of wounded was still moving toward the distant camp of families, but there were about eight more men climbing the southern slope of the ridge. Two wore bloody rags, indicating that they were indeed wounded from the night battle, but the rest appeared to be courageous fighting men. Wes couldn't help but admire them. They thought their friends had been ambushed, though as only a few men, they were attempting to flank their enemy.

When Wes fired at the eight, he started with those who were closest to tree or cliff cover. After that, he tranquilized the last four who were caught in the open.

Wes turned in a slow arc, aware of a sudden silence—the ridge was quiet and still. None of the Kindred moved except Wes as he returned to his original firing position. The sun was at his back and to his right as he surveyed the highway and meadow below. All was silent. He looked at his watch. Only twenty-three minutes had passed since the first shot had been fired. That left about thirty-five minutes to gather the men.

"Let's go!" Wes shouted to Rick, who passed the call to the others.

The five younger Kindred slid and leaped down the north slope, while Wes and Chevy followed more slowly. The two older men steadied their rifles and watched for any pretend-sleepers, protecting the men as they worked. Starting on the western end, one Kindred gathered the rifles as the four others worked in pairs to bind the wrists of the soldiers. They didn't have time to bind the ankles as well, nor did they have anything but the men's own belts or jackets to hastily tie them up. The binds weren't permanent, but representative, Wes told them. Without their rifles, the soldiers were defenseless, anyway.

After the soldiers were bound, they were dragged to be lain in the middle of the highway, if they weren't already there. Within twenty minutes, at a speed that had them all winded, the one hundred and thirty were bound and their guns had been deposited in a pile in the thick foliage at the base of the ridge. Wes told the others about the attempt to flank them on the ridge, and those eleven were rounded up as well, tied and dragged down to join the others.

By that time, according to Wes's watch, the first of the men were soon to wake. At the front of the column, Wes found Kevin Avon. Although he was sleeping soundly at the moment, Wes remembered very well the man's commanding presence and firm gaze. With some effort, Wes picked up the leader's body, hefted him over his shoulder, and walked down the highway with him. Behind a thicket off the highway, Wes laid the man on the ground and sat down to wait for him to wake. For the first time in an hour, Wes was able to rest. Blood had dried on his cheek where a bullet had ricocheted off a rock and grazed his face, nearly blinding his only eye, but otherwise, he was unscathed. He hadn't seen the others wounded any worse, but they were certain to have a few scrapes and close calls as well since so many bullets had been flying.

Instead of waking gradually, when Avon opened his eyes, he was instantly alert, acknowledging his bound wrists. He glared at Wes, the bullpup, then back at Wes's face. Wes set his rifle aside, and instead drew his Desert Eagle sidearm. He rested the firearm on his knee, the gaping muzzle aimed loosely in Avon's direction.

Avon's jaw clenched, then relaxed. Wes saw the man take a deep breath, and exhale slowly, perhaps accepting that he was definitely not in control of the situation.

"All of your men have become my prisoners," Wes stated.

"Yeah. All of them? Right." Avon scoffed, then frowned. "You're serious?"

"I've been awake for thirty-six hours. I'm sore, wounded, and saddened by this whole mess. I'm absolutely serious."

Avon turned his head to acknowledge his surroundings for the first time, maybe trying to locate his men. But Wes had taken him to a point where even the highway couldn't be seen through the trees thirty yards away.

"I'm listening."

"Right now," Wes said, "I'm sitting here, trying to figure out if you value life at all."

"I value it enough to punish anyone and everyone who takes it unjustly." Avon's gravelly voice was fierce, but an instant after he spoke, his face softened, as if he'd just heard his own words. "You're talking about what happened at the Junction."

Wes felt his own emotions rise as he remembered the single, sporadic gunshots in the early morning darkness.

"Did you leave anyone alive?" Wes asked.

Avon wouldn't meet his eyes.

"Someone might have escaped.

"But no one you saw?"

"No, no one I saw."

Wes tapped his forefinger on his drawn handgun. This man was responsible for the very slaughter the Kindred had been trying to avoid.

"One or two men were responsible for the kidnap and death of your two scouts."

"Where is he?" Avon's nostrils flared. "Tell me or I swear I'll—"

"You'll kill the women and children who are gathered around your injured scout? Kill the doctor who is nursing him back to life?" Wes slowly shook his head. "No, you haven't exercised justice here, Kevin. You have stolen lives. You've responded to a threat by acting emotionally. Soldiers respond stoically, honorably. Wait until your families meet all of the Lune Lake families, and they begin to look at you as the one who slaughtered dozens who barely knew how to hold a rifle."

"But they were each holding a rifle!"

"I told you last night they weren't even hunters!" Wes checked his voice, then spoke softer. "I told you to give us time, that we would sort it out. I have a question to ask you, and much of your future depends on the truth of what you tell me. Where is Oleg Saratov?"

"He's with my people. Honest. When he came in the night with news that one scout was dead, and the other had been badly beaten, I placed him under arrest and left him with a small contingent who stayed back with the women and children. I couldn't allow him to warn you that we were coming."

"It wasn't me he needed to warn. Me and the Kindred weren't a part of Matthias' actions against your scouts or your people. The Kindred didn't get involved until we heard and saw the massacre at the Junction a few hours ago. That's when we put you and your men down."

Avon looked down at his body, as if taking account of his uninjured legs and arms for the first time.

"The tranquilizers. Oleg told me about your methods. So, it's true. You have some sort of high-velocity tranquilizer round. That's the rifle you use?"

"It is. Let's get back on subject." Wes holstered his sidearm since he'd sufficiently used it to make his point. "What follows next must be accomplished in three phases, and you clearly haven't thought about it."

"I'm a chess player." The commander sneered. "I think of everything."

"With whatever reason you justify it, you've just slaughtered forty husbands, sons, and brothers of the families you intend to settle next to as neighbors. How do you think that's going to go over?"

Avon blinked as the truth stung and the social ramifications apparently crossed his mind for the first time.

"We'll just have to settle in those cabins you said were near those other lakes, on the far side of Lune Lake Loop."

"No, it's too close to us to ignore you and live peacefully beside you." Wes tilted his head. "You'll need to go somewhere else, maybe Mammoth Lake, or up into Yosemite. Most of you will die, of course, since winter is approaching, but I see no alternative, since you've made yourselves the sworn enemies of the people of Lune Lake. Of course, even if you go on to Mammoth Lake, you'll run into other settlers who've claimed those areas, too. You'll need to kill them off before you take their cabins. But again, you'll need to hurry, because the snow will be here in a couple months. It takes time to prepare for winter around here, especially with people who are from the desert or cities."

"Well, we're already coming late in the season." Avon seemed to do the math in his head, and saw the math was against him. "We can't go anywhere else. There's no time. We have to make it work here. Somehow."

"I don't see how, Kevin. You've made yourselves unwelcome here. You've already shown yourselves to be unworthy neighbors. And as trained as you think your men are, seven of us just took down one hundred and forty of you."

"Yeah, right. Seven." He cursed. "Go try bluffing someone else, but I know how skilled my men are. I trained them. They're veterans. You may have tranquilized me, but it would take an army to take us all down."

"Yeah—an army of seven. Like I was saying, we won't have you settle here. You'll have to move on."

"And I was saying," Avon pressed, "half of our women and children will die if we're caught unprepared by winter at this elevation!"

"If only there were some compromise to save the lives of your people." Wes frowned and looked away. "I mean, the Lune Lake people—forty families' worth—now have no men to care for them. And you can imagine the fortitude this mountain region requires. Your caravan has an overwhelming number of men, and maybe they could each care for a family, but it would require a significant example of humility to bring peace between our two groups. Offenses on both sides, an unreasonable degree of blood has been shed, and winter is on its way. The pressures of leadership, huh?"

"Aren't you the savage?" Avon cursed. "You've been setting me up this whole time. I'm boxed in. My people can't go any further. What do you think I'm going to do—

sacrifice myself or something? Yeah, I know you're Christians, and that's why you use the tranquilizers, but I'm no messiah, I assure you. Pick some other soul to be your sacrificial lamb."

"No, you'll do fine." Wes finally smiled. "The people you've brought hundreds of miles depend on it. Otherwise, you fail, they die, and everyone left alive barely survives winter, including those of us who remain in Lune Lake."

"You people killed one of our own. My men will never be at peace!"

"What will they do, revolt?" Wes held out his hands. "With what? We've taken all your weapons. You might have twenty or thirty rifles left back in your caravan, but I remind you that seven of us took down your whole army. No, to survive, we all need to humble ourselves. Matthias, who started this mess, is dead, but he's not gone."

"What's that supposed to mean?"

"He'll need to be buried, along with his men. Since your men no longer have rifles, their hands are free for digging a mass grave. You've survived Pan-Day, so you know what a mass grave is."

"You're crazy. My men aren't burying our enemies!"

"Yes, they will, or they won't be welcome here. And you'll help them. And over their graves, in front of everyone in Lune Lake who lost someone, you'll admit your fault in the needless massacre. Then, you'll be free to go settle into your new homes around Silver and Grant Lakes. But it still won't be enough."

"What else?" Avon asked passively, as if he were finally seeing the wisdom in Wes's words.

"Lune Lake has about forty families that'll need to be tended to through the winter. They'll be heartbroken from the loss of their fathers and sons, but the only helping hand that will be available to them will be from those who killed their loved ones. If you tell me your men have any honor, then they will step up in this way."

"But will the families receive them?"

"How can they not? If your men are humble, they'll learn even to be loved and to love again. This is what the Kindred know something about, so we can help heal the wounds that are so fresh, even as we speak."

"What you're proposing sounds impossible."

"I think we've already reasoned out the alternatives."

"Death isn't an alternative. Believe me, I live my life—and keep others alive—by calculating the odds. I've never factored in the kind of reality you're proposing."

Wes studied the man in front of him, then looked away. Avon was younger, stronger, and probably faster than Wes. If he misjudged the commander, a lot could go wrong.

"So, three phases," Wes repeated. "Burial, funeral, winter preparation. All of it stems on the reversal of the aggression you arrived here with. You need to move hearts at the funeral, Kevin, or the healing won't begin."

"I'm not someone who . . . moves hearts." He scowled. "That's just not me."

"Empathy isn't natural, I think," Wes said. "By nature, we're selfish. If the last twenty-four hours—or the past year—hasn't taught you that, nothing will."

"I don't empathize."

"You'll need a miracle then, and that's where God comes in."

"I'm not religious. Keep that to yourself, Wes Trimble."

"Imagine this: the wife of Matthias, the man who started all this mess, has two teenage children. One of them is mentally handicapped. Matthias' wife—I know her—has spent her whole life taking care of their handicapped child. Think of that burden through Pan-Day. Not easy, especially with a husband who's hateful and argumentative. Now this woman is alienated, because Matthias was so controlling of her life, and she has no friends. They live in the Village, but no one will help take care of her, because very few people in the Village are capable of even taking care of themselves."

"How did Matthias convince forty men to try to ambush us, if he was such a jerk?"

"He played off their fear, and he was able to do that so well because he was afraid himself. Right now, his family is afraid. And they'll be even more afraid when they realize they're all alone in this world. The Kindred Seven are definitely a force to be reckoned with in this canyon, but we can't fill in the gaps of forty men, even forty who were struggling to figure out how to live out here in the wild. You have to provide a stable presence here, Kevin, or these people will continue to act on their fears. This violence needs to end, or it'll go on and on. It'll be uphill work, yes, but God has given us each other. No one else."

Wes leaned forward and Avon held up his wrists for him to unwrap his belt. It wouldn't have kept someone like Avon from freeing himself after a few moments of struggle, but the belt had done the job temporarily.

Avon rubbed his wrists.

"My men are near?"

"I'll take you to them. They'll need your leadership right away."

"You said you haven't slept for a day and a half. Neither have we. I should take them back to their families and get a fresh start tomorrow."

"Get a fresh start tonight," Wes corrected. "It's barely seven in the morning. Get the men back to their families and sleep for a few hours. Then we'll meet you at the Junction. We should be able to bring back all the dead bodies in one trip, if we work together."

"You have everything figured out, don't you?" Avon offered his hand to Wes, and Wes took it. He rose to his feet, and drew Wes up with him. "I suppose I'll have to get used to that, at least until we get our rifles back."

"We've got time to adjust." Wes laughed lightly and slapped the man's shoulder as they walked out of the thicket together. "After all, we're going to be neighbors for a while."

When they reached the road, Wes paused on the pavement when he noticed Avon had stopped.

"What's this?" Avon asked gesturing toward the line of men seated belly-to-back down the middle of the highway. "You were serious? Only seven of you?"

Wes waved to Chevy and the other six Kindred who stood guard over the one hundred and forty-one men.

"Well, we'll be eight as soon as you send Oleg back to us."

"Okay." Avon held out his hand again. "You have my word. For all of us, this is a truce. It won't hurt for them all to see us shake hands right now. Is this what you had in mind when you proposed that I make an effort?"

"It's something we can work on together.

"You're not leaving me alone to do this—the three phases?"

"I'll see you tonight." Wes gripped the commander's hand. "And we'll get started."

Wes stood at a distance as the Kindred backed off to allow Avon to gather his men. They freed themselves from their belts or hastily-tied coats from their wrists. They mingled for a moment as the word was passed from Avon, and the men turned to the east.

"We'll need our weapons back soon, Wes Trimble," Avon said loud enough for the Kindred to hear.

"That's Phase Four, Kevin Avon," Wes waved back.

The leader shook his head, as if he'd heard enough about Wes's phases, but he waved back anyway.

"Phase Four, Wes?" Chevy asked. "I take it things went well? Let me guess—you led him to Christ already."

"No, I didn't." Wes chuckled. "But that doesn't mean there won't be an opportunity for that to happen."

"So, he'll be our neighbor? He went for it? Yeah, I guess I'd call that an opportunity!"

Chapter 5

When Wes felt Wynter's hand on his shoulder, he woke and sat up on the bed in their cabin. He shifted his eye patch from his right eye to his left so he could see, and groaned internally over the aches and weariness he still felt from the night's toil.

"You said you wanted to sleep only a couple hours," Wynter said as she fit Mia into a sweater. "I see people already moving around outside."

Wes drew on his boots, then looked out the open door. Sure enough, a couple of the Kindred families were already waiting in the evening light for the funeral to begin. At least two of the men held unlit torches, which they would light as soon as darkness fell.

"Let's hope this is the last of the horrors we need to see around here." Wes fit his shoulder holster and firearm over his shoulder. "I know real peace won't come until Christ Himself reigns on earth, but it would sure be nice for a little preview of that peace around here."

"Oleg came by while you were sleeping," Wynter said, "so that's a sign, isn't it?"

"Yes." Wes smiled. "It means Kevin Avon is keeping his word, so far."

Outside, Wes greeted many of the people who had gathered, and more were coming by the minute, all who lived around the bottom end of Lune Lake Loop. These were the Kindred families, and those who were also Christians or close friends of the Kindred. A couple of them had lost a fighting man overnight due to siding with Matthias. Nevertheless, as if he didn't remember their offense at all, Wes embraced the family members of those who'd stood against him the day before.

Led by Bill Jevans, pushing his all-terrain wheelchair, the funeral procession started up the highway. Many of the men, led by Wes, pulled, pushed, and walked beside a recovered flatbed wagon. One wheel wobbled, but at a walking pace, the long bed, used probably for hay rides from a lost era, would do the job of carrying the dead. Wes held the long tongue of the wagon under one arm, and with the other men's help, the wagon rolled easily.

A few feet away, but clear of the wagon, Wynter walked with a solemn face, matching everyone else's mood that evening. Wynter carried Mia on the front of her, and a small pack on her back. Wes didn't know what she held in the pack, but knowing Wynter, she probably carried extra water or a little food, besides baby-changing supplies. That was Wynter, Wes thought—always thinking, planning, and preparing for others.

Chevy walked behind Wes, also drawing on the tongue of the wagon. Jill, Chevy's wife, walked beside him, along with Dalia, their teenage daughter. Several neighbor children strolled along with Dalia, including Elio, who had grown attached to the young woman.

As the procession approached and passed the Village, the fatherless and brotherless remnants of families came out from their houses and apartments. They'd been notified of the funeral plans, and everyone had responded, it seemed. Instead of a bitter merging, Wes saw the Kindred families welcome those who had lost family members, and the procession hardly stopped rolling forward. Stifled sobs now followed Wes as he followed Bill Jevans, and he prayed that this day of great loss wasn't quickly forgotten by the living, so that nothing so cruel and wicked ever happened there again.

Although he recognized the heartbreaking beauty of the Kindred families embracing the Matthias family and friends from the Village, Wes knew there would be greater obstacles to surmount that evening. He prayed for calm as they approached the Junction where the Las Vegas refugees were to meet them. If Kevin Avon and his army didn't show, Wes didn't see how the healing between the two groups of people could happen. He was counting on it so much, Wes had asked the Kindred not to bring their rifles, but he'd simultaneously instructed them to carry concealed handguns, loaded with gel-tranqs, just in case there was some sort of aggression.

It was dusk as the Lune Lake community arrived at the Junction. The stench of death was heavy, and several of the women who'd lost husbands wailed freely as the wagon was drawn into the midst of the massacred men. It was a sight of horror even to Wes, who'd buried hundreds in the past year, yet he knew everyone else had seen the same as well. And although many present that day had witnessed such carnage, Wes hoped they would also witness for the first time something precious. But it would require Avon to show up.

The women and children stayed by the highway as Wes and the men, in groups of four, gently carried the deceased over to the wagon, and laid them on the bed.

"How is this supposed to work without Avon?" Oleg asked quietly as they went together for a second deceased man.

"We might bury these men tonight," Wes said, "but you're right. There will be no peace if both parties aren't here."

At that time, someone from the Kindred crowd started singing *Amazing Grace*, and the emotions seemed to pour out afresh. The torches were lit and burned bright for the men to continue their work, but Wes's heart was breaking for another reason now. He begged God for help in understanding how peace hadn't been orchestrated—peace he'd fought for and even bled for.

Then, out of the darkness, a milling mass of humanity arrived. Oleg elbowed Wes, and Chevy gently punched Wes's opposite shoulder, as if both men were quietly celebrating their own pleasure in the refugees' arrival.

The melancholy singing of the hymn faltered as the families who'd lost men looked upon the families who'd killed them. But through the tension, Wes heard Wynter's clear, strong voice continue the chorus. Others caught on, and the singing spread.

Just as the Kindred families had embraced the families once led by Matthias, now the Kindred families went to the Vegas refugees, so that the two people groups merged in shared grief and relief. Strangers were greeted in silent acknowledgement, and Wes and Kevin Avon shook hands, slapped each other on the back, then stood awkwardly apart, watching their people mingle.

"I'd wondered if you'd show," Wes mumbled to the man.

"I had to calm their fears that we weren't walking into an ambush, since we did this to your community."

"What won them over?"

"Forgiveness."

"How so?"

"I told them that we were placing ourselves in the hands of people who had promised us forgiveness, proven by the fact that they had used tranquilizers instead of lethal bullets during the battle. And then they saw the wisdom of us needing each other."

"We'll need to keep reminding both peoples of that truth," Wes said. "We can't expect everything to be sorted out tonight, but it's a start."

With Kevin Avon at his side, Wes led the men to continue the gruesome work of collecting the dead. With the new arrival of over two hundred men, the rest of the dead were loaded onto the wagon in mere minutes. It was also this same mass of new arrivals that helped get the wagon rolling back toward Lune Lake. Wes surrendered his place at the front to men he'd only seen through his rifle scope, and he took Wynter's hand in his own as they walked. Bill Jevans still led the procession, while the people continued to sing *Amazing Grace*.

"This is amazing!" Wynter gasped, tears on her cheeks glimmering in the torchlight.

Bill Jevans, knowing the canyon best, led everyone past the Village, then off to the left to a meadow that lay before the mountain slope. There, a dozen men took up picks and shovels and began to dig. More torches were lit, and the crowd completely encircled the burial site so that everyone was forced to look across the circle at one another. And the men who dug weren't Kindred men at all—some men were from Lune Lake, and some were from the refugee group.

During a lull of *Amazing Grace*, Wes and Wynter agreed on a new hymn, and they started the crowd on *It is Well with My Soul*. Very few joined in chorus at first, but after repeating the first verse twice, others picked up the words the third time through, and a new spirit was realized throughout the crowd.

"When peace like a river, attendeth my way,
When sorrows like sea-billows roll;
Whatever my lot, Thou has taught me to say,
It is well, it is well with my soul."

When the grave was dug—a long and deep trench fit for forty men—the diggers gave way to men who had volunteered to carry the dead and lay them side-by-side in the dirt. Wives wailed louder now, and children cried for their loss. When all the deceased were laid out, Wes nodded to Kevin Avon. Together, they stood between two torches held out from the circled crowd. Avon cleared his throat and seemed to be nervous as he took in the sea of faces. For assurance to continue, Wes placed his hand on the commander's shoulder. The singing quieted, then ceased.

"My name is Kevin Avon." The man's gravelly voice broke, and he looked to Wes again, maybe pleading that he not have to speak.

"Go ahead," Wes urged, knowing that his personal approval of Avon's speaking would cause the Lune Lake crowd to give the stranger a chance. "Speak up."

"My name is Kevin Avon." He raised his head. "I've never been part of a funeral service like this before. My guess is that none of us have, even though we've seen lots of dying since Pan-Day. I wish we were coming together under different circumstances, and maybe even sharing a meal together to find out who our neighbors are, or will be. But instead, we're saying goodbye to these men. Maybe you knew these men. Or maybe, like me, you're saying goodbye to them, having never met them. I can't help but think that if we would've met and talked about things, we never would've fought. And we never would've been gathered here like this.

"All my life, I've been a fighter, a soldier, like some of you. For me, I've always dedicated myself to discipline and victory. But tonight, I don't know victory. I don't feel any satisfaction. A battle was fought early this morning, but I'm here to tell you that no one won. We have all had to face our humanity, I think. Me, most of all. I'm looking at these men before us, and I see lives that could've been saved if we would've approached things as Wes Trimble approaches things. If I would've listened, and if others would've taken time to— Well, by what we've seen here tonight, I've changed.

"You people of Lune Lake, we stand with you tonight as strangers, but in the months to come, you'll see that we aren't your enemies. You'll see that we need your help to settle in this canyon, and you'll see that we're eager to be your neighbors. And so we mourn with you right now. And we'll stand with you, because Wes Trimble has shown us a better way, so that nothing like this ever happens again. This gravesite and these men will be a reminder of many men's haste—including my own—to shed blood. And as a reminder so we won't repeat a night like this ever again. We'll remember. We *will* remember. That's all."

Kevin lowered his head and took a step back. No one applauded, but it would've been inappropriate to applaud. Wes still sensed the fragile uncertainty in the air, and though he wished he had the words to heal everyone, he knew what the people needed most was the comfort of God, and God's words.

Wes gestured to the nearest man with the torch to hold the flame closer so Wes could read from his Bible. He read from Psalm 38, which spoke much about suffering and sorrow, but also of a soul in grief over sin. Since so many present that night weren't believers, Wes found the words of the psalmist especially appropriate. And perhaps what he read would incline hearts to face their own mortality as well as their need for salvation from sin.

Although Avon wasn't a believer yet, and his speech of reconciliation hadn't been perfect, Wes figured that along with the reading from the Bible, enough had been said. So, he closed his Bible and raised his hands to the sky.

"Lord God, please forgive us as a people. Not as a divided people, but as a people who have all traveled and journeyed from somewhere. We're all strangers from somewhere, Father, and we need Your direction to learn to live together. We need to realize the forgiveness You have shown us, because of Your Son, Jesus Christ, and only then will we learn to forgive those who stand beside us. In the months to come, let us work together to survive the winter, and to use the forest that You have provided to live with contentment. And one day, Lord, each one of us will be laid to rest in death. But help us to remember, my God, that while we remain, we have the gift of life with which You intend us to love You and to care for others. Thank You, Father, for Your comfort and Your promises. In Jesus' name, amen."

Wes lowered his arms, and those with shovels seemed to understand it was now their turn to work again. Softly, people wept as the dirt was shoveled over the deceased.

Wes moved across the circle and embraced the widows one at a time, having known them in Sandburg, or while in Lune Lake. To his surprise, he noticed in the darkness that Kevin Avon was doing the same. Some might've thought it was awkward or even inappropriate for the commander of the army who had killed the men to be comforting the families of the deceased, but it was a night of firsts, and Wes privately thanked God for what it could mean for them all.

"Tomorrow, I recommend you do two things," Oleg said when he pulled Wes aside. "First, you need to gather everyone again, and keep this momentum going. Explain to them how you're all going to work together through the winter, to take care of everyone. Committees need to be organized, and representatives need to be held accountable to take care of the widows and orphans. But more than anything, these people need revival. You need to preach the straight gospel message tomorrow!"

"Noted," Wes said. "And the second thing?"

"I'll be leaving, heading back to San Diego. And you know what? I can't wait to tell Titus what a success Lune Lake has become!"

"Even through the massacre and your own captivity?"

"Especially through those things." Oleg shook Wes's hand. "I've learned that it's not the hard times that define us, but how we grow closer to God through the hard times that shows who we really are."

"Thank you for the help, Oleg, and for the extra rifles you brought. There's a future for the Kindred up here in these mountains."

"I think so, but I won't be sticking around to see it bear fruit. I'm getting out of these hills before the snow falls. After breakfast, I'll be heading out."

"We'll just have to make sure it's a hearty breakfast, then," Wynter said as she joined them. "We'll miss you, Oleg, but I know my brother is probably anxious to have you back at his side."

The crowd gradually dissipated, and Wes said goodbye to the Village residents, assuring them he'd make sure they were cared for. Soon, only the Kindred and the several hundred Vegas refugees were left at the burial site.

"Bill Jevans will show you where you can camp for the night," Wes said to Avon and his prominent men. "By midmorning, Chevy and I will find you and see you to your new homes around the other side of the Loop. Then, in a day or two, we'll find lodgings over here for the single men you're assigning to help with firewood and food gathering for the fatherless families."

Avon nodded, calmly, accepting the new way of things.

"It's strange, don't you think?"

"What's that?"

"How enemies can become friends." He threw a hand into the air, like he was flabbergasted. "I've never heard of anything so strange as tonight. How could these people really forgive us?"

"Tomorrow, when we meet, I'm going to start teaching you about reconciliation. That's the word for it, when enemies are made friends. It's something God is obviously wanting you to understand."

The Kindred left the refugees in Bill Jevans' hands, with Wynter and Wes following casually behind.

"A bittersweet night, huh?" Wynter commented as they watched the other families go before them.

"Yeah. But one with hope, too."

"What do you think God has next in store for the Kindred?"

"More of the same." Wes chuckled. "There will be other battles and more storms. Conflicts will come and go, and we'll still experience opposition and discomfort. But we'll keep looking to our Lord. And one day, Jesus Christ will return and set all things right."

"You know, with all these new people coming into the canyon, we're liable to see a lot of converts to Christ—and new Kindred recruits."

"That's true. It's something to pray about." Wes put his arm around his wife and stroked Mia's chin. "We also need to pray about Mia's little eyepatch."

"What are you talking about? Our daughter's eyes are perfectly fine!"

"Her father wears an eyepatch, so it's only natural that he would want her to have one, too, hon. Just a cute, little, baby-blue one. It'll make her unique."

"Ridiculous!" Wynter laughed into the night. "You and your eyepatches!"

~ End of RESOLUTION Book Four ~

Thanks for reading this *RESOLUTION Collection!* I pray it blessed you as well as entertained you. Please leave your input wherever you bought this book so I know if I hit the mark. Thanks! —*David Telbat*

What's Next?

Now that you've read *The RESOLUTION Series*, you might be wondering what's next. If you've not yet read *The STEADFAST Series*, it is **next on America's Last Days timeline**. There are **six novellas** in that series, which are also available in one volume called the *STEADFAST Collection*. And, after the *Steadfast* novellas, you may want to move into Telbat's full-length *Last Dawn Series*. Book One, *Dawn of Affliction*, has many of your favorite characters, and is followed by three more novels for your enjoyment. Happy reading!

Bonus Chapter 1 of *Steadfast Book One* is ready for you to read! The novella was first published in May 2017. Just flip a couple more pages and enjoy!

Character Sketch

Anthony "Ant" Bartlik (bk3) is the owner of a new way-station—Ant's Place—in the Sierra Nevada Mtns; husband to Liana, father of two boys

Avery "Chevy" Hewitt is the only surviving COIL operative from the courageous Kindred of Nails team. With selfless abandon, this ex-con is still throwing himself into harm's way to help the afflicted.

Bill Jevans (bk3) is the handicapped caretaker of the Lune Lake buildings.

Dalia Austin is Jill's temperamental fifteen-year-old daughter.

Hoxborn and Nicole (bk2) are a brother and sister team who help organize the survivors in the town of Sandburg. Hoxborn was once the local high school's janitor, and Nicole was the lunch lady.

Ivory White (bk1) is an old man, almost blind, barely surviving in a house as he takes care of a three-year-old Hispanic boy.

Jill Austin is an aging single mother and ex-actress, struggling to move on from being famous in a society that no longer exists.

Kevin Avon (bk4) is a gravelly-voiced military leader of a Las Vegas group of refugees.

Matthias Seaver (bk4) is a frightened and rash survivor in his fifties, whose attitude more often wounds than heals.

Oleg Saratov (bk4) is a veteran COIL operative from Russia who became a believer and accompanied Titus Caspertein for many years.

Roy Mallinger (bk1) is a young man who's searching for an edge on survival. Though once a highway bandit, his providential interaction with God's people teaches him about Christ's sacrifice.

Valles (bk3) is a scout for the Diablos.

Wes Trimble was once a top CIA man. Later in life, God led him to work closely with COIL, wherein he fell in love with Wynter Caspertein. He has only one eye, but his physical impairment doesn't hold him back from facing down the seemingly insurmountable, as he shares about Christ.

Wynter Trimble is the wife of Wes and a COIL operative when needed.

Glossary

COIL is the Commission of International Laborers, a Christian organization made up of specially-trained operatives.

The Diablos (bk2) are California's Central Valley raiders. They number in the hundreds, and their hand in murder and kidnapping has oppressed the region for months.

Lune Lake (bk2) is a resort community on the eastern slope of the Sierra Nevada Mountains. It is comprised of lodges, ski runs, and lakes, and is sandwiched between rugged mountains on the west and desert to the east.

Sandburg (bk2) is a town in the San Joaquin Valley, now comprised of only a few barricaded blocks of buildings.

Bonus Chapter

STEADFAST Book One

Chapter 1

STEADFAST Book One

Bonus Chapter 1

"Therefore, my beloved brethren, be ye steadfast, unmovable, always abounding in the work of the Lord, forasmuch as ye know that your labor is not in vain in the Lord." I Corinthians 15:58 (KJV)

~

Eric Radner was starving to death. It had been weeks since he'd eaten an actual meal. Like a wild animal, he'd begun to eat grass and insects, even worms and snails. The only thing that scared him more than starving to death was the possibility of dying by the virus.

Now, a cold rain chilled his shriveled skeleton. The Wyoming forest was quiet except for the static of falling rain and Eric's chattering teeth. This was the end, Eric thought, as he sat on the ground and leaned against a tree. In a couple of days, he'd fall asleep and never wake up. His body couldn't take much more torment from the elements.

The thought of death saddened him most of all because he never understood why he'd been born in the first place. What was the point of life? It all seemed so insignificant. His malnourishment mixed with hopelessness brought upon him an overwhelming depression. There seemed no escape from the pending doom.

He tightened his designer belt around his midsection, but his belt wouldn't fasten any smaller. His clothes hung off him in tatters. The sole of one shoe had fallen off, and two of his toes had been cut on rocks while crossing a creek a week earlier. Though he knew nothing about living in the wilderness, he decided it was still better this way. In his imagination, he saw mountains of bodies in every city—infected, rotting, discarded ... No, he wouldn't die from the virus.

Using the tree to stand, he studied the terrain around him. The movies always made it seem like the mountains were plentiful with caves, but he hadn't found a single one in weeks. His nights had been spent at the base of trees, covering himself with leaves and branches, restless from bug bites and nightmares of coyotes tearing at his corpse. Living like this, he'd never survive the winter.

Above the tree tops, he glimpsed a steep mountain slope, rocky and jagged. It seemed like a potential place for a cave—or to cast himself off a cliff to end his suffering. Why was he prolonging the inevitable? An instant later, he answered his own thoughts. He wasn't rushing into eternity because he didn't know what eternity held. He'd never taken the time to find out.

Using his hands, Eric climbed the mountain slope. In his city footwear, he slipped many times in the first few minutes, bloodying his knees and even his brow. He paused after ten minutes to scan the terrain behind him. Now above the trees, he looked down on the still green and gray forest, a sheet of rain barring him from seeing beyond a mile.

The world was finished, he guessed. Humanity, at least, would be wiped out by the virus. It all seemed so pointless—births and weddings, barbeques and vacations. Eric felt that he'd never done anything significant for anyone but himself, and even if he'd used his money to build homes for earthquake victims or fed the homeless, what would it all matter if everyone was to die now by a contagion?

To his right, Eric spotted a ridge that angled upward. On the spine of the mountain, the climbing was easier. In his pursuit for a cave to hide and die in, he exposed his thin frame not only to the pelting rain but now to a driving wind. A cliff face stretched beside and below him, and he contemplated a hasty end. His soul was pierced by defeat, deeper even than his fear of the virus or of the eternal unknown.

As he crawled over a boulder the size of a van, he slipped and tumbled off sideways. He landed a few feet below on his back, breathless, staring up at the cloudy afternoon sky. The rain stung his eyes. Slowly, he sat up and noticed he'd landed on a narrow ledge above the cliff. He'd heard of mountain goats and deer that had game trails where people couldn't safely walk.

Too dazed and weak to stand, he crawled along the cliff as a barely discernible trail cut up the mountainside. His knees were numb from the gashes. His head hung heavily, his untrimmed hair filthy and matted against his sopping skull.

His head bumped into something. He lifted his eyes to find not a tree, but flat boards. Several seconds passed before his mind recognized a manmade structure. A door and a wall were disguised by bark and slabs of rock set up against a small cabin, as if to hold it upright against the wind. An antique latch clicked under his thumb, and the door swung inward on modern though rusty hinges.

Was this real? A dark interior welcomed Eric, and he crawled out of the rain to roll onto his side on the plank flooring. Tilting his head, he looked up at a one-room habitat, large enough for a wide kitchen counter, a narrow bed, and a small wooden table. Open shelves lined the walls with books, charts, and cans of food. A rifle hung on a sling by the doorframe, and a closed trunk sat under the bed.

Eric drew his tired bones upright, leaning heavily on the kitchen counter, and hesitantly selected a can from one shelf. His deliverance was here before him. Through gasps and sobs, he fumbled for a manual can opener amongst a set of knives. After three attempts with the can opener, he tossed it aside and went for a sturdy kitchen blade. Impatiently, he stabbed weakly at the top of the can until he could pry open the top. His knees nearly buckled at the aroma of shredded beef in thick gravy.

For a man who'd eaten worms and insects for days, eating beef with his filthy fingers straight from the can was still a banquet.

Halfway through his feast, he clutched his midsection as cramps seized him. His stomach had shrunk. He was already stuffed. Setting the can aside, he took three hasty steps, then lunged at the bed. Facedown, he slept where he fell, one leg and arm hanging off the rustic structure.

The following day, Eric woke to a chill on his back. He rolled off the bed and stood upright. Though weak, he felt rested. The cabin still seemed like an illusion, but the cold morning breeze was real. With a nudge, he closed the door and more thoroughly studied the interior of his sanctuary.

Miles from civilization, the mountainside cabin overlooked a vast, dense forest. Thick plastic windows had been set into the sturdy walls. The roof was angled sharply to avoid snow accumulation. Binoculars sat on the table next to a late generation radio and transmitter. A plaque on the wall confirmed what Eric had already surmised—it was a U.S. Forest Service cabin.

He'd found a forest ranger lookout post, probably only manned during fire season. Maybe occasionally by hunters. The lack of much dust indicated someone had been there within the last few months, but vacated, Eric guessed, when news of the virus had been heard.

"Why me?" Eric asked aloud.

Never before had he asked that question for anything but bad circumstances. But now, he understood he was being blessed, or honored, and he didn't know why. This wasn't luck. Death had surrounded him. Now, he stood in a mountain shack that contained everything he needed to survive.

In the trunk under the bed, he found men's jeans and flannel shirts. On one shelf, a row of books leaned against boxes of rifle cartridges. There were volumes on survival, hunting, and North American herbs, as well as a musty collection of crime novels and a set of encyclopedias—yet missing several volumes. And a Bible. Eric reached out and touched the binding of the Bible. None of this was an accident. Though he'd never read the Bible, he knew he was about to. He needed answers—about life and death and the end of the world.

The radio! He sat on a wooden chair at the table. After a moment, he found the power switch and turned it on. Using a dial, he clicked through static only briefly before he heard voices. With startled attention, he listened as reports poured in from around the country. Most of what was said were recordings. When the tapes looped for a second time, Eric changed the frequency to hear another.

Only weeks before—maybe four—he'd run to hide in the Wyoming mountains. Now, whole cities were closed off. The virus had spread to every metropolitan area. Half of Atlanta had burned. New Orleans was a ghost town from the dead and dying, or those who'd run for safety. Los Angeles was a war zone of looting survivors and a military force trying to regain control. Martial Law had been initiated nationwide, but the virus had depleted the National Guard ranks. Or soldiers had left their posts to care for their own families.

For the next several days, Eric ate canned food and listened to the radio. Something they called the Meridia Virus had swept across America like a vengeful wind. Some said it was a biological weapon accidentally loosed. Others said it was intentionally released by the Russians, or Chinese, or jihadists. No one knew where it had started, or if it would end. The nation's infrastructure was collapsing, and the death count hadn't even peaked.

While the Internet was still online and radio stations were still broadcasting, one hundred million had been reported as infected. Rumor had it, once infected, no one lived beyond two weeks. Death came after symptoms of skin boils, rashes, and dehydration.

The public, as a whole, seemed to accept the virus as an evolutionary response to overpopulation and unrestrained chemical consumption. Therefore, people reacted passively, with no desire to pursue ways of survival. Hopelessness prevailed.

Apocalyptic theorists boasted in their own reasonings for the pandemic, and offered numerous ways to overcome. None of them agreed, Eric found, and as the days passed, they went silent. Or died.

There was even a religious report that looped nonstop. The Christians were looking toward the heavens for answers. Many guessed that Christ would have returned while America was still eating and drinking, marrying and partying, texting and gaming. But the clouds seemed silent. So, believers understood the virus to be a warning, a final flag for all to repent. The wealthiest nation, the proudest people, had been brought to its knees. But while on its knees, would the remnant call upon the Lord?

Two live operators broadcasted what they knew or suspected—one from Denver and the other from Chicago. But after another week, only one remained, then the last operator went quiet as well. All that was left for Eric to listen to were announcements and warnings he'd already heard about the virus: avoid contact with everyone, even family. The virus could be airborne, or it could be transmitted by touch. No one knew for sure.

Eric finally turned off the radio and walked outside. The early autumn sky was blue. Below his cabin, the forest stretched like a blanket to the south. Lakes and ridges interrupted the green trees, but he was otherwise isolated. Yet, for how long? He couldn't stay in the ranger cabin. Someone might return, someone with the virus. Or someone with murderous intent for survival. They'd take his remaining possessions and he'd be starving in the wilderness again.

If he were to survive, he'd need to relocate in secret. Shielding his eyes, he gazed to the east. He was pretty sure he'd abandoned his car in that direction. The forest was dense there, and the mountains high. There was plenty of water, and trees to build a cabin, and game to hunt.

But he had much to learn first. He'd never hunted deer, let alone cut meat off a carcass. Reaching for the survival book, his fingers brushed the Bible again. How to gut a deer would have to wait.

Opening the Bible, he paged through its crisp pages. Someone had made notes in pen in the margins of almost every page. This was someone's personal Bible, the object of untold hours of attention and devotion. Where were the answers he sought? He flipped to the beginning and started reading.

Over the next two weeks, Eric turned on the radio only twice more, but found the same looped recordings. His Bible reading was interrupted only by meals, sleep, and studying the survival guide. As his strength grew, he considered which items he would take from the ranger's lookout, and which items he would leave behind for someone if they returned. However, it seemed no one was coming back to that mountain.

From the Bible, he found the truth of a just God, wrathful against rebellion and sin, but gracious toward repentant sinners. Eric was forced each evening to look honestly at his own heart. The words in the Bible had awakened something inside him. The fear of the virus and his concern of being around other people remained, but it lessened in the face of God's apparent plan for all of humanity. Even him. Mankind had entered a path of destruction. God alone promised to show Himself as Victor. Jesus, God in the flesh, had proven Himself as that Victor, and man was meant to be His followers and ambassadors to bring Jesus glory. It began by faith, Eric read.

He didn't see how he could possibly obey much of how the Bible guided him to live, since he was isolated from other people. But there were steps he could take now, privately, between himself and God. Faith, for the first time in his life, came alive. And he believed.

※

"The following announcement is a pre-recorded statement in coordination with the Public Broadcasting System, in case of emergency. State and federal authorities are asking all citizens to remain in their homes. Because of the current health risk, specialists are advising all citizens to refrain from contact with your neighbors. Do not share food. Do not shake hands. Do not touch.

"The virus seems to have a long incubation period. Eight to ten days after exposure, the symptoms begin to show. Fever is the primary symptom, followed by other extreme flu-like symptoms. Due to dehydration, dry patches or sores may appear on the skin, possibly erupting as boils that may make transmission more possible. If someone has a fever, then they are contagious by touch, though airborne particles haven't been ruled out. Tylenol may be taken to reduce the fever, but the infected will still be contagious.

"Hospitals are not trained or equipped for this emergency. Do not bring your symptomatic loved ones to a hospital or any public treatment facility. You'll only be endangering others. At this moment, a vaccine is being prepared for distribution.

"You are encouraged to use sanitation services sparingly. As you accumulate trash, do not place it in front of your home. The piling up of trash will hinder emergency personnel in the cleanup effort. It's advised that community volunteers coordinate neighborhood burn factories, to eliminate trash. Burn factories and related furnaces should have a chimney that extends a minimum of thirty feet above the ground or street level to disperse toxic particles safely.

"In the event of the death of family members or neighbors, a quick private burial is necessary, unless an immediate cremation is possible. If cremation is not feasible, a grave in the ground should be dug at least five feet deep. Do not wrap the body in any material so that it may decompose quickly. If you need assistance in urban centers with body disposal or contaminated waste removal, hang a black flag or large dark-colored cloth outside your front door. Sanitation volunteers are asked to proceed with caution, with bio-hazard suits whenever available.

"Water shortage requires careful rationing. Fill sealable containers only, and never drink dirty or discolored water. Boil any water you collect from a source outside of your tap water if your tap water ceases to work. During rain storms, place water containers outside to collect rain water, but only five minutes after the rain begins. The first few minutes of rain may be contaminated or toxic, depending on your locality to a neighborhood burn zone.

"Food shortage also requires careful rationing. In rural areas, garden produce grown under the soil is recommended and safe for consumption. In urban areas, roofs and windowsills may be utilized for gardening space. Potatoes, carrots, turnips, onions, and radishes are advised. Do not eat meat without cooking it well.

"In cold months, or for cooking purposes, you may require a private source of heat, especially if electrical power restoration is delayed. All burning restrictions have been lifted in all counties. However, it is advisable that you burn wood and wood products only inside your private residence. Wood that is painted should not be burned unless the paint is first removed. The interior framing of your house, inside the walls, may contain wood that you can burn safely. If you do not have a stove, a fire below a window is acceptable, but it is not advisable to light fires near or inside ventilation systems. When not cooking, the fire should be extinguished to preserve fuel and decrease possible fire hazard.

"As specialists and government agencies restore utilities and management, it is advisable that you find pastimes that do not require physical contact. Reading books aloud with a mask is acceptable in the vicinity of family members. Board and card games are discouraged, due to accidental virus transmission. Exercising indoors is encouraged.

"Due to the threat of accidental transmission and virus carrier potentials, all family pets should be put down and buried immediately. The limiting of animals within residences will extend the availability of water and food resources, as well as diminish the threat of disease transmission.

"Patience and understanding are necessary through this difficult time. Depending on access to your community, utilities and services should be restored within weeks rather than months. In the meantime, under all circumstances, do not make physical contact with anyone until the contagion is better identified and a vaccine can be implemented nationwide.

"The following announcement is a pre-recorded statement in coordination with the Public Broadcasting System, in case of emergency . . ."

The End of Bonus Chapter 1
STEADFAST Book One
(First published May 2017.)

About the Author

D.I. (David) Telbat is a Christian author best known for his **clean, Suspenseful Fiction with a Faith Focus**. This includes his bestselling and award-winning *COIL Series, Steadfast Series, Last Dawn Series, Hidden Humanity, Called To Gobi*, and other Christian Suspense and End Times novels. He wrote his first book at age 14, and he hasn't stopped since!

David studied writing in school and worked for a time in the newspaper field. Getting into serious trouble with the law as a young man became a turning point in his life. The Lord used that experience to draw David into a personal relationship with Him. Re-focusing his life for Christ, he now seeks to honor God with his life and writing by doing what he loves most—writing and Christian ministry.

Subscribe to receive David Telbat's FREE, bi-weekly **D.I. Telbat Newsletter** with one of his Christian short stories, or an Author Reflection, or his Novel News Update. Also receive **exclusive subscriber gifts**, such as his *Three For Free*—three-novels-in-one eBook! Come join the adventure, discover D.I. Telbat books, and subscribe to his newsletter through his ditelbat.com site or his author pages at books2read.com/ditelbat/.

www.ingramcontent.com/pod-product-compliance
Lightning Source LLC
LaVergne TN
LVHW091625070526
838199LV00044B/939